BORN IN JERUSALEM in 1936, A.B. Yehoshua is the author of nine novels and a collection of short stories. One of Israel's top novelists, he has won prizes worldwide for all his novels, and in the UK was shortlisted in 2005 for the first Man Booker International Prize. He continues to be an outspoken critic of both Israeli and Palestinian policies.

"an excellent, nicely tuned translation by Stuart Schoffman."
Ethan Bronner *The New York Times Book Review*

"Mr Yehoshua, Israel's most distinguished living novelist, is a dove. But he is one who, like his fellow writers Amos Oz and David Grossman, joins love for the unique qualities of his people with despair over their failure to make room politically and economically – but above all imaginatively – for the Arabs among them.

With Mr Oz and Mr Grossman this despair comes out as a fine anger. With Mr Yehoshua . . . it comes out as a finer and ultimately more shattering Talmudic questioning."
Richard Eder, *Books of the Times, The New York Times*

"*Friendly Fire* goes beyond Israeli and Jewish issues to touch on universal issues affecting all of humanity. Intensely realized, thoughtful, and stunning in its unique imagery and symbolism, this unusual novel deals with seemingly everyday issues, offering new insights into the human condition – life, love, and death . . ."
Mary Whipple, Amazon.com

". . . these lives haunted by loss are powerfully evoked."
David H̶e̶l̶m̶a̶n̶ ̶J̶e̶w̶i̶s̶h̶ *Chronicle*

Also by A.B. Yehoshua

Friendly Fire

A Duet

A.B. Yehoshua

Translated from the Hebrew by
Stuart Schoffman

HALBAN
LONDON

This paperback edition published in Great Britain by
Halban Publishers Ltd.
22 Golden Square
London W1F 9JW
2010

www.halbanpublishers.com

A CIP catalogue record for this book is available from the British
Library.

ISBN 978 1 905559 19 0

Originally published in Hebrew under the title *Esh Yedidutit*

by Hakibbutz Hameuchad, Tel Aviv, 2007
in the imprint "Hasifria Hahadasha"

Typeset by Spectra Titles, Norfolk
Printed in Great Britain by
MPG Books Ltd, Bodmin, Cornwall

For the family, with love

Second Candle

1.

THIS, SAYS YA'ARI, holding his wife tight, is where we have to part, and with a pang of misgiving he hands her the passport, after checking that all the other necessary items are tucked into the plastic envelope—boarding pass for the connecting flight, return ticket to Israel, and her medical insurance certificate, to which he has taped two of her blood-pressure pills. Here, I've put everything important together in one place. All you have to do is look after your passport. And again he warns his wife not to be tempted during the long stopover to leave the airport and go into the city. This time, don't forget, you're on your own, I'm not at your side, and our ambassador is no longer an ambassador, so if you get into trouble . . .

"Why get into trouble?" she protests. "I remember the city being close to the airport, and I've got more than six hours between flights."

"First of all, the city is not that close, and second, why bother? We were there three years ago and saw everything worth seeing. No, please don't scare me just as you're leaving. You haven't slept well the past few nights, and the flight is long and tiring. Set yourself up in that nice cafeteria where we parked ourselves the last time, put your feet up and give the swelling in your ankles a chance to go down, and let the time pass quietly. You can read that novel you just bought . . ."

"Nice cafeteria? What are you talking about? It's a depressing place. So why—for your peace of mind should I be cooped up there for six hours?"

"Because it's Africa, Daniela, not Europe. Nothing is solid or clear-cut there. You could easily get lost, or lose track of time."

"And I remember empty roads . . . not much traffic . . ."

"Exactly, the traffic is patchy and disorganized there. So without even realizing it, you could miss your connection, and then what do we do with you? I beg of you, don't add to my worries . . . this whole trip is distressing and frightening as it is."

"Really, that's too much."

"Only because I love you too much."

"Love, or control? We really do need to decide, at some point."

"Love in control," her husband says smiling sadly, summarizing his life as he embraces her. In three years she'll be sixty. Since her older sister died, more than a year ago, her blood pressure has gone up a bit and she has grown absent-minded and dreamy, but her womanliness continues to attract and fascinate him as much as it did when they first met. Yesterday, in honour of the trip, she had her hair cropped and dyed amber, and her youthful look makes him feel proud.

And so they stand, the man and his wife by the departure gate. It's Hanukkah. From the centre of the glass dome, radiant in the reddish dawn, a grand menorah dangles over the terminal, and the light of its first candle flickers as if it were a real flame.

"So . . . ," he thinks to add, "in the end you managed to avoid me . . . We didn't make love and I didn't get to relax before your departure."

"Shh, shh. . . ." She presses a finger to his lips, smiling uneasily at passersby. "Careful . . . people can hear you, so you'd better be honest, you also didn't try too hard in the past week."

"Not so," says the husband, bitterly defending his manhood. "I wanted to, but I was no match for you. You can't escape your responsibility. And don't add insult to injury: promise me you won't go to the city. Why is six hours such a big deal to you?"

A twinkle in the traveller's pretty eyes. The connection between the lost lovemaking and the stopover in Nairobi has taken her by surprise.

"All right," she hedges. "We'll see . . . I'll try . . . just stop looking for reasons to worry. If I've gone thirty-seven years without getting lost, you won't lose me this time either, and next week we'll treat ourselves to what we missed. What do you think, I'm not frustrated too? That I lack desire, the real thing?"

And before he has a chance to respond, she pulls him forcefully towards her, plants a kiss on his forehead, and disappears through the glass door. It's only for seven days, but it has been years since she left the country without him, and he is not only anxious but also amazed that she was able to get what she wanted. The two of them made a family visit to Africa three years ago, and most of today's route he knows well, but until she arrives, late at night after two flights, at her brother-in-law's in Morogoro, she will have plenty of dreamy and absent-minded hours alone.

OUTSIDE, IT'S STILL dark. The reddish dawn reflected in the terminal's glass dome was, it turns out, an optical illusion. He feels a first twinge of longing as he spots a scarf left behind on the backseat. True, he can look forward in her absence to freedom and control of his daily routine, but her surprising declaration of "real desire" revives the itch of missed opportunity.

Despite the very early hour he knows there's no point in going home. He won't climb back into the big empty bed and get some rest but will instead be seduced by the dirty dishes left for the cleaning lady and then seek out other needless chores. For a moment he considers paying a morning visit to his father, but the Filipinos are displeased when he descends on them during the old man's ablutions. Therefore he quickly drives past his childhood home and heads for the south of the city, to the engineering design firm he inherited from his father.

The treetops tossing in the morning wind bring to mind a complaint that landed on his desk several weeks before. So he changes course and heads west towards the sea, to the recently erected Pinsker Tower. He presses the remote control to lift the parking gate and descends carefully into the belly of the building.

The thirty-storey tower was completed by the end of summer, yet even at this early hour he sees very few cars parked in the gloomy cavern of the underground garage. Apartment sales must be slow; meanwhile, the building's small population of residents has already banded together to protest defects in its construction. The first winter storms brought the latest grievance: an insufferable roaring, whistling, and rumbling in the shafts of the elevators designed by Ya'ari's company, which also supervised their installation.

Indeed, as soon as he pushes open the heavy fire door separating the garage from the elevator landing, a wild wailing assaults him, as though he'd walked onto the runway of a military airfield. The previous week, one of the firm's engineers had been sent to investigate the phenomenon and had returned mystified. Are the winds being sucked in from the car park? Or are they invading from the roof? Are the anxious whistles the result of some flaw between the elevators and their counterweights, or perhaps a crack has opened in the rear stairwell, and from there the shaft sucks the winds from the outside? It was conceivable that the wind came in by a less direct route, through one of the vacant apartments. A few days earlier, the elevator manufacturer had seen fit to dispatch to the tower a technician specializing in the diagnosis of acoustic disturbances, but at that moment the winter retreated and folded its winds, and the silence prevented the sensitive woman from forming an opinion.

The children are afraid to ride alone in the elevators when the winds are blowing wildly, complained the head of the tenants' committee yesterday, following the resumption of the winter storms—having been provided with Ya'ari's cell phone number by the construction company and encouraged to call him directly. Babies are bursting into tears upon entering the elevator. Tears? Hard to believe, Ya'ari thinks, picturing his two little grandchildren. Can it be that bad? But he did not try to make light of the complaint nor to shirk responsibility. His professional reputation and that of his people is precious to him, and he has promised that if the noises persist, he himself will come to tilt his ear to the winds.

And so, at dawn, he keeps his word. Focused and alert, he

stands silently facing the four elevators—each of which is currently landing at a different floor of the tower—bringing his seasoned intuition to bear on the violent wailing of the winds. Finally he calls for one. The closest descends and opens its doors. He sends it one flight up, then presses the button again, to see if a more distant cab responds or if the first one returns after concluding its upward mission. Yes, the control panel is properly programmed: the faraway elevators stay put and the nearest one comes back. There is no superfluous movement between floors; energy is being properly conserved.

Now he enters the car and with the master key detaches it from the group system and bends it to his will. This way he can navigate its movements from floor to floor and try to identify the point where the wind flows in. He crouches against the rear wall mirror, leaning on his own reflection, and as the elevator slowly climbs he listens to the howling outside the steel cage. Here the roaring he heard underground is muted, a growl of stifled fury that at certain floors shifts into mournful sobbing. Without question, within this shaft that was meant to be completely sealed off from the outside world swirl uninvited spirits. But are they also breaking into the cars? Have his elevators let him down? For Ya'ari, over the objections of the engineers at his firm who preferred Finnish or Chinese elevators—which might actually have proven, bottom line, to be cheaper—had for once insisted on using an Israeli model.

Before he orders the technicians to shut down the elevators and examine the shaft, there is still time to summon to the tower not only the acoustic expert with her sensitive ear, but also a fresh and creative intelligence. Ya'ari is thinking of his son, who joined the business three years ago and has demonstrated an ingenuity appreciated by his father and co-workers alike.

He rides to the top floor, and before he emerges from the elevator he cancels his control and returns it to the main system. Here, on the thirtieth floor, all is silent. It would seem from the plastic wrapping on the door that a buyer for the deluxe penthouse has yet to be found. He enters the machine room opposite; to his surprise he hears neither growl nor whistle, only the precise, pleasant whoosh of the European cables, which now begin to stir as the earliest-rising tenants leave the building. He edges between the huge motors and walks out onto the tiny iron balcony, which the building's architect opposed but Ya'ari insisted upon, so that maintenance technicians could flee into the fresh air in the event of fire.

Slovenly, dark clouds enfold Tel Aviv. The Pinsker Tower has sprung up in the midst of a quiet, low-rise urban environment and thus commands a wide view and can even conduct a respectable dialogue with the downtown skyscrapers that sparkle in the greyish southeast.

The yellow brushstrokes now visible on the horizon are no trick of the light, and the passenger plane silently gaining altitude is also very real. No, thinks Ya'ari, checking his watch, it's not her plane yet. Even barring a delay, she won't take off for another ten minutes, and there's no point waiting for her in the freezing cold, since there is no way of knowing which plane is hers.

But his love for his wife rivets him to the little balcony. Her journey has begun and can't be stopped, but he can watch over her from afar. In principle he could have gone with her, but it wasn't his workload alone that made him stay behind. Knowing her so well, he understood that his presence would prevent her from fulfilling her desire to focus on the loss of her sister and to resurrect, with the help of the bereaved husband, the sweet sorrow of childhood memories in which he, Ya'ari, had played no part. He knew that even if he were to sit quietly with his wife and brother-in-law and not take part in the conversation, she would feel that he was insufficiently interested in the morsels of distant memory, of her sister or even of herself, that she hoped to coax from a man who had known her as a child, back when he was a young soldier soon to be discharged who came to the house as her sister's first and final suitor.

He leans with his full weight upon the iron railing. As an experienced elevator expert, he is unaffected by dizzying heights, but he does wonder what has become of the winds that ought to be stroking his face.

2.

As SHE LEAVES the duty-free shop she is surprised to hear her name called on the public-address system and is struck anew by the recognition that on this trip there's no one at her side to keep track of time. All she'd wanted to do was buy some lipstick that her housekeeper had asked for, and when she couldn't find it at the cosmetics counter she had turned to leave, but then one of the older saleswomen, sensing the disappointment of a nice lady her own age, had talked her into buying another brand in a similar shade and of equal quality.

Indeed, she is aware that since her sister died she has been increasingly drawn to older women, as if she might find the image of her loved one in them. And these women, for their part, respond to her attentiveness and her slightly abashed smile inviting sympathy, which is why she gets stuck in endless conversations with teachers at her school and with women met by chance, in cafés, the doctor's waiting room, the beauty parlour and, of course, shops; women such as this friendly saleslady who began to talk about her own life, managing at the same time to cajole her patient listener to add onto her purchase (at a significant discount) a fancy face cream guaranteed to rejuvenate her dry skin.

And the passage of time must be apparent in her face if the young steward bounding towards her identifies her as the tardy passenger and nabs her without asking her name, tears the stub from her boarding pass, and insists on escorting her to the plane, as if it were in her power to escape the sealed sleeve. It's okay, he says, his arm around this woman who could be his mother, the main thing is you're on board, and he hands her over, as if she were a confused child, to the stewardess, who takes her carry-on bag, stuffs it into an overhead locker, and shows her to her seat. "I was sure you weren't going to make it," confides the young man who hesitantly rises from her window seat under the stern eye of the stewardess.

She blushes, but won't give up her window. Even though she usually naps on planes or is immersed in a book and rarely looks out at earth or sky, being by a window is important to her, and even more so this time, with no husband beside her. As the doors are locked, and the engines rumble, and the flight becomes an irreversible reality, a wrinkle of worry furrows her tranquil brow. Is this trip necessary? Will it be helpful? Will Yirmi, her brother-in-law, help her revive the pain that has dulled over the past year? She doesn't lack consolation. Her friends and loved ones still remember to say something nice now and then about her sister, and her husband and family try to lift her spirits. But it's not consolation she wants. On the contrary, she is looking for precise words, forgotten facts—or maybe new ones—that will inflame her pain and grief over her big sister, whose death has claimed a portion of her own youth. Yes, she has a clear desire to breathe life into her loss and crack open the crust of forgetfulness that has begun to envelop her. She longs to spend a few days in the company of a man she has known since childhood, whose love for and devotion to her sister, she is certain, were no less strong than her own.

At the request of the concerned-looking stewardess she fastens her seat belt, takes the newspaper that is offered to her, and adds a request. If possible, at the end of the flight, could the stewardess save her some of the Hebrew newspapers and magazines that have been left on board? For out there deep in the Syrian-African Rift is an Israeli who would surely love to have them.

3.

YA'ARI IS STILL standing on the tiny balcony, shivering, hypnotized by the sunrise that expands the broad horizon and highlights the passenger planes that take off from the airport one after another, bound westwards for the sea. His discerning eye has already picked out one deviant craft that is gracefully bending to the south. It's *her,* he thinks excitedly, as though his wife herself were steering it, and he narrows his gaze to follow the dot till it vanishes in the distance. Then he relaxes. Yes, his wife will arrive in peace and return in peace. And he leaves the tiny balcony, locks the engine room, and calls the elevator to take him down to the car park.

On her own? On her own? Brother-in-law Yirmiyahu had been astounded when Ya'ari had phoned with the round-trip flight times of his wife's holiday visit. On her own? he repeated. Yes, on her own, said Ya'ari, rising to defend his wife's honour, why shouldn't she? Of course she's capable, the warm, familiar voice from Dar es Salaam said with a chuckle, and if it's for seven days and not more, she might even survive here without you. But can *you* handle it? Can you accept the separation and not change your mind at the last minute and join her?

His brother-in-law certainly knew him well—perhaps from knowing himself. Until two weeks prior to the trip, Ya'ari had vacillated as to whether he should allow Daniela, whose blood pressure had gone up a bit since her sister's death, to travel alone to Africa even to see a close relative, almost an older brother, a responsible and trustworthy individual, and also a man stricken by fate more than once in recent years.

Ya'ari, unlike his family and friends, was not so ready to condemn the man who hadn't waited for the end of the thirty-day mourning period for his wife, but instead, after sitting shivah for a week, had rushed back to his post as chargé d'affaires at the Israeli economic mission in Tanzania. Half a year after Yirmi's return to East Africa it was decided in Jerusalem, whether due to budget cuts or other considerations, to eliminate the small office and ease into retirement the widowed diplomat, who apart from a security man and two local employees had no one working with him. In truth, more than once Yirmi himself had joked to relatives and friends about the pointlessness of his little outpost, which sometimes seemed to have been invented especially for him—an overdue bonus for an old worker in the administrative wing of the Foreign Ministry whose retirement had been delayed, as provided by law, because he had lost a son in the army. Therefore he accepted without rancour the elimination of his position, even though it came so soon after his wife's death. And it was only natural that on his final return from Africa, after giving notice to the tenants renting his Jerusalem apartment, he had allowed himself a little detour, family time with his daughter and her husband, still toiling towards their academic degrees in the United States.

But America did not appeal to the new pensioner, and the visit was cut short. Without consultation—which in any case he owed to no one—or any prior warning, he surprised his relatives and friends by extending for two years his tenants' lease in Jerusalem and returning to Africa, not to his former location but to a place two hundred kilometres southwest of Morogoro, near the Syrian-African Rift, to take a vaguely defined administrative position with an anthropological research team.

Why not? he apologized to his brother- and sister-in-law by phone from Dar es Salaam, en route to the new place. Why hurry back to Israel? Who really needs me there? Not even you. After all, I'm in Jerusalem and you're in Tel Aviv. You're busy with work, your kids, now your grandchildren too, and I'm free as a bird, without a wife or a career. You have no money worries; on the contrary, you worry how to spend your money, and I've got only the mediocre pension of a government worker, because we handed over our "friendly fire" payment to support our perennial doctoral students. Tell me honestly, why should I not take advantage of an unexpected opportunity to save a little money for my old age, before the inevitable collapse of my body or soul? Am I no less entitled than old Ya'ari to be cared for, if not by a Filipino couple, by at least one quiet and devoted Filipino to push my wheelchair in the park? Here in Africa living is cheap, and with the research team I get free room and board, and they'll pay me a decent wage for administrative duties and some minor bookkeeping. And meanwhile my rent comes in every month from Jerusalem, and the tenants even fix the place up at their own expense. Look, they replaced the stained kitchen counter, repaired cracks and ancient holes in the walls, and replastered the entire apartment. They've also promised to dust all the books and rearrange them by subject. So what's the hurry? Is there a chance or danger that the country will run away or disappear? Sometimes it seems you forget that you'll always be a few years younger than I, and you'll still find time to travel to new places, but I won't have many more opportunities to take in foreign experiences like Africa, of which, believe me, I haven't yet had my fill. So, *please*, to whom do I owe anything here? Would it not be pathetic for a man like me, already pushing seventy, in his first year of bereavement, to start a relationship with some new woman for whom I could have neither desire nor passion? After all, who knows better than you, that my wife and I shared a love that was every bit as great as yours?

And therefore, my dears, and Daniela especially, let go of your sense of responsibility and stop worrying. I won't disappear. And if you still feel that you miss me, and you can't get over your longing, come for a short visit, even though you were here three years ago and nothing has changed since then and there's nothing new to see.

"It's totally his right," was Ya'ari's verdict, though Yirmi's sudden decision continued to unsettle his wife. "None of us is entitled to judge him."

4.

THE FULL FORCE of her fellow passenger's slumber is now directed her way. All her attempts to shrink into her seat and shake off the young head yearning to lean on her shoulder are futile. This man—maybe he partied last night, counting on a chance to sleep it off on the plane—is now avenging in his sleep the loss of his stolen window and also looking for a bed, not caring if that bed is the shoulder of a woman more than twenty years his senior, with two grandchildren, who will soon enough take out their photos to draw comfort from their sweet faces. Now she understands the weight of the responsibility she took on when electing to travel alone. Her husband's controlling, protective love has spoiled her, anaesthetized her own sense of reality. Especially on trips, when he carries her travel documents and navigates unfamiliar roads and shifting conditions, so that in planes and trains and cars and hotels she coasts in a safe bubble while at her side is an alert and attentive person, who always has the correct foreign currency and the necessary information. Nor is there any reason for her to feel grateful for his devotion and concern, for she knows that by her very existence, even when she sleeps, she repays him fully for all his services.

But now she is on her way to Africa with no one to organize the world around her. And the stewardess passes by and notices the insolent sleeper, yet doesn't offer to help, as if this trespasser she'd earlier evicted from his seat were now under her protection. So Daniela has no alternative but to wake the fellow herself and return him politely but firmly to his territory. The young man curls up a bit and mumbles an apology, though apparently only in his dream, for his eyes immediately close again, and his head droops.

She folds up the newspaper and places it for safekeeping in the bag from the duty-free shop, next to the lipstick and the skin cream that according to the chatty saleswoman would work wonders on her face. Then she extracts from her bag the photo album of her two grandchildren, whom she still swaddles in the adoration of a new grandmother. She lingers a long time on each picture, as if deciphering an esoteric text. Her older granddaughter, age five, is the image of her mother, Daniela's pretty daughter-in-law, but the child's blue eyes radiate innocence and wonder, nothing like her mother's distant, alienated look. She dwells more on photos of her grandson, a restless, agitated two-year-old always shown gripped tight by his father or mother or harnessed into a high chair or buggy. It's too early to tell whom he'll choose to resemble. Though his round face and the slight crease in his eyelids bring vaguely to mind the features of her son, or maybe even her husband, she's not willing to leave it at that. In photo after photo she strains to make out in this grandson signs of resemblance to herself as well. And since the flight is long and she will not, despite her fatigue, let herself doze off beside the territory-stealing stranger, she has more than enough time at her disposal to discover what she hopes to find.

5.

THE ELEVATOR BEGINS its slow descent from the thirtieth floor, but stops immediately at the twenty-ninth, and opens its doors. A woman clad in spandex and crowned by a headset is startled to find someone coming down from the thirtieth floor at such an early hour. At first she continues to groove on her music while sizing up her fellow traveller with a penetrating gaze, but as the elevator slows down and approaches the garage, she can't hold back and pulls off her earphones.

"Don't tell me the penthouse has been sold," she says peevishly, as if the sale of the luxury apartment, which she naturally craved but could not afford, were a small personal defeat.

"The penthouse?" Ya'ari answers, smiling. "I wouldn't know. I don't live here. I came to check out the complaints about your winds."

"*Our* winds?" the woman says, brightening. "Maybe you can actually explain to me what's going on here? They promised state-of-the-art construction, a luxury building, we paid a lot of money, and with the first little bit of winter, this insane orchestra starts to run wild—do you hear it?"

"Of course."

They step out onto the elevator landing. The roaring gets louder. He shrugs and turns to leave, but the athletic tenant won't let him go: "So what are you? A wind expert?"

"Not really, but I was responsible for the planning of these elevators."

"So what went wrong in your calculations?"

"Mine? Why mine? It could have been someone else's. It needs to be checked out."

And Ya'ari gets the feeling that it's not the howling wind that is now bothering the energetic woman, but his very existence. Who is he exactly? And why? So before he breaks off contact and goes looking for his car in the twilit garage, he adds, almost in passing, "Don't worry. We'll find the cause of the winds and get them under control. My engineers will get to the bottom of it." And he nods good-bye.

But the woman persists. She feels entitled to a precise definition of this well-built man of more than sixty whose stylish cropped hair is flecked with white. His dark eyes radiate confidence; his windbreaker, unfashionable and threadbare, adds a simple, unaffected touch.

"'My engineers?'" she repeats, in the quarrelsome tone that seems natural to her. "How many do you have altogether?"

"Ten or twelve," he answers quietly. "Depends how you count them." Then he disappears into the shadows of the garage. He glances at his watch. His wife has not even left the territorial waters of Israel and already his free-floating love is attracting strangers.

6.

EVEN THOUGH HER husband is not at her side to safeguard her sleep in this unfamiliar place, her eyelashes drift downwards, the photo album falls to her feet, and the engine noise insulates the intimacy of her experience. Then the warm aroma of something freshly baked rouses her, she opens her eyes and sees the young man in the next seat hungrily consuming his breakfast.

"Real desire," she had tossed at her husband almost

offhandedly as they were about to part, and it's still not clear to her what she'd had in mind, what compelled her to say it at the last minute. Was it to hurt him for not insisting on coming with her, even though she really had wanted to go alone, or was it to strengthen his longing for her, leaving him with hopes for her return? Yes, he's right. She was responsible for his frustration. He wanted to, he tried, but she, despite her willingness to give him the pleasure he craved, hadn't considered it quite fair for him to be satisfied while her own desire was blocked by anxiety over the trip, and in any case she never found sex so important, either in her youth or in maturity, and certainly not now, as she ripens into the third phase of her life, yet she knows that her husband's love needs to be requited more often. It's just that she's not always able to focus her energies at the expense of her own desires and the need to be good to herself.

She looks out of the window. While she was sleeping the clouds broke into soft cottony tufts, and in the light of day she sees the desert plain kissing the gulf. Is this Africa? From her visit three years before she remembers the arresting redness of the soil and the Africans wrapped in colourful fabrics walking upon it with barefoot grace. From the window of her brother-in-law's office, adjacent to the apartment where he housed them in violation of the rules—not only to save the cost of a hotel but also so they'd be together the whole time—she once saw her sister, early in the morning, buying milk and cheese from a plump African woman wearing a headdress with a flamboyant green feather. Daniela's heart reaches out to her sister's slender silhouette, wrapped in an old woollen shawl she remembers from their parents' home.

The photo album of her grandchildren has made its way while she slept to the feet of her neighbour, who is now unwittingly stepping on it. She politely asks him to pick it up; he apologizes, saying that he hadn't noticed. The stewardess, who is already clearing away empty trays, asks whether she would still like her breakfast, and after a moment's uncertainty she decides not to decline. But when she removes the aluminium cover from the main course and tastes the first bite, she feels a wave of nausea, like the ones she felt so many years ago at the beginnings of her pregnancies. Her husband is always ready and eager to finish off her leftovers, indeed expecting that his wife will always leave him something of hers, and so even when she wants to clean her plate, she restrains herself and leaves him something symbolic, as a concrete expression of her fidelity. But now there is no one to rescue her from this repellent meal. And she senses the gaze that lingers on her abandoned knife and fork. Would it be a gesture of friendship to offer a total stranger food she has already tasted? After all, if she were younger, perhaps a young man would try to get to know her over such a meal. She offers him the tray politely and cordially. The young man hesitates and blushes. He seems like a well-brought-up fellow who does not eat from the plate of strangers.

"Why not eat it yourself? It's excellent . . ."

"Please take it." And giving him no time for second thoughts, with a sure motherly hand she calmly shoves the tray his way before the stewardess can pounce and remove it to her cart.

The young passenger grins with embarrassment, but the hunger of youth gets the better of him, and with sheepish care he wipes with a napkin the fork that has lately been in her mouth and plunges the knife into the omelette. She nods encouragingly, but does not want to commit herself to a chat occasioned by the odd kindness she has forced on him, and she therefore gathers up the newspaper that blankets her feet and begins to flip from pictures to text.

7.

THE MAIN ENTRANCE to the design firm is unlocked. Someone has arrived before him. His seventy-five-year-old accountant, who worked with his father for many years, is drinking coffee and enjoying a croissant, his face illuminated by the glow of the news he reads on the computer screen. A year ago, Ya'ari brought him out of retirement and back to active duty to assist in the expansion of the business and compliance with new tax regulations. The ex-pensioner, unwilling to give up his afternoon nap, comes early to the office and disappears before twelve. Ya'ari is not sure that his productivity warrants the handsome salary he earns on top of his pension, but because the man remains loyal to Ya'ari's invalid father and now and then goes to play chess with him and keep him abreast of goings-on at the office, it's convenient to have him on the staff.

"What got you out of bed?" The accountant gathers the pastry crumbs from his trousers and swallows them.

With nonchalant pride, Ya'ari tells of Daniela flying off that morning to her brother-in-law in Africa.

"To that consul?"

"Actually just a chargé d'affaires, and now not even that. Half a year after his wife died they closed the mission for lack of funding and they pensioned him off. But because living is cheap in Africa, he decided to stay there, and now he does the bookkeeping for some research dig, so he can build up his savings for old age. After all, in the Foreign Ministry they would never consider taking someone back out of retirement . . ."

But the pensioner is oblivious to the boss's subtle jab, so confident is he of his indispensability.

"What are they digging for?" he persists.

Ya'ari doesn't know exactly what his brother-in-law's team is digging for. When his wife gets back in a week, she will tell all.

The accountant eyes his employer a bit suspiciously. He still thinks of Ya'ari as the high school student who would come to the office after class to try out the new electric typewriter.

"You always travel together, so what happened this time? You weren't afraid to let your wife travel alone, never mind to Africa?"

Ya'ari is a little uneasy. The intimate tone bothers him, but since his father keeps his old employee up to date on family matters, he finds himself patiently explaining the reason for the rare separation. Daniela could take advantage of the Hanukkah break at her school, but for him it was hard to get away from the office, this week in particular when decisions needed to be made about changes in the Defence Ministry facility. Besides, it's not clear that Moran will be able to get out of his army reserve duty. Most important, his wife will not be alone there for a minute. Their brother-in-law will be with her and look after her the whole time.

"How old is your brother-in-law? Seventy? Older?"

"Something like that."

It turns out that Ya'ari's father talks about Yirmi now and

then, with affection and sadness. But the accountant only met him once—at Ya'ari's wedding.

"At my wedding?" Ya'ari is amazed. "Thirty-seven years ago? You were there?"

Why not? The accountant was invited to the wedding along with other employees of the firm. And from that celebration he remembers the tall man who danced energetically all night with the two sisters . . .

"Yes, there was a natural joy in him, until the blow came…" Ya'ari mumbles, and goes into his office, which has shrunk during the firm's recent expansion—a process which involved tearing down their floor's inner walls and turning it all into one space. Only Ya'ari did not relinquish his private space, because this is where his father once sat and because he loves the view: a window on the backyard framing a big tree whose branches in recent years have intertwined with an unidentified plant that in springtime produces a riot of red flowers. He considers whether it may not be too early to phone his son and ask him to hop over to the tower on his way to the office and listen to the roaring winds. The fine line between a father's right and an employer's, which was clear between him and his own father, hasn't yet been fully defined between them, and his son has become preoccupied since the birth of the second grandchild, a moody boy who requires special attention and frequent visits to doctors. But because it seems to him that his son, too, has been unsettled by the idea of his mother heading off alone to Africa, he decides to call him now, if only to set his mind at ease.

"Hey, habibi," he says, when his sleepy son picks up, "I hope I didn't wake you. I just wanted to let you know Imma has taken off, but she promised to stay at Nairobi airport until the connecting flight. So for the time being we can relax and hope the day will go smoothly."

8.

SHORTLY BEFORE THEY landed, the stewardess handed her a bag bulging with Israeli newspapers. Ah, Daniela exclaimed, how nice of you not to forget, but why is the package so heavy? We only have three newspapers.

"I don't know," the stewardess apologized. "I collected everything. Also the financial supplements and sports, want ads and real estate; I didn't know what you wanted for your Israeli and what you didn't."

"No problem . . . thank you . . . I'll find room for it."

And it is her hungry young neighbour who crams the bundle into her suitcase, and helps her wheel it to the bus taking the travellers to the terminal. Here, he jokes, I've already paid you back for the meal you gave me. And with laughing eyes she says, you see, it wasn't for nothing that I strengthened you with an extra meal. Then the young man finally allows himself to express interest in the purpose of the trip of this genial older woman, and she tells him about her brother-in-law, who used to be some sort of chargé d'affaires, but doesn't get around to mentioning the death of her sister, because there is someone excitedly pushing towards her from the other end of the bus, calling out: I don't believe it, is it you? In Africa?

This large, red-headed woman, no longer young, was her student long ago. For many years she has been living in Nairobi with her husband, a representative of a big construction company, but in all that time she has never forgotten the young teacher of English who managed so enjoyably to instil in her a knowledge of that all-important language. You won't believe it, chatters her former pupil, who looks not much younger than Daniela, I still haven't forgotten *King Lear,* which you taught us with patience and love. And back then English really was a foreign language for us, and wasn't easy. When did you stop teaching? I haven't stopped, Daniela says, smiling wearily. I still teach in the very same school; I'm not quite as old as you think. No, God forbid, says the woman, embarrassed, I didn't mean that, they just say that teaching burns people out fast. But if you still have the energy and passion for Shakespeare, good for you...

Daniela laughs. No, they removed Shakespeare from the curriculum a long time ago and replaced him with American short stories. But in recent years she hasn't been preparing students for the matriculation exams, but teaching in the lower grades. Lower grades? Why? There were some disciplinary problems with the older students. With you? Disciplinary problems? Her former student is amazed. We not only loved you, she says, we were afraid of you. It's true, smiles Daniela, who at times has sensed her students' fear. But what can you do? Since my older sister's death I've become a bit slow and self-absorbed, and there are students who take advantage.

Now her old student looks genuinely pained. But it's only temporary, she suggests, trying to console the teacher who is not asking for consolation. Surely you'll go back to teaching the higher grades. Could be, Daniela replies, rolling her bag from the bus to the terminal. For the moment it suits me. It's easier and less time-consuming to correct the younger ones' exams.

When her former student, who herself has lately become a young grandmother, realizes that Daniela is headed not for passport control but rather towards the dreary transit lounge, where she is to wait more than six hours for her next flight, she urges her to go through the passport line now and spend the stopover at her house. She has a nice big house, with a pleasant, quiet living room. True, the house is away from the city centre, but she'll make sure her husband sends his driver to get her back to the airport in time.

Daniela hesitates. She really needs a rest, and the woman seems efficient and reliable. But the promise she made to her husband not to leave the airport silences her. If, God forbid, there should be a foul-up, some unexpected delay, how could she justify violating a promise, even one extorted from her at the last minute? Ever since her sister's death his fears for her safety have grown more intense.

She looks at her student, now locating in her memory the flaming red hair. Really, why not go and rest at her place? After all, what could happen? This is a responsible woman who's been living here a good many years and will surely take care to get her back in time for her flight. She looks down the hall leading to the transit lounge, which overflows with waiting Africans and their children, who are racing around among bundles and baskets. Spending six hours amid this multitude will not be easy. But it would be harder still to break her promise to Ya'ari. Does he know things about her that she doesn't see in herself? An increased absent-mindedness, a distracted depression that could lead her astray? The way she lost track of time in the duty-free shop still bothers her. True, she had wanted to make this trip alone, yet she had not believed that her husband would not insist at the last minute on coming with her. So even if the promise she made him now seems annoying and unnecessary, can she break it?

"It's all right," she says regretfully to the woman, who has already steered her towards passport control. Six hours is long, but not impossibly so. Best not to burden your husband. I'll find myself some quiet corner; I bought a novel this morning at the airport, so the time should pass quickly.

And to the great dismay of her old student, she heads for the transit hall, wheeling her suitcase between the baskets and bundles of other passengers, looking for the cafeteria where she waited with her husband three years ago .

It's still there, and though as unattractive as ever, it is no longer gloomy. The place has been expanded with added tables and chairs, and the walls are decorated with colourful posters advertising hotels and restaurants in the city. Even as she wonders where she'll find that quiet corner in which to pass the long hours, she catches the eye of a waiter, who opens a folding table for her. In the corner, she points, the corner please, I'll have to be here a very long time.

Now she regrets having passed up the airplane meal, and so she orders a sandwich and a cup of coffee, and opens the novel. She chose it with no prior knowledge, purely by its name and cover illustration. But because it was written by a woman, naturally the main character will be a woman. Admittedly, Daniela is not always comfortable with women's novels. In general, the heroines don't like themselves much, making it hard for the reader to identify with them, and without that identification, no matter how smooth the writing and well-made the plot, the time won't go quickly.

She reads the long, closely printed blurb on the back cover. The editor promises the readers of this novel a dramatic reversal. An elusive secret only implied at the outset will by the end turn everything upside down. So the reading will not be simple; it will require concentration, and that's not going to be easy with two African youths standing near her table and staring at her. On the previous visit, at a table near this one, she waited with her husband for an evening flight back to Israel. That wait had lasted only an hour and a half, and with her husband by her side, attentive to her every word, the time passed quickly. She remembers that despite the anticipation of going home, and a satisfying visit with her sister and brother-in-law to think about, sadness overcame her. Something must have told her that this separation from her sister would be a long one, but she could hardly have foreseen that less than two years later a sudden heart attack would take her sister from the world in an instant, and her brother-in-law would bring back to Israel not a coffin but only an earthenware jug filled with ashes. What's the matter? he would argue to the hushed astonishment of his relatives, none of us, after all, believes in the resurrection of the dead.

9.

YA'ARI SHIFTS WITH finesse from the role of concerned father to the role of employer, asking whether Moran's release from army duty has been confirmed.

"It'll be fine, Abba, don't worry."

"When's it supposed to start, your reserve duty?"

"It started already. Yesterday."

"And you have a release? You're covered?"

"Nobody can give me an official release. I'm just ignoring it."

"But why don't you explain to them that this is a critical week at work, with many important decisions . . ."

"They don't need explanations. They've got them from everybody and his brother. Better just to keep quiet. Even if they discover I'm missing, the adjutant is a friend of mine; we were in officers' training together."

"So did you at least tell this adjutant?"

"No. If I tell him, he'll have to order me to come in. Best just to ignore the order. Like last time. I didn't show up and nobody noticed. They have enough soldiers and officers."

"And this time, too?"

"I'm sure of it."

"We have those meetings coming up at the Defence Ministry. I'm sure that if you told them about the Defence Ministry, they'd free you up."

"The Defence Ministry impresses nobody. Every dropout has a fantastic excuse. Don't worry, it'll be fine. I'm here, with you."

"You know, because I wasn't sure you'd be free, I couldn't go on the trip with Imma."

"And I thought it was because she wanted to be there alone."

"That, too. Where's your unit going?

"West Bank, but not too deep inside."

"Maybe you can cook up another excuse?"

"Such as?"

"A matter of conscience . . . conscientious objection . . . after all, your cousin . . ."

"Enough, Abba, I'm not going to masquerade as something I'm not. This army is always in flux, it's unfocused and aimless. There are surplus soldiers everywhere. Nobody'll notice that I didn't show up."

"But this adjutant, your friend . . ."

"Even if he notices, he won't bat an eyelid."

"I'll take your word for it. You know how crucial you're going to be to me in the coming days. So on the way over here, go down to the Pinsker Tower and listen to the wailing winds. The tenants are livid, and rightly so. I was there this morning, and the roaring is enough to drive you mad. I have a couple of theories about what exactly is going on, but I won't say a word till I get your opinion. And you haven't forgotten the noon meeting at the new site?"

"I haven't forgotten."

"Now what about Nadi, is he a little calmer at night?"

"Sometimes."

"Last night?"

"So-so. Maybe before nursery school I'll take him to the clinic. Are you coming over tonight to light candles with the kids?"

"Not tonight. In the late afternoon I'll light them with Grandpa. I haven't seen him for two days. From there I'll go home. I slept maybe three hours last night. But we'll have plenty more candles to light before your mother gets back."

Through the big doorway, engineers and draughtsmen, technicians and secretaries pour into the office, and their computer screens light up one by one. People warm their hands on coffee mugs and enter Ya'ari's office to say hello and show him sketches. Some years back, Ya'ari lost direct touch with the latest design technologies and the specifications of the elevators planned by his firm, but he can still suggest lines of thinking to his employees and judge the quality of their work.

The sunlight comes and goes and a soft rain continues to fall, but outside the window the branches on his tree are still. The morning's storm has quietened down, and he fears that his son will listen in vain for the moaning of the winds.

The phone rings, the secretary brings the day's mail, but Ya'ari's thoughts are with the beloved passenger. Soon the long stopover in Nairobi will begin, and though he is certain she will not break her promise and go into the city, he feels sorry that she'll be sitting alone for six long hours in that crowded and unpleasant restaurant. It would be better if she could find herself a nice quiet corner near the departure gate. In his mind he strides ahead of her through the airport, recalling its layout to help her find the right spot, somewhere not too isolated. And he hopes that her pleasant disposition and friendly smile will engage a fellow passenger who is waiting too. A man or a woman, Israeli or European, even a local African, someone who will watch over the internal logic of her movements.

10.

BUT SHE HAS not sought out a small, quiet corner; instead, she has tried to improve her seating arrangement in the big cafeteria. A white-haired African helped her relocate her little table to a more remote corner, and after a waiter set down her sandwich and coffee, she wandered among the tables and found two more chairs, set her rolling suitcase and bag on one of them and put her feet up on the other, to rest them thoroughly and restore her ankles to their normal shape. When she opened her suitcase, she was tempted at first by the bundle of Israeli newspapers, but instead, with a small sigh and few expectations, took out the new novel she had bought at the airport.

And so, amid the racket of cups and dishes, the babble of unintelligible languages, and smells of coffee and roasted meat begins an encounter between an older woman, who is an experienced reader, with a fictional woman of thirty or so who from the first page is prone to self-pity. In a feverish but confusing monologue she seeks the reader's sympathy for her unspecified plight. But what exactly am I supposed to care about or identify with, complains the traveller, if the author has no sympathy with her own character? Out of respect for the written word she keeps turning pages, while now and then glancing at her ankles, propped on the chair as if on the sofa back home. Eventually she kicks off one shoe and then the other, and contentedly rubs together the soles of her small feet.

The windows of the coffee shop are narrow and filthy, and the light that filters through is insufficient. The noise and smells also inhibit concentration, but she has got used to the small territory she has captured and is settled in for a long wait. True, right now she could be enjoying the hospitality of her former student, whose husband would surely have returned her to the airport on time, but then she'd have to listen to her hostess, thank her, smile, and act impressed. Yes, conversation comes easily to her, nor is it hard for her to accept kindness or even coddling from others. But the distress she would have felt over breaking the promise to her husband would have poisoned the pleasant interlude. When she's with him, she can easily deflect or defy his loving concern, but when she is alone it paralyzes her and makes her feel ashamed.

Never mind, she removes her glasses and wipes them clean, thinking the hours will pass. I have no choice, and neither does Time. Despite the chaos around her, she feels confident, and she is close to the departure gate. She takes out her passport to check her boarding pass, which normally her husband would carry, and after trying to decipher its details uses it to mark the page in her book, returns the passport to her bag, and puts the novel in her suitcase. Then she smiles warmly at a young couple seated nearby, a European man and an African woman playing merrily with a child who is an attractive mix of his parents' genes. After securing their agreement to guard her territory for a few moments, she puts on her shoes and heads bag in hand down a dim corridor towards a kiosk she recalls from the previous layover. It's still there, colourful and well-stocked as before, and the vendor, an older, very black man, fills for her a good-sized bag of assorted sweets and bars of chocolate. After a brief hesitation she also selects, from a bright glass bowl, a lollipop in the shape of a parrot, glittering with specks of coloured sugar and perched on a little branch. She'd coveted it the last time, but Ya'ari had vetoed it as unsanitary. Now, loaded with sweetness, she returns happily to her table and after insisting that not only the boy, who is her own grandson's age, but his parents, too, partake of the sweets, she opens her novel to the bookmarked page and with dignified and guilty passion begins to lick the forbidden lollipop.

11.

THE HOURS PLOD along, the rain continues to fall, the wind stiffens. Francisco phones and in his gentle English requests Ya'ari's guidance. Despite the storm, his father is insisting on his morning walk.

From time to time Ya'ari is called upon to adjudicate a dispute between his father and the Filipino, and generally he decides in his father's favour, even when the old man's wishes seem eccentric. He has no reason to believe that the disease that in recent years has caused trembling in his father's hands and feet and greatly slowed his gait has also undermined his judgment. True, since the onset of his illness the old man has sunk into depression and his speech has grown halting and spare, but Ya'ari, who has always honoured his father, feels that his core remains strong and that despite being cooped up at home he has kept his clear sense of reality.

"It's okay," the son assures Francisco. "Just dress him warmly, put the black poncho on him, and make sure he wears a scarf and hat."

"But Mister Ya'ari, Abba's hat is missing."

"Then find him another. Just don't take him out without one. The last time you forgot, he caught a cold. Attach the canopy I made for the wheelchair and don't walk around the streets. Take him to the playground, so if the rain gets worse you can shelter under the awning by the slides. It's okay if he gets a little wet. The smell of the rain makes him happy. He likes the wind, too."

"You want to say something to Abba?"

"Not right now. Just tell him that I will come to light the

candles with him in the early evening."

"Hanukkah candles . . ."

"Bravo, Francisco. You've got it."

Still preoccupied by his wife's stopover, Ya'ari postpones one of his meetings until midafternoon and sets out early to meet his son. But when he sees that the rain has not let up, indeed has intensified, he decides to detour to the playground near his childhood home to watch his father's excursion.

Beyond the windscreen wipers he sees the slight figure of Francisco, all bundled up, slowly pushing his father's wheelchair among the slides and seesaws of the empty playground. The caregiver has indeed wrapped the old man properly in a scarf, covered him with the black poncho, and placed on his head a red beret from Ya'ari's army days.

He waits till the wheelchair has completed its tour and begins to head in their direction. Though his old beret nearly covers his father's eyes, Ya'ari senses and savours the pleasure of this old man who is stronger than wind and rain.

12.

NEITHER THE AUTHOR of the novel nor the character she has invented succeeds in arousing Daniela's sympathies. She reads conscientiously, never skipping a line, but still has no sense of the heroine's inner life, not even when, on page 20, she pays a belligerent visit to her parents' home, intending to bolster her self-pity by reviving a childhood grudge. Daniela finds the nasty fight that breaks out between daughter and parents artificial and unconvincing. The author doesn't seem to understand that at the heart of family animosities there is a warm intimacy that does not exist among warring strangers. She props her legs up on the suitcase that stands on the floor, since the waiter has reclaimed one of her chairs for a group of tourists who came flooding in, but when he returns to swipe the chair holding her big bag—implying that the old white lady's mere coffee and sandwich do not justify her taking root—she puts on her shoes and wheels her case towards the departure gate.

The gate is at the end of the corridor. The door to the runway is locked, and there is no fellow traveller in the small, desolate waiting area. The three hours remaining until takeoff are a dreary and demoralizing prospect. For the first time since she decided to make the long trip to her brother-in-law in Africa, she is annoyed with her husband for not insisting on joining her. True, she knew that his presence would not always fit in with the memorial she planned for her late sister. But now, in the empty room with the locked door, she needs him. She has depended on his presence for so many years that now it is like a soothing drug in her bloodstream. He should never have allowed her to go off alone. Yes, in a few hours she will be welcomed by her brother-in-law, who calls her Little Sister, but on the phone he seemed unclear as to the purpose of the visit she is imposing on him, and she sensed that he might even fear it a little. For her part, she finds his reasons for returning to the continent where his diplomatic job had been eliminated equally vague. Was it really just to save money for his old age? And what exactly does he do there? He is already past seventy, and she knows that her sister, who loved and trusted him, would be happy to know that someone from the family was watching over him.

Out of hunger and fatigue, but even more out of boredom,

she eats a whole bar of chocolate, which leaves an unpleasant aftertaste in her mouth. She should never have given her airplane breakfast to that random young man as if he were her husband. The next flight is not a long one, and they won't be serving a real meal, so she had better return soon to the cafeteria and satisfy her hunger with something hot. Meanwhile she can stretch out on one of the benches facing the locked departure gate. Of course it's not fitting for a mature bourgeois woman to stretch out like a vagrant on an airport bench, but she's alone here, and if her lying down bothers anybody, she'll sense it and sit up.

The bench is hard and she has nothing to cushion it with. She returns to her novel. Having failed to convey the heroine's internal anguish, the author resorts, predictably, to her external woes, and begins to complicate the plot. A former secret agent appears suddenly as a standoffish lover, a device that does nothing to revive the reader's flagging interest. Daniela's eyes grow heavy, and she quickly marks her place with the boarding pass and sticks the book in her suitcase, lest it tumble open to the floor as drowsiness overcomes her.

Fatigue ripples through the solitary woman who lounges near the locked gate. Despite the uncomfortable conditions, her sleep is deep and soothing, and the passengers who arrive for the flight preceding hers do not demand that she cut it short. From time to time she hears fragments of warm and pleasant voices speaking European languages and also strange African tongues, but does not open her eyes to ascertain whether the people beside her are white or black. They all wish her well. A soft smile glides over her face. The missing husband is replaced in her sleep by many husbands, utter strangers, but lovable all the same.

13.

FROM AFAR YA'ARI sees his son waiting for him by the closed gate of the construction site, wearing a short military-style jacket similar in colour and cut to his own, but made of fabric instead of leather. Knowing that his son has not brought a helmet, he takes two from the boot of his car, yellow ones, places one on his own head and gives his son the other, teasing him, here you go, it's instead of your reserve duty helmet. They open the gate and enter the main site, where the frame of the building is still unfinished. The foreman, who has been charged to keep secret the building's ultimate purpose, shakes their hands cordially and steers them into a wobbly yellow cage, operated by a sad Chinese, that rises slow and screeching towards the grey girders at the top, while they peer through the bars like monkeys at the fine rain that streaks the horizon. You won't be cold up there? the supervisor asks Moran. If my father's not cold, neither am I, the son smiles. Ya'ari protests: I'm me and you're you. Then, without warning, the cage stops with a shudder, and they walk out onto a pitted surface covered with building materials, and peek into the grey abyss of the elevator shaft, from which sprout iron cables and scraps of scaffolding.

Ya'ari kneels down and inspects the shaft, warning the supervisor about cracks and holes. I've already got my share of trouble from shoddy work on a shaft in an apartment building in the western part of town, and even though I'm responsible for the elevator, not the shaft, the tenants, as you can well imagine, are on my back to deal with every stray wind that happens to get sucked inside.

Moran takes out a metal tape measure and extends it along the top of the shaft. Be careful there, his father calls out, don't get too close to the edge. A flash of sweet memory takes him back thirty years, to the night of passion when he sired this boy. What was that "real passion" line she tossed his way when they parted at the airport? Was it just the delusion of a woman no longer young, or a veiled challenge to the man who had not fought hard enough for love in the days before her trip?

Moran pulls out more of the tape. He is checking to make sure that the shaft's actual dimensions match those that were planned in the office, before they begin to deal with the new request that occasioned this visit: to add a fifth elevator, a private one for top-level agents whose identities cannot be exposed.

Ya'ari warns the foreman: "Even if we succeed in installing an extra elevator at the expense of the other four, it'll be very cramped, with room for only one person, preferably not a fat one."

But the size of the fifth elevator is unimportant to the supervisor, so long as it works.

A tear in the clouds sends a shaft of light onto the shaved head of Moran, who is not happy with the measurements. You've already clipped four centimetres from the width we requested, he tells the foreman, and if you keep building the shaft at the same angle, in the end we'll be fifteen centimetres short, so how can you demand an additional elevator?

He loudly zips the metal tape back into its case, replaces it in his pocket, and shakes the construction dust from his hands.

The missing centimetres do not worry Ya'ari. We'll manage, he reassures his son, and signals to the Chinese, who is mesmerized by the sea, to open the yellow cage and take them down to ground level. And as he looks around at the ever growing city, he thinks of the distant traveller. Yes, she is surely exhausted and irritable from the long wait in the transit area that he has imposed on her, but he has no doubt that her smiling eyes will enchant everyone who comes near her.

14.

AND INDEED, AS the swift equatorial dusk darkens the narrow windows, she is cheered by the new passengers who are gathering for her flight. A steward writes the name of the airline and the flight number and destination in chalk on a small blackboard, and hangs the board by the exit door. She evaluates the human qualities of her fellow passengers, black and white, making note of who might be approachable for support should anything go wrong en route, or should her brother-in-law be late picking her up in Morogoro.

She goes to the toilet and methodically applies her makeup, looking with approval at her reflection in the less than clean mirror. When boarding is announced she does not wait, as she usually does, till the line shortens or disappears, but rather gets up quickly to be among the first. And when the steward asks to see her passport she presents it readily. But her boarding pass is missing.

The line is held up while everyone waits patiently for the smiling woman to find the pass in her bag; when she doesn't she is asked courteously to step aside and hunt more thoroughly. Is it really necessary? she inquires in her precise English. Can't one do without it? After all, the return ticket is proof enough. But it turns out that the actual piece of paper is required, for even though this gate has no machine that swallows the passes and then ejects them, but only a human hand, soft and delicate, the pass is still the sole guarantee that she has in fact boarded the flight and not disappeared.

A few more minutes of futile searching go by, until an airline employee in an orange uniform, which goes nicely with her dark skin, gently moves her away from the lengthening queue and suggests that she look in her suitcase. It will turn up, she assures the mortified passenger. It's bound to turn up.

She smiles in agreement with the amiable woman, even as she feels embarrassed and desperate, as well as furious at her husband. This was predictable. He did warn her to keep all the documents together, and now he might even be pleased that his anxiety was justified and that he cannot rely on her, and thus it is his duty and mission to paralyze her with his ministrations, anaesthetize her, cushion her very being as if she were a princess.

But she does remember it well, that rectangular boarding pass. She had it, she saw it, she didn't disrespect or neglect it, she remembers what it looked like, its colour, so why is it betraying her now, disappearing and leaving her bereft in a transit lounge?

Travellers pass by her, a European family with children, gaily boarding the short evening flight to the game reserve of their dreams. The bus that is to take them to the plane turns on its lights and starts its engine. Has your suitcase already been loaded onto the plane? they ask her. No, she assures them, it's only a week-long trip, to visit a relative; her wheeled carry-on is all she has. For a moment she considers adding that her host was until a few years ago a chargé d'affaires in the region; perhaps, owing to his high status, they might forgive her the boarding pass, but on second thoughts such credentials strike her as useless, so she says nothing.

This makes it easier for the airline staff. No need to delay the flight and hunt for a suitcase on the plane. They can simply leave the flustered passenger here and send the plane on its way. It occurs to her that if she'd had another bag, they might have had to forget about the boarding pass and let her travel with her suitcase, but no, Yirmi had advised her not to bring too many clothes; the weather is pleasant, he'd said, and if it gets cold, I still have your sister's sweater and windbreaker.

She is on the verge of tears. Suddenly the disappearance of her boarding pass merges with the death of her sister.

But she *will* remember where she put that damned pass. She will summon all her strength, she will wake up. It is not just her husband who put her in this stupor, but also her sister's death. She must snap out of it, otherwise there's no point in this trip to far-off Africa that was meant to prevent the pain of her loss from diminishing. If she doesn't wake up, how will she be able to revive memories of her forgotten childhood? Her brother-in-law can't do the work for her. Deep down she knows that he has reservations about her visit, even if it's only for seven days. He doesn't understand its purpose, and is also wary of her criticism, open or implicit. He fears having her dig into his affairs. And if she arrives in a scatterbrained, stupefied state, then he, like her husband, will anaesthetize her, cushion her very being, and increase her dependency, just as he had done with her sister.

Which is why she must find that boarding pass. She will not

degrade herself and go like a naughty schoolgirl to the transit counter and ask that her flight be rescheduled for the next day. She will pull herself together, she will not allow the love lavished upon her to demolish her independence. She needs a dash of misery, genuine anger at herself, like that masochistic heroine in the novel that so far she doesn't care for very much.

Suddenly it becomes clear. No, the pass is not lost, it is in the book, in the suitcase, marking the place where she left off, where the heroine had exhausted her capacity for empathy.

Wait, wait, she calls to the steward, who is about to shut the door on her. She gets down on her knees and opens the suitcase, and beside the package of newspapers she finds the novel, and the boarding pass protrudes from it, safe and sound. She pulls it out, making a mental note of the page number before closing the book.

"We've been looking for someone to take care of you," the steward says, tearing the stub from the card, "but I see you've taken care of yourself."

Since she is the last passenger, he rolls her bag to the bus, though now it seems to roll happily by itself. Once there, she is welcomed with enthusiasm, people getting up to offer her a seat, and she smiles and sits down, taking care to insert into her passport, as her husband had instructed, the remaining portion of the boarding pass, even though in a few minutes she will have to take it out again and present it to the stewardess who is at the door of the plane.

15.

THE SUNSET, DIMLY visible between the heavy clouds, casts grey shadows in Ya'ari's office. But he does not turn on the light, tilting back instead in his comfortable desk chair, closing his eyes in a moment of contemplation before fulfilling the final obligation of a day that began before dawn. His father is eating dinner now, but because it is hard for Ya'ari to watch Francisco's wife, Kinzie, feeding him with a small spoon, he prefers to arrive at the end of the meal, when his father's bib has been removed and his face washed clean.

It's quiet in the office. Because of the holiday, the women finished their workday at lunchtime, and not all the men who went out for lunch made it back to their desks, either. A few years ago, after his father could no longer conceal the trembling in his extremities and finally retired, Ya'ari did away with clocking-in, expecting that hours missed would be stamped upon the individual conscience of each employee. He was right. Sometimes at night, when he and Daniela are on their way home from a concert or a movie, he will detour past the office to show her the bright flicker of busy computers in the windows.

"Listen, Ya'ari," says Gottlieb, the elevator manufacturer, on the telephone. "I see that the wind is up again, and as I told you this morning, even if our work is not to blame, I'm willing, if only for the personal and professional peace of mind of a friend who trusted us, to send my expert there right now, but on condition that you, or someone from your office, will go with her."

"Why?"

"Because at the site she can advise you better on how to deal with the tenants and prove to them that the noises are not caused by your design and certainly not by my elevators, but

43

exclusively by the construction company's lousy job on the shaft and maybe also a mistake of the architect's in the placement of the fire doors in the garage. I don't need to hear any howling myself to know that the wind is getting in from the bottom, not from the top, and my technician will diagnose for you exactly what's causing the uproar. So listen, my friend, don't be lazy; tomorrow the weather will improve and the storm will be gone and they won't hear a thing. Take yourself over there and meet her in half an hour, and don't change your mind. Or send your son. She's a rare type, a gifted person, professional, who will relieve you once and for all of the guilt you decided to take upon yourself this morning just so you could pin it on me this afternoon."

"Not guilt, responsibility."

"Then she'll free you from responsibility."

"But what's so special about her?"

"She can pinpoint, just by listening, malfunctions in motors or cables long before they cause serious problems. With such a finely-tuned ear she could conduct a philharmonic orchestra plus a big choir, instead of working with us in the service department . . ."

"Israeli?"

"Totally Israeli. She was sent as a child to some musical kibbutz in Galilee, where she developed perfect pitch among the tractors and combines and ploughs."

"How old is she?"

"Thirty, forty, maybe more. But tiny, ageless, athletic . . . She can slide herself into any crack . . . A fearless little devil."

"All right, I'll find someone to meet her in the garage."

"Better if you go yourself . . ."

"Can't do it, my father's Filipinos are waiting for me with the Hanukkah candles."

"What's going on with your old man?"

"Stable."

"Give him my regards. You know how much I loved and respected him."

"So keep on loving and respecting him, because he's alive and well."

"Obviously, no question . . . but still, my dear Ya'ari, on your way, hop over to the winds, and we'll be done with this whole affair."

"No. My workday is over. I got up at three in the morning to take my wife to the airport."

"Where'd she go off to in the middle of winter?"

"To Africa."

"An organized tour?"

"No, she went alone."

"To Africa? By herself? You never told me you had such an adventurous wife."

Ya'ari would like to explain to the elevator manufacturer that his wife would not be there alone. But he holds off. Adventurous? So be it. This lends his wife an aura she never aspired to, and that suddenly appeals to him.

16.

THIS TIME SHE leans her head against the window, as if it were a spouse's shoulder, and keenly watches the moving world below. The aircraft is a propeller plane, new, not large, that cruises with a steady and pleasant hum through the clear evening sky at low altitude, so that she can see not only the bend of a river and the contour of a small lake but also the lights of houses, and here and there even a campfire. Her pride over not missing the flight has made her uncharacteristically alert and aware. She takes out her passport, checks the accompanying travel documents, and then turns its pages, one after the next, as if it were a small prayer book.

In the adjoining seat is an elderly Englishman, blue-skinned, white-haired and heavyset, already accepting from the stewardess his third glass of Scotch. But he doesn't worry Daniela. The flight will not be long, and the man seems solid and essentially sober, and appears to be looking at her with secret appreciation. Yes, despite her age, she is well aware that she has not lost her feminine charm. If she were to turn to the English gentleman with specific questions in her excellent English, encouraging him to talk about himself, he might well fall in love with her by the time they landed. But instead she turns towards the window, because the expanse of Africa, lit by the moon, is what now engages her.

17.

THE WIND IS back, says Ya'ari, detaching his son from the computer. Gottlieb is sending his acoustic technician to the Pinsker Tower to figure out the source of the winds and to free us—and mainly him—from responsibility to the tenants. But he insists on one of us joining her and hearing her explanations. I'm in no mood for any more wind, and I'm rushing to light candles with Grandpa, so do me a favour, habibi, go and meet her in the garage, and we'll put an end to the complaints. It's unacceptable that individual tenants are pestering me on my cell phone.

In the ample living room of his childhood home, positioned in front of the Channel One news, his father sits trembling in a wheelchair; by his side is six-year-old Hilario, the Filipinos' son, whose Hebrew is fluent, and accent-free. Hilario has his own little hanukkiah, the eight-branched holiday menorah, made of yellow clay and set with three candles of different colours, which await Ya'ari's arrival together with the three candles in the big, old menorah.

When his father's illness worsened, Daniela insisted that they bring in not one Filipino carer but two, a married couple who would add to caring the stable and secure embrace of a small family. It's a big house, she said, there's room for everyone, and for a little extra money we'll buy peace of mind for all of us.

Is the house actually big? Ya'ari has been asking himself lately, when he comes to visit his father and sees how the living area has shrunk, what with the buggy and playpen, the bassinet in the kitchen, and the rack for drying laundry. The couple,

Francisco and Kinzie, who themselves look like teenagers, a few months ago became the parents of a daughter, who requires her own substantial space, and then there's little Hilario, born in Southeast Asia, who occupies Ya'ari's childhood room and who, having left the local kindergarten that Ya'ari himself attended as a boy, is a devoted and studious pupil in the first grade. He sits now at the ready beside the trembling grandfather, an unlit candle in his hand and a kippah on his head, waiting for Ya'ari to give him permission to recite the blessings and light the menorah.

"Don't overdo it . . ." says Ya'ari, reaching to remove the skullcap from the little Filipino's head.

But Ya'ari's father stops him, what do you care? He's not hurting anybody with his kippah. He has a new teacher now, who has come from a religious school, and she gives the kids a little religion, more than the zero you got.

Ya'ari has already grown accustomed to his father knowing every detail of Hilario's life, more than he ever knew about Ya'ari or his brother when they were children. And no wonder: his father's English is minimal, so he speaks with his two carers through their firstborn son, and along the way learns about the world of his young translator.

"Fine," sighs Ya'ari in English. "I'm exhausted, so first of all let's finish with the candles."

The old man motions to Francisco to turn off the lights, so that the flickering flames will delight the boy. And then Hilario lights the shammash, the candle in his hand that lends its fire to all the others, and in a whisper, but without a single mistake, he chants the two traditional blessings, while touching the friendly fire to the candles in his little clay hanukkiah. When he is done, he offers the shammash to Ya'ari, but Ya'ari gestures for him to continue, and the child, his face aglow with excitement, stands on tiptoe and repeats the blessings, while with an unsteady hand he lights the shammash and candles in the grandfather's menorah. Afterwards he turns to his mother, who sits in a corner with her infant in her arms, and gets her permission to sing a Hanukkah song. To Ya'ari's relief it is not "Maoz Tsur," which he loathes, but rather an old Hanukkah song whose melody is modest and pleasing to the ear, and since Francisco and Kinzie do not know the words nor even the tune, Ya'ari has no choice but to back the boy up with some humming of his own.

When the ceremony is over, the father wants to know if Daniela has arrived safely at Yirmiyahu's place. Two days ago she came to say good-bye and told him at length about the purpose of her trip, and although the father listened intently and kept nodding his head, not merely from his illness, but in approval of her wish to return and recover the grief and pain that had begun to fade, he was uneasy for his beloved daughter-in-law, travelling to East Africa alone.

Ya'ari looks at his watch. As far as he knows, there is no time difference between Israel and East Africa, so if everything is all right she is in mid-air and due to land in one hour.

"But Yirmiyahu is no longer an ambassador there . . ." the father recalls.

"He never was an ambassador, just a chargé d'affaires in a small economic mission, which closed down after Shuli died."

By the soft light of the six flames Ya'ari can see that his father's eyes are blazing. A blush spreads over his cheeks, the tremor in his body worsens, and his hands shake uncontrollably. His gaze drifts away from his son and into a corner of the room. Ya'ari turns his head and sees that the Filipino woman is taking advantage of the darkness to nurse the baby. Despite the natural duskiness of her skin the darkness of the room does not conceal her naked bosom; the flickering fire of the Hanukkah candles reveals the sweet shapely splendour of a young woman's breast, which apparently stirs the soul of the old man.

Francisco should be warned, thinks Ya'ari, not to let his wife expose herself like that in front of his father. Because she dresses him and feeds him, it would be bad to afflict him unduly with a longing for her flesh.

But the moment is unsuitable for warnings, especially in front of the boy, who is fascinated by the flames, so he shifts the wheelchair slightly, depriving his father of the sight of his carer's bare breast, and also casually attempts to distract him with a description of the winds whistling in the elevator shaft of the Pinsker Tower, which sucks them in from the outside world in a way that remains mysterious.

18.

THE MOMENT OF arrival is announced, and the stewardess rises to distribute sweets to the passengers. But the Englishman, gulping the last of his Scotch, declines to ruin the taste of good Scotch with the acid drop he is offered, so with sheepish generosity he offers his to the silent lady traveller beside him. And in the few minutes remaining before they land, she is willing not only to accept the sweet, but also to ask him about the climate and scenery awaiting her on the ground.

It turns out that the elderly Englishman adores the Morogoro nature reserve and even owns a small farm there. Because of his fondness for the wildlife, he returns here every year, as it is absolutely clear to him that the animals miss him, too; but he has never heard of an anthropological dig in the area. To tell the truth, he has no interest in such excavations; indeed, it seems to him a bit strange that such a pleasant and elegant woman as herself is about to join up with bone-hunters searching for prehistoric monkey men, given that the spectacular natural world of the here and now veritably teems with mystery. Therefore, as the wheels of the aircraft touch down on the runway, she feels compelled to correct the misguided impression he has formed of the nature of her journey, and to reveal its true purpose. And the Englishman, whose melancholy grew after the empty glass was taken from him, empathizes greatly with her tale of loss and wishes to add a tear of his own over the dear, dead sister and the soldier who was so needlessly killed. He even seems prepared, time permitting, to fall in love with her, and before unbuckling his seat belt he hands the Israeli woman a business card with the name and address of his estate: perhaps she might like to come and visit. Daniela accepts the card, as she did the sweet, and faithful to her husband's order to keep everything together, she tucks it in beside the medical insurance papers in the passport envelope, because now, as she descends in darkness the steps of the plane, she is conscious not only of the time and distance she has covered, but also of the erosion of her capacity to carry on alone, so she wheels her suitcase in the faltering footsteps of the inebriated Englishman, who is swiftly installed in a wheelchair by two brawny Africans, so that he may make a more dignified exit from the tiny airport.

Even after she exits passport control and is surrounded by porters and greeters, Daniela keeps her eye on the wheelchair, since at first glance she notices that among the dozens of black faces crowding behind the fence and in front of it too, there is no familiar-looking white one. But a sense of her own worth protects her from any worry or fear; only a strange smile alights on her lips. She is entirely certain that even if the visit she has imposed on her brother-in-law is not much to his liking, he would never think of not coming to welcome the woman who in her childhood had been integral to his courtship of her sister and had championed their love with her whole young heart. And he, for his part, would always call her Little Sister and help her with her homework in arithmetic and geometry, and would be dispatched late at night to fetch her in her father's car from youth-group activities or school parties.

Even as her strange smile begins to compete with a look of mild panic, there arises from the middle of the crowd a little sign, with her name and flight number in a familiar hand.

It is not Yirmiyahu waving the sign, however, but a noble emissary, black as night, very tall and erect. A red scarf is wrapped about her neck and she wears the white gown of a doctor or nurse. And when Daniela signals that she is the sought-after passenger, the emissary hurries towards her through the throng of greeters, who judging by their great number must be mainly curious onlookers who come each evening to this rural airport in case the plane might need their assistance in taking off or landing.

The thin, very tall woman bends towards Mrs. Ya'ari and in simple, correct English, albeit of indeterminate accent, introduces herself: Sijjin Kuang, Sudanese, a nurse attached to the anthropological research team. That afternoon, she took a patient to the local hospital, and was asked to stay around till evening to pick up a guest from Israel. Naturally, after such a long wait, she is in a hurry to get back. The distance to the base camp of the excavations is not great, thirty miles, but half of that is on dirt roads. She is pleased to learn that the visitor has no luggage apart from her small suitcase, and advises her to use the toilet, since the road ahead will not offer proper facilities. But Daniela, eager to get going, says without a second thought, thank you, I'm all set.

In the car park a dust-covered vehicle is waiting, with shovels and hoes and earth-strainers strewn inside. The nurse is also the driver. Before she starts the engine, she hands the visitor a bag containing a thermos and a large sandwich, food for the journey sent by the brother-in-law, whose absence remains unexplained.

Daniela wearily removes the thick wrapper (which appears to be a page torn from an old encyclopaedia), revealing a sort of giant pita, brown and thick, with sliced egg inside, layered with strips of aubergine fried with onion.

Sijjin Kuang manoeuvres deftly between the cars scattered in the car park, at the same time studying the passenger, who gazes with amazement at the enormous sandwich.

"Jeremy said you would love it . . ."

Daniela's eyes sparkle. Yes, he's right. She and her sister always loved aubergine, maybe because this was the first vegetable that their mother, a finicky immigrant, had learned to cook in the Land of Israel. Despite the hunger rumbling inside her since she skipped the meal on her first flight, and which the sandwich and sweets at the airport had failed to quiet, she offers to share her pita with the Sudanese woman, who declines, no, this is meant only for you—a peace offering from a person who was afraid to come to the airport himself.

"Afraid?"

"That other passengers from your country would be with you."

"Israelis?"

"Yes, Israelis."

"What is there to fear from them?"

"I don't know. Perhaps I am mistaken," the nurse corrects herself, "but I think he does not want to meet anyone from his country right now, not to see them, not to feel them, not even from afar."

"Not even from afar?" Daniela repeats with astonishment and pain the words of the Sudanese woman, who for all her thinness and delicacy displays great expertise in speeding the heavy vehicle down the dark road. "In what sense? By the way, on my plane there was not a single other Israeli."

"He could not know that in advance," smiles the driver, whose upright head threatens to bang into the roof of the car.

The guest nods slowly in agreement and adds not a word. In truth, she has come from so far away not merely to summon pain and memory, but also to understand what is going on with her brother-in-law. And now this messenger may offer a first clue. She unscrews the cap of the thermos, carefully pours in the warm tea, and offers it to the nurse, who repeats and explains in good English, it is all for you, Mrs. Ya'ari, I have eaten and had something to drink, it is best for me to concentrate on driving, since the roads here are sometimes difficult to follow.

The sweet tea refreshes Daniela, who pours herself a second

cup and a third. Afterwards she begins to bite carefully into the fragrant sandwich, and after swallowing the last crumb with great contentment, she receives permission and indeed encouragement from the Sudanese to enhance the good taste with a soothing cigarette, the last of the five or six she smokes every day. Only then, as the tobacco ash flickers in the darkness, does she turn to Sijjin Kuang and begins a polite and cautious interrogation.

19.

ON HIS WAY home in the wind and rain, grey-faced from an exhausting day, the father phones his son to hear the technician's diagnosis of the winds in the tower. And who is this expert, anyway, whom Gottlieb showers with praise?

Moran sounds amused and excited. "No, Gottlieb's not exaggerating. You missed out on a magician and juggler. Right out of the circus."

"How old is she, anyway?"

"Hard to tell. She's a kind of child-woman, who at first glance looks twenty, but by the time I left she seemed over forty. The face of a child, huge eyes, nimble and a bit hyper. She worked for years in the regional auto garage at Kfar Blum, up north . . ."

"Whatever," Ya'ari says with a yawn. "What's the verdict with the winds?"

"Wait a minute. Listen, she has incredible hearing. First, imagine this, as soon as we start going up in the middle elevator, she can already tell that we replaced the original seal with a different one. You remember?"

"Moran, I remember nothing. I got up at three A.M., lit candles with Grandpa, and I'm wiped out. Give me the bottom line. How are the winds getting in?"

"She claims that the shaft is cracked and pocked with holes in more than one place, which produces an unusual sound effect, like the sound from the holes of a flute or clarinet. She recommends that at three in the morning we shut down all the elevators and ride on top of one of them in order to locate the exact spot of the penetration."

"Forget it. Flute or clarinet, what does it have to do with us? The defect, just as I thought, is in the shaft, so we're not responsible. The tenants need to go to the construction company."

"I'm not sure you're entirely right, Abba. Gottlieb was obliged, and so were we as the designers, to check the shaft carefully before installing anything."

"Now listen, Moran. The shaft is not our responsibility. Period. Cracks and holes can develop even after the installation is finished."

"She claims, according to the sounds, that these are old defects."

"*She* claims . . . *she* says . . . habibi, calm down. This little girl is not God around here. Anyway, we'll talk tomorrow at the office."

"And Imma, did you hear from her?"

"According to my calculations, she's still in the air, unless I'm wrong."

20.

HE IS WRONG. It's remarkable that a practical man like him is unaware that East Africa is one hour ahead of Israel, meaning that the beloved traveller is no longer in the air, but on the ground, on a dark and desolate mountain road—though her fate is in the capable hands of an intelligent driver, whom she is briskly quizzing about her life story.

In the bloody civil war of southern Sudan, Sijjin Kuang's relatives and many other members of her tribe were slaughtered because their skin colour was blacker than that of their murderers. She, alone among her entire family, was saved. Her rescuer was a United Nations observer, a Norwegian, tall like her, who arranged for her rehabilitation and education in his country on condition that when she received her nursing degree she would return to serve in a field hospital on the Sudanese-Kenyan border, where she could take care of the wounded of her tribe. But the hospital was never established, and while going around Nairobi looking for other work, she learned that UNESCO was funding an anthropological expedition made up solely of African scientists, whose goal was to discover, using their own research methods, the missing link between the apes and man. She applied to the director of the mission, a Tanzanian named Seloha Abu, offering her services as nurse to the team.

"You are a Christian, of course," says Daniela, who is highly impressed by her personality and the details of her story. But Sijjin Kuang is neither Christian nor Muslim, but rather an animist, as supporters call them, or *mushrikun,* as their opponents call them, or, in cultural-scientific terms, simply pagan.

"Pagan?" The Israeli is overwhelmed by such intimate contact, in the dark, with an idol-worshipper. "Really? In what sense? This is so interesting . . . because for us, pagans are only in legends . . ."

And the Sudanese, with a slightly embarrassed smile, explains very briefly the principles of her ancient tribal faith.

"Spirits? Winds?"

"Yes. Sacred spirits in trees and stones."

"And this kind of belief," Daniela inquires cautiously, "does not interfere with the rationality of the medical science that you studied?"

"No belief can interfere with care for the sick," the Sudanese declares. "Least of all animism, since any person may approach the spirits individually and according to his understanding, without any pope or ayatollah to do it for him."

"Marvellous . . ."

Daniela now wonders how a white person such as her brother-in-law was accepted to join a scientific mission composed only of Africans, all the more because he is neither a scientist nor a doctor, and moreover is a citizen of a country not generally well-liked. But the Sudanese has a simple explanation. To prevent conflicts on sensitive matters among Africans who have joined the mission from all over the continent, it was decided that financial management and supervision of expenses would be placed in the hands of a white man, a foreigner yet an experienced person, someone familiar with the region and its ways. Then a white widowed pensioner, a former diplomat in Africa, offered them his experience in administration and finance, and struck the members of the team as a reliable and objective person, immune to outside temptation.

"Temptation? In what sense?"

"Temptation that might prevent him from handling the accounts with honesty and precision. But soon he will explain this to you himself."

A warm summer wind streams through the open window of the car, scented by the thick flora. This is hill country, and the car climbs and descends the lower slopes surrounding Mount Morogoro, which appears periodically and then vanishes from view. The moon that accompanied her flight has disappeared behind the clouds, but its light is reflected by the lush roadside foliage that brushes the sides of the car. Not long ago, following a small road sign, the driver turned off the asphalt onto a dirt road. Though narrow, the road is tightly packed and free of potholes, and the engine maintains its powerful rhythm. But Daniela now has a bit of a problem. The huge sandwich she consumed, and the great quantity of tea that preceded it, demand relief. Had she known about those in advance, she would not so blithely have passed up the chance to use the toilet at the airport. No choice now but to ask the kind driver to stop at a spot appropriate for both car and passenger and inquire as to whether there might be some paper handy; otherwise, she will have to open her suitcase.

"You will have to open your suitcase," Sijjin Kuang says, laughing, and slows to a halt.

She cautions the traveller not to try to seek privacy in the bush, where she is likely to arouse the interest of some small creature. You can simply stay on the road, you can see there is no traffic here, and even if a car should happen to pass by, no one will remember you.

But Daniela is uncomfortable being exposed in the

moonlight, even in front of this licensed nurse, who in the meantime has turned off the engine and got out to stretch her legs and light up some sort of long pipe, thin and black like its owner. So she goes off to a bend in the road. Even there, despite Sijjin Kuang's warning, she is reluctant to crouch on the road, and blazes herself a trail a few steps into the bush.

Under the whispering branches of an African tree she pulls down her trousers with great emotion. The senior schoolteacher at ease with herself, the wife, experienced mother and grandmother is visited by the memory of a mortified little girl who at a family outing at the Yarkon River, while basking in the love of aunts and uncles and cousins, suddenly lost control, and whose soaked panties threatened to destroy her happy world. But neither her mother nor her father had been aware of her distress, and her older sister had rushed to shield the crying child and discreetly take her to the riverbank, to a clump of bushes not unlike the one where she squats now, and with kind words wiped away her shame, soothed and consoled her, until she smiled again.

And now, with her pants at her ankles, by the light of a hidden moon whose movement in the sky speckles the surrounding foliage, free of the controlling love of her husband, who could not begin to imagine how far the arrow has flown from the bow drawn at the airport at dawn, she surrenders to the agony of losing a beloved sister, who always knew how to comfort her but had not succeeded in comforting herself. She lingers in her crouch, drinking deeply the grief that floods her, and slowly, slowly consoles herself, stands up, and straightens her clothing, but does not leave the place until she gathers a few stones to hide what she has left behind.

Total silence. As she returns to the dirt road the Israeli briefly loses her way to the car that holds her suitcase and her travel documents, but she does not lose her nerve, and loudly calls the full name of the nurse. Sijjin Kuang! Sijjin Kuang! Sijjin Kuang! Three times she repeats the name of the tall idol-worshipper. And the animist, who is probably at this very moment seeking the blessing of the wind and trees and stones for the successful continuation of the journey, switches on the headlights and honks, to show the white woman the way back.

21.

Late in the evening, Ya'ari collects the newspaper that was flung onto his doorstep at dawn and turns on the lights in the clean and polished apartment. With amused curiosity he looks for innovations made in his absence. Their long-serving housekeeper, whom Daniela respects and even admires, has carte blanche to run their home as she sees fit, which is truly a great liberty, since besides cleaning and cooking she often whimsically rearranges furniture, closets, and bureaux so that the owners, returning home of an evening, may discover that an armchair has moved to the other side of the living room, underwear and socks have migrated to foreign drawers, and a plant that has forever dwelt peacefully on the porch is now a centrepiece on the dining room table. Some relocations are happily accepted, others rejected and reversed, but out of respect for the cleaning lady, never a comment is made.

Today there are no changes at home. Only in the Hanukkah menorah, cleansed of last night's wax, has the housekeeper before leaving work stuck two new candles and the shammash, for tonight's lighting. But this evening Ya'ari has no intention of reciting the blessing alone over more flames, so he adds a fourth candle, for tomorrow night, and moves the menorah to a corner of the kitchen.

From the quantity of food still sitting warm on the kitchen counter he guesses that the housekeeper has not quite grasped that in the coming week only one person will be eating here. As he samples each dish with his fork, he flips through the TV channels to make sure that no plane has crashed today. His brother-in-law warned him that communication between the base camp of the dig and the wider world had to run first through Dar es Salaam, but Ya'ari was adamant: That may be so, but since I'm sending you a woman who for many years has not travelled abroad by herself and who, since her sister's death, has become even more dreamy and absent-minded, I must receive a sign of life within twenty-four hours. If not her voice, then yours, and if not yours, at least an e-mail to the office.

22.

JUST BEFORE MIDNIGHT, they arrive at the base camp of the scientific mission, set upon a colonial farm, built at the beginning of the last century. Following Tanzanian independence, the property was confiscated from its European owners and turned into an elite training camp for army officers and public officials favoured by the government. But tribal conflicts and violent regime changes made it impossible for officers and officials to maintain domestic tranquillity within a single locale, and the place was abandoned and forgotten for many years, until two African anthropologists discovered it and approached UNESCO with a request for help in renovating it as a service facility for new excavations.

In the darkness, the outline of the farmhouse seems a ghost of the colonial past. But a light is burning on the ground floor. That is the kitchen, where he is no doubt waiting for you, says Sijjin Kuang to her passenger, who suddenly feels too exhausted to lift her small suitcase. After the Sudanese woman picks up a package from the backseat, she leads the visitor towards the light.

If Shuli only knew how far Daniela has travelled, alone, to rekindle her memory, she would be pleased, perhaps even proud of her, but surely also apprehensive—as Daniela is now—about her encounter with the widower left behind.

"Here he is." The nurse points to a tall silhouette in the doorway.

Instead of running to his sister-in-law, to embrace her and help wheel her suitcase, Yirmiyahu waits at the entrance for the two women to come to him. Only then does he hug Daniela tight, and fondly pat the shoulder of the black nurse who brought her.

"What happened?" he asks in English, "I thought that maybe you changed your mind and cancelled at the last minute."

"Why? Did you want me to change my mind?"

"No, I did not want anything."

He insists on continuing the conversation in English, on account of Sijjin Kuang, who stands as still as a statue beside him, holding the package in her arms like someone offering a sacrifice. Then, as if feeling sorry for his sister-in-law, who has made this long journey all by herself, he hugs her again and takes the handle of her rolling suitcase. At that moment she senses that his body has a new, pungent smell.

"The water is heated," he says, still in English, though he sounds a bit rusty. "But if you wish to drink a glass of tea before bed, let's go into the kitchen."

The three enter a large hall containing an enormous refrigerator and stoves for cooking and baking, and also what looks like an ancient boiler, the kind used to heat water for washing. The huge pots and frying pans, the ladles and spoons, graters and knives, testify to generous cooking for a good many people. A pile of firewood stands in the corner and dozens of empty plastic boxes are arranged on tables. While the newcomer looks around wonderingly, her host relieves the Sudanese nurse of the bundle in her arms, thanks her for her trouble, and bids her good night.

"I asked her to buy you new sheets, so you'll feel safe and sound in your bed."

Daniela blushes. She ought to say, "Why? Really, no need," but she can't deny his display of sensitivity. He knows well that in strange lodgings she requires, as her sister did—a pristine bed.

As he sets a kettle on the fire, she studies him. The white hair that she remembers from their last meeting has fallen out, and his bald skull, resembling the fashionably shaved heads of young men, arouses in her a slight anxiety.

"I brought you a bunch of newspapers from Israel."

"Newspapers?"

"Also magazines and supplements. The stewardess collected them on the plane and filled a whole bag, so you can pick what interests you."

An ironic smile crosses his face. His eyes flash with a sudden spark.

"Where are they?"

Despite her fatigue, she bends over the suitcase and extracts the bulging bag. For a moment he seems loath to touch it, as if she were handing him a slimy reptile. Then he grabs it and rushes to the boiler, opens a small door revealing tongues of bluish flame, and without delay shoves the entire bag into the fire and quickly shuts the door.

"Wait," she cries, "stop . . ."

"This is where they belong," he smiles darkly at the visitor, with a measure of satisfaction.

Her face turns pale. But she keeps her composure, as always.

"Perhaps for you it's where they belong. But before you start burning things, you could warn me."

"Why?"

"Because there was lipstick in there too, which I bought at the airport for my housekeeper."

"Too late," he says quietly, without remorse. "The fire is very hot."

Now she regards him with hostility and resentment. In her parents' house, he was the one who had devoured every old newspaper. But he returns her look with affection.

"Don't be angry. No big deal, just newspapers, which get thrown out anyway. So instead of the rubbish I threw them in the fire. You'll make it up to your housekeeper with something else. I hope you don't have any more gifts like these in store for me."

"Not a thing," she winces, "that was it. Nothing else. Maybe only . . . candles . . ."

"Candles? Why candles?"

"It's Hanukkah now, did you forget? I was thinking, maybe we could light them this week, together . . . It's one of my favourite holidays . . ."

"It's Hanukkah? I really didn't know. For some time now I've been cut off from the Jewish calendar. Tonight, for instance, how many candles?"

"It started yesterday, so tonight is the second candle."

"Second candle?" he seems amused that his sister-in-law thought to bring Hanukkah candles to Africa. "Where are they? Let's see them."

For a moment she hesitates, but then takes out the box of candles and hands it to him, in the odd hope that he might agree to light them here, in the middle of the night, and ease her sudden longing for her husband and children. But again, with the same quick, slightly maniacal movement, he opens the little door and adds the Hanukkah candles to the smouldering Israeli newspapers.

"What's the matter with you?" She stands up angrily, but still maintains her calm, as with a student in her class who has done something idiotic.

"Nothing. Don't get angry, Daniela. I've simply decided to take a rest here from all of that."

"A rest from what?"

"From the whole mess, Jewish and Israeli . . . Please, don't spoil my rest. After all, you've come to grieve."

"In what way spoil it?" She speaks quietly, without rancour, feeling pity for this big man with the pink bald head.

"You'll find out soon enough what I mean. I want quiet. I don't want to know anything, I want to be disconnected, I don't even want to know the name of the prime minister."

"But you do know."

"I don't, and don't tell me. I don't want to know, just as you don't know the name of the prime minister here in Tanzania, or in China. Spare me all that. Come to think of it, maybe it's too bad I didn't insist that Amotz come with you. I'm afraid you'll get bored here with me on such a long visit."

Now, for the first time, she is offended.

"I won't be bored, don't worry about me. And the visit isn't long, and if it gets hard for you having me here, I'll cut it short and leave earlier. Do what you need to do. I brought a book with me too, and don't you dare throw it in any fire."

"If the book is for you, I won't touch it."

"The nurse you sent to get me warned me . . . By the way, is she really still a pagan?"

"Why still?"

"You mean, she believes in spirits?"

"What's wrong with that?"

"Nothing wrong. A very impressive young woman . . . aristocratic . . ."

"You can't remember, but before the state was established, on street corners in Jerusalem there stood Sudanese like her, very tall and black, wrapped in robes, roasting these wonderful, delicious peanuts on little burners, and selling them in cones made of newspaper. But that was before you were born."

"Before I was born . . ."

"Her whole family was murdered in the civil war in southern Sudan, and she's grown up to be a woman of great tenderness and humanity."

"Yes. And she said that you didn't come to meet me because

you were afraid to run into Israelis. Why would there be Israelis on the plane?"

"On every plane between two points in the world there is at least one Israeli."

"I was the only one on the plane that brought me here."

"Are you sure?"

"I'm sure."

"And a Jew?"

"A Jew?"

"Maybe there was a Jew on the plane?"

"How would I know?"

"Then imagine that I didn't want to run into him either."

"That bad?"

"That bad."

"Why? You're angry at—"

"No, not angry at all, but I am asking for a rest. I'm seventy years old, and I'm allowed to disconnect a bit, and if it's not a final break, then it's a temporary one, or let's call it a time out. Simply a time out from my people, Jews in general and Israelis in particular."

"And from me too?"

"From you?" He regards his sister-in-law with fondness, pours boiling water into her teacup, puts a flaming match to the cigarette she clenches between her lips, absolutely her last one of the day. "With you I have no choice, you'll always be my Little Sister, as I told you when you were ten. And if you came all the way to Africa to remember Shuli and mourn her with me, it's your right, since I know better than anyone how much you loved her and how much she loved you. That's all. I am warning you, grieve, but do not preach."

Third Candle

1.

IN THE MIDDLE of the night, Tel Aviv brightens for an hour or so, and the moon, freed of its grey blanket, rolls the husband from his wife's abandoned territory back to his own side of the bed, and from there, after a slight hesitation, lifts him to his feet as well. Yes, Yirmiyahu cautioned him not to expect any electronic sign of life until the next day, but still he wanders, one more time, among the television channels, so that—with the collusion of a mild sleeping pill—he will be able to fall asleep again, reassured that no plane has crashed or been hijacked, and in the meantime, till his bloodstream carries the pill's chemical message to his brain, he tries, with a few quick strokes on the pad of graph paper he keeps by the bed, to work out a scheme whereby the secret fifth elevator could not only be independently controlled but also have doors at right angles to each other, so that it could be squeezed into the southwest corner of the shaft without stealing much space from the four elevators already designed. Just a preliminary sketch, inspired by a design flickering in his memory, maybe from some old magazine. And as he long ago taught himself to do, so as not to disturb his wife's sleep, he works under a small reading lamp that blends its light with the miserly moonbeams. Despite his excitement over the idea and his faith in the sketch that embodies it, he adds a small note to the bottom of the page: *Moran, check if this is realistic!*

2.

IN THE CLEAR summer night south of the equator, the very same moon, rich and profligate, does not disturb the sleep of the woman, whose natural serenity has pleasantly blended into the bed provided by her host, fitted with new linen. From many years' experience, Yirmiyahu knew that Daniela, like her sister, would not sleep well between old sheets washed in a dubious laundry. Even though he did not invite her to visit, he made sure she got new sheets and witnessed their packaging being removed. That was how the sisters would pamper each other, and the death of Shuli has not freed her husband from her obligation to the other, on top of his own obligation to let her have his room and bed.

This kind gesture of his does not trouble her. Six nights is a short time. On the other hand, she is dismayed that he threw the Israeli papers in the fire, and the destruction of the Hanukkah candles really does offend her, even though he promised with a smile that he had no intention of burning anything else. After midnight, in the big kitchen, as she smoked her very, very last cigarette—deducted from tomorrow's quota—he also told her not to misunderstand him, that his need to criticize, judge, or lodge official protest evaporated long ago, that all he wants now is disengagement and separation, at least for a while. Is she not a mature woman, who has known this man and his history since her childhood? Why, then, should his words not put her at ease?

After her teacup was washed and returned to its place, he took her suitcase and said, come, let's go upstairs, get ready for seventy steps, because here of course there's no elevator, though your Amotz would doubtless be surprised to discover that the architect who designed this place between the two world wars did not entirely rule out the possibility. There's a narrow round concrete shaft next to the stairwell. Now it's full of old furniture, probably tossed in there for years from all the floors.

And maybe there's no need for an elevator, since the broad shallow steps are easy to climb, even to the room on the top floor. This room was the one stipulation of this white man who joined the African team: a private room on a high floor, with a view of the broad landscape. The room is not large, but it is tidy and clean; and unlike his study in Jerusalem holds very few books, though on the desk is a pile of papers and ledgers, held in place by a shiny skull.

"Don't be alarmed," he told her, picking up the skull and stroking it. "It's not human. It belonged to a young ape, more than three million years ago—maybe an early ancestor of ours. And it's not real, either, but reconstructed on the basis of a single wisdom tooth. But if you think it will bother you at night, I'll take it away. Shuli would definitely not have been happy to sleep alone with it in the same room."

But Shuli's little sister has no such fears. Why should a replica of the skull of a young monkey a few million years old disturb her sleep? Doesn't he remember that as a child she would bring her parents greenish toads from the banks of the Yarkon and suggest they stroke them at bedtime? Yes, Yirmi agreed, as a grin brightened his face, and he also remembered the toads jumping in her sister's bed. And maybe he would remember other things too. For a moment it seemed that he was glad his sister-in-law had come to visit. Yes, he admitted, this last mourning period was hasty, perhaps because the previous one had gone on and on. He left the country before the end of the thirty days not because he wanted to run away, but for fear that if he stayed away too long, the authorities in Dar es Salaam would take advantage of his absence and shut down the diplomatic office they had long since regretted approving, because of the security costs. The great irony was that in the end it was the Foreign Ministry in Jerusalem that decided to shut it down, to save money, and maybe the whole economic mission had been created in the first place as some sort of compensation for the "friendly fire" that had killed his son.

She sat on his bed and listened, careful not to appear tired so as not to offend him, but he gathered himself and before leaving her to her fatigue, he showed her how to work the taps in the shower, and with an ironic smile promised plenty of piping hot water, since the boiler on the bottom floor was still consuming the Israeli newspapers and lighting the Hanukkah candles.

After washing herself long and thoroughly she got into bed, and to wind down from the trip and drift off without a husband by her side, she made herself drowsy with a page from the mediocre novel. Then she turned out the light, and with her rare talent for transmuting worries and fears into memories and dreams she put her palm to her mouth like an infant at the breast, and fell asleep.

At dawn, when her brother-in-law entered on tiptoe to

close the shutters and protect her from the blazing sunrise, she simply smiled her thanks, and since she could rely on him to send, in her name, an electronic sign of life to her husband, she allowed herself many more hours of untroubled slumber.

3.

IN THE MORNING Ya'ari is pleased to find, in his e-mail at the office, the long-expected message. Now, with his wife under his brother-in-law's supervision, he may let go of his anxiety until her return trip begins five days hence. With his mind unencumbered, he tries to perfect on the computer his nocturnal vision of a narrow corner elevator, independently controlled, that would rob hardly any space from the four others. But he is still reluctant to enlist any of his employees, lest one of them glibly dismiss the idea out of hand. First he had better ask Moran, since his criticism, however harsh and negative, will remain between father and son.

But Moran is late. Has Nadi again deprived his parents of sleep, and, as usual, was it his father who got up to calm him, not his mother? For all his sweetness, this two-year-old grandson is a stormy little scamp, and the grandfather and grandmother concur in blaming their daughter-in-law, who while assiduously trying to find herself has apparently neglected her child. But the two continually caution each other not to say a word of criticism to her or Moran. When they first met her, seven years back, she was a shy, pale girl; no one could have foreseen the beauty that would later bloom. Now, after bearing two children, her body has filled out, and her skin has a new lustre. She now goes about in heels that increase her height and show off her attractive legs, and her face, sculpted by cosmetic art, has been drawing attention. Yet the beauty only recently revealed, to her as well as to others, confuses her somewhat. It has helped her find jobs, but also undermined her determination to stick to them. Out of cocky confidence that the world will always pay homage to her good looks, she tends to make light of her obligations, quits a situation without thinking it through, switching jobs arbitrarily, out of caprice.

Outside it is grey and quiet. Rain and wind have stopped, yet this wintry calm does not prevent that stubborn, depressive head of the Pinsker Tower tenants' council from calling Ya'ari's cell phone once more to demand that he do something to stop the whistling noise in the elevators. Unwilling to debate the limits of his responsibility with a private individual, Ya'ari merely inquires politely whether the winds are still raging in the tower while on the big tree outside his office window not a leaf is stirring.

"Not one leaf?" snickers the tenant. "Maybe for you, Mr. Ya'ari, but these elevators of yours don't need any winds from the outside, they create their own."

Ya'ari laughs, hanging up with a vague promise.

It's now nearly nine o'clock and Moran is still not in. Ya'ari calls his cell phone, but gets only the voicemail. And though he knows that his daughter-in-law is doubtless still asleep, he also calls their home phone, but that, too, goes unanswered. Given no choice, he calls his daughter-in-law's cell, and as usual a lovely disembodied voice invites him to leave a message. A few minutes later, she gets back to him, sounding confused.

"Right, I forgot. I forgot to let you know that Moran left this morning for reserve duty."

"Reserve duty? After all that? What changed?"

"I mean, he didn't exactly leave by himself, they took him."

"Who?"

"A military policeman."

"A military policeman? They still exist?"

"Apparently so."

"Dammit, I warned him. But he thought they'd forget about him."

"They didn't forget."

"Forgive me, Efrati, but you too are not totally blameless on this. You should have pressured him not to provoke them."

"Great, Amotz, now I'm to blame," she retorts, as if her beauty were a permanent guarantee of her integrity. "Why me? Why are you so sure that he involves me in his little pranks?"

"Okay, sorry. So what happens now? I need him urgently in the office."

"If you need him, you'll find a way to get to him."

"And the children, Efrati?" he says, softening, "and the children? You don't need help with them?"

"Of course I need help. I have a training class up north till late tonight. My mother promised that they could sleep at her place, but if Nadi falls asleep again at his nursery, she won't be able to cope with him at night."

"And I had planned to light candles with you this evening."

"Very good . . . so you two go to my mother, light candles with her, and help her out a bit. The kids will be happy, too . . . and if my mother's already worn out, maybe you and Daniela could take them home to sleep at your place."

"No, wait, listen, Efrati, it's just me. You forgot that Daniela flew to Africa yesterday."

"Oh, right. I'm not used to thinking about the two of you apart; I forgot all about it."

4.

THE SHUTTERS, CLOSED at dawn, have indeed enabled the visitor to sleep till late morning, and as she becomes aware of the hour she realizes how worn out she must have been from the emotion and anxiety of the day gone by. Yirmi has apparently not deemed a few days' visit sufficient reason for clearing a shelf in his small armoire, so her little suitcase will have to serve as a clothes closet. Only her African-patterned dress which Amotz encouraged her to buy three years ago in the market in Dar es Salaam and which she never dared wear in Israel, she hangs at full length beside her brother-in-law's khaki clothing, to rid it of wrinkles before trying it on at last, here on the continent where it belongs.

The old shutters open with an agreeable creak, revealing a landscape of low-lying reddish hills covered with stumpy but abundant vegetation. The thick wayside foliage that had accompanied her nocturnal trip around Mount Morogoro is gone, and the vista now before her, for all its greenness, has a flavour of the neighbouring desert. Near the entrance to the farm she recognizes the Land Rover that brought her, parked between two pickup trucks.

She descends unhurriedly to the ground floor, where she is surrounded by a whirlwind of human activity accompanied by the singing of women, the rush of flowing water, the clatter of dishes, and the cackle of chickens. Into the oversize sunny kitchen comes cooking equipment and tableware, sticky and coated with dust, sent back overnight from the site of the dig—plastic containers, plates and cups, mounds of spoons, forks, and knives—all of it taken to the sink at once, for soaking and scrubbing. A cornucopia of supplies is arranged on the dining tables: fresh vegetables, brown eggs, corn bread, slabs of bloody meat, fish still quivering their last. On one of the tables stands a cage full of squawking chickens, and tied to the entry door is a black goat nursing her kid, which is also destined for slaughter.

The stoves are ablaze, covered with enormous pots, kettles, and skillets; beside them, black men and women in white toques and headscarves chop the heads and tails from fish, hack up cuts of meat, boil, stir, and roast. Yirmi takes full and active part, too—not in cooking, but in commerce. Wearing a colonial pith helmet, he sits at a table with old-fashioned scales, banknotes, and coins arrayed before him and lists the details of all supplies entering the kitchen, scrutinizing each bill before paying it. His very being projects the authority of a white man, bald and old, against the abundant vitality of Africa.

"Well, you slept very well," he says, in a tone of mild rebuke towards his sister-in-law, who has come to mourn a dead sibling but behaves as if she were on vacation. And he calls Sijjin Kuang, the nurse, who is making the rounds of the stoves, supervising the cooks—perhaps watching over their culinary hygiene—and requests that she bring the guest a selection of the day's dishes, for a combined breakfast and lunch.

Food is prepared at base camp, then packed in plastic containers and sent in insulated coolers to the dig. The scientific team there is not big: ten people, all Africans, most of them born in the region, who acquired professional experience working with European teams in Kenya and Ethiopia and South

Africa and are now conducting their own excavation. The workers assisting them at the dig come from local tribes; the idea is that the ethnic and linguistic ties between the scientists and their labourers will facilitate the discovery of the fossils they seek.

Daniela is ravenous, but unaccustomed to dining alone. She invites the Sudanese nurse to keep her company, and Yirmiyahu covers up the banknotes and coins with his helmet and joins them too. When the head chef comes to clear the dishes at the end of the meal, she praises his cooking and offers to help wash up. The black man, amazed by the older white woman's friendliness, bares his teeth as if about to swallow her whole.

Yirmi bursts into laughter. "Wash the dishes? You? Here?"

"Why not?"

"Why not? Back in your parents' house, on Saturdays after lunch, you resorted to all kinds of tricks to avoid the one chore they imposed on you, till finally Shuli would get fed up and go and wash them herself."

"Instead of me?" Daniela's face turns red. "That's not true… maybe she would sometimes come and help me dry them."

"No, no." He insists, for some reason, on this childhood memory now more than forty years old. "You were quite the artist at shirking."

"I didn't shirk anything, I just wanted to do it at my own pace."

"At my own pace." He chuckles, as if speaking of something that happened yesterday, "But in the end there was no pace at all."

Daniela smiles. Yes, "at my own pace" had indeed been her avoidance tactic. She always hoped that someone whose patience had run out would do it in her place, or at least help her. Although washing the Shabbat lunch dishes had in fact been her sole housekeeping responsibility, she'd sit gloomily through the meal, and because in general she was a cheerful child, the other family members easily diagnosed her "dishwashing depression" and joked about it, yet they refused, for educational reasons, to coddle her. What's so hard about washing dishes? her mother would sympathetically ask her adorable daughter. And Daniela would struggle to describe the humiliation of being stuck in the small dreary kitchen—which actually repelled her mother as well—while everyone else was indulging in Sabbath-afternoon naps.

"At her own pace," when they were all curled up in their beds, she would enter with mild disgust that sunless room in their workers' apartment and stand beside the scratched, greying sink, crammed with dishes each more revolting than the next, douse the lot of them with copious quantities of soap, and then go off to leaf through the newspaper or chat awhile on the phone, hoping the soap would do the job on its own. And when the parents awoke from their nap to find a sink still full of filthy dishes and she heard the redemptive sound of a running kitchen tap, she would hurry in, perky and smiling, and say, hey, what's the rush? Didn't I promise I'd wash them myself? How come you never have enough patience to let me do it at my own pace?

Now, as she watches the joyful collective labour in the giant kitchen, it occurs to her that it wasn't the scrubbing itself that made her suffer, but the loneliness. After all, she had always happily helped her father tend their little garden or paint a porch railing, but her spirit had rebelled against being left alone to face the grimy leftovers of her sleeping family, much as she loved them all.

And if it sometimes happened that because of "my own pace" there remained by the evening not one clean glass, plate or spoon, and the household swelled with righteous anger at this immobile "pace," her sister would rise to her rescue and without complaint would placate everyone by entering the kitchen as her full partner.

"She really was never mad at me?" Daniela asks now, with wonder. "It would have been so natural for her to be angry, too…"

"Angry? No, I don't remember . . ."

The little sister, who in a few years will be sixty, lifts her eyes with relief and thanks and stifled tears to the blue skies and red and green hills of the African savannah.

5.

IN TEL AVIV the winds have risen, and with them a stormy phone conversation between Gottlieb and Ya'ari.

"All the same, Ya'ari, explain to me again, this time logically, please, what exactly is driving you right now? Why do you keep obsessing over these noises when you know as well as I do that they are not the fault of your design, and certainly not of my manufacturing. You want to waste a day's work, shut down the elevators, dismantle the doors, run up expenses, and all you'll discover is what is obvious to everyone, that the construction company skimped on iron and screwed up the casting, and that they're the only ones who should be butting heads with the tenants."

"You might turn out to be right in the end, but in any case Moran met with your expert, the woman technician . . ."

"Rolaleh."

"And in her opinion the defects in the shaft are old and apparently existed before we installed the elevators, so that even if we are not formally responsible for them, morally . . ."

"Morally?" The manufacturer is taken aback. "That's a new one. Where'd that come from?"

"Listen, and don't get angry. Your technicians had a moral responsibility, and so, I admit, did our engineer who supervised the job, to make note of any defects and alert the construction company before installation."

"No, no, you're wrong. We've been working together for more than thirty years, but despite the professional experience you've built up, I've been doing this longer. Between your father and me there were always agreements and understandings regarding the limits of our joint responsibility. And even after you took over, we agreed to continue in the same spirit; in other words, to coordinate our position vis-à-vis contractors and construction companies, so they can't pull a divide-and-conquer. How then does morality come into this? In the past we never used such a strange expression, and there is no need to use it in the future either. We spoke of joint legal responsibility, and determined what its financial implications would be, and that way our partnership was conducted honourably, and we saved money too. So why not let sleeping dogs lie? The construction company is keeping quiet and not making any claims on us, but only trying to wear us down in a roundabout way, through the head of the tenants' committee. Even if he is a bereaved father, that's no reason to lose our heads."

"A bereaved father? How do you know that?"

"It's not only you that he's hassling, but me too, so I decided to find out just who this guy is and what gets him so worked up, and it turns out he is a bereaved father; his son fell in action a month or two before he moved into the tower. And even though one must treat such people with respect, you also have to remember that they have a different agenda in their heads. Unfortunately, over the various wars, I've had any number of bereaved workers at my plant, and I'm always careful not to get into any confrontation with them. I listen to them politely, and nod sadly and promise to consider their request and try to take it into account, and afterwards, carefully and delicately, I manage to get round them and do what I need to do. Because if you start to get tangled up with grieving parents, they can drag you a long way."

"You know that… in our family… too"

"Of course, I was at the military funeral."

"You were there, too? I don't remember. I was taking care of Nofar, my young daughter. She fainted at the graveside, and I was so distraught I didn't notice . . ."

"Yes, I also remember how alarmed your father was; even then he used a cane . . . How old was she?"

"Nofar? Maybe twelve. Of the four of us, she took her cousin's death the hardest, and I think even now, almost seven years later, she hasn't really got over it."

"That happens sometimes with cousins: they fall madly in love, in secret."

"Could be… who knows what goes on in the hearts of your own children, even your wife can surprise you… But listen, let's get back to the complaint and agree that we'll devote one workday to it, to keep up our good name, yours and mine, and we'll split the expenses. We'll ride up on the top of the big elevator, scanning the shaft very slowly with a torch, and figure out once and for all where the winds are sneaking in and what they're wailing about."

"No, habibi, I strongly object. I learned long ago that a machine is like a human body. You open it up and start poking around, you discover things you'd rather not know. Yes, my technician is very sensitive to sounds and noises, but believe me, she's also a little crazy."

"Crazy?"

"Too sure of herself. And therefore you have to set limits for her. Bottom line, as long as there's no formal complaint, we sit quietly in a corner. And if this man, head of the tenants' committee, hassles you again, tell him, You're right, sir, we are looking into the matter, sir, but it will take a little time, sir, and gently get him off your back. Howling winds aren't wolves who eat people alive. As for morality, my friend, that belongs in the family."

6.

THE CHEFS REMOVE the white hats from their heads and fan them over the cooking pots, to cool the food a bit before it is ladled into containers and placed in the big refrigerator. The meals won't be sent to the excavation site until three. In the meantime Yirmi proposes a short walk to his sister-in-law, to see a very unusual elephant.

"Elephant?" She laughs happily. "Lovely, but why unusual?"

"When you see him you'll understand."

"Why on foot? We can't drive?"

"It won't be a long walk."

"You're sure?"

"I won't take you for any hike your sister couldn't have handled."

She goes up to her room to put on gym shoes, thinks a minute, then also changes into the African dress, figuring that whatever remote corner of Africa they are headed for will be the right place to see whether its bold colours are compatible with her personality. To her surprise, her brother-in-law recognizes the dress that she bought years ago in the market near the Israeli mission. He had tried to talk his wife into emulating her sister and buying herself such a dress, but Shuli had firmly refused.

"I didn't dare wear it in Israel, because the colours are not only loud, they also clash."

"Pity, because African women of your age know that loud clashing colours only rejuvenate them."

"So now I'll be a rejuvenated African woman," says the visitor lightly as they step outside the farmhouse and into the blinding sun.

"Just a moment," she says, "stop. I'm not prepared for a sun this strong. You forget that I come from a stormy land of rain and wind."

But Yirmi scoffs at the ferocity of the Israeli winter. How stormy can it really be? He takes off his pith helmet and places it on her head—here, this is in honour of the equator—and leads her to a dirt track, easy to walk on. Even as she adjusts to the day's fierce light, she feels the purity of the air.

After a short and pleasant walk they come upon a stream with black cows grazing on the bank. Yirmi addresses the tall herdsmen with a few words in their own language, and they reply at greater length.

Since her arrival last night she has not spoken about her family. She has not mentioned Amotz, Moran, or Nofar, and has taken special care not to bring up her two darling grandchildren, and oddly he too has ignored their existence, hasn't asked after them or taken any interest, as if they had been swallowed by the abyss of his detachment. As they stroll now along the bank of the stream she decides to say something about them, for they have always been dear to him. And he walks at her side indifferent and silent in his loose khaki clothes, a tall man, his bare skull reddening in the powerful light.

"Excuse me, does this interest you at all?"

"To tell you the truth, not really . . . but if it's important to you, talk, why not?"

She is shocked, trying not to recoil from the direct blow. True, she insisted on this visit not so she could tell him about her husband and children, but rather so they could both talk about her sister, from whom he, perhaps, wants to disengage too.

Half an hour later they arrive at a broad river lined with huts and thatched sheds.

"See, that's where they keep the elephant." Yirmi points to a distant shed. Several youths gathered beside it suddenly run towards them. An elderly white-haired African, sitting by the entrance to the shed, recognizes the pale man from afar and calls out his name. It turns out that Yirmi has visited a few times and paid an admission fee.

The elephant is not especially big, but his presence and smell fill the shed. One of his legs is tied with a long chain to a tree trunk whose boughs have been chopped off. Without paying attention to the visitors, he continues to scoop up vegetables daintily from the small feeding trough with his trunk and toss them into his pink maw. The African shouts a curt command, and the animal stops eating, raises its head and moves it closer to his guests. Now the tourist understands the reason for the visit. The elephant's left eye is narrow and normal, sunk into the black flesh of its cheek, but the right one is huge and wide open, a wise and curious cyclops eye, with a wandering blue-green iris that gazes at the world with melancholy humanity.

"What is this?" She is shaken and moved. "Is that a real eye?"

"Yes, it is. This man, who was a ranger in one of the nature reserves, noticed this unique eye the moment the elephant was born, and also saw that because of this birth defect the mother elephant rejected her baby and was even prone to attack it, so he got permission from the authorities to isolate the baby elephant, in order to protect it and also to show its wonders to the world. Now he roams around with him from place to place, puts up a shed, and charges admission."

The African issues another command, and the animal takes a few steps towards Daniela, curtsies ceremoniously, and bows its head to give her a close view of the miraculous eye and to receive a reward in return. The visitor falters. The sharp stink of the elephant makes her dizzy. Stroke him, orders her brother-in-law, and she extends a hand towards that mesmerizing blue-green orb, then quickly pulls back. Yirmiyahu gives a strange little laugh.

Daniela looks at her brother-in-law, who seems pleased and

serene. Yes, from the very start he displayed certain idiosyncrasies that bothered her parents, but his love and devotion to her sister banished all their worries. Now, without Shuli, he seems to be shedding his inhibitions.

The elephant stands up again and in honour of the guests dumps his turds, which plop softly onto the straw matting. The African studies them with satisfaction and grins at Yirmiyahu, who nods in agreement.

"I see you are happy here," Daniela snaps as they leave the shed. "You've cut yourself off and left all troubles behind. You burn newspapers, you live without a radio or telephone. But have you really succeeded in disconnecting, or are you just playing games? Don't tell me, for example, that you don't know that we have a new prime minister."

"I don't know," he says, lifting his hand to silence her, "and I don't want to know."

"You don't care who the new prime minister is?"

"I really don't," he shuts her up, "and don't say another word. I do not want to hear his name or those of the ministers and deputies. I don't care and I'm not interested. Please, Daniela, try to understand where I am and what's important to me now. I mean, you came to revive your grief, not to poison my disengagement."

7.

YA'ARI TRIES UNSUCCESSFULLY to reach Moran. It's hard for him to accept the fact that his son's cell phone, ever ready for his calls, has suddenly become a mere voice mail, indifferently storing messages with the cell phone company. So he calls his son's apartment, not in the hope of finding him, but rather to leave on a real answering machine a short, pointed message—a father's worry masquerading as an employer's demand to know exactly when his worker will be available. Afterwards he again tries Efrat on her cell phone, aware that if she responds at all it will only be a return call later on. Since Ya'ari knows that his daughter-in-law can identify his number on her screen and ignore it at will, he leaves her the strongest message that a father-in-law can leave the mother of his grandchildren without damaging his relationship with her. Efrat, my dear, he says in a voice tinged with desperation, if you've managed to locate your deserter, let me know right away, because I need him urgently.

In truth, today there is nothing at the office so urgent as to require Moran's presence. But the father seeks him not as an employee but as a son whom he can control with his love. Especially now, more than twenty-four hours after parting from his wife, whose absence, not physically but emotionally, irritates him. His wife knows how to articulate problems that he has a hard time defining by himself, and is also capable of easing them and minimizing their importance. And even though he would not degrade himself by complaining to his son the way he would to his wife, he wants him now as her reflection.

He phones his daughter in Jerusalem, but she doesn't answer either, which pleases him, since now he can leave her a message without getting into an argument. I hope, Nofar, he says, choosing his words carefully, that you haven't forgotten that Imma flew yesterday to Yirmi in Africa. Moran has gone off on reserve duty, or more precisely, he was taken, and it's not yet clear whether he'll be back tonight or tomorrow. Efrat has yet another training course, and her mother is taking the children.

So this evening I'm on my own. If you're not on duty, and there's nothing keeping you in Jerusalem, maybe you could come home, to spend a little time with me and light candles together.

Silence. The pleasant aroma of tobacco strikes his nostrils. He stands up, takes his jacket and goes out of his office into the main hall. Though it's well before noon, the hall is nearly empty. In a corner, isolated by a small glass divider, sits the chief engineer, Dr. Malachi, peering pensively at a diagram of a large elevator on his computer screen. Dr. Malachi has given himself licence, with no one else around, to puff on a pipe. Ya'ari draws near to savour the fragrance.

"The smell of tobacco is a big part of my childhood, from the good old days when people were still allowed to smoke at the office. If I didn't have my meeting at the Defence Ministry, I'd hang around to inhale some more. But please, before you go home, make sure not to leave any burning ashes in the waste-paper basket…"

"And you make sure not to promise them a fifth elevator before they commit to additional payment for all the design changes we'll have to make."

"We'll see," Ya'ari mutters, putting on his jacket, "we'll see," but does not reveal the night-time sketch tucked in his pocket, for fear of a dismissive response from the man to whom he pays the highest salary in the office.

8.

"So you're not sorry I dragged you here to see the elephant," he inquires gently.

"No," she answers. Under the visor of the pith helmet is a glimmer of childlike sweetness in her no longer young face, as she continues, "So an elephant with a freak genetic defect is more interesting to you than the prime minister . . ."

"Why? He's also a freak?" Yirmi laughs, turning his gaze towards the distant hills.

The sun has climbed high in the sky and the path is awash in blazing light; the trace of shadow that earlier she imagined was trailing them from behind has vanished. They return to the little stream and tramp among the cows and sheep, and the tall herdsmen lean on their staffs and regard them solemnly. Not far off, on the side of a hill, a plume of smoke rises from a hut she didn't notice earlier. Tell me, she asks her brother-in-law, could we have a peek inside a hut like this? Why not? he answers, you'll see how people live; you'll understand the depth of the poverty and inhale its heavy stench. And they turn and trudge up the hillside. Beside the shack a cow munches grass. A big African woman stands on a tree stump to spread fresh cow dung on the roof of the hut. Yirmiyahu says something to her, gives her a coin, and nudges his sister-in-law towards the entrance.

The hut is empty. Here and there are scattered blankets with tin plates on them. In the corner, ringed with black basalt stones, burns a purplish flame. Its smoke caresses the tufts of straw that protrude from the ceiling.

"They're not afraid the straw will catch fire and burn down the hut?"

"If a hut burns down, it's easy enough to put up a new one. That's an eternal flame, and from generation to generation they keep it burning, even in the heat of summer."

"Friendly fire," she whispers unthinkingly, as her eyes tear up from the smoke.

"Yes." He flinches in pain. "Friendly fire, indeed . . . Who the hell knows how we all got infected by that revolting expression. You know who first blurted that out?"

"No."

"Guess."

"I don't know . . ."

"Your favourite person . . ."

"Moran? No. Just don't tell me that Amotz . . ."

"Why not? Yes, Amotz, back in Jerusalem, at the Foreign Ministry, when the army officer and doctor came into my office. It was Amotz who brought them, because when Eyali filled out the forms, back in basic training, he listed you and Amotz to be notified in case of bad news. They could not conceal the fact that a soldier had been killed by our own forces, because this had already trickled into the media, and so, while I am standing there with the poisoned lance stuck in my heart, and this angel of death, in uniform, brings me the message that the gunfire came from our soldiers and he trembles as he explains what happened in the battle, as if there really had been a battle and not simply the killing of a soldier who was mistaken for the enemy, a wanted man, it somehow seemed to your Amotz, my Amotz, our Amotz, who had come from Tel Aviv with this bearer of bad news, that I didn't comprehend the explanations—or the opposite, maybe he was actually trying to console me, to loosen the rope that was wound around my neck, since being killed by our own forces is a hundred times crueller than 'enemy fire'—and then he grabs my hand and hugs me tight, and says to me, Yirmi, what they mean is friendly fire."

"Amotz?" she whispers.

"Yes, Amotz, and not only once, but several times, he repeated that wretched expression, and at first I wanted to rip him apart, but then suddenly, amid all the shock and anger, I also understood that inside this stupid oxymoron, this *friendly fire*, there was something more, some small spark of light that would help me navigate through the great darkness that awaited me and better identify the true sickness that afflicts all of us. And from then on I fell in love with this expression, and I started to use it a lot, relevantly and also irrelevantly, and to pass it on to others . . . See, even you, Little Sister, you walk into a crappy little hut in Africa and you say, totally naturally, *friendly fire* . . . right?"

9.

THE MINISTRY OF Defence is walking distance from Ya'ari's office, but a river of parents and children milling towards Tel Aviv's Hall of Culture impedes his progress. Ya'ari inherited a security clearance from his father, who in his day also worked with the Defence Ministry, and his entry into the heavily guarded building therefore goes smoothly, with no unnecessary delays.

A few years ago they expanded the old structure, adding new floors and basements. Ya'ari's firm designed most of the elevators in the new wings, and there were periods when he participated in many meetings of the ministry's construction department, to protect his plans from cost-cutting contractors. As someone familiar with the workings of the ministry, he now notices that it, too, is short of many workers today. The computers are blank and the offices abandoned, including that of the division manager he is scheduled to meet. What's going on, he asks the loyal secretary, who is still at her post: is the Defence Ministry upgrading the holiness of Hanukkah to give time off to its workers?

"Why not?" she answers, surprised that Ya'ari is unaware of the Hanukkah performance organized at the Hall of Culture for the children of ministry employees. Especially since his son, Moran, managed to cadge free tickets from her for the children of Ya'ari's firm.

"And he didn't bother to tell me, and even my daughter-in-law doesn't know. This morning he needed to go off for some clarification regarding his reserve duty, meaning that my two grandchildren are missing the show."

"How old are they?"

"The boy is two and the girl is five."

"Then don't be upset. My grandchildren were around those ages last year, and they only suffered through the stupid play."

"How do you know it's the same play?"

"How much originality can there be in the moonlighting of unemployed actors?"

"So there's nobody left here to dicuss this case."

"The new deputy, she's here."

"Why? She has no kids?"

"Kids? No. Determinedly single. Go and see her."

The deputy, a construction engineer with a Ph.D., is a

woman of fifty or so, tall and cheerful. She welcomes Ya'ari with enthusiasm and locates the file, marked SECRET in red ink.

"This fifth elevator," Ya'ari begins, with a sigh, "which all of a sudden popped up after we finished the planning—tell me, is it really necessary?"

The deputy examines the file and sighs, too. "What can I do? We also get orders. It turns out that they need an extra elevator here, independent, which will go straight from the top floor to the lowest level of the garage without picking up any passengers in between. And in addition to an internal telephone, they want a screen and video hookup trained on the outside world. In other words, a very private elevator."

"All right, then we'll have to deal with it. But I hope you've taken into account that it will require a complete overhaul of the design of the shaft, and will involve further payment."

"The redesign is only natural," the deputy admits, "but as for more money, we've already milked the ministry budget for this project down to the last penny."

"Thanks very much, but what does that mean? That I now have to subsidize the defence forces of the State of Israel?"

"Why not?" she laughs, "they protect you too."

Ya'ari shrugs but doesn't argue. Budgets in any case are determined in a different department, and in that one he'll know how to hold his own. He's not sure whether to show the deputy the idea that came to him by moonlight and finally decides to risk it. A gracious woman, good looking and elegant in her own way, can't take it upon herself to kill a technical idea that's outside her area of expertise. Look, he explains with a cryptic smile, he's a grass widower whose wife flew off to Africa and he can't sleep well at night, so he came up with this idea, which might placate, even satisfy all parties. A corner elevator, with perpendicular doors, squeezed into the south corner of the shaft and operated by independent control: this would require no significant appropriation of space at the expense of the four currently planned elevators, so the finished design won't need complete redoing. The deputy takes out a scale ruler and measures the diagram.

"This elevator of yours is very narrow, Mr. Ya'ari." She smiles ironically. "Our secret passenger will have to lose weight in order to ride in it."

"You're right," Ya'ari admits, "it is very narrow. But don't forget it has another corner, for another person, presumably the wife of the secret passenger."

"His wife?" remarks the deputy with surprise. "Well, it wasn't really her I pictured in your spartan elevator. But if his wife insists on chaperoning her husband everywhere, then she'll have to slim down, too."

10.

THE BIG KITCHEN at the farm is clean and quiet. The cooks have disappeared. Yirmiyahu opens one of the doors of the big refrigerator for his sister-in-law. What can I heat up for you? But the strong sun, and the memory of the African woman smearing her roof with cow manure, have dulled her appetite. No hurry, she tells him. First I'll go up and rest awhile, and then, if possible…

Yes, they can postpone lunch, but they will have to finish it by three, because then he must go out with the food to the excavation site and won't return till late at night.

"Is it far?"

"Not terribly, but the driving is very slow."

"So what about me?"

"Rest, read. After all, I didn't burn your novel."

"And who else will stay here?"

"There is always a security guard."

Suddenly she is seized with the fear of abandonment.

"Can I join you? Is there room for me?"

"Yes, but on condition that you don't wait like your sister till the last minute, but be ready down here by two-thirty, and we'll eat and hit the road. You want me to wake you?"

"No need," she says, suddenly a bit dejected. "I don't think I'll be able to sleep."

She slowly climbs the broad and easy stairs that spiral around the old elevator shaft. The room she left that morning now smells of Lysol, reminding her of the toilets at her school. In her absence the floor has been mopped, the bathroom cleaned, and her bed remade. She looks at the bluish haze of the summer sky. On a distant hill are two zebras, either fighting or copulating, not clear which. She thinks about her husband. Was Amotz in fact the source of the phrase *friendly fire*, which even during the week of mourning began to trip from Yirmi's tongue with a sarcasm that depressed and paralyzed her sister?

She pulls the wooden shutters closed and surrounds herself with darkness. The room is pleasant, but is missing a large mirror to reflect her full image. The small scratched mirror hanging over the sink can't satisfy her curiosity. She takes off her gym shoes and her dress. Remembering the appreciative looks of the locals, she is pleased that she took Amotz's advice to try out its bold colours on their native soil. For years she has worn only trousers, convinced that dresses make her look heavier. But here she is free and not compelled to look after her figure. The dress added a light touch to the morning visit to the elephant.

She stretches out on the bed in her bra and pants, then after a few minutes undoes the bra and liberates her breasts. Then she wraps herself in a lightweight robe she found in Yirmi's closet. Amotz had too easily turned down the chance to come with her. True, she was concerned that on this trip he would be in the way, but for now she is not swept up in childhood memories or in sorrow, and who knows what might happen in the short week ahead. The detachment to which her brother-in-law is so fervently addicted is damaging the simple and natural bond she always had with him. And it is implausible that he's living here merely to build up his savings. Surely his intentions are more radical. As she leafs through the three volumes of anthropology and geology that she found in the room she realizes that they are not there simply for reading or browsing. They are a clear statement on the part of a man whose bookshelves in Jerusalem were always filled to overflowing.

She gets up to make sure that she has locked the door. If she had gone with Amotz that day to the Foreign Ministry to bring the horrible news, he would have chosen his words more carefully, and not blurted out "friendly fire," the words Yirmi has fallen in love with and is amplifying into a new religion. But she got to her sister's side in Jerusalem too late. Moran was so anxious about the heavy blow he was about to deal her that he hung around the school for a solid hour till she finished her lesson. Everyone knew about Eyali's death before she did.

The door is locked. Despite the heat she takes one of Yirmi's woollen blankets and curls up under it. For years she has been faithful to her afternoon nap and tries not to miss it even when travelling. And since in their first year of marriage, it had already become clear to Amotz that afternoon napping enhanced her sexuality, he would loyally join her. Was it because of the mysterious power of the afternoon sun? Maybe this feeling of sexual awakening in the afternoon was tied to her teenage years, when every day after school she would be surrounded by several admiring boys, who would tag along on her way home and dawdle in front of the apartment block, while her mother waited upstairs to serve her lunch.

Whatever the reason, years after her mother's death, with her suitors long since happily united with other women, she still retains that afternoon flame, which Amotz won't allow to go to waste, even cutting meetings short and driving the long way home to their northern suburb to try his strength in the darkened bedroom, in which a teacher has fallen asleep after her long day in class.

11.

BUOYED BY THE fact that his night-time sketch has been met, for now, with humour and not scorn, Ya'ari shuns his own elevator and skips down the stairs to the exit. The skies have cleared and a friendly winter sun caresses the passersby. The streets are calm, now that the Hall of Culture has swallowed up the children and their parents. But can it be that the Hanukkah show has also consumed his chief engineer and financial manager? The office is locked. The smell of tobacco is all that remains.

He phones Moran, but his son's sophisticated mobile device, paid for by the firm, is only taking messages. With low expectations he calls Efrat's cell phone, which his experienced bookkeeper has also managed to list as an office expense, and hears her phone's parrot recitation of its usual ingratiating but heartless recording. Everyone is shirking his duty. Is he the only one at his desk today? Taped to his computer screen is a note from the chief engineer. *An elderly woman from Jerusalem, Dr. Devorah Bennett, wishes to speak to your father regarding a malfunction in the private elevator in her home. I intentionally did not take down her number, so that she won't expect us to call her back. But she will probably call again this afternoon. Should I give her your father's home number?*

No, scribbles Ya'ari with a black marker, *don't give her anybody's number. The tenant from Pinsker is enough for me. Just remember that we're a design firm and not a service company.* And he pastes the note to the engineer's computer screen, locks up the office, and drives home. If he's not entitled to a ticket to a children's play, maybe he deserves a free dream in his double bed.

And so, desiring only to dream, he threads his car through crowded streets, marvelling at the sight of the many ultra-Orthodox Jews who have excused themselves from Torah study and, lacking a children's show of their own to attend, are filling the playgrounds along the banks of the Yarkon River, sliding and swinging, despite the cold weather, the fringes of their ritual undershirts flapping in the breeze.

Before entering his building he clears the leaves the wind has amassed at the front door. The near perfect neatness of the apartment underscores the absence of his habitually messy wife.

He restores to its place a red candle that has fallen from the menorah set up for the evening's lighting, heats his lunch, and eats it rapidly. Then he goes into his bedroom and gets undressed. Is dozing off alone, without making love, a good enough reason to disconnect from the world?

Without hesitation he unplugs the phone. Tomorrow afternoon Yirmiyahu will take Daniela to Dar es Salaam, as agreed, and place a call to Israel. So for now he can let things go. The Filipinos are looking after his father; the army has taken Moran, whose mother-in-law is supposed to deal with the children, counteract and Efrat's good looks will excuse her failings. Nofar in any case is out of his control, even if she does show up this evening. He draws down the blinds, turns on the heater, gets into bed and pulls the blanket over him. It's nice, this unaccustomed silence, undisturbed even by the rustling of newspapers by his side. Yes, out of love he should have offered to go with her, but the wiser love was not to insist on it. And he did make sure to warn Yirmiyahu to be extra vigilant in the face of her absent-mindedness and dreamy confusion, which have lately grown worse.

He knows that his brother-in-law would have preferred him to accompany her. But had he made the trip, he would have weighed down the visit with his polite silence, which would have been interpreted as ironic. Nor was another visit to Tanzania worth the expense and aggravation of travel. It was only three years ago that they were there. He remembers exploring a huge crater with Shuli and Yirmi, an enclosed nature reserve filled with predatory animals and rare plant life. Yes, sometimes he has pangs of longing for the soothing expanse of the savannah or the swirling colours of the sunsets, but just to indulge in nostalgia, would it have been worth neglecting his business for a whole week and instead sit mutely between his wife and brother-in-law? After Yirmi jumped on that "friendly fire," which he haplessly uttered at a terrible moment, and began to cling to it so absurdly, Ya'ari realized he should be wary of spontaneous conversation with him. Gottlieb is right. Bereaved fathers have a different agenda in their heads.

He gets up to draw the curtain and darken the room, and notices that his cell phone is on the bureau, alive and well. Should he turn it off completely, or set it on silent vibration? He finally decides on vibration, but also stuffs it under his pillow.

12.

SOON, ON THE African farm, it will be three P.M. From outside the locked door of his bedroom Yirmiyahu calls to the sleeping woman: We're leaving! Why did you think I didn't need to wake you?

Daniela apologizes, even though she does not feel she is to blame. On trips abroad she always keeps her watch set on Israeli time, to stay in sync with her children and grandchildren. Amotz takes care of local time.

"But Amotz isn't here," her brother-in-law points out with mild annoyance, and tells her to hurry up; otherwise he'll leave her here to finish her novel.

Though this is a woman who adheres to "her own pace," the threat of being left alone at the farm with an elderly African watchman gets her moving faster. Besides, there's no fussing over what to wear. Deftly she slips back into her African dress, not only because of its comfortable fabric and her memory of the admiring gaze of the tall shepherds leaning on their staffs, but also out of the knowledge that only here, in Africa, can she get away with wearing anything so colourful.

In front of the farmhouse the vehicles stand ready for the journey. The food coolers are stacked one upon the other, and next to them are jugs of milk and water and small bags of flour and potatoes and white beans for individual cooking, a few big kettles of soup, and the freshly washed cooking pots and dinnerware. The goat, its slaughter apparently postponed, surveys the scene with interest. The cooks, who have removed their white uniforms and put on short grey sheepskins, finish the last bits of preparation for the trip, oiling the hunting rifles and poking around under the hoods of the old pickup trucks.

There is no one in the kitchen, except for Sijjin Kuang, wearing a greenish smock. She places a plate and cup for the visitor on one of the long tables.

"We'll heat something up for you," Yirmi tells Daniela, "but only on condition that you eat fast."

But the hungry guest will not degrade herself and eat alone before the eyes of strangers, and certainly not at a pace to which she is unaccustomed. No, she says, she'll hold out until it's time to have dinner with the diggers. That way their journey can begin right away. But the Sudanese nurse is not pleased by the guest's foregoing of food and expertly fixes her two sandwiches for the road. Nor does she stop at that; even as the pickups' engines sputter into activity, she vanishes into the building and returns with a windbreaker. Your dress is pretty, but at night you'll need something more against the cold, she tells Daniela, before taking her place behind the wheel of the Land Rover.

Yirmi has long legs, and therefore, apologizing to his sister-in-law, who has been relegated to the backseat, amid the luxury items designated for the researchers—bottles of whisky and cognac, packets of cigarettes and chocolate—and medical supplies for everyone. She places Sijjin Kuang's windbreaker on her lap and looks around her and nibbles at a sandwich. The Land Rover travels between the two pickup trucks, and in the lead truck ride the Africans with their hunting rifles.

"Why rifles?" wonders the visitor, and they tell her that sometimes animals and birds of prey are attracted by the travelling feast and need to be chased away.

The convoy first heads towards the small village they visited in the morning, where children are still congregating by the shed housing the elephant with the cyclops eye. From there, the road slopes gently down to the vast, silent savannah, where the air and the dry grass, patchy and scorched, shine golden in the western sun. The vehicles drive slowly, keeping their distance from one another, to avoid the clouds of dust kicked up by the tyres. Now and again they are stopped by a herd of plodding gnus or unhurried zebus, who take their time before deigning to move on and clear the road.

The great expanse before them stirs a feeling of respect in the visitor. Yirmiyahu directs her attention to a giant baobab with a trunk wider than his room at the farm and branches that look like thick roots shooting skywards, as if the tree were growing upside down. On one branch crouches a golden beast of prey.

On this plain the dead, animal and human, are not buried, says the Sudanese nurse, but rather left exposed in the wild, to be eaten by animals and birds, re-absorbed into the natural world that gave them life. Their bodies will not be resurrected, but a good soul may hope to find a strong wind that will agree to carry it.

Two hills stand out on the horizon: this might be their destination. For as soon as the hills appear, the convoy shifts its formation from single file to side by side, with the brotherly freedom—or rivalry—of those whose goal is clear to them and who have no need for a defined pathway or any rules of the road. They advance under the sheltering sky, whose palette of colours deepens towards evening, and a dizzying swirl of ravening birds swoops towards the travelling food stores, undeterred by occasional gunfire. The Africans gaily wave from the pickup trucks at the Land Rover, especially at the Israeli visitor, who only yesterday morning took off from her homeland and whose country and husband and children and grandchildren already appear strangely distant to her. Yes, she muses, maybe it would have been a bit much to light Hanukkah candles in a place where one is seeking the primal ape who never anticipated that Jews, too, would spring from his loins.

Now and then, the Sudanese and her brother-in-law exchange a few words, muffled by the engine noise. She pulls the windbreaker lent to her by Sijjin Kuang tightly across her lap and rubs it with her fingers, then lifts it to her face and inhales its smell. She gasps. As the Africans fire with cries of joy at a stubborn hawk and bring it down, she quietly taps Yirmi's broad back and holds up the windbreaker. Before she can ask, he answers:

"Of course. It was Shuli's. Didn't I tell you that I'd have a warm coat for you here?"

13.

IN ISRAEL, IT'S still three o'clock. The pillow beneath the husband's head has stifled not one vibration but five, thanks either to the quality of the feathers or the soundness of his sleep. But each vibration has left in its wake a message, and now Ya'ari is on his feet, listening to all of them.

The first, to his surprise, is from Nofar. Okay, Abba, if Imma isn't there I'll come around seven. A friend whom you don't know will come with me and also won't stay long. So okay, we'll light candles. But that's it. Please don't sit this friend down for an interrogation and don't ask him what his parents do. He's just a friend. Here today, gone tomorrow. As for the candles, my condition is no 'Maoz Tsur' or any of the other songs I loathe. Do a short blessing, if you must, and that's it. And if you're dying to sing, sing to yourself after we go. Not a tragedy. Because if you want your daughter's love, obey her. Sorry.

The second message is in a feeble voice. This is Doctor Devorah Bennett speaking from Jerusalem. If this is in fact your number, Amotz Ya'ari, then please don't hang up on me now in the middle, and call back at zero two six seven five four double zero and six at the end. I repeat: zero two is Jerusalem, and then six seven five four double zero and at the end again six. I urgently need your father. If you tell him my name, Devorah Bennett, he will certainly remember me. Because we were great friends. I know he has been ill, but at my apartment there is a private elevator that your father built many years ago, and he gave it, gave me, a lifetime guarantee, the lifetime of the elevator I mean, or more correctly my lifetime. I know that your firm doesn't do repairs but only design, but mine is a special case. All

I ask of you is your father's telephone number. That is all I ask. Please, Ya'ari, if you would be so kind . . .

The third message is from Efrat. Well, that's that. Moran for starters has been sentenced to a week's confinement to his base, and they also took away his cell phone battery. He said that he would try to reach you tomorrow morning to explain what happened exactly. He is still awaiting a trial for his previous absences. In the meantime I've arranged with my mother for her to fetch the kids from nursery—the Hanukkah holiday starts tomorrow for them—but if you could help her out at least in the beginning, that would be great. I'm still up north and won't be back till late . . .

The fourth message is from the tenant in the Pinsker Tower. I've been waiting in vain for an answer. Therefore we have no alternative but to be more explicit with you. We consulted with people from the construction company, and they claim that those who designed and manufactured the elevators are responsible for the winds. Therefore you and the manufacturer are obliged at least to determine the source of the problem prior to a meeting at which we will all figure out how to deal with it. If you continue to ignore us, we will be forced to take legal action. We know that such a lawsuit could drag on for years, but as you know, the court would compensate us for damages incurred in the meantime.

The fifth message is from Yael, Efrat's mother, a highly-strung and good-hearted divorcee, whose wry locutions Ya'ari always finds entertaining. You have doubtless already heard from Efrat that your son was hit with a week's confinement to base for his arrogant casualness. But on top of it all, Efrat insists on staying at her terribly important training course today. With problematic parents such as these there is no choice but for grandpa and grandma from both sides to join hands so that the grandchildren will not be abandoned. So please, Amotz, get back to me immediately; I am, as we speak, in the dentist's chair as he plots to extract one of my teeth, but my cell phone is always close to my heart, ever-ready to inform you of your role in the current mess."

Without delay he calls his son's mother-in-law, who asks him through semi-anaesthetized lips and a mouth full of cotton rolls to fetch the children from nursery at four and wait for her at the Roladin Café across from her house.

"A café?"

"Why not? They know the children there. Order each of them a scoop of vanilla, and remind the waiter not to put chocolate sprinkles on Nadi's, because he thinks they're flies. It's a nice place, and as soon as my tooth is pulled out I'll dash over and relieve you. Sorry, but what can I do? Today in any case is Daniela's turn, but she told me that she's going all the way to Africa to console her brother-in-law who's stuck out there, and who could begrudge her such a noble gesture?"

14.

THE EVER SHIFTING African sky now promises an imminent sunset, and the purple hills on the horizon assume the shape of a prehistoric snail. The ground beneath the tyres is rougher and bumpier now, covered with stubborn scrub and hidden potholes. The drivers no longer have the freedom to choose their own path, and they resume their small caravan formation, feeling out the best way to go. In the distance, bands of zebus flicker into view at times, disappear, then return. Foxes or hyenas peek out amid the scattered trees, having smelled the soup from afar, and try to join the crawling food convoy. One of the Africans, who has donned his chef's hat in honour of the approaching meal, gets on top of his truck's tarpaulin and opens fire over the heads of the wild animals—not to do harm, just to warn them off.

Since dusk falls rapidly in the region, it is already dark when the caravan arrives at the large encampment of the excavators, pitched on the slope of a bare volcanic canyon. In the depths of the canyon, one can just glimpse a bluish sparkle of water. Closer by, the UNESCO flag flaps on a tall pole, and small flags in a variety of colours are planted all around it to mark the locations of fossils. A crowd of diggers, men and women, are already unloading the contents of the vehicles, including the live goat, with cries of joy. Sijjin Kuang rushes with a medical kit to one of the big tents, while the white administrator stays with the alcohol, the cigarettes, and the chocolate, awaiting the arrival of the scientists.

Now they draw near, climbing up from the canyon, young and dusty and most of them naked to the waist, Africans differing one from the next in appearance and hue but all of them astonished to find a middle-aged white woman clad in a colourful African dress and an old windbreaker. "Who is this?" they inquire in English, in a variety of accents.

And Yirmiyahu presents the sister of his late wife, who has left her husband and family and country and come for only a few days to try to connect with the spirit of her beloved Shuli.

The black researchers greet her heartily, impressed by the boldness of this older woman who has come all the way to their excavations of the origins of the prehistoric man who split off from the chimpanzee millions of years ago, in order to grieve for her sister. Daniela is beside herself with excitement, and with the assertiveness that comes naturally to an experienced teacher wants to know the names of the half-naked people standing before her, their countries of origin, and the professional expertise of each and every one. Yirmiyahu did not exaggerate in describing the multinational nature of this group that has gathered from all over the continent. Here is an archaeologist from Uganda, and with him a botanist from Chad, and two tall South African geologists, and a Tanzanian anthropologist as black as coal who is the leader of the mission. Behind them stand a physicist from Ghana and an American zoologist from Kansas City who has not forgotten his ancestors and has come from the New World to help verify that humanity began right here.

And as they introduce themselves with their musical-sounding names and their professional titles and energetically shake the hand of the older woman whose English is so fine and precise, she wonders with slight concern if her daughter-in-law has remembered that today she won't be able to pick up the grandchildren from nursery school and day care, even though it's her turn to do so.

15.

THE MILD CONCERN of the woman in East Africa coincides with panic in Tel Aviv, as Amotz arrives to pick up his grandson from nursery and discovers to his amazement that this is not one small nursery but an entire network of them sharing a single schoolyard; in the bustling crowd of toddlers in motion he has a hard time picking out his own.

From the moment he agreed to collect the grandchildren he has been under pressure. First he tried to move the child seats from his wife's smaller car to his own, but after getting tangled up with straps and buckles and losing valuable time, he gave up on his car and took hers—which, besides being slower, was almost out of petrol. On the few occasions he accompanied his wife to this narrow, crowded Tel Aviv street, he would wait for her double-parked or in a disabled-parking spot till she returned with the precious cargo. Sometimes he would wonder how it was possible that from the gate of a yard that looked so small there emerged so many little children. Only today, entering the yard himself, does he realize how big it is. His inability to locate his grandson's group fills him with alarm, especially when he discovers that because he is a bit late, or perhaps because of Hanukkah, some of the rooms are already empty. And because he is not known here as a grandparent, he cannot simply loiter in the yard and wait, but must dash around till he finds the right child, dressed and buttoned up properly, clutching a little backpack, wearing on his head a paper crown with a Hanukkah candle, staring distantly at the grandfather who joyously falls to his knees before him.

"What happened to your wife today?" the young nursery-school teachers wonder.

For a moment Ya'ari considers whether this is the right moment to list the reasons for her absence, but in the end he gives them an abridged version.

"All the way to Africa?" they marvel, and urge him to warn Nadav's parents that during the holiday jam-doughnut free-for-all, their son managed to sneak off and join some other kids in an afternoon nap. On normal days they never forget to prevent him from doing so, and of course they tire him out in the playground, so he won't exhaust his parents till midnight.

Ya'ari nods his head and grins. It won't be a problem for his parents, but for his other grandma; he'll be sleeping at her house tonight together with his sister. Right, Nadi?

But the child is listening in suspicious, unfriendly silence, and there's no knowing what he has in store for anyone.

Then the two of them go to pick up Nadi's sister, Neta, a sweet and friendly child, who rushes towards them clutching a small clay menorah. She instructs her grandfather how to buckle her brother into his car seat.

In the little café across from his son's mother-in-law's house they know the children well. There's no need for long explanations to get scoops of vanilla ice cream in colourful bowls, one scoop with chocolate sprinkles and the other plain.

"Grandma," Neta remarks to Grandpa, "always takes off Nadi's coat, because he gets it dirty."

Ya'ari complies with his granddaughter's instructions and removes the Italian coat from its gloomy owner. Unlike his spouse, he is incapable of recalling in which European city the children's clothes were purchased on various visits, but this particular store in Rome he remembers well, because of the coat's ridiculous price.

He tries to help his grandson work at his ice cream, but Nadi doesn't need any assistance. With his little spoon he digs and burrows intently into the depths of the white ball, till the spoon taps the bottom of the dish.

"Another scoop," he firmly demands, but Ya'ari refuses. "In

the summertime you can eat two scoops of ice cream, but in the winter one is enough. When I was your age," he tells his grandchildren, "my father would never think of giving me ice cream in the wintertime."

"Is your father still alive?" asks Neta.

"Of course, don't you remember you visited him at Rosh Hashanah?"

Neta remembers her great-grandfather's shaking, which made her scared, but what impressed Nadi was his wheelchair.

Outside, a drumbeat of rain begins. Whether because of the weather or because of Hanukkah, so many people are packed into the café that Ya'ari feels mild pressure to give up the table. But where to go? Daniela knows how to chat with the grandchildren, because she knows the names of their teachers and also their friends. But Ya'ari knows no names, and his attempts to draw the kids out with general questions about the world elicit a neutral "yes" or "no" from the girl, while the tough little toddler doesn't even turn his head. Fewer than forty-eight hours have passed since his wife left, and already he longs for her to be seated by his side and in her wisdom help him engage his grandchildren. He offers to order them jam doughnuts and hot chocolate, but they're sick of jam doughnuts, and he has no choice but to violate what he just decreed and order them another ice cream.

Ya'ari is fascinated by the little boy as he expertly sculpts away layer after layer. He reminds his grandfather of someone—but who could it be? This question still lacks a clear answer. Day by day Neta grows to resemble her mother, but the genetic inspiration for her little brother's features, the colour of his eyes, is less easy to divine. Moran sometimes jokes that thanks to all of Efrat's screaming in the delivery room they didn't notice that their darling newborn had been switched with a bad baby.

Daniela always objects strenuously to that: Bad? How dare you? He's just an active child, full of imagination and turmoil, which is why he is afraid to fall asleep by himself. But he is also a thinker, and at nursery there are children who admire him.

Only after the thinker's spoon has rapped the empty dish over and over again does Grandma Yael merrily arrive, wrapped in a fox stole, or possibly wolf, her cheeks red from the cold, a lollipop in either hand. The two kids cling to her with great affection and an obvious sense of relief: she has rescued them from the supervision of a grandfather who asks stupid questions.

"Where's the tooth?" Nadi demands.

It seems that Grandma Yael told her grandchildren about the aching tooth, and promised to show it to them after it had entered the wider world.

"This kid is fantastic," she says, giving the boy a mighty kiss, "he remembers everything," and she quickly removes a handkerchief from her bag in which a large wisdom tooth, with its little root, has been respectfully wrapped.

Neta recoils. "Yuck," she says. But the little one does not fear his grandma's tooth and even strokes it gently with his finger.

"Does it still hurt if I touch it?"

This is a straightforward woman, without any so-called repression mechanism. So concluded Daniela when she and Ya'ari first got to know their in-law. Yael's lack of inhibitions made it easy for Daniela to weave a warm telephone relationship with the other grandma, who is a longtime divorcée. But Ya'ari is wary of her. At the last minute, without asking beforehand, she invited to Efrat and Moran's wedding, which the Ya'ari family financed, fifty more guests than the number allotted to her, and only the caterer's ingenuity prevented anyone from going home hungry. She is an emotional and unpredictable woman, yet all in all a happy one. Even her ex-husband, a bitter, cynical playboy, danced with her at the wedding till after midnight, breaking the heart of his young date.

Ya'ari gets up and puts on his jacket.

"That's it, Grandpa's going," he announces, then suddenly remembers that the teacher asked him to report that Nadi had again succeeded in stealing an illicit nap.

"*Oy*," sighs the grandmother, clasping her hands with dismay, "what's going to happen, sweetie? Another white night for Grandma without sleep?"

"Black," the child corrects her. "Abba says, Nadi gave me a black night."

16.

A BLACK, VELVET night softly blankets the other grandmother at the edge of the basalt canyon. Above her, unfamiliar African stars spin the Milky Way of her childhood into a torrential river of light bursting into the depths of the universe. Somewhere down the slope, an unseen generator putters, shattering the stillness, powering the strings of grimy electric bulbs that line the paths between the tents. Closer by, flames dance bashfully under big pots propped on stones and filled with good food.

The Tanzanian team leader, Saloha Abu, invites the guest to

the researchers' table, where the cooks are already dishing out generous portions.

"Ask them about their excavations," whispers Yirmi. "Take an interest in their work, they need attention and appreciation."

Daniela nods.

"With your fluent English you'll be able to communicate with them and understand their anthropological explanations, which I can't make head or tail of. Maybe also because my hearing is bad."

"Hearing or concentration?"

"Maybe also concentration . . . like any other solitary person."

"Don't worry, I'll show great interest," says the guest, her eyes sparkling as they near the fire, "and not merely out of politeness, but also habit. A teacher knows how to engage young people."

They sit down with the researchers in a square of collapsible tables, at whose centre, ringed by stones, a bluish fire hovers on its coals like a hen on her eggs. The aroma of the hot food on Daniela's plate is giving her a huge appetite. She has eaten nothing since Sijjin Kuang's sandwiches. Even so, she doesn't tuck in before asking the scientists to explain the nature of their project to her.

The Tanzanian team leader chooses Dr. Roberto Saboleda Kukiriza, an archaeologist from Uganda, to explain the essence to the white woman.

Dr. Kukiriza is a handsome man of about thirty-five. His studies in London polished the English he learned as a child, and he is eager to explain and demonstrate their work. He immediately abandons his plateful of delicacies and hurries to fetch a folding wooden board that has glued to it a multi-coloured map of Africa, indicating anthropological sites both established and potential.

He sets the map up for the guest, adjusting its position to catch the firelight, then turns to this woman who is at least twenty years his senior and says, "I will explain it to you, Madam, but only on condition that you eat."

The scientific lecture has a political prologue: Dr. Kukiriza begins by deploring the violated honour of Africa and the developed world's loss of faith in its future. Famine, disease, and especially vicious conflicts and wars, have sown this despair. Indeed, one cannot bend the bitter truth that under colonial rule the extent of famine and disease and killing on the continent was less than after independence. Worst of all, the disdainful attitude of the first world, the second—and even the third—which calls Africa the last world—is being absorbed more and more deeply into the African soul itself: depression threatens to dry up the wellspring of the people's joy. That is why this group of scientists has decided to transcend tribal and national rivalries and try to raise Africa's stature through original and independent research. Without state-of-the-art laboratories and sophisticated equipment, with only simple and inexpensive tools, they are digging and probing the earth to find the source of all humanity, the evolutionary link between the chimpanzee and *Homo sapiens,* in order to put Africa back on the map of the world as the cradle of civilization.

Yes, although fossils of a human nature, prehistoric hominids, have been discovered in various places around the world, there is consensus in the scientific community that the original human, *per se,* came from the great apes of Africa. It is only when the chimpanzee branches into *Australopithecus afarensis* that the evolution that leads us to ourselves begins in earnest. In these times, when the developed world is giving up on this continent and may yet abandon it, it is perhaps proper for Africa to remind humankind, if not of where it is headed, then at least of where it has come from.

This, of course, is an ideological goal and not a scientific one, admits the eloquent speaker to the white visitor, yet in the end a modest goal, not a revolution, for in any case we remain obliged to evolutionary science, and ideology is merely a frosting that can be scraped off. Indeed, evolution itself is not a revolution, but, rather, a process of transmission, like a relay race. Chimpanzees are still running around the world with no intention of turning into humans, but five to seven million years ago was born one chimp who handed down something new to its descendants. And one of those descendants passed this same something, with a minor addition, to its own offspring. And what is this "something"? One may call it a new trait, physical or mental. *Trait* of course is an imprecise literary word, but there is none better to explain the whole matter. Because what it describes might be an extra wisdom tooth, or a twisted one, or a more rounded design of the hip joint, or a keener, subtler sense of smell that increases the animal's curiosity about its environment.

The various transmitters of this trait, continues the Ugandan archaeologist in his superb English, were not aware of what they passed along of themselves, nor what this transmission would lead to. They remained bound and loyal to their own kind, to their existence as apes of various species, most of which became extinct over time. But what they handed down continued under its own power, to develop or alter from transmission to transmission, now getting stronger and now weaker, sometimes clear and sometimes blurred—until through countless transmissions there gradually arose our primal direct ancestor, the first *Homo sapiens,* who was human in every regard.

And this development from the chimpanzee was not a highway, but rather a road that branched into many byways, and there were relatives who strayed or were expelled from the main road and got stuck in dead-end streets. For example, three and a half million years ago, our family members known as the robust australopithecines, who included *Australopithecus boisei,* which was discovered right here in East Africa, were cut off from human evolution. They were, to put it bluntly, eating machines, or as they are more fondly known, nut-crackers. A million years ago they became extinct owing to their small and limited brains, which inhibited their culinary flexibility.

"Eating machines?" Yirmiyahu loves the expression.

"Yes, they had faces the size of dinner plates and huge jawbones, but they were vegetarians nonetheless."

Here the team leader interrupts the flow of his colleague's lecture before it strays further still from the main path. The food is growing cold, and this communal meal must be concluded honourably. Later on we will be able to show our guest some of the fossils we have found.

The food pleases the Israeli woman's palate, and she heaps warm praise upon the chefs and does not decline a second helping.

And at the meal's end, after the remains have been cleared away, the truths unearthed in this remote volcanic canyon can finally be made tangible for the unexpected visitor. On the table are arrayed not sweets but a dessert of highly significant fossils: a fragment of a huge lower jawbone, with two big teeth still planted in it. Two great eye sockets in a section of skull. A twisted hipbone from which a world of knowledge might be derived.

Now the Ugandan is joined by the Kenyan and Ghanaian, who assist him in explaining the dramatic importance of the bones. Daniela senses, with pleasure, not only their desire to share this chance to show off their accomplishments to a stranger willing to express interest for an hour or so, but also their hunger for mature, womanly, motherly protection, all the more, perhaps, because she is so very white. She therefore takes pains not to miss a single word and to encourage the speakers with nods of agreement. And even as millions of years of anthropology are jumbled between the jaws of an eating machine, with the empty eyes of a prehistoric ape looking on in wide amazement, she steals a glance at her brother-in-law, to see if he is working as hard as she is to follow the explanations. But the newly exposed skull of the old man is facing the fire, his eyes fixed on the flame, and his illuminated face wears an expression of sorrow.

Again the Tanzanian team leader is compelled to exert his authority. That's enough for now, he tells his friends. If we want our guest to remember anything, let us not burden her with too many dates and fossils. Though she is here for only a short visit, perhaps we will be fortunate enough to see her again. Daniela can sense the disappointment of the speakers, whose opportunity to impress a woman has been cut short, and therefore, before departing, she turns to them with a challenging question, but one surely in keeping with the spirit of the times: Here you are a purely African group, a team of black men, and this is an honourable scientific accomplishment; but why have you not thought of including a woman?

"We do have a woman among us," they protest, "an Arab paleontologist. Please, come and meet her."

They lead her to the infirmary tent, where Sijjin Kuang sits beside a cot on which lies a light-skinned young woman with delicate features. She is introduced as Zohara al-Ukbi, a North African Arab, and she smiles through her pain at the unexpected visitor, extending to her a fevered hand.

17.

THE OFFICE IS dark and locked, and when he enters only the rich scent of tobacco lingers in the empty hall. He turns on all the lights and discovers that none of the employees has thought to return to work after lunch. This is something new, grouses Ya'ari to himself, upgrading dubious ancient history into a holy vacation. But it was he who decided to do away with clocking-in and rely on the individual consciences of his employees, and he remains quite certain that the work will not suffer. Therefore, he's not going to stick around either. He checks his e-mails and finds no new signs of life from either his wife or his son. But tomorrow, according to plan, Yirmiyahu will take Daniela to Dar es Salaam, and there will finally be a real conversation.

The office is located one flight up in a quiet residential building, in the heart of Tel Aviv. Outside the streetlights are on, and the lovely windless evening carries the bright chatter of passersby in through the window. Hanukkah is a holiday beloved by all. If Daniela were here, they'd go and see a movie at one of the shopping malls, or would be invited to friends'. For a moment he considers calling his father, but decides he should limit his presence over there. Best not to encourage the Filipinos to depend on him too much.

If his son were by his side it would be easier to bear the absence of his wife. He turns off all the office lights, and as he is about to lock the door the cell phone suddenly sounds its melody, and he pounces on it in the darkness without first identifying the caller. No, it's not the soldier confined to his base. It's the old lady in Jerusalem, Dr. Bennett, whose voice quivers at him in the darkness. Finally she has caught him and will not let him go until he reveals how she can reach the original Mr. Ya'ari who installed the elevator in her home and promised her a guarantee for a lifetime—the elevator's and hers.

Yes, she knows that his father has long since retired from the business, and that he is unwell, but she considers herself a special case. An old friend, for whom, she is certain, the real Ya'ari will rise from his sickbed and come to her with all that is required, with spare parts and technicians.

"No," Ya'ari patiently explains, "we are a design firm and not a service company, we have no parts and no technicians, we only sit in front of computers and think. Have you heard perhaps of the Yellow Pages? There you will find the help you need."

She is familiar with the Yellow Pages and also how to use them. But his father made her swear to call only him should anything go wrong. For this is an internal elevator, personal, his own original invention, and only he knows how to maintain it.

"And when was the last malfunction?"

Not for many years has there been any serious problem. That's because the elevator always received regular care and maintenance. Whenever his father was in Jerusalem, he would come over and tend to it.

"Strange, he never told me about either you or your elevator."

Perhaps there were other things he never told him.

"Could be," Ya'ari softens, "but my father, Mrs. Bennett, for all his good intentions, can no longer come and see you. He is ill now. He has Parkinson's."

So what?

"What do you mean, so what? His hands and legs are shaking and he can't repair anything."

So he should at least come and give a diagnosis. She has good friends who also have Parkinson's, but their minds still work.

"Yes, his mind still works, but not for your elevator."

Now the woman from Jerusalem stands up to this man who is behaving so unfairly. Why does he speak for his father and not allow his father to decide for himself? How dare he infantilize his father to her, she remembers him, Amotz Ya'ari, as a child.

"Me? As a child?"

Yes, at her own house, in 1954, not so long after the State was established, when they installed the elevator. His father brought him along, to show his son to her. She thinks he was seven then.

"Eight."

And she gave him a whole ice cream. Maybe that will help him remember.

"A whole ice cream? I don't remember, but I believe you," Ya'ari laughs and surrenders. "If I got a whole ice cream from you at the age of eight, then tell me, what exactly do you want from me now? I don't think I'll be able to fix the malfunction."

But she has already told him what she wants. She needs his father's telephone number. There are several Yoel Ya'aris in the Tel Aviv–Jaffa phone book, and she is an old lady who cannot begin calling them all.

"But I warn you that speaking is not easy for my father either, so please make it brief."

Of course, very brief. She belongs to a generation that prizes actions and not words.

18.

IT IS THE Land Rover that leads the small supply convoy home. Sijjin Kuang tracks their way across the desert plain, the two pickup trucks closely following. Now that the food containers are empty, the off-duty cooks, no longer on guard, can curl up contentedly, but the aroma of food still clings to them, and gleaming eyes still follow the convoy in the darkness.

In the front seat, Yirmiyahu's head bobs as if freed from the will of its owner, and sinks on its own as he falls asleep. But in the backseat his sister-in-law is wide awake.

"How can you manage to navigate in this darkness," she asks the silent driver.

"From the bends in the road, but the stars also help."

And Daniela lifts her eyes and sees skies such as she has

never known anywhere. There are stars she has never seen and will likely not see again. This pure emerald glow, when has she ever experienced it before? When has she ever contemplated nature alone? Even in the distant past, in the summer camps of her youth movement or during military service, her contact with nature was accompanied by human chatter. And after that Amotz was with her. She married him at a very young age—she had barely finished her army service. He trapped her with his love and quickly furnished her with a comfortable nest.

The young black scientists have moved her. Not for some time has she felt so needed, desirable in this way. Maybe it's the dearth of women, along with her foreignness and the whiteness of her skin, that drew them to a woman more than twenty years older than they themselves.

Despite the twists in the road engraved in her memory, and despite the helpful stars, the Sudanese woman is not always sure of her way across the monotonous plain. Now she stops and waits for the other two drivers to stop also and get out of their trucks to consult with her about the right direction. The three speak quietly, in tones of mutual respect. One of the men bends to sniff the ground, and his friend stretches out his arm and points to the sky. Yirmiyahu straightens up and yawns, glances indifferently at the drivers' conference, in which he takes no part, and observes to his sister-in-law that it is always at this exact spot that they deliberate about the remainder of the drive.

And the guest sits behind this standoffish man thinking that she has not yet come anywhere near the ultimate purpose of her trip. On the contrary, in the two days since she set out on her journey, she has only grown more serene. Tomorrow, in Dar es Salaam, she will hear the live voice of her husband, and she expects no special news from him. She trusts him to watch over the family.

Yirmiyahu looks behind him and yawns again, apologizing. Yes, sometimes they exhaust him with their stones and monkey bones, but all in all these blacks are very gentle people.

"Just a minute, tell me, so I won't be confused—they don't get insulted when you call them blacks?"

"Why should they be insulted? They know that beyond the first millimetre of black skin they're exactly the same as us. The whole difference is that we're *muzungu* and they're not."

"What?"

"We are *muzungu,* white people. Not actually white, but peeled. Our black skin has been peeled from us."

"Peeled? This is the difference?"

"So I hear."

A bicycle rider who suddenly emerges from the darkness settles once and for all the quiet debate among the drivers, and the caravan makes a full U-turn and follows him until the moon bursts into view beyond the hills and illuminates the wilderness.

Yirmiyahu goes back to sleep. The air is cold, and Daniela zips up her sister's windbreaker. She hugs herself with both arms, and her thoughts wander to Tel Aviv. Did Amotz go tonight to light candles with the grandchildren again, or did he manage to cajole Nofar to come home? Now here again are the stream and the huts; the caravan picks up speed. The elephant shed is surrounded by torches and a sizeable crowd. Daniela has an urge to go back and look again, alone, at the miracle of the giant eye. She taps Sijjin Kuang on the shoulder and asks her to stop for a few minutes.

Unescorted and fearless she hurriedly makes her way through the African crowd. When she reaches the entrance to the shed, the elephant's owner has already recognized the white woman, and sees the return visit as a sign of respect for the elephant and for himself. He therefore does not ask for an admission fee, but she takes a few dollars from her purse and sets them on his table.

And at this late hour, she sees the same sad wisdom revealed in that enormous eye. Daniela asks herself if this genetic defect will remain an oddity and eventually be lost, or if perhaps by some pathway not at all understood something of it will be transmitted into a new human evolution.

19.

AS HE OPENS the door Ya'ari hears water running in the shower. If so, Nofar is already home, he thinks, and this pleases him, though he is nervous about meeting her new friend.

Yes, the friend is here. Not a lover or a boyfriend, just a friend, who nonetheless is not sitting and politely waiting but rather taking the liberty of sauntering around the living room as if he belonged there. This time, a new twist, it's not someone young like her, but rather older. His cheeks are unshaven and his temples are flecked with grey. A man who has met the request of a young friend to come with her, just as a friend, to light candles at the home of her father, who has been left alone on the Hanukkah holiday.

Ya'ari heeds his daughter's warning to curb his usual curiosity regarding her friends' education and training, and does not pry into the visitor's activities to get an inkling of his purpose in life. To avoid an interrogation that will anger Nofar, he talks about the weather, applauds the rain and deplores the strong winds, which sometimes sneak into apartment towers. He adds a gripe about the holiday, which in the past amounted to jam doughnuts and spinning *dreidels* and has now been upgraded into a holy respite from work. For example, all the engineers in his firm left at noon for a children's play at the Hall of Culture and never returned.

The friend drifts around the room, his expression pained and suspicious, voicing neither sympathy nor agreement with Ya'ari's remarks. His small deep-set eyes keep reverting to the family photos that Daniela has planted everywhere, on walls and bookshelves. Not like a passing acquaintance, here today and gone tomorrow, but like someone with a stake in the matter, he studies each picture carefully, as if trying to decipher the structure of the family. And when he gets to the photograph, framed in black, of Eyal, he asks in a fevered whisper, "Is this the cousin Nofar never stops talking about?" Fear makes the host's heart beat faster. "I wonder how old he would be if he were alive."

"About your age, thirty-two. He was only three years older than Nofar's brother."

But the curious friend doesn't let up. Perhaps he agreed to attend a candle-lighting in a strange home only so that he could learn more details about the soldier who was killed by his comrades' fire.

"Nofar told me that you had to break the news to his parents."

"To his father. I wasn't alone; an officer and a doctor were with me."

"And he really was killed accidentally, by our own forces?"

"Yes, by friendly fire, something like that…" Ya'ari whispers.

"And they had to tell that to the family?"

Ya'ari's face darkens at the stranger who has the nerve to burrow into his intimate life, but for his daughter's sake he controls himself.

"Of course. The media in any case would have made the truth public. But they call it 'our own forces,' and I put it slightly differently, to soften it."

"And did it really soften it?"

Ya'ari does not answer, because at that very moment Nofar enters the living room with her hair wet from the shower. She is wearing black, and her almond eyes, her mother's eyes, shoot him an arrow of warning.

"So, at last we get to see you," he kisses and hugs her tight.

"So come on, Abba, let's light the candles, because we're going to a party. But remember what I asked, only the basic blessings."

He nods and goes to the big silver menorah, already prepared with its four candles, removes the shammash and lights it with a match. Printed on the blue box of candles are the two blessings, which he reads while applying the flame to the first candle. Then he hands the burning shammash to the friend, who uses it to light the second candle, then passes it to the young woman. Nofar heats the tip of the third candle to expose its wick, and when the bluish flame intensifies to yellow-red, she returns the shammash still lit to her father, who restores it to its place.

20.

And in East Africa, on the top floor of the farmhouse, Daniela turns over on her bed in the dark and has a hard time finding the point of fatigue from which she can confidently slip into sleep. It is almost midnight, and even if in her homeland it's an hour earlier, the candles have surely gone out long ago at her house, and her son and daughter-in-law's too. As for Nofar, she is probably boycotting all lights of happiness till she exhausts the grief in her heart.

Yirmiyahu's detachment could become contagious: she had better be careful. He seems content with his primitive surroundings, and the memory of his wife is growing dimmer. If she can't find a way of arousing memories in him of Shuli, and of her too, he won't do it for her.

She gets up from the bed and opens the shutters wide and looks out on an expanse with no artificial light. Right now she very much needs the touch of her husband's hand. His attentive eye. How easily she could have made him come along.

She turns on a light and examines the skull of the young monkey that sits on the desk. A relative who became extinct a few million years ago and has returned as a replica. She pries his mouth open with her fingers to study his jaws. There's only one real tooth here—which one she can't tell. No, she strokes the smooth skull, you were not an eating machine.

Sleep continues to elude her. If Yirmiyahu hadn't been so quick to burn the Israeli papers instead of just handing them back, she could have lulled herself with old news from home. But there is not a letter of Hebrew in sight, apart from the novel. Last night she read two more pages, and they bored her.

Given no choice, she opens the book where she left off yesterday and moves the lamp closer. The heroine has found herself a new love, or a boyfriend, or merely a friend. Someone involved in shady business. To the author's credit it may be said that she does not raise false expectations in the alert reader. It's obvious that the relationship will not last till the end of the novel, but attraction and lust will do for now.

Okay, the reader squints, let's see how and why they get sick of each other. On page 95 the heroine travels to Europe with her friend. They arrive at a hotel in a capital city, and the author begins without much ado an elaborate depiction of their lovemaking. Daniela is quite tolerant of sexual descriptions in novels; they seldom last for more than two or three paragraphs—a page at most. But this author has decided to go into detail and continue the episode until the end of the chapter: eight full pages dense with foreplay and intercourse. Is the passion that erupts between these characters realistic, that is, equal to the capacities of the heroine as portrayed up to now, or has the author decided to inflame her artificially, to satisfy her readers' expectations? The descriptions are very physical, and, as usual with such episodes, repetitive. The language is precise, and for that very reason also revolting. This author is shameless, no word is off-limits to her. Daniela feels cheated. Previously the characters, in spite of their weaknesses, have manifested a certain spiritual longing; now all of a sudden, this crude naturalism. She examines the back cover to see if the editor's blurb contains any hint to prepare the reader for this vulgarity. But it would appear that although the editor could have attracted more customers, he preferred to keep quiet and protect his reputation for fine literary taste.

Should she skip over this chapter, and go to the next? The reader considers this as her breathing grows heavier. But since she is not in the habit of skimming, she soldiers on, page after page, till the light goes out in the room of the lovers, who have reached supreme satisfaction.

And the furious reader drops the novel to the floor, turns off the light, and waits patiently for merciful slumber.

Fourth Candle

1.

THE CLOUDS THAT descended before dawn on the coastal plain have spread thickly over Tel Aviv, and at six A.M., when Ya'ari pulls up his bedroom blinds, he is surprised to discover that not only has his neighbour's house been engulfed by the milky mist, but also the tree that was planted in the garden a decade ago to hide the homes from one another. He shakes dead damp leaves from the newspaper flung on his doorstep and tries to detect a breath of wind in the fog, or any trace of movement in the hidden world.

The world is bundled in silence, at ease with its air of mystery. As Amotz drinks his morning coffee, checking *Ha'aretz* for yesterday's rainfall, patiently waiting for the sun to free his neighbour's house from its shroud of haze, he remembers the idea floated by Gottlieb, who appeared to him in last night's dream pushing the buggy of an alert baby girl clad in a technician's jump suit, with a screwdriver dangling from her neck, who gazed at the dreamer with starry eyes. Here, this is my expert, Gottlieb grumbled, and you would send her all alone, unsupervised, into the shaft? But Ya'ari awoke before he could answer the elevator manufacturer.

The young tree in the garden emerges from the thinning fog, and beyond its branches appears the house next door, with its lights on and the owner, a famous gynaecologist, marching along with religious devotion on his treadmill. The phone rings, and Ya'ari scoops it up with the certainty that at this hour it can only be Moran. But to his disappointment it's his father, who should just be getting up and being washed, which requires time and concentration. Something wrong, Abba? No, says the old man, I'm the same as always. But I wanted to ask, before you fix your schedule for the day, that you come here earlier—in the morning, not the evening. The candles I'll light with Hilario, but you, if you can, come to me this morning. It's something urgent—no, not medically, just humanly.

"Let me guess. That woman in Jerusalem finally got hold of you."

"Not hard to guess."

"But tell me, Abba, honestly—isn't it ridiculous for me, or someone else in the office, to try to repair a private elevator from fifty years ago? By the way, did you tell her you're in a wheelchair?"

"No, no, Amotz, we won't talk like this on the phone about Devorah Bennett. You try and get here soon, before work, and we'll sit and discuss quietly how we can help her. Give your father half an hour. No more."

"It's not a question of half an hour. You know how Francisco doesn't like it when I interrupt the morning routine."

"Francisco will forgive us this time. I've already talked to him."

2.

THE ANTICIPATION OF hearing her husband's voice over the phone in Dar es Salaam, reporting on the welfare of her loved ones, rouses Daniela from bed, and she is up and about before sunrise. She opens the shutters and leans out to refresh her spirits in the dark chilly air. Then she turns to pick up the novel from the floor and leafs through it to find the place where she stopped the night before. Since her sister's death, she finds herself rereading pages, but by the time she notices, it's too late to skip ahead. Only rarely does a second reading reveal hidden aspects of the characters and events. In fact, sometimes it makes the writing seem even shallower.

She skims the final page of the chapter she finished last night. The sexual descriptions now seem to her less degrading. Is it daybreak that tempers the vulgarity of the night-time reading, or have her fragmented dreams reconciled her to it? Either way, she has no intention of re-reading that chapter, and anyway, it would be better to save the rest of the novel for the trip home, to take advantage of every free minute here for seeing nature and conversing with Yirmiyahu and the locals. So she removes the stub of her used boarding pass from her passport and marks the page.

Despite the open window, it feels stuffy in the smallish room, and after a brief hesitation she puts on her African dress and wraps herself in her sister's windbreaker and walks down three flights, noting three or four doorways per floor. She needs to clarify which is Yirmiyahu's temporary bedroom. Though she feels well, and well-rested, it's still a good idea for a woman whose blood pressure has gone up to know on which door she can knock at night if something weighs heavily on her heart.

She wouldn't dare to explore outside, even around the main building of the farm, until the sun climbed higher and human voices were audible in the vicinity. But she will try to fix herself a cup of coffee. The huge kitchen is silent, and because she can't find the light switch, she makes do with the glow of dawn in the windows, rummaging among the utensils hanging on the walls until she finds a little pot that resembles a Middle Eastern *finjan*. She fills it with water, certain that she will also find some coffee, maybe even sugar and milk.

On the day of the terrible news, in her sister's home in Jerusalem, feeling miserable about being late and annoyed that it was she who was assigned to the kitchen, she dropped a big jar of coffee, scattering shards of glass and black grounds all over the floor. The lateness hadn't even been her fault. Moran hadn't set foot in his old school building, not even to share the news of his cousin's death with the principal and the secretary. Instead, with shaking knees he had paced the empty schoolyard for more than three-quarters of an hour, waiting for the bell, and only when it rang had he rushed to the staffroom to stop his mother at the doorway, and hug her tight and lead her to the exit.

By the time she reached Jerusalem, she had been preceded not only by Amotz, but by relatives and friends who had already been informed, so that when she first saw her sister she found her already surrounded by the kindness of others, depriving her of the personal time and space to wrap her arms around the bereaved mother and absorb some small measure of the grief roiling inside her. In those first moments in the crowded living room, she had felt helpless in the presence of women who did not hurry to yield her the place she deserved; it even seemed that they blamed her for being late and it was therefore she who was sent to the kitchen to make a cup of coffee that might keep her sister from fainting.

Now, in this kitchen that takes up the entire ground floor of a farmhouse, she opens cupboard after cupboard in search of coffee and sugar. But the shelves are bare of food, holding only baking pans filled with fossils. Perhaps these are remnants of extinct animals, but judging by the clutter they seem not to be rare or valuable, like those she was shown last night at the scientists' dining table, and, since they are not destined to cast new light on the origins of man, may merit one more quick look before being thrown in the rubbish.

An elderly African enters the kitchen soundlessly, walking with a slight limp. He nods lugubriously upon hearing the white woman's request for coffee and sugar, and opens one of the great refrigerator doors, taking out black coffee, brown sugar, and some greyish milk—but whose? From what animal? She questions the old man, who knows some English. And he pronounces the name of some beast utterly unfamiliar to her, though it might be familiar if pronounced otherwise, and she decides she can do without milk until someone more authoritative and precise can clarify its provenance.

3.

ON HIS EVENING visits, when his father's house is clean and organized, Ya'ari typically gives one short ring and then opens the door with his key, but this morning he rings longer and waits, to allow those inside to prepare for his arrival. In fact, the Filipinos send Hilario to open the door, hoping that his sweet fluent Hebrew, and maybe also his adorable turban, will help the boss's son forgive the unaccustomed mess.

The father's morning ablutions have left the apartment very warm, and its residents' identity is more pronounced now than in the evening: it is there in the pungent smells of food cooked the night before, still cooling in a corner of the living room; the infant girl clad only in a diaper and set upon the dining table; the pyjamas decorated with pictures of Asian birds, strewn on unmade beds; and the baby's mother, her nakedness swathed in a silken robe of many spectacular colours.

"What is this, Hilario, no school today?"

"It's vacation, Mr. Ya'ari. The holiday of the Maccabees," announces the little student, excited as ever by the mysteries of Judaism.

On the way to his father's bedroom Amotz peeks into his own childhood room, now occupied by Hilario and his Israeli-born sister. Amid the electronic war toys, beneath the posters of mythic figures from children's movies, he can discern a few prehistoric items, such as the Monopoly game of his youth.

His father has been returned to bed after the morning's elaborate bathing, and Ya'ari is not used to chatting with a father wrapped comfortably in two blankets with only his head visible, collared by a colourful towel, and showing no sign of the tremors of his disease.

"Don't be angry with me for insisting that you come this morning," he says, "but this friend of mine, Devorah Bennett, told me she had been trying to reach me for days, and that you and others at the office were hiding my phone number from her. So listen, habibi, this woman is a dear friend, and after Imma died she helped me a great deal during a difficult period. By the way, before I forget, what about Daniela, did you hear from her?"

"Today she goes to Dar es Salaam, where Yirmi will connect her to me by phone."

"If you get the chance, give her my regards, and tell her I hope her visit to her brother-in-law will help her get herself together."

"The problem with her is guilt . . . she always felt guilty towards her sister, for no reason, and after she passed away the guilt only intensified."

"A little guilt, even for no reason, can still be something productive and healthy," says the elderly elevator designer, "particularly if it is towards family or friends, and it should always be listened to. This is why I want you to help me with my little guilt regarding the friend in Jerusalem. She is nine years younger than I am, meaning she should now be eighty-one years of age. What can I say, a slip of a girl, and many years ago I helped her out with a private elevator, so she could go straight from the apartment to the roof and make some use of it. A simple elevator, small, just for one floor, with a Czech mechanism from before the world war that works on oil pressure with a piston that lifts it from the side. But the construction was all mine. Gottlieb built it according to my plans. And when your mother and I visited Germany in the early fifties, we found a few spare parts in an old scrap warehouse, and I shipped them back to Israel as research materials. You'll soon see it for yourself."

"What makes you think I'll see it?"

"Because I gave my friend a lifetime warranty. She is an intellectual lady and a bit artistic, and during the British Mandate she had an English husband, one-quarter Jewish, who didn't last long here after the establishment of the State. The building is in the centre of town, and after a beauty salon opened up on the ground floor, I suggested to her, so she could have a quiet corner, an elevator straight from her flat to the roof, which was not being used and could be reached only by a ladder from the stairwell. So this way she made herself a nice, quiet retreat, which is also cool in the summer evenings, as you'll see."

"Why do you think I should see it?"

"Because your father is asking you to. This is a woman who helped me a great deal after Imma died. She hasn't got the means to bring in a technician, who in any case will not be familiar with such an elevator. It's a building on King George Street, opposite the old Knesset, and she apparently doesn't plan to leave it while she is alive, and therefore she needs the elevator that gives her access to the roof. When Jerusalem was divided, before '67, you could see the Old City from there. And I gather that the elevator is still alive and only needs adjustment, and to have its seal changed. You'll check for yourself."

"But what good can I do? I'm a design engineer, not a technician."

The father shuts his eyes and falls silent.

"All right," he finally says, "if you are just a designer then don't go and see her in Jerusalem. Forget my request. I'll ask Moran. He has more patience, which is why he has golden hands, even though he, like you, is an engineer and not a technician."

"As you wish, ask Moran, he is an independent being, but just so you know, he's in the army right now."

"How come? He told me he's ignoring the army."

"He ignored the army, but the army didn't ignore him."

"So what's going to happen?"

"What's going to happen? Eventually they'll let him go."

"No, I mean in Jerusalem."

"In Jerusalem the slip of a girl can wait a bit. If you gave her a lifetime guarantee, then there's no danger that the warranty will run out. Meanwhile it's winter, so she won't need to go up on the roof."

"You're now talking without an ounce of compassion. But it doesn't matter. If you refuse, and the army is holding Moran, then I will ask Francisco to get me a taxi that can handle a wheelchair and bring along two Filipino friends from the old people's home, and they'll take me to Jerusalem, at least to give her a diagnosis."

"Good God, you are really stubborn. But tell me, what's wrong with that damned elevator?"

"First of all, it's not damned, and second, as I told you, it's not dead at all, it's still alive, but it has, so she says, kind of a tremor when it starts moving, and also when it stops."

"Maybe it got a little old, Abba? What do you think?"

"Of course it got old, but because it is not a person, it's possible to adjust the oil pressure and replace the seal . . . no?"

"Anything is possible."

"And besides which, she also says, Devorah Bennett, that there's now a wail that was never there before, as if a cat on heat were riding in it with her."

"A cat on heat?"

"Yes, that is how she describes it."

"No, Abba, for God's sake, don't talk to me about more wailing noises in elevators."

4.

THIS IS EXACTLY the same road, travelled in the opposite direction, and in the light of a broiling summer morning it goes faster, and the visitor may take in all that was hidden on the night she landed here. This time she is not in the front seat, but sitting a bit cramped in the back, behind her brother-in-law's bald head, though the driver is the same driver, quiet and precise. This morning Sijjin Kuang has her shoulders and slender arms wrapped in a sunflower-coloured shawl that highlights the coal black sheen of her skin. At ten they must be in Morogoro to board a Chinese freight train carrying copper ore to the port of Dar es Salaam, where, as firmly agreed, their first order of business will be to establish a living link between the guest and her husband; only afterwards will they attend to the needs of the excavation team. And even though Sijjin Kuang is plainly of different stock from the locals, Daniela is very pleased to be visiting in the company of a black African woman, whose presence affords her a quiet legitimacy.

Yesterday, visiting the excavation site, she imagined for a moment that perhaps there had developed between the elderly widower and the nurse a bond deeper than their professional one, but this morning her impression has been erased by the profound sadness she sees in this young woman, whose whole family was murdered. She observes that when her brother-in-law's hand or shoulder happen to bump into the driver's as the

141

car rounds a bend or suddenly swerves, the Sudanese shrinks from him, as from some enemy who wished to harm her.

They drive around Mount Morogoro on a wide red-dirt road, hard as asphalt, that twists through a thick bushy forest that now and then vanishes for no reason, replaced by a barren hilltop. She asks her brother-in-law, is the earth redder here? I remember your explaining it to Amotz and me last time, but I don't remember what you said.

"The red colour comes from the iron in the soil, which also decreases its fertility."

"Iron . . . I remember now, that's what you told us then too."

"See, here's proof that I'm a stable person, who doesn't easily change his mind. But if you ask Sijjin Kuang, for example, why the earth of Africa is red, she will flatly tell you it's because of all the blood that has been spilled upon it."

The driver, hearing her name mentioned, glances back at Daniela.

"And maybe because of the blood she can't forget, it's also good for you to be with her, because her tragedy is greater than yours. Next to her you can forget your own."

Yirmi does not respond at first. Maybe he didn't hear. Maybe he disagrees with what she said. But suddenly he turns around, pulls his sister-in-law's little hand towards him and puts it to his lips in a gesture of gratitude. Sometimes you amaze me with your accuracy, the way you touch, as if casually, the heart of the matter. Of course this woman's tragedy is greater than mine, and I realize that, but that's not the only reason why I like her to drive the car and go on my rounds with me. You will be amazed, but she does not know about our Eyali, because I told her nothing, nor have I told the others, so that no one here will have any emotional purchase on what I myself want to forget. This woman helps me peel off my identity.

"How?"

"With all those things you also like about her. She is a genuine animist, a pagan who believes in trees and stones and spirits, not as a confused appendage to some failed abstract religion, and not as a cry for help out of weakness and despair, but as a natural act, a whole different faith. And therefore, unlike Christians or Muslims, she has no connection or commitment to Jews, for either good or ill, love or hate. We are not the source she comes from, or a cause for struggle or competition. For her we are simply not relevant, nor does she see herself as relevant to us. For me she is a place where we do not exist in any memories. Not religious, not historical, not mythological. For her I am only a man—admittedly white, but that's a minor detail, because it was blacks, after all, who murdered her family and her tribe. And therefore, without talk or effort, simply as one person to another, she helps me peel away my identity, like the white man who has peeled off his blackness. Everything that has oppressed me begins to fall off, without argument or debate, so that even if a dear and familiar guest happens to descend on me, that person can't reverse the process."

"You mean me, of course."

"For example. But up to now I have no complaints: you are behaving courteously and keeping within bounds."

5.

"Okay, I surrender," Amotz says to his father. "Tomorrow's Friday; I'll try to get up to Jerusalem."

"But why not go today? You have all this free time now."

"What free time?"

"Your wife's not here and you have no one to take care of or worry about."

"Don't exaggerate. I have someone left to take care of, and there's always something to worry about. So I'll hop up to Jerusalem tomorrow, not because of the yowling of an imaginary cat on heat, but purely for your peace of mind."

"My peace of mind isn't a good enough reason? So before you go, let me give you a kiss."

Ya'ari can't remember the last time his father asked to kiss him. He himself, when he comes to visit and finds his father in the wheelchair, sometimes squeezes his trembling hand and lightly kisses, out of obligation, the cheek of the man from whom he has learned so much. But he doesn't recall his father ever once initiating a kiss, not for several dozen years. Now he does, as he lies naked in bed, under two blankets, and Ya'ari has to bend over him as he offers only his forehead to his father's lips.

"If you find the cat on heat inside her shaft, bring it with you so I can see it," says the father, then closes his eyes and plants a kiss on the forehead of the man of sixty.

Judging by his father's excitement, it would seem that she was a love of his, Ya'ari muses as he heads south to his office on a grey windless day. The old father even yearned to confess, but his son wouldn't let him, lest it turn out that the woman in Jerusalem had been his lover while his mother was still alive.

And even if he were told that the woman only helped his father restore his manhood after his wife's death, Ya'ari has no great desire to meet her, and certainly none to service her ancient, shaking, wailing elevator. In any case it lies beyond his power to heal its afflictions, or even diagnose them. If Moran were in town, he would certainly send him to Jerusalem to satisfy his grandpa. But Moran has sunk into the abyss of the army and has exchanged not one word with him; Ya'ari suspects that his son has begun to enjoy the freedom of his confinement.

The office is teeming. Those who took yesterday off have come in early today to complete their projects. Where's Moran, ask colleagues whose work depends on him. Moran is doing reserve duty, says Ya'ari, avoiding the whole truth. But he said he would ignore the army? So he said it. Not everything he says comes true.

For a moment Ya'ari considers whether it would be right to ask one of the younger engineers to go to Jerusalem in his place. But anyone sent there would likely feel foolish and helpless, confronted with a prehistoric private elevator, and bear a grudge over the Friday needlessly stolen from him, and the imposition of a technician's chore on an engineer.

He phones the lady in Jerusalem and speaks to her in practical army language: You've won, Mrs. Bennett, I will come to see your elevator tomorrow morning, but I warn you, have no illusions, I am coming only to look, not to repair. So please, don't budge from your house from nine A.M. on.

After that, he convenes the weekly staff meeting in his office earlier than usual, to ensure that at the appointed hour of noon both he and his telephone will be free to receive his wife's African voice.

6.

AND AT THIS moment Daniela is not far from Dar es Salaam. She sits in a makeshift passenger compartment in the Chinese freight train, her brother-in-law dozes on the bench beside her, and across from her sits Sijjin Kuang, whose gentle gaze indicates that she gathered—at least from the Hebrew word *pagani*—that the conversation between the two Israeli relatives had something to do with her. And even though the tragedy of the young Sudanese woman, who lost both family and homeland, is greater than the disaster that befell the elderly administrator—whose head droops on his chest and appears to be nodding in agreement—the visitor would still like to give her some hint about the fire that needlessly killed the white man's son.

But Yirmiyahu does not want to tell his driver anything about himself, lest one story lead to another, and one history get tangled with another, until even an idolator could find herself connected to him. And so, since his sister-in-law has not come here to thwart his wishes, she steers the conversation to injuries and illnesses. Perhaps she can learn from the African nurse's experience about an ancient and proven cure for some malady she has yet to contract.

Now through the window a few houses can be seen, then streets. Here is a city. And, for a tiny moment, a sliver of smooth sea with a gliding sailing boat.

Yirmi, again alert and energetic, confidently leads the two women along streets he clearly knows well, between vegetable stalls and buckets of fish and sacks of coal. If possible, Daniela says, let's start by calling Israel. We promised Amotz, and I know he's waiting with his hand on the phone.

"If we promised, we will deliver." Yirmi calms her with a smile. "From the time I met him, forty years ago, I've known it's dangerous to make him wait."

He guides them into a darkened shack, a public telecommunications centre, filled with a jumble of wires, plugged into elderly computers and antique phones, that brings to mind a spider's web. The proprietor, a beefy woman named Zaineb, greets them happily and seats the tourist by a telephone with a well-worn dial.

"I have learned from experience that from here you speak frugally and clearly," Yirmi says self-righteously, "since every month I call America to report to Elinor that I am surviving, and to hear how many words she has added to her dissertation. Write down the exact number for Zaineb, with the codes for Israel and Tel Aviv, and you will be able to put your loved one at ease. We shall wait patiently outside."

"You don't want to say a few words?"

"Only if you don't overdo your conversation. Look, don't be so sure that I don't think about him too sometimes."

The connection from the spider's web is made efficiently, and is actually clear and strong. And in Tel Aviv the office receptionist is happy to hear the African voice of the boss's wife, though she is a bit surprised by the early hour. There's a staff meeting going on in his office, but not to worry, she'll pull him out of there right away. Just don't hang up.

"Why do you say I'm early? We arranged to talk today at twelve."

"But it's now eleven," the secretary chides her. "You seem to have an hour's difference in your favour."

"In my favour?" Daniela says, laughing, "in what sense?"

But the secretary has already gone to fetch her husband.

147

7.

Standing by the receptionist's desk, using her telephone in front of other people and maybe being overheard, was not the way he had wanted to conduct the much anticipated conversation with his wife. But is it proper to cut short the meeting and dismiss everyone from his office, just so he can complain about his troubles without an audience? Given no choice, he grabs the receiver and retreats to a corner, stretching the phone cord as far as he can, and tries to speak confidentially. His tone comes out sounding both accusatory and defensive.

"That's right," he says, "I got the times wrong. I was sure you were on the same longitude, and all of a sudden Africa is not only southwest but also east of us. So everything I imagined you doing on your trip you had finished an hour before."

"No big deal. It's only an hour's difference. But if it's hard for you to talk now, I'll try again later."

"No, absolutely not. I'll just talk quietly, because there are people here. Can you hear me?"

"Perfectly. First of all, tell me about the children."

"Just a minute, the children can wait. You tell *me* what's happening. First of all, how was the trip?"

"The flight to Nairobi was nice, but to spend six hours in the airport just for your peace of mind, that was cruel. And I ended up almost missing the connecting flight anyway."

"Missing it? How is that possible?"

"My boarding pass disappeared in the novel."

"Novel?"

"The book I bought at the airport."

"But I warned you beforehand to keep everything with your

passport, and I put it there myself. So how did it wander into the novel?"

"No big deal, I found it."

"Watch out. You can only afford to dream when I'm with you. And how was the second flight? I worried the whole time that on an internal flight in Africa you'd have a small, shabby plane."

"It was a small plane, but clean and nice and not shabby at all, and they even served unlimited whisky."

He laughs. "Not to you, I hope. And where is it, this farm of Yirmi's? Is it far from the airport?"

"Not very. But the road is mostly dirt and a bit complicated, part of it through a forest. Fortunately, the pagan who drove me—"

"Pagan?"

"A charming young Sudanese woman, an idol worshipper... a tragic figure, I'll tell you all about her..."

"Idol worshipper? What idols?"

"No, not now. I'll tell you everything later. How are the children?"

"Leave the children aside for a minute. Yirmi forgot you and didn't come to the airport?"

"No, no, it's a long story. I'll tell you all about it. He's the one who sent her; she's the nurse of the research team."

"And what about *him?*"

"Stranger than ever. But also pleased with himself. I brought him a package of Israeli papers from the plane and he burned them all."

"Burned them? Good for him. Why should he read Israeli papers in Africa? Where's the fun in that?"

"The Hanukkah candles I brought, he threw them in the fire too."

"What, he has a campfire burning there?"

"The fire of the boiler."

"But why the candles?"

"No reason. He's looking for ways to disengage himself. From Israel. From the Jews. From everything."

"Disengage? Why not? A great idea. I wish I could do that sometimes. But why detach himself in Africa? There are nicer places in the world to get detached."

"Not now, Amotz. He's right outside. We'll talk about everything next week. But tell me what's going on with the children."

"Nofar came home yesterday with an older friend to light candles."

"Very good."

"But she only stayed a little while."

"That's not important. What's important is she came."

"But here's the big news, listen carefully: the army didn't give up on Moran. They caught him and put him in confinement."

"Actual confinement?"

"The real thing, confined to base for a week or so. But he's in Israel, not the West Bank, with the adjutant corps. I haven't got through to him yet, because they confiscated his cell phone, but he's in touch with Efrat occasionally. And yesterday I took your place and picked up the children from nursery and waited with them at a café till Yael was able to take them. Tomorrow's Friday, and I'll light candles with them then."

"It's good that her mother always volunteers to help."

"The mother is okay, but the daughter of the mother keeps running around on empty. A training course up north, then a seminar down south. She drives me crazy."

"Go crazy quietly and keep it to yourself, be careful not to make any remarks. It's not your business to educate her. Let Moran take care of her."

"But Moran is a prisoner. An officer in the IDF. Imagine the disgrace."

"Leave him alone too. Don't reprimand him. For a long time I've had the feeling that he's afraid of his reserve duty."

"Afraid? Moran? Where'd you get that idea? Moran was never a coward, certainly not in the army. He just felt like ignoring them, and he's like you, he is sure that the whole world revolves around him."

"And I'm sure the whole world revolves around me?"

"More or less."

"Where'd you get that idea?"

"Not now. I'm not alone either. This is my secretary's phone. But where's Yirmi? Is he with you? In any case, I want to say a word to him."

"What word?"

"That he should keep an eye on you."

"Don't you dare."

8.

YIRMIYAHU IS WAITING in an alley with Sijjin Kuang, whose tall aristocratic figure next to the awkward old white man's has attracted the curiosity of people in the marketplace. From time to time he glances inside at his sister-in-law, who sits smiling and content in the depths of the communications hut, surrounded by young Africans riveted to computer screens, as she, in a girlish pose he finds charming, presses the worn-out phone receiver against her short-cropped head, crosses her legs, and plays with the hem of her dress, exposing her shapely calves.

Even if the phone call here is cheap compared with other places in the city, it is going on longer than he expected, and the warm chattiness of his relatives is beginning to make him impatient. They've only been apart for two days, they'll be back together in three, and they still insist on such a long conversation. He remembers that even as a girl she would tie up her parents' phone for long periods, chatting and laughing, without thinking about the cost—or other people. And the daily calls between her and her sister in the years before Eyal fell would sometimes go on for more than an hour. It was his death that cut them short, those calls. Her son's death shrank and compressed Shuli's world. She lost her patience for the stories of strangers and family members alike; even so close a sister interested her less.

Now Daniela is waving for him to come in and join her. Amotz wants to say a few words to you too, and maybe in any case we should hang up, she suggests, and let Amotz call us back from Israel. No, that's impossible, Yirmiyahu says. The owner doesn't like it when her income is undercut like that, so she doesn't give out her phone number. He takes the receiver, and without saying hello he teases his brother-in-law.

"Well? Already after two days it's hard for you to be alone?"

But Ya'ari ignores the sting and asks with heartfelt concern, "Yirmi, habibi, how's it going?"

"No complaints. So far the woman you sent us is behaving well, and we'll therefore return her to you whole and not feed any part of her to the lions."

The elevator man is in no mood to joke. "And you? What about *you*?"

"Things are the way things should be with me."

"When will we see you?"

"When you too come here. But first let me recover a little from your wife's visit."

"Not in Africa. I mean, when will we see you in Israel?"

"Israel? What's the rush? I spent most of my life there, and it's not going anywhere. It looks to me as if the country can't get destroyed no matter how hard it tries. Here in Africa it's quiet and comfortable, and above all cheap. I also want a nice Filipino to take care of me when I'm old. And anyway, my dear Amotz, I've developed slightly different ideas about our world."

"What kind of ideas?"

"Not now in the middle of the marketplace, on an international call. Other people are waiting to talk to the outside world, and I'm hogging the line. Daniela will tell you what she understood from me, and what you don't understand from her, you can always ask me. And maybe it's totally unimportant. The main thing is, take care of yourself, and also don't forget the children."

As he is about to hang up, Daniela snatches the receiver and manages to ask her husband how his father is and what's new with the winds in the tower.

But when she goes out again into the sunny street she realizes that this call to Israel has not brought her any relief, as if Yirmi's alienation has infected her as well. Her brother-in-law lingers in the hut, waiting to pay her bill, and at her side Sijjin Kuang stands serenely aloof from the colourful mob around her. And she aches for the grief and pain still buried inside her. For it was here in this marketplace, that her sister had her fatal seizure. It was from one of these alleys that strangers rushed her to a nearby clinic, where she departed this world alone.

Where did it begin? Where was Shuli taken ill?

And where was your diplomatic office? So far she does not recognize anything from her last visit.

He will show her the place. With a little patience she will remember everything. It is all nearby, and he is willing to show her around, but first they must go to the bank, before it closes for the midday break.

So, while Sijjin Kuang goes off to replenish the camp's medical supplies, he and his Israeli guest enter a fairly decent-looking bank and go up to the second floor. He seats her in a waiting room beside a heavyset African clad in a tribal robe, and disappears into the manager's office.

Her smile immediately enchants her neighbour, and she does not limit herself to a mere smile, but dares, in English fashion, to inquire about the weather. The African at once grasps the white woman's meaning, but lacks the English to answer her. Instead, he gets up excitedly and with a grand gesture of his arm invites her to come with him to the big window, where he pours out words in an utterly foreign language, pointing to the sky and the clouds, then just as suddenly falls silent and retreats humbly to his chair. But she stays by the window, as if trying to digest what he told her.

The weather has indeed changed. The day has turned grey and the first drops of rain dot the windowpane. Her conversation with her husband was in the end technical and lacking in feeling. If he was concerned about expressing feelings in front of his employees, why didn't he go back into his office and end the meeting, so he could lift her spirits with a few words confirming his love. He didn't sound loving, or as if he missed her, but rather annoyed by her absence, impatient, needing to control. The purpose of her trip is still not clear to him, so he needs at least to be reassured that African planes aren't rickety, that he hasn't risked losing her on a pointless journey.

And maybe he's right, and this trip really wasn't necessary.

At the edge of the rain-streaked sky she can see a grey-green patch of the Indian Ocean, with bobbing fishing boats. So the beach is not far from here. On her last trip, Shuli took her along more than once for her long daily walk on the beach. Alone, without husbands by their side, they strolled with complete confidence on the fishermen's dock. Her sister had really enjoyed Yirmiyahu's economic posting in Tanzania. Once Elinor gave her some grandchildren, she said, maybe she'd want to be nearer to them, but in the meantime she was comfortable in these foreign surroundings, which dampened her pain over the loss of the soldier who had drawn the fire of his friends. Daniela was surprised, at the time, to have confirmed what she had already suspected—that behind the veil of silent, noble grief, strange and difficult feelings burned in her sister regarding her son, and because she feared exposing those feelings inadvertently, she was grateful for the sojourn in an out-of-the-way country not on the map of friends or relatives. Even as she walked next to the person who was closer to her than any other, alone together on an ocean beach, Shuli preferred to reveal nothing, instead replaying over and over long-forgotten moments from their own childhood and clinging to memories of their own parents.

Later on, in her calls from Israel, Daniela took care not to dwell too much on her own children and grandchildren, and given her sister's little interest in other family members, and in mutual friends, and even less interest in political news from her home country, there was not much the two sisters could do but rehash their last visit, marvel time and again at the animals in the nature reserve, recall the naked children splashing in the waves, as if from now on only these would be the subjects they had in common that were worthy of discussion.

The guest again focuses her gaze on the beach and asks herself whether on that terrible day when her sister began to die in the marketplace of Dar es Salaam, she had managed that same morning to walk the length of the fishermen's dock.

She turns around in a panic. No, it's not the African man touching her, but rather her brother-in-law, holding two bags in his hand, one filled with banknotes and the other with coins. Beside him is the bank manager, a young cheerful African in shirtsleeves and tie, who knew her sister well and twice even sat next to her at a meal, in the days when her brother-in-law had more significant dealings with the bank than simple transactions on the account of a remote research dig. Yes, says the bank manager, Jeremy has just told him about her visit to Tanzania, which seems to him worthy and important, for indeed one must not forget the dead, especially those whose souls have departed from them in a far-off place, for only in this way can they return to their homes.

"What? Are you also a pagan?" Daniela blurts out; her impertinence surprises her as much as anyone.

"I wish I could be," sighs the young black man. "It is too late for me. I was born a Muslim, and for me to return to paganism the rules of the bank would also have to be changed."

And he bows slightly to her and goes to invite the dozing African into his office.

"Do you have more errands?" she asks her brother-in-law impatiently, "or can you show me now where it all began?"

"I do have a few more," he says calmly, "but they're all in the right direction."

9.

YA'ARI DOES NOT require words of love and affection from his wife. It's enough that he has clearly heard her sane voice and his brother-in-law's jesting one. Her last-minute interest in the outcome of the Pinsker Tower controversy also warmed his heart. It's hardly a sign of absentmindedness that from so far away she remembers what troubles him in his daily work. True, she has always known how to surprise him with her unexpected interest in some office problem he happened to mention offhandedly. And because technical matters themselves are foreign to her and beyond her ken, she has made it her business to uncover the hidden sensitivities of employees and clients in order to support her husband in his deliberations and even give him a little advice. When he told her rather flippantly about the complaints regarding the building on Pinsker Street, for some reason she was intrigued and wanted to hear for herself the howling of the winds that had crept into the elevators her husband designed. But so far her free time had never coincided with a typical windstorm.

He returns to his office. The meeting has continued without him, but has deteriorated from the technical problems of adding a fifth elevator to an argument about how much the redesign would cost. The chief engineer has just named a substantial figure, and the younger ones all object: until we figure out exactly how to squeeze it in, it's impossible to set a price. But the chief engineer is speaking from financial, not technical, experience. If you don't give a government ministry a big number up front, and lock it down with their budget department, at the end of the job instead of a cheque they'll present you with a book of the minister's speeches, autographed with a warm personal message.

Ya'ari interrupts them with a geographical question: "The African continent is west of Israel, or east?"

"The African continent? What does that mean? West, in general."

Ya'ari laughs. "What does 'in general' mean?"

Now the engineers sense that the boss wants to trip them up with a trick question, so they concentrate and try to imagine a map of the world.

"Both east and west," says one young man finally. "It's a big enough continent for both directions."

Ya'ari explains how his brief absence involved Israel lagging behind his wife in Africa. He chuckles as he admits, to the amazement of his engineers, that despite the distance he was sure that they were at the same longitude, but apparently not. Then he quickly returns the conversation to technical matters, but is careful not to drop any hints about the night-time sketch folded in his pocket.

At noon he invites his secretary to have lunch with him, to clear up a few things forgotten yesterday. The clear skies and calm air enable the waiter to ask an unseasonable question: Inside or out? Outside, decides Ya'ari, that's a fine idea. Though the secretary feels chilly and would have preferred the warmth inside, she cannot refuse the challenge of the open air, for in winter a sunny day has added value. But she has to keep on her jacket with the synthetic fur collar, making it hard for her to manoeuvre between her fork and the pen she uses to write down his instructions.

The weather is getting warmer, and with the calming of the winds his cell phone relaxes, too. The bereaved tenant in the tower is quiet, the old woman in Jerusalem has fallen silent, and Gottlieb has also broken off contact. Ya'ari returns to work, looks affectionately at his employees, their faces glowing with digitized wisdom, and enters his office and opens the window. Around the beloved tree are scattered branches and twigs torn off by the recent storms, but this natural pruning has not detracted from its charm. Soon enough, the unknown vine that has colonized it will produce its spectacular red blossoms.

Can it be that Daniela is right? Did Moran actually fear his reserve duty, was his dismissive attitude meant to mask his fears? Ya'ari has never seen any sign of cowardice in his son. Moran, like his cousin Eyal, served in a combat unit, and even took on an extra year as an officer. Yet Daniela often reads their children's minds better than he does. But still, fear? Now? With the territories at the moment on a low flame? Can't a father with two children, whose family has already paid its debt to the homeland, ask for a little consideration?

He phones Efrat's cell phone, and to his utter astonishment it is picked up at once, but the voice is his granddaughter's.

"Neta, darling, where are you? Not at school?"

"Today's a holiday, Grandpa. Nadi is also off today."

"So where are you two now?"

"Home."

"Home? Great. That's the best place. You're playing?"

"No. We're watching TV."

"TV? What would you do without TV?"

"Nothing."

"Sweetie, give me Imma."

"Imma went out."

"Went out without her phone? How can that be?"

"It can be because she forgot it."

"And who's with you? Grandma?"

"No. A girl is looking after us."

"A girl? Whose girl? Which girl?"

"A girl."

"Who is this girl? What's her name?"

"She didn't say."

"Neta, sweetheart, give me this girl."

"But she's watching TV now."

"That doesn't matter. Tell her your grandpa wants to tell her something important."

The receiver is handed to the girl amid the shouting of children on television.

"Who are you, young lady?"

Her name is Michal, babysitter of the moment, all of ten years old, who lives in the next building.

"And what's going on there, Michal?"

"Nothing."

Ya'ari begins to fume at his daughter-in-law—

10.

In Dar es Salaam the rain is soft and languid, and upon leaving the bank Yirmiyahu buys his sister-in-law an umbrella, and hires a barefoot porter with a large straw basket belted to his back to carry their purchases through the market.

"Is it really so important for you to see this place?" he asks again. "It's just a place in the market, next to some stall. There's nothing special about it."

But the guest is determined to stand on the very spot where death began to grip her sister. For this is also why she made the long trip from Israel.

He holds her arm and guides her carefully between the puddles as he leads her to a tool shed, where after checking a list he loads the porter's basket with small spades, soil strainers, batteries of various sizes, torches, and kerosene lamps. He tops off his order with some steel knives, which are also stashed in the basket. Then they walk among fruit and vegetable stalls until they reach the meat and fish market. There, in a small square where a torn net is spread out, two Indians wait for the white administrator, who pays them for last month's shipment of fish and hands them a new order.

"On that morning, did she take her walk on the beach?"

Yirmiyahu shrugs. "Who knows? I hope so with all my heart, because she so much loved her walks on the beach, and from the time you walked there together it was also bound up with a shared memory. There were days, after you returned to Israel, that she didn't feel like walking there alone."

"Because I wasn't here?" Daniela's voice quavers, and this knowledge of her sister's sorrow finally awakens her own.

They enter an open area of clothing stalls, hung with dresses and robes and colourful shirts and stacked with rolls of Indian fabric, and as if from the centre of the earth there appears beside them another porter, and Yirmi loads his basket with army blankets which will warm the bones of the scientists on cold nights. The Israeli visitor, wedged between passersby of various races, is struck by a clear recognition of the place. She stood exactly here on her previous visit. Shuli took her and Amotz to this very stall. She looks up at the rope stretched lengthways above her head and sees hanging on it a dress that is the twin of her own. This is the spot, she says to herself, this is the spot, and in her memory arises an image of Shuli, firm and decisive, rejecting Amotz's aggressive suggestion that she buy herself a dress to match Daniela's, as an occasional substitute for her mourning clothes.

The administrator of the scientific team piles coins and small bills into the African's open palms, and then takes leave of him with a hearty embrace. But before he can go to another stall Daniela tugs at his shirt.

"Am I right that this is the place where she stopped and first felt dizzy?"

For a moment he is amazed, and studies his sister-in-law with affection.

"More or less. Not far from here. You see that big rock? She sat down on it. And this man, the one I just bought the blankets from, noticed her distress from far away, and she managed to send him to alert me. But when I got there, she was already gone. She had lost consciousness, and four people picked her up and began to run with her to the hospital. But where did you get the idea this was the place?"

"Because we were here with her on the last visit," Daniela cries, "here is where we bought the dress I'm wearing now, and Amotz pleaded with her to buy the same one . . ."

And she points to the dress dangling above them.

"No," he says decisively, "don't start looking for mysticism that isn't here. That doesn't become you. This is no place in particular. This is simply a stop along the way to the diplomatic office; she passed by here every day. And don't get too worked up about your dress either. Dresses like these, if you look closely, are hanging on every corner."

The visitor shakes her head. Her heart is pounding.

"And where is the hospital they took her to?"

"They didn't make it to the hospital. Along the way they took her to an infirmary, sort of a small public clinic."

"Please, Yirmi, take me to that clinic."

"But it's already a bit late. The train leaves in an hour, and I thought we'd get something to eat."

"I don't care about food. Take me to the clinic."

"But why? It's just a clinic. Why does it matter to you?"

"Because that's why I came all the way from Israel."

11.

Now FURIOUS, YA'ARI backs up the file he was working on in a futile attempt to calm down, exits the program, and turns off the computer. He closes the window, puts on his jacket, and says to the secretary, I have to go to my grandchildren. If someone needs me, I'm on my cell phone. He drives to his son's building in the north of the city, and this time does not hesitate to commandeer the apartment's vacant parking spot. He doesn't bother to ring the bell; he uses his own key, enters a dark apartment and calls out cheerfully: Children, look who's here.

On the floor in front of the television sit his grandson and granddaughter. The short, pudgy girl between them must be that ten-year-old babysitter, who does not however lack initiative and ingenuity, since she has located the electric switch that shuts the blinds, darkening the living room and enhancing, as in a cinema, the illusory reality of the characters prancing on the screen. Neta and Nadi gape for a moment at their energetic grandpa, but they are drained and lethargic from long hours of staring at that addictive screen, and do not rise to greet him.

The first thing he does is lower the volume on the TV. Then he raises the blinds and restores the daylight, and only afterwards begins his interrogation of the babysitter, as if she were to blame simply for being there.

"Has their mother called?"

"No."

"And their grandma?"

"No."

"So who has called?"

"Just you."

But Nadi jumps up and says: "Not right, Abba also talked to us."

"Abba called?"

"Yes." The babysitter remembers now. "After you called."

"And what did he say?"

"He was looking for Imma," Neta says helpfully. "He said that the army is still keeping him, and Imma should send him warm clothes."

"Underpants," Nadi adds, "Abba needs underpants. And also T-shirts."

"And that's it?"

"That's it," says Neta.

"No," her little brother corrects her, "he also kissed his telephone."

Now Ya'ari's anger has cooled and he allows the babysitter to turn up the roar of some forest animals who at the moment are dancing merrily with the programme's host. Then he goes to the fridge, to see what's in it before asking whether anyone is hungry. They are all hungry, especially the chubby babysitter. He eagerly volunteers to remedy this, and swiftly prepares little sandwiches, garnishing them, as he has learned from his wife, with graceful curls of cucumber, and serves them to the entranced children on the floor. Then he makes a bigger sandwich for himself and strolls with it around the apartment.

Because he sees Moran every day at the office, and Daniela prefers to look after the grandchildren in her own home, he does not often visit that of his son and daughter-in-law. Now, in their absence, he takes the opportunity to get to know it better. First he explores the living room, checking out the CDs and videos, then moves to the children's room, to have a look at their drawings and games, and from there he heads into the bedroom and finds a very messy double bed, looking as if the previous night two people slept there, not one. He examines his son's clothing, and finds that unlike the conjugal bed, the clothes in the closet have merited orderly arrangement. Trousers and shirts are hung up, sweaters are neatly folded and stacked on the shelves, and in the underwear drawers nestle carefully sorted boxer shorts and T-Shirts.

What happened with the army this time? Why have they suddenly become so heavy-handed? Next to the bed his son's palm computer is blinking. He easily locates the number of Moran's army unit, and after a second's hesitation, he calls it. The young female soldier who answers knows of Lieutenant Ya'ari and even has an idea of where he may be confined. For though the soldiers have already been sent to man checkpoints in Samaria, the adjutant officers of the reserve battalion remain inside the 1967 border, at the training camp near Karkur.

"Karkur?" Ya'ari closes his eyes a moment and conjures a map of Israel. "Karkur? That's not so far away."

"What can you do," grumbles the clerk, "everything is close by in this country."

Ya'ari returns to the living room and finds that the babysitter has again shut out the daylight, the better to bond with the TV. The jungle animals have completed their dance, and now a sharp-tongued human is conducting a heart-to-heart conversation with a group of boys and girls on the subject of proper parenting. His granddaughter Neta, still a bit young to pass judgment on her parents, has repaired to her room to begin a drawing. Nadi, meanwhile, is sleeping soundly on the floor, and the young babysitter is not strong enough to lift him onto the sofa. Ya'ari hurries to gather the slumbering toddler in his arms, marvelling at how heavy the boy is, as if something extra were hidden inside him. Wanting him to sleep soundly, he passes by the children's room and Neta's artistic activity and carries him to his parents' unmade bed. With loving compassion he removes the child's shoes and covers him with their blanket. Then, observing the high forehead and strong, almost cruel line of the child's jaw, he asks himself: This boy, who does he remind me of?

"How much do you get an hour?" he asks the young

babysitter, whose eyes are still fixed on the screen, when he goes back into the living room.

He then learns that she is not the original babysitter: that's her older sister, who collects the salary and pays her a portion as subcontractor.

"Subcontractor?" says Ya'ari, laughing.

"That's what she says I am."

"What's your sister's name?"

"Yuval."

"You should know that Yuval is exploiting you."

The babysitter is stunned; and glittering tears appear in her calf eyes.

"I was only joking . . ." the grandfather says. "It's certainly not your fault." He feels the need to console the chubby girl, but is careful not to stroke her. Enough, it's time for him to get out of here. But the menorah displayed on top of the television bothers him. It is blotched with drops of wax, and the stumps of two of last night's candles are still stuck in it, as if a natural or man-made wind had prevented their peaceable extinction. He extracts the bits of candle, takes the menorah to the sink, puts it under hot water from the tap, and then scrapes off the wax drippings with a knife. Before returning the menorah to the television he sticks in four white candles plus a blue shammash, for the evening's lighting.

If Nadi were awake, it would be possible, though it's still daytime, to light candles with his grandchildren and even sing a brief song with them. He smiles at the babysitter, but the girl has not forgiven him for insulting her big sister. So what is he doing here, dammit? He takes hold of himself, and an urge to exert control snaps him into quick action. In the kitchen he finds a large clean rubbish bag and tiptoes with it into the bedroom. Nadi is still sleeping soundly. He carefully opens the closet and stuffs two pairs of trousers into the bag, along with a heavy sweater and a light one, adding handfuls of boxer shorts and T-shirts, as if this were not a confined soldier but a long-term prisoner. Afterwards he writes on a slip of paper his cell phone number and that of Grandma Yael and gives them to the girl.

She looks at the phone numbers.

"Yael is your wife?"

"No, Yael is the other grandma. My wife is in Africa."

And when he goes to say goodbye to his granddaughter, she clings to him, why are you going? Stay, Grandpa, but he kisses her with finality. I have to take Abba warm clothes, so he won't be cold, but Imma will be back soon.

He slings the rubbish bag over his shoulder and leaves the apartment, doesn't call the elevator but rather stamps quickly down the stairs, out into a twilight world and a gorgeous winter sky, blue and orange and white.

12.

UNWILLINGLY, DRIVEN BY his sister-in-law's firm demand, he signals for the two porters to follow him, and under a colourless sky, into a cold wind and a light rain that prickles their faces marches their small and singular procession, led by a white man, old and bald though tall and fit, clutching the arm of a middle-aged white woman shielding herself with an umbrella, and a short distance behind tread two barefoot porters with baskets on their backs, and as the four pass the building of the former Israeli diplomatic mission, now occupied by a Chinese tobacco company, they are suddenly joined, as out of thin air, by the stately nurse Sijjin Kuang, also attended by a barefoot porter with a straw basket affixed to his shoulders. Now all six walk together along a street of whitewashed houses and up to the door of the clinic. The entrance is clogged with patients and their companions, but Yirmiyahu, in the strength of his whiteness, leads the procession past them into the building, where without asking either doctor or nurse he confidently navigates his way to a sickroom with five beds, and points to a bed by the window: the last stop on Shuli's rapid departure from this world.

And now in her sister's bed there lies a young man, a Tanzanian who looks with alarm at the white man and woman who stand before him staring, and at the Sudanese woman who towers behind them, and Daniela, unable to contain the emotions that emerge as powerfully and gloriously as she had hoped, approaches the bed and takes the hand of the young patient and squeezes it in friendship, adding a few words of encouragement in English. And the African, though he may not comprehend their meaning, understands their kind and consoling tone, for he takes the liberty, this young man, of stroking that friendly white hand. And the caress of the delicate black fingers of a sick young man, beside the window through which her sister's soul left this world, justifies absolutely the long journey she has made from Israel to this place.

Now the three porters, who with their baskets still on their back also followed the imperious white man into the room, make way for the doctor and nurse, arrived in haste to demand the reason for this unprecedented invasion. Yirmiyahu introduces himself and his sister-in-law and explains. They nod with understanding and sympathy, and because they are new to the infirmary, they call for the older doctor, who well remembers the white woman who died here the year before. And although he has nothing to say about the treatment they never had a chance to begin, or the respirator that was late to arrive, he can at least testify that she passed away quickly and without undue suffering, lying in the bed by the window.

13.

WITHOUT CHECKING THE map for the Karkur exit, Ya'ari heads north on the coastal highway, working his way into a three-lane crawl of thick rush hour traffic. The air has grown milder, and Ya'ari does not hesitate to roll down the passenger window, hoping to inhale the aroma of well-watered fields and maybe a hint of distant orchards. At this hour the light is at its best, and in the Israeli sky, so boring and monotonous most days of the year, a small drama is unfolding. The setting sun, blazing itself a westward path through the crest of puffy clouds moving in from the sea, sculpts snowy peaks and antediluvian beasts, and ignites the fiery beard of a hoary giant.

In a hundred hours, more or less, he will pick up his wife at the airport. Some of these hours will melt away while he sleeps or works, but at times he will be gripped by longing, mainly for her attentive ear. If his love could take control of time, she would return home sooner. At this moment, however, her absence is an advantage. Ya'ari has no doubt that his wife would have sternly forbidden this sort of expedition. Moran is nearly thirty years old, and his father does not need to show up in his quarters to humiliate him with a bundle of T-shirts and boxer shorts. His wife, that Efrat, should be attending to his underwear, instead of her endless training courses.

Moran, however, is not only his son but also an employee of his firm—thus will Ya'ari justify himself at times, half seriously—and as an employer, it is his right and his duty to attend to his personal business. Daniela, of course, rejects this disingenuous double-dipping, which gives him, but not her, additional rights in the son they share, and if she were here now she would say, that's nonsense, for you he's only a son, and besides, how can you be so sure that you'll find him or that they'll let you see him? This trip is useless, and afterwards don't complain that you're pressed for time. Thus, with her wily wisdom, would she have prevented this trip.

But at the moment her wiles and wisdom are detained in Africa, and he is master of his fate, betting that his ingenuity will save the journey from being pointless. And if he doesn't find Moran, that's not so terrible. Karkur is not far away, the snail-paced traffic allows him to admire the beauty in the winter light and the movements of the clouds, and Hanukkah lends a festiveness to the overflowing car parks at the shopping malls of the kibbutzim near Tel Aviv—Ga'ash, Shefayim, and Yakum. The old fields, now pricey real estate, are dominated by an old-fashioned water tower crowned by a big rotating menorah, already releasing light from all nine candlesticks, though the holiday is only half over.

Ya'ari, too, feels released, a pleasant feeling. Only rarely has he the patience to drive trapped in the middle lane, with no chance of passing or manoeuvring. And since in the lanes to his right and left he has been escorted for the past kilometre by women whose upper bodies and profiles he finds attractive, now he lowers the window on the driver's side, so that the two open windows, right and left, create a living, though silent, communion between the two of them, and to his great surprise they indeed notice each other and try to signal right past him.

Now he spots the magnet that has drawn this heavy traffic: an IKEA outlet. Once he passes the commercial strip south of Netanya the flow of cars speeds up, creating a strong wind that forces him to raise the windows again and turn down the heater. After a bit of hesitation he phones Nofar, and gets her voicemail. Happy to be saved from a frosty, anxiety-provoking conversation, he leaves a warm but carefully worded message. Next he calls the apartment he has just left, to see if the woman of the house has returned, but a new voice answers: the babysitter's older sister, come to replace her subcontractor.

"Don't worry, Grandpa," she addresses him officiously, "your grandchildren are already fast asleep. Neta also nodded off in the middle of her drawing. Everything is just fine. If anything pops up, I'll call. I've got your number right here."

Again his thoughts return to the phone conversation with his wife. Now it seems to him there was a mild tension in her voice, as if she were uncertain that her visit was really welcome. And it's true that in the course of his long friendship with his brother-in-law he has sometimes been aware of various oddities in his behaviour. If since his wife's death he has chosen to stay in a wild and remote place not just as a means of fattening his retirement funds but also as a way of detaching himself from the family, maybe he is not pleased with the sisterly visit she has imposed on him.

North of Netanya the charms of freedom wear off. The three lanes shrink to two, the traffic slows to a crawl again, and sometimes stops altogether. The car in the lane to his right, sealed and dark, with tinted windows, keeps trying to cut him off. If he were to start a political party, he would run on a one-line platform: Widen the highway between Netanya and Hadera. Surely that would win a few seats in the Knesset—though it would never occur to him to run for office. Sometimes he too yearns to burn all the Israeli newspapers in a big furnace. But his wife reads them avidly. She who would teach high school must understand reality, in order to explain it to her students.

Beyond the bridge spanning the Alexander River flaps a small, improvised-looking formation of migratory birds that have lost their larger flock. Daylight is down to its last rays. He takes advantage of the creeping pace to have a look at the road map. Good thing: if he'd relied on instinct, he'd have turned east too early, at the Hadera junction, instead of at the big power station at Caesarea.

Now that he is sure of his route, he begins passing other cars. It's not good to arrive at an army base after dark, when the guards at the gate are more strict.

And indeed, at the entrance to the training camp, surrounded by rustling eucalyptus trees, two skinny Ethiopian recruits in full gear, armed with rifles, come forward and demand from the civilian a signed entry pass.

"I'm not even here for you," he objects. "I'm going to the adjutancy of the reserve battalion. My son is an officer at their headquarters, and he urgently needs a parcel of clothing."

And he points to the rubbish bag.

But there is no separate entrance for the reserve battalion, and the well-disciplined recruits have not been trained in the rules governing parents who bring urgent bundles of clothing. And because they are forbidden to leave their post, they recommend that he wait for a patrol that is soon due to pass by.

"When?"

"In about an hour."

"No," Ya'ari protests, "I am very sorry, I have no intention of waiting here in the dark for a whole hour. Now listen, you're new recruits, but I am a bereaved father. Seven years ago my oldest son fell in a military action in the West Bank, in Tulkarm. So please, don't be hard on me now. It's already late, and the one son I have left is here with the reserves, a combat officer who needs warm clothing. Here, please, I'm opening the bag so you can see for yourselves it's only T-shirts and boxer shorts and not bombs or grenades."

14.

DANIELA WILL NOT let go of the doctor. His English is not rich with imagery, but it is generous in detail, and she drinks up her sister's final moments, reconstructing an image of her to replace the urn of ashes that her husband had brought to Israel, saying with infuriating certainty that "none of us believes in the resurrection of the dead." Now after the doctor reassures the Israeli visitor that the young black man lying in her sister's bed will recover fully, she is ready to leave this place where the void in her has been filled with the pain she longed for. As they exit the infirmary and hurry towards the train station, she feels that even if her visit were to end at this moment, its true purpose would in a sense have been realized, now that she has learned where and how her sister died. If a flight home from Dar es Salaam were suddenly offered to her, so she could be with her grandchildren on Friday evening, to light candles with them, sing Hanukkah songs, and eat a jam doughnut, she would leave her brother-in-law on the spot. He would go on his way in this summer rain, with his three porters and the grief-stricken nurse, along streets whose Africanness cannot hide the Muslim identity expressed in minarets and verses from the Koran on walls in curlicue script.

But because departing early is impossible, not least since it might be interpreted as an open insult, she must remain patient with this host upon whom she has imposed herself. During the remainder of her stay, she realizes, she will not discover much about her sister that she didn't know before. She can see that her brother-in-law is disinclined to dwell on shared memories. Until her departure, then, it will be up to her simply to volunteer her warmth and humanity.

The three porters, who know their destination, now break into the lead, and Yirmiyahu is forced to hurry behind them, glancing backwards as he does so to be sure his sister-in-law is not lagging behind Sijjin Kuang, sailing tall at the rear of the little company like the mast of the last ship in a convoy.

The image of the bed and window at the foreign clinic stays with Daniela, and sorrow wells up within her like a hot potion, and pity too, for the bald man, her seventy-year-old brother-in-law, a constant in her life since childhood, whose long springing strides lend him a faint resemblance to a peeled monkey.

At the station the train is waiting, already packed with passengers. Whole families, bunched like grapes in every window, peer out at them and at first she fears they will not find seats. But the head of the local UNESCO delegation, who takes this train regularly, has arranged a compartment for them. At the doorway of their car they pay the porters, not merely for their labour but also for the tools of their trade, since the three big baskets are coming aboard too. And because the visit to the clinic took the time they might have spent lunching at a comfortable restaurant, Sijjin Kuang has bought food for the road. To Daniela's disappointment, the diverse bounty she produces does not include any dessert. Meanwhile, the guest has spotted a peddler bearing a well-stocked snack emporium on a tricycle, and asks her brother-in-law, a little sheepishly, if she has time to add a few sweets to the meal. To her surprise he approves her going alone to the moveable kiosk, not even warning her to hurry, as if unconcerned by the possibility that she might miss the train and be left behind.

Still, he watches her every move from the train window—a middle-aged woman who despite her years has a nice figure and good legs, like her sister, though the sweets she consumes freely have thickened her a bit. There she stands, eagerly picking out one treat and then another, like the young girl in her school uniform with her book bag on her back who would dawdle on the way home at the kiosk near their apartment block.

And indeed, as she returns all excited to the compartment, and sets before her companions bags of chocolates and toffees imported from the Asian continent beyond this shared ocean, her brother-in-law reminds her of the kiosk of her youth, where she would take sweets without paying.

"Don't exaggerate, it was all written down."

"In an open account, which your mother would pay off on the first of every month."

"Something like that . . ."

"I don't get it, was there a system like that for other children in your class?"

"I don't think so."

"That's what always amazed me, that your father and mother, who were modest and almost ascetic, agreed to give a girl an open account. In your home, after all, there were almost no sweets."

"Which is why they didn't care that I hung around the kiosk."

"They weren't afraid of spoiling you?"

She smiles.

"You've known me more than forty years. Do I seem spoiled to you? Money was never important to me. When I earned money from babysitting or as a camp counsellor, I would give it all to my mother and didn't care about it. No, Yirmi, my mother and father didn't lose anything from my open account at the kiosk; they only gained smiles and a good mood."

"And your suitors?" he teases her. "They also benefited from that open account?"

"Who do you mean?"

"The boys who would walk you home after school."

"They weren't looking for sweets."

"Of that I am sure." Yirmi chuckles, as if the visit to the clinic has lightened his mood. While the train toots and flexes for the journey with a little lurch forwards and then back, he derives enjoyment from his sister-in-law's youth, taking the opportunity to ask why, with so many suitors, it was Amotz she had picked.

"Why not?"

"Because you had boyfriends who were more successful. At least that was what Shuli used to say."

"Successful?" Her eyes flash, as the train sets off with a screech. "Successful in what way?"

Suddenly anxious, Yirmiyahu shrugs and doesn't answer.

15.

SINCE THESE ARE raw recruits—just ten days earlier they were civilians—they are not aware that one may violate a military order out of misunderstanding, but not out of compassion, and so they open the gate for the bereaved father bringing warm clothes to his remaining son. But as for the location of the reservists' command, they do not know where it is.

No problem, he will find it himself. All he asks now of the guards, who have displayed such genuine humanity, is that they keep an eye on his car. Then he sets out briskly through the wintry dusk on the paths of the big military base. Above him the wind rustles softly in the eucalyptus trees, which grew to great heights after the fetid swamps were drained, back in the early Zionist era. He asks no one the way, but finds it for himself among sheds and tents, walking quietly past the evening formation of a platoon of recruits in full gear, who listen to a lecture on morality from their arrogant sergeant. Ya'ari wanders, possibly in circles, mud accumulating on his shoes as in the blackening sky two or three wayward stars appear. Just as the fast-falling darkness might have begun to undermine his confidence, he notices two civilian cars and a dusty army Land Rover parked by a shed thumping with dance music.

In the belief that the darkness will conceal his face he creeps up to the building and peeks into window after window, verifying by the equipment and uniforms and beds that reservists are quartered here. One room is only a darkened office, but the next one is lit, with two unmade army cots, and there on a blanket spread out on the floor beside a small heater sits Moran dressed in a civilian shirt, playing backgammon with a diminutive major sporting a mane of wild red hair. Ya'ari is in no hurry, he stands close to the pane and continues to watch his son. Suddenly Moran looks up, but does not seem surprised to see his father's face at the window, and doesn't get up or stop the game. With a friendly wave he invites his father inside, and says to his companion, don't say I didn't warn you that my father would try to rescue me from here. And the short red-haired officer looks at Ya'ari affectionately and says, welcome, Abba of Moran, just give us another minute to finish the game, so I can chalk up another victory.

"By all means, beat him as much as you want, he deserves it," Ya'ari replies facetiously. "Just so you know, I did not come here as a father, but as an employer."

Moran smiles and groans, "Sure, an employer," and vigorously throws the dice.

Within a minute or two the game is over, and the two slowly stand up and stretch. Now Moran hugs his father warmly and without embarrassment presents his cheek for a kiss, as the major introduces himself to the visitor with a cordial handshake: Hezi, maybe you remember me, I was with Moran in officers' training school.

"And you're also locked up here? I see that the two of you are having a good time in confinement."

"No, Abba, Hezi is not a prisoner, he's on the side of the jailers. Hezi is the adjutant of the battalion. He had nobody to play backgammon with, so he decided to latch onto me for ten days."

Ya'ari is amused.

"So you're the adjutant? You should know that I kept warning your friend here to request a release from duty in the proper formal manner, and not to count on people just forgetting about him."

"And he was right not to," says the adjutant. "He knew very well that he wouldn't get any release from me."

"Even if he's in the midst of an important project for the Ministry of Defence?"

"I have soldiers whose wives are eight and nine months pregnant, I have soldiers with a father or mother in hospital, I have soldiers for whom every day of reserve duty hurts their business—why should I care about the Ministry of Defence? From his standpoint Moran was right to decide just to ignore us and hope that we'd forget about him."

"But . . ."

"But unfortunately it's not so easy to forget someone like Moran, so I sent a military policeman to get him, and believe me, Abba of Moran, it was purely out of mercy that we didn't send him to jail and instead kept him here attached to the adjutancy—also so I would have someone to play backgammon with, even though he is a mediocre player without much luck."

Moran laughs. "Don't believe him, he's just ragging me."

"But . . ."

"But what?"

"But . . ." Ya'ari hesitates, "why didn't you send him to serve with the rest of them?"

"They don't really need him there. We assigned another officer to his platoon. And I have an iron rule: an extra soldier is a vulnerable soldier. Overall, too many reservists showed up this time—there are many unemployed workers in Israel."

"So why not let him off?"

"Why let him off? He damaged the solidarity, thumbed his nose at the camaraderie, so he'll sit here confined to base till the end of his reserve duty and take stock of himself, and in the meantime improve his backgammon."

Moran laughs, and it seems he also enjoys his friend's rebuke. But his father studies the officer to determine if he's being serious.

"How did you get to be a major, and Moran is still only a lieutenant?"

"Because I don't have a rich father like Moran, so I stayed on a few more years as a career officer to save money for my studies."

"And what did you study?"

"In the end, I didn't study."

"So how do you make a living?"

"This and that."

"In any case I think I remember your face from somewhere."

"Maybe you saw his mug on television," Moran says.

"On television?"

"Because just as you see him here, the adjutant of reservists, distinguished major, bursting with patriotic values, on television he's on a satirical show, rattling off bad jokes, and lucky for him there's canned laughter so he won't fall flat."

The officer-comedian punches Moran in the ribs with an affectionate fist.

"So what do you say, Hezi,"—Ya'ari turns to the adjutant, man to man—"I came to bring the detainee warm clothes, but better still why don't I free you of him. So he can do something useful for the world instead of wasting away here."

But the officer-comedian puts on a grave face, and answers firmly: It is all right to give the clothes to Moran, but it is not all right to give Moran to his father. He is sentenced till the end of his unit's reserve duty, and will be released when the others are. And as for usefulness to the world—his cell phone has been confiscated, but he is allowed one call a day to his wife, and if she's not home, or her cell is turned off, that's not the army's problem. And anyway, how did you get permission to enter the camp?

"I told the recruits at the gate that I am a bereaved uncle."

"Bereaved uncle?" marvels the adjutant. "What on earth is a bereaved uncle?"

Moran, surprised by his father's words, reminds his friend about his cousin who was killed seven years before.

"By friendly fire," Ya'ari quietly adds.

16.

THE TRAIN ACCELERATES, the cars emit a metallic rumble, and the three straw baskets, left in the corridor, embark on little independent journeys, and need to be reined in. Sijjin Kuang rises from her seat, pulls them into the compartment, ties them together, and shoves them against the door, blocking the entry of any curious passengers strolling through the train. Then she takes a newspaper from one of the bags of food she bought at the station, gets down on her knees, and spreads the paper on the floor. Then she lays out the feast: brown eggs, smoked sardines, fried calamari, a wedge of hard white cheese veined with red, a few greenish bananas, moist dates, and a hairy coconut. With her long delicate fingers she takes a large smoked sardine and begins to gnaw at its flattened head.

Daniela watches with admiration as the tall and graceful Sudanese flexibly folds her legs to allow room for others on the floor of the compartment, and after hesitating a moment she gathers up the hem of her skirt and also assumes a kneeling position. Avoiding the smoked fish and seafood, she cuts herself a slice of the cheese with the blade of a penknife that Sijjin Kuang opens and offers her. Yirmiyahu, without leaving his seat, fashions himself a cone out of newspaper and fills it with sardines and squid and tears off a generous piece of pita bread. They lunch together in silence, as at a mourners' meal, but with a warm sense of conviviality in this compartment set apart by its wall of big baskets, which glow golden in the afternoon light.

Sijjin Kuang does not eat sweets and is content to offset her salty spicy lunch with some coconut. Yirmiyahu happily tops off his meal with the Indian toffee procured by his sister-in-law, then tilts his head back next to the window and closes his eyes. Daniela finds that the sweets she bought are too sickly and have an unfamiliar aftertaste, and makes do instead with a few dates. Since long silences are generally difficult for her, she tries to draw out Sijjin Kuang on the subject of rituals of fire and winds and trees and animals, and from the pagan's short answers gathers that among idolators as well as monotheists, materiality carries less weight than metaphors and symbols. Indeed the Sudanese woman thought that when Yirmiyahu threw the candles in the fire he was performing a religious rite.

There's no telling whether he is asleep or listening to their conversation with his eyes closed. Daniela helps the nurse gather up the food-stained newspapers, and when Sijjin Kuang slips out of the compartment, stepping over the baskets, to dispose of the bags of rubbish, Daniela resumes her seat by the window, opposite her brother-in-law. Yirmiyahu opens his eyes and smiles. Well, this is surely not how you imagined the visit, being hurried from place to place. But it's not so bad—in the remaining days you'll have a chance to rest.

"It's absolutely fine, this travelling. Resting I can do at home."

He nods.

"All in all, it's good that Amotz didn't come with you. He always wants to accomplish something clear and practical, and a trip like today's, back and forth just to see a window and a bed, would have driven him crazy."

His mildly critical tone makes her uneasy. The train suddenly speeds up and blows its whistle repeatedly. Yirmiyahu sticks his head out of the window to see what the noise is about. They are riding through a sea of short yellow grass. Had her sister really told him about more successful suitors in her youth, or was that his own idea? When she was in high school, Yirmi and Shuli were already married and living in Jerusalem, only on Saturdays would they visit Tel Aviv. And who talked then about "more successful" anyway? Certainly not her parents. They never characterized her friends that way, but would only express an opinion about who seemed nice, and who less so. From the first, they found Amotz likeable and, most important, trustworthy.

Suddenly she has the desire to confront her brother-in-law and defend her husband. "It's strange," she turns to him with a serious look when the train's whistle blasts die down. "Strange that you mention boyfriends from more than forty years ago, as if you had actually known them."

"That's true, I didn't know a single one of them, but sometimes, years later, Shuli would recognize someone's name in the newspaper, someone who went far."

"Far where?"

"Do I know?" he says, uncomfortably. "For example, that guy who ended up becoming the attorney general."

"Why do you think I should have married the attorney general? I was never involved in any crime."

He laughs. "How about medical problems?"

"What's the connection?"

"I'm thinking about that chubby professor we ran into at a concert in Jerusalem a few years back, the famous heart surgeon, who was so excited to see you . . . no regrets?"

"About what?"

"Do I know? Don't get upset, I'm just making conversation. That you didn't pick him rather than Amotz?"

"He was a limited, boring man. Anyway, you're funny— what do you know about him?"

He places his hand on her shoulder. "Little sister, don't mind my jabbering away here, at the end of the world, the end of life, about suitors you had forty years ago. I'm just curious. I would also ask Shuli sometimes, what is it about your sister that attracts the boys? I mean, you were never especially beautiful."

"Certainly not. There were always prettier girls around."

"But the men were drawn to you anyway like bears to honey. Especially the intellectuals."

"You're exaggerating . . ."

"And in the end, out of all of them, you picked a technician…"

"He's not just a technician."

"And you picked him out so early, you were maybe twenty."

"What's this about?" she says indignantly. "What do you have against Amotz?"

"Who said I have anything against him? Why are you putting words in my mouth? When all these years we've been not just brothers-in-law, but also friends."

"So why are you suddenly uneasy with him?"

"Who said I'm uneasy? What's the matter? Why can't we just chat about your youth? It's so rare that we're alone together, without Shuli or Amotz. So tell me why you picked him over everyone else?"

"He lived in our neighbourhood, but didn't go to our school. In his second to last year he switched to a vocational high school."

"Why?"

"Because his father wanted to prepare him better for the technical side of his business. But afterwards, you know, he became a certified engineer."

"Of course. I never doubted his abilities. Only . . ."

"Only what?"

From behind the straw baskets guarding the compartment appears the beautifully sculpted ebony figure of Sijjin Kuang. She enters and remains standing in the middle of the floor, gazing out of the window. All at once she turns with a big smile to Daniela, gesturing with her long arm for the white woman to look outside. From within the railway car shouts of joy can be heard, and the train seems to be slowing down.

Not far from the track, in the branches of a lone baobab tree in the open plain, perch lions and cubs, blinking peaceably at the passengers in the train.

But Daniela, unwilling to be distracted, is trying not to lose the thread of conversation.

"Why was Amotz in my eyes the best of all? Because from the start I not only felt but knew that this was the man who would be able to protect me from unnecessary suffering. He wasn't a doctor or a lawyer, and not an especially talented engineer either, and maybe he can be a little oppressive and tedious at times, but he is a person who has love and loyalty stamped in his soul, which is why he won't let despair near me."

"Despair?" Yirmiyahu recoils. "What are you talking about?"

"Despair, despair," the word sears her mouth, and the Sudanese watches her, mesmerized. "The despair of pain, the kind that killed my sister. You know exactly what I am talking about."

17.

"So if that's the case," Ya'ari says to the adjutant, "at least let me consult with your prisoner about something urgent at work."

"What kind of work?"

"Elevators that we are designing for the Ministry of Defence."

"Can't it wait till next week?"

"What's the problem, man? What am I asking for? For Moran just to have a glance at a sketch that I brought."

"Just a look, then. Not a full work session. Because dinner is beginning right now in the mess hall, and I promised the rabbi of the base that I would bring him some reservists for the recruits' candle-lighting."

Ya'ari pulls his son into a corner and anxiously takes his nocturnal sketch from his pocket. Don't look at the details, he warns, just get a general impression. I haven't shown this to anyone in the office yet, but I couldn't hold back and showed it to the new deputy director of the building department, who knows nothing about elevators.

Moran brings the drawing closer to the light.

"And what did the deputy say?"

"Nothing, really . . . she made a joke that the passenger would have to be very thin . . . even though there's room here for two."

Moran is immersed in the sketch. His father looks at him nervously, fearing that deep down his son is snickering at him.

"Strange. How did you get the idea for a corner elevator?"

"It came at night . . . conceived in a dream . . . maybe, because Imma isn't beside me now at night I'm a bit less calm and more creative. And maybe I came across something similar in some old magazine. But why does the source matter to you and who cares what inspired it? The main thing is, tell me frankly—does it look feasible, or did I draw something absurd? I don't want to look stupid with a useless idea."

Moran moves the diagram from side to side. The adjutant straightens his uniform, puts on an army jacket, sets a beret on his head, adjusts his epaulettes, watches impatiently.

"I don't dismiss the idea."

"Really?" Ya'ari is flooded with joy. "It's feasible?"

"I don't know . . . we have to check it out. But in principle, I don't dismiss the idea. Could be that this is the right direction. Because otherwise we'll be in trouble. You saw for yourself how the deviation in the shaft already makes us minus ten centimetres at this stage, so that when we get up to the roof and discover that they shaved half a metre in width from the shaft, we'll have another bone to pick with the contractor."

"That was exactly my reasoning," his father says, with enthusiasm. "Instead of trying to squeeze together everything that's already been designed, we'll just shove the damn fifth one into the south corner."

"Has anyone at the Defence Ministry explained what it's intended for?"

"Nothing. Total secrecy. More than twenty years we've been working with them, and all of a sudden a mystery. And over what? An elevator? In that case, we'll also be a bit mysterious in our design, and whoever insists on riding in it can please shrink and stand in the corner."

"Enough," calls the adjutant from the doorway. "Your quick glance has already turned into a full meeting, so please say good-bye now. The rabbi and the candles are waiting."

And he turns out the lights. In the sudden darkness Ya'ari hugs his son tight, and they go out into the night, while the adjutant calls out to other people, officers from headquarters, female clerks, drivers, maybe other soldiers who are confined to base.

Ya'ari, too, is drawn into the group advancing along a winding path marked by whitewashed stones. Really, why shouldn't he take part? The rabbi will be happy to show the recruits that even an old civilian has come to his candle-lighting, providing the soldiers with a feeling of brotherhood and deepening their identity and sense of belonging. Together with the group he enters a large dining hall packed with Ethiopians and Russians, blacks and whites, shaky new recruits battered by their first month of training. They sit crammed together at long tables where tin pots of tea are steaming beside platters stacked with huge jam doughnuts.

On a small stage stands a Hanukkah menorah fashioned of big copper shell casings from helicopter cannons. Four thick white candles stand at attention, dominated by their commandant, a giant red shammash.

The rabbi gestures for the reservists to come forward to the seats saved for them, and asks them to silence their cell phones. Ya'ari prefers to remain in the doorway, where his cell begins to play its tune, compelling him to retreat outside, into the dark.

Efrat has finally returned home and demands to know where *he* has disappeared to.

"You won't believe where I am," he proudly declares. "I'm with Moran in Karkur. I brought him T-shirts and boxer shorts. But he's not with me at the moment. They took him to the mess hall to light candles."

The army rabbi, an officer with the rank of lieutenant colonel, lights the shammash, but instead of proceeding immediately to intone the blessings, he takes the opportunity to begin with a sermon about the wonders and miracles of the holiday, waving the huge shammash like a torch.

"I don't get it. When did you leave the children?"

"About 4:30. That girl, your babysitter, didn't tell you?"

"But I don't understand why you decided to put Nadi to bed at such an hour."

"I didn't put him to bed. He fell asleep on the floor in front of the TV, and I just moved him to the bed."

"But why our bed and not his?"

"Because Neta was drawing in the children's room, and I didn't want the light to disturb him."

"If he's already asleep, nothing will disturb him," she scolds, "but what do you care if the light bothers him? Did you want to ruin my night on purpose?"

"To ruin your night on purpose?" Ya'ari is dumbfounded but tries to construct a logical response. "You just said a moment ago that no light would bother him, so even if I had put him in his own bed, he wouldn't have woken up."

"Be that as it may," she continues in the same angry, imperious tone, "why in our bed?"

Something has gone wrong for her, has wounded her, thinks Ya'ari. Maybe the world has stopped marvelling at her beauty.

"And if it's your bed, why is it a tragedy?"

"Because he wet my blankets and sheet."

"Nadi still wets the bed? I didn't know."

"I very much hope that you really didn't know," she says, with a biting sarcasm that he never imagined she was capable of.

Ya'ari is stunned. But he heeds his wife's warnings and avoids a harsh response; instead he speaks to the young woman with warmth and tenderness.

"Efrati, what happened? Why are you so angry?"

Now her voice cracks a little.

"Nothing. I'm tired and worn out from all this Hanukkah stuff. And Moran's confinement, and also Daniela's trip. I had so much hoped she would help me during the holiday with the kids. All of a sudden everything is on my head and making me crazy. Anyway, I'll get over it . . . only please, don't forget to come over tomorrow night, as you promised, for candle-lighting. When Nadi got up, the first thing he said was where did Grandpa disappear to and when is he coming back?"

"He's a sweetheart."

"So you'll come tomorrow?"

"Of course."

In the dining hall the sermon has ended, short and sweet, and the four candles and the shammash are burning as the recruits sing. Ya'ari, meanwhile, has found his way to the front gate, where the Ethiopian guards have lit a holiday campfire of their own. Apparently they have added a foreign substance to the fire, perhaps brought from home, which turns the flame from red to purple.

18.

LOOKING OUT AT the tracks as the train pulls into Morogoro, Daniela is stunned to discover that the three porters who carried the straw baskets in Dar es Salaam have already arrived and are there to greet them. No, Yirmiyahu corrects her, it only looks like that to you, because these are members of the same tribe, maybe relatives of the others—though exactly how they got the news that we'd be on this train and would need assistance, that's anybody's guess.

Led by the three new porters, they walk to the petrol station to pick up the trusty Land Rover. Freshly washed, its bonnet raised, it awaits the inspection of the Sudanese driver: the oil filter has been changed, the carburettor cleaned, and the spark plugs polished to assure quick, precise firing. As the porters empty the big baskets and organize their contents into cardboard boxes, Sijjin Kuang bends over the recesses of the engine, making sure that all her wishes have been fulfilled.

Yirmiyahu distributes bills and coins all around. The big straw baskets will change hands again, and more than once, in their serpentine journey back to the marketplace in the capital.

An airplane lands on a nearby runway. Only two days have passed since I landed here, Daniela reminds herself, and in another four I'll take off for home.

For the third time during the visit Yirmiyahu apologizes to his guest for exiling her to the backseat. Sijjin Kuang takes her place behind the wheel.

"What's this? You've stopped driving in Africa?" Daniela asks Yirmiyahu with some asperity. "I mean, you always loved to drive, and when you were over at our house, you never minded taking me home at night from wherever I was."

Yirmiyahu still loves to drive, even though in Africa the roads are difficult, but when the Sudanese woman is with him he gives up the wheel because for her, control over the car helps console her grief and replaces her lost sexuality.

Daniela is astounded by his loose tongue. How vulgar. And what does he know about her sexuality?

Yirmiyahu turns his body around to speak directly to his sister-in-law, who shields her eyes with her hand. As it ploughs westwards, the car heads into the sun.

He knows nothing. A white man like him cannot understand the sexuality of an orphaned African woman. And it would never occur to him to spy on her to get at the truth. He appreciates her femininity, he has no racial hang-ups, but he senses from within his own soul, the soul of someone whose own sexuality has faded, that the memory of a family massacred before her eyes has snuffed out her womanliness. At least this is how he feels, because this is also what happened to Daniela's sister. The friendly fire burned out what little sexuality she still had.

"No, please don't use that expression again."

"Why?"

"It sounds cynical. Drop it. For my sake."

"You're wrong, no cynicism intended. It's a realistic description, and also a poetic one . . ."

"You're stubborn as a mule, Yirmi . . ."

"The original mule wasn't me, but Shuli, your sister. And because I, in contrast to Amotz, failed abjectly to protect her from suffering, I agreed not to claim her sexuality, and rightly so, for it was there and only there that he could not join us."

"Who?"

"How can you not understand?"

"Eyal?"

"Obviously."

Now she is very frightened. To join us? What do you mean?

The sun is swallowed up by a great cloud, and Sijjin Kuang turns on the headlights and concentrates on the road. After many hours spent in close quarters with the two white people she can sense their conversation is becoming important.

After Eyal's death he was allowed to be with them everywhere, all the time. It was possible to connect him to any subject, to talk about him any time he or Shuli wanted to remember him. They didn't always want to, but they knew they

194

could. They could cry for him, they could cry for themselves, they could take pity or get angry and curse the soldier who had been so quick to shoot him, and so quick to explain his mistake.

Yes, if a character in a film, or music at a concert, brought their son to mind somehow, either one of them was permitted to say a word in the middle of the movie or the performance, or sometimes to be content with a sigh, a touch, or a glance. They knew and agreed that he was available at every moment, and neither of them was allowed to say, Enough pain, now let him rest in peace. During a meal or on a trip, or at a party with friends, even while shopping, it was always possible to connect with him, even through a joke or a laugh.

But not during sex. Here there exists only two, a man and a woman, and their son, dead or alive, has no place in their bed or their bedroom. Because if the dead son slipped into the shadow of a passing thought, or became embodied in a bare leg or the movement of a hand, the sex would die down at once, or else be putrid. And perhaps to preserve Eyali, from the day of the funeral to the day she died, her sister resolutely put an end to her sexuality, and thereby his as well, for how could he impose himself on her when he knew that at any moment she might open the door of her mind and say, Come, my son, come back and I will grieve for you again. Could he have said, in the middle of lovemaking, Just a minute, son, stop, wait a bit, you arrived too soon. Just like that day at dawn, this, too, is a battleground, and if you take one more step into the soul of the naked woman I am holding in my arms I'll spray you with friendly fire . . .

Raindrops slide down the front windscreen, although minutes ago it was sunny. The road is gradually engulfed by

195

hilly forest. When Yirmi sees that his sister-in-law, who has listened attentively to him, is shocked into silence, he slowly turns his face to the front, towards the road, as a sign that the confession is over and there is nothing more to be said.

But for Daniela the conversation is not over. Without trying to raise her voice over the engine noise, she leans forward and brings her lips close to her brother-in-law's bald crown, and as he freezes in place she says in a near whisper:

"This confession of yours is so painful and understandable and natural. For weeks after he died, when we were thinking about you, we also couldn't touch each other. And Amotz, who always wants it—in that period he was careful not to try to persuade me. Without a word of explanation he just went celibate. Then something strange happened, which sometimes happens to him even now. He started crying in movies, in the dark, sometimes over silly things . . . and when I look over at him, he's self-conscious and ashamed . . ."

Yirmiyahu's skull freezes. Then slowly he turns around.

"Crying in the dark? Amotz? I don't believe it . . ."

"Maybe now you can understand why he was the one I chose."

Fifth Candle

1.

ON FRIDAY MORNING Ya'ari stands by the rubbish bin weeding *Ha'aretz* of unnecessary supplements—national and local, real-estate sections, inserts of big retail chains—and while so doing he pictures the furnace where his brother-in-law burned all the Israeli papers. If the newspapers get any fatter we'll have to install an African furnace here too, so as not to overload the bin. His newspaper reading is quick and selective, though he makes sure not to miss the millimetres of rainfall, the level of the Sea of Galilee, and the synoptic weather map. When the radio chimes in with a report of dry but strong easterly winds replacing the humid westerlies, he wonders whether a new type of wind will produce a different sort of roaring and howling at the tower, or whether the wind-sucking shaft doesn't discriminate between east and west.

He washes the breakfast dishes in the sink, it being only fair that in the absence of the mistress of the house the dishwasher also get a rest. But the silence around him feels oppressive, especially as he looks ahead to a long, slow Saturday. Though he told the owner of the Jerusalem elevator to expect him by nine A.M., he knows from experience that it's impolitic to barge in on an older woman before she gets properly organized. His mood is good. He pleasantly replays in his mind Moran's favourable reaction to his nocturnal sketch. So on his way to Jerusalem he is willing to go and listen again to those whining winds before agreeing with the manufacturer on where to hold firm and where to give in. Until candle-lighting time with the grandchildren there is no important person on the horizon he can or should arrange to meet. For many years now, he and his wife have made all their visits together, and if he should invite himself somewhere two days after Daniela left on her trip, it might seem suspicious, as if he were taking advantage of her absence to tell his friends something new about himself.

Once again he transmits the electronic signal to the iron gate and descends into the underground garage. He is careful to wait for the car that has followed him inside to claim its parking spot, and only then steers his own to one of the empty spaces, which are fewer now than on his last visit. As he opens the fire door that separates the parking from the elevators, it seems to him that the easterly winds have worsened the roaring— perhaps because of their dryness. No doubt about it, this noise is a major nuisance and ought to prompt some soul-searching on the part of the architect and the construction company— though the elevator factory and his own design firm are not exempt from scrutiny either. Ya'ari does not call for an elevator right away, but instead stands still and listens, and when the tenant who has just parked his car walks up, the stranger standing stupidly before the elevator doors understandably arouses his suspicion.

The tenant is an older man with a melancholy face and sunken cheeks. He wears old khaki pants, and his shoes are covered with fresh mud, as if he were returning from a tramp through the fields. Though his apartment keys already dangle from his hand, at the sight of the visitor standing as if in silent prayer opposite the motionless elevators, he, too, refrains from calling one, merely tilting his head and listening with a grave expression. Each man steals a sidelong glance at the other; already they are forming suspicions. Finally the tenant steps to the side and takes his cell phone from his pocket, and just as Ya'ari, who has had enough of the wailing winds, is about to open the fire door and return to his car, a melody tinkles in his pocket and stops him short.

The voice of the tenant talking in the corner merges with the one on Ya'ari's phone.

"Yes, Kidron, it's me."

"Now do you believe that the winds are real and not a hallucination?" The tenant continues to talk from mobile to mobile at a few metres' distance.

But Ya'ari, who prefers face-to-face conversations with real voices, hangs up.

"Real, obviously. I never accused you of hallucinating. But I doubt, or rather, I deny, the responsibility of my firm for this condition."

"The building company is also ducking out, and the architect is AWOL, and your friend Gottlieb is hiding in a hole, so who in the end will assume sole responsibility?"

"There's no simple answer to that. Responsibility still needs to be determined and assigned. But forgive me if I ask you something that may seem impertinent."

"What?"

"Is this howling really so horrible?"

"*What?*"

"After all, stormy winds are rare in this sunny country, and in Tel Aviv they're especially rare, and the ride in an elevator, even to the top floor, takes no more than a minute . . ."

"So what?"

"So what's all the fuss about? Because in a certain sense, from another standpoint, the sound of the wind in a sealed apartment block in the heart of the city only adds a touch of living nature—a taste of clouds, or maybe the aroma of mountains . . ."

"Aroma of mountains? Have you lost your mind?"

"I'm only suggesting an option, a different way of looking at the whole thing."

"Maybe it's an option for you, Mr. Ya'ari, but certainly not for the people who live here. And if you think that with oddball fantasies like these you and your firm can weasel out of the responsibility for your defective design, let me tell you, it won't work. Because we'll hound you all the way to a court of law."

"Don't you have anything more important to do?" Ya'ari asks with a cordial smile.

"I do," the man answers firmly, "but I also have a great deal of free time to get involved with many things. As you see, here it is only six-thirty A.M., and I have already finished my workday, which began one hour ago."

A little chill runs down Ya'ari's back.

"That's because my work is brief," the tenant continues, "though not easy. I go every morning to the military cemetery, to my son's grave, walk around the gravestone a bit, pull out a few weeds, remove an old pebble and replace it with a new one. Sometimes, if a tear comes, I also have to wipe it. All in all, not much employment. Which is why I have plenty of time to demand that others fulfill their obligations."

Ya'ari hangs his head and recalls Gottlieb's words, that people like this have a different agenda and with a touch of inner satisfaction he says, "I may not be a bereaved father like you, Mr. Kidron, only a bereaved uncle, but I have insider knowledge, family knowledge, of your grief, and I respect it a great deal. So please, don't be angry that I made a little joke. You can rest easy: this is what I came here for, and I'm going to arrange a four-way meeting with the elevator manufacturer and the contractor and the architect, so that with a team effort we can determine where the winds are sneaking in, and after we discover the source and maybe also the cause, we'll try to calm them down."

2.

As SOON AS they return to the farm, Daniela, exhausted from the journey to Dar es Salaam and the walk down her sister's *via dolorosa*, excuses herself to her brother-in-law and the nurse, takes what remains of the sweets, and goes up to her room. With uncharacteristic speed she strips off her dress, which she can now no longer wear on this trip, takes a long shower, and decides to forego the sweets, whose aftertaste and excessive sickliness she finds repellent, and to go to bed hungry. She does not touch the novel lying beside her bed, opting instead to turn out the light immediately, find the right position, and fall into a deep sleep.

The next morning she wakes early. When five A.M. dawns on her wristwatch she knows her night is over; she has no magic up her sleeve to eke out any extra sleep. For half an hour she stays curled up in the darkness with her eyes open, taking a mental inventory of all her family members in their familiar beds, but finds it hard to imagine the sleeping arrangements of the military prisoner. In the end, hunger forces her to rise in the hesitating dawn, if only for a cup of coffee and a slice of bread.

In principle she could speed up time by returning to her novel. If the editor only made it clearer on the back cover what sort of rewarding surprise awaited the reader, maybe anticipation would lend her some patience. But her hunch is that there will be no real dramatic twist in the plot, or acquisition of self-knowledge on the part of the main character. The most she can expect is a change in her own understanding of the intention or genre of this novel. Which is ultimately not much of a reversal, and depends upon the willingness of the reader. But this novel is not broad or deep enough for the effort.

No, she has no desire to go back to the novel. But if she had Friday's *Ha'aretz* spread open in her hands, she could use that to satisfy her hunger, and keep lying in bed. Unlike her husband, she knows how to glean from its various columns new signs of human compassion in the world.

But until she gets back to Israel she will not have a newspaper. So she dresses in the clothes she wore on the airplane and makes her way down the dark stairway to the vast kitchen. I'm already a little bit of the landlady here, she thinks to herself, amused. But in the kitchen a small light is on. The old groundskeeper who yesterday helped her locate coffee and sugar stands up straight as she enters. Was it his idea to wait for her, following her previous failure to find the coffee and sugar on her own, or is he here on the secret orders of her host?

But she's glad of his company, and warmly takes his hand in both of hers and squeezes it firmly. In lieu of her husband, she has at her disposal a shrivelled old man who has already boiled the water and placed a plate and cup and silverware on the table as well as jars of coffee and sugar, and now removes the greyish milk from the fridge. Maybe in the meantime he has learned to pronounce the English name of the animal that produced it, so that the white woman can consent to lighten her coffee.

Even if most of the sights and details of this visit to Africa fade with the passage of time, she knows she will never forget till her dying day the old wizened African who serves her like a husband, in a huge kitchen before dawn.

3.

MUCH AS YA'ARI would like to delay his mission of mercy to Jerusalem, which will almost certainly come to naught, the drive goes quickly. All wheeling and dealing in the capital sloughs off to the coastal plain at the weekend. Jerusalem on the eve of the Sabbath becomes a provincial town, not locked shut, exactly, but nearly abandoned and therefore very easy to get into. It's not even nine in the morning, and already he is parking his car on a small street near the old Knesset building.

Sometimes design jobs in Jerusalem come Ya'ari's way, though no longer in the city centre, but rather in the suburbs, primarily the newer office parks. His visit to the area near the old Knesset, now the headquarters of the Rabbinical Court, is almost a tourist excursion, and he takes a moment to enter the building and examine a small exhibition of black-and-white photos of days long gone but not forgotten. Although he never lived in Jerusalem, and in the fifties and sixties there was no television to inflict the city's politicians on the public, he still remembers well the newsreels screened in the cinemas. The prime minister and his cabinet would walk around simply and naturally, without the trappings of power or burly security men, in the middle of King George V Street where he is walking now, and exactly two policemen were needed to direct the traffic around them.

But why wallow in nostalgia for the good old days? Wasn't this same modest, innocent Knesset building pelted with stones and bottles during the stormy debate whether to accept German reparations for the Holocaust? It's better not to romanticize the purity of the past; better to concentrate on the present. He locates his destination, then steps into a pleasant café at the corner and orders a fresh croissant and a large coffee. This way he can excuse himself at the outset from whatever refreshments Mrs. Bennett might offer and be able to make a quick getaway from her home. Not only does he not want to be regarded by anyone as a technician of old elevators, he is also particularly reluctant to meet a woman who meant something to his father, maybe he loved her, even if today she is just a girl of eighty-one.

But for all his efforts he hasn't turned the clock very far forwards. When at last he climbs the stairs to the fourth floor it is still only 9:20, so he lingers on every landing, checking the names of the tenants. On the top floor, beside an iron ladder that ascends to the roof, there is a single door, with a name on it in Hebrew and English: Dr. Devorah Bennett, Psychoanalyst. He doesn't ring the bell, but instead knocks lightly, to test her hearing.

A conversation is apparently going on inside, since the tenant's voice is loudly audible. Nonetheless she is aware of his tap on the door, and opens it. There she is, an elderly light-haired woman, shrunken and wrinkled but also nimble and elfin and cheerful, who holds a phone in her hand and keeps talking: Yes, it's your son. Punctual, like his father.

Ya'ari's mood sours at once: clearly this old girl was a good-looking woman in her day, and if she was never actually his father's lover, she was surely the object of his lust. The only question is whether all this happened before or after the death of his mother.

"It's your father on the phone," she says, gracefully waving the receiver. "He called to see if you had arrived. Would you care to speak to him?"

"No," retorts Ya'ari, "I'll report to him after my visit."

"No, Yulik," she shouts into the phone, pressing it close to her ear, "your son has decided to speak to you only after the visit, so good-bye for now, my dear, and don't bother us any more." She gently replaces the phone receiver and extends a liver-spotted hand to Ya'ari.

"Thank you for agreeing to come and see me after all. Don't worry, I know you're only an engineer and not a technician, but if you give me a diagnosis, it'll be possible for me to look for a cure. Your father said he isn't going for his walk in the park today but is staying by the phone, so if you want to ask him something during the inspection, he's ready."

"I have nothing to ask him," Ya'ari interrupts, "and by the way, did you know that my father is confined to a wheelchair, and takes his walk with a Filipino who pushes him?"

Mrs. Bennett wasn't told about the wheelchair, but she'd

guessed, having known for years about the Parkinson's disease, and she was very cross with the man who was ashamed of his illness and stopped visiting her, because what was there to be ashamed of? To tremble is human too.

Ya'ari studies her. "He visited you, in recent years?"

"Of course. After your mother's death we were more than friends . . . so far as our age permitted. But sit, please, drink a cup of tea, so you'll have strength to listen to the yowling of my elevator. It's all ready, it won't take much of your time."

On a table in the living room, beside a menorah prepared for the evening with five candles, are waiting two shiny white cups, a sugar bowl, packets of Sweet 'n' Low, teabags of various types, and little saucers of cookies and chocolate squares. Dominating this array is a vase stuffed with flowers.

"Thank you, I already had mine at that nice café next to the Knesset."

"So you didn't count on me," she says, without complaint. "A shame that you didn't hear from your father how good I am at pampering. It's my loss, as they say these days. But at least sweeten your bitterness a little with a piece of chocolate."

A little smile crosses Ya'ari's lips. He nibbles a chocolate square and looks around, but sees no trace of an elevator.

"You are obviously looking for the elevator. Please, come with me."

She leads him into the corridor of the apartment, which, it turns out, is not at all small. The clutter that typically accumulates in old people's apartments is not oppressive here. The ancient furniture is polished and the upholstery shows no signs of wear or neglect. On the hooks on the backs of the doors, coats hang in orderly fashion. He follows her, looking at the whitish flaxen hair braided and bunched at the nape of her neck. They walk past her consultation room, where photos of Sigmund Freud in youth and age peek out from shelves stuffed with journals and books, then the bathroom and kitchen, and finally her bedroom, in the centre of which stands a big double bed covered with a spread decorated with flowers and peacocks and scattered with many silk cushions.

There is still no sign of an elevator. Now she goes over to a large closet and opens wide two of its doors, as reverently as if it were the Holy Ark of the synagogue. But instead of a curtain, she slides open a thin metal grille, revealing, at last, the elevator—small, narrow, and the incarnation of his nocturnal vision of that fifth elevator in the corner. Inside the car are three buttons: green for up, blue for down, red for help in an emergency.

4.

WHILE SHE DRINKS her coffee Daniela offers her pack of cigarettes to the elderly African, who is watching her from across the table. The man accepts a cigarette, selects a small branch from the stack of firewood, opens the door of the stove and pokes it in, and before lighting his own brings the flame to the cigarette between her lips.

His name is Richard. There is no way to tell whether this is his original name or a name given to him in the days when he worked at a local English farm. It has been many years now since he used much English, and he remembers only bits of the language—fossilized remains whose meaning he can still reconstruct. When spoken to, he tilts his head with great attention, as if to encourage the speaker to rattle off more and more words, until one comes up that will enable him to figure out the rest.

She likes this old man, and since the morning is young and Yirmiyahu and Sijjin Kuang haven't yet arrived, she is willing to chatter to him indefinitely, without expecting him to understand much or reply. She just wants him to feel that she respects him and is grateful for his help, and she also believes that among all the words she generously heaps upon him eventually there will be one that registers. And that word must have arrived, she thinks, when suddenly he rises from his seat and leads her up to the first floor and opens the door of the room temporarily occupied by her brother-in-law. It isn't large, and the bed inside is narrow and dishevelled. For some reason Daniela is relieved that there is no second bed, unmade or otherwise, even though she really doesn't care and has no right to worry about something no longer significant. The groundskeeper quietly limps over to the bed and straightens the sheets, and she is drawn to the little window, which looks out on the dirt road she took to the village of the sadly wise elephant. The rain of the night before has cleansed the world and sweetened the morning light, and before the sun gets too strong she can take a walk and not sit around idly waiting for her brother-in-law to show up.

But is she allowed to walk alone? Why not? She remembers the tranquil road very well, and has no intention of going too far. For a moment she considers asking Richard to escort her, but really, why impose upon him and also on herself? She hurries up to her room, before the sun can get stronger, takes her sister's windbreaker, gets some dollar bills and sticks them in a pocket—money Amotz put in her purse for emergencies—and returns to the ground floor, hoping the old man will witness her departure. But he has already vanished, gone as silently as he came.

The air is fresh, the road a bit muddy. Not overdoing it, she climbs the hill slowly, feeling liberated but a bit fearful too. Now and then she looks behind her, but no one is there. Even when she reaches the top there is no one to be seen. She does not think about animals. Everything here is open and exposed; if some animal is hiding nearby, it must be small and harmless.

As she descends the slope the farm disappears from view. But she recalls the road clearly and feels serenely confident that she'll find her way back. Two young women at the river are busy with laundry. When Daniela draws nearer she notices that their breasts are bare, so she bows her head in a gesture of respect and gives a friendly smile. She greets them in simple English, and also points behind her, towards the farm hidden behind the hill, in order to explain to them where she belongs and where she will return. But the two young women seem unconcerned by the presence of the older white woman. They laugh and splash each other. Their breasts are perfectly formed, smooth and solid. Thatches of youthful pubic hair are visible between their long legs. One of them says something to her friend, and suddenly they point towards the village, and each cups a hand over her eye as both try in vain to find the right word to spur the lone tourist to keep walking. *"Elephant,"* they finally exclaim. "Elephant!" they shout, delighted to have lit upon the word.

Daniela confirms that she gets their message. Indeed, she tells them, she has already twice visited this elephant, once at night. But the girls don't understand her, and in order to encourage her to continue up the next slope they emerge from the river and begin to dance for her, attracting her attention with the charming sway of their well-formed buttocks and showing her the right direction. Daniela laughs, and tells them, "If you say so, I'll keep walking," and she looks back and sees the elderly groundskeeper standing on the first hilltop. Apparently someone is looking after her and taking care of her, as always. And so she presses bravely on to a third visit with the melancholy elephant.

But as she draws near, she can't spot the shed: the elephant must have moved on to display his wonders somewhere else. She advances further and sees she has arrived just in time to say good-bye. The shed has been dismantled, but the elephant himself is still chained to the tree stump, and his energetic and experienced owner is struggling to cover his prized asset, that blue cyclops eye, with a colourful bandage, apparently to protect it from the dust of the road and perhaps from the evil eye of demons. The elephant rebels, flopping his head from side to side, projecting his trunk skywards and protesting with a strange roar, which the surrounding Africans mimic with joyous laughter.

Finally some onlookers volunteer to help the owner subdue the huge animal, and the bandage is bound tight behind the opposite ear. Though it seems unlikely that these Africans have seen the cartoon elephant her grandchildren love on TV—an elephant suffering from a toothache who comes to the rabbit for a cure—they laugh gleefully nonetheless at the sight of the great animal tied in a bandage.

Her heart beating fast, Daniela pushes into the crowd. They

are indifferent to her presence now; they are riveted by the creature who is desperately shaking his enormous head, trying to shed the bandage. Daniela shudders at the elephant's suffering, as if he were a member of her family. She makes her way to his owner, who stands stubborn and determined before the rebellious beast, holding his chain, ready to take to the road, and she unzips her sister's pocket and takes out a bill and offers it to the owner in front of the entire crowd, on condition that he remove the bandage and again show her the unique eye.

The man, who doubtless recalls and recognizes the white woman, seems amazed and excited by the offer. For the money in her hand—and only now does she realize her mistake—is a hundred-dollar bill; and although he has laboured greatly to tie the bandage, he cannot pass up a donation of a single dollar, much less a hundred, offered to him with such decisiveness and likely to change his life. He therefore hurries to fasten the chain to the tree stump, to command the elephant to kneel and even lie down completely before the magnanimous, demanding woman. He searches behind the ear, which is flapping like a fan, and finds the knot, and undoes and removes the colourful cloth, to the delight of all assembled.

And within the welling yellow-green blueness that peers at her with longing, moisture slowly condenses into a tear, and after the first flows another, and the tears of the mute animal, who may also be expressing thanks, melt the tourist's heart, as if this moment finally fulfils the wish she has brought to Africa on the holiday of Hanukkah.

5.

"HELP FROM WHOM?" Ya'ari is perplexed.

"From a partner, for example, if he were here," smiles Mrs. Bennett, and Ya'ari appreciates her sprightly humour.

"But why the bedroom?"

"Because only here, in that corner, did your father feel confident we wouldn't run into a water pipe in the wall, or telephone wires, or electricity. He was sure that if he went from here into the roof, he wouldn't endanger or ruin anything."

Ya'ari hesitates a bit before cautiously entering the tiny car. Indeed, a sophisticated engineering feat, almost devilishly clever, was accomplished here in the 1950s. His father had succeeded in fitting into a corner of the bedroom a hydraulic elevator with an oil-driven piston attached sideways to the wall, with a small hand-shaped fork lifting the elevator cab along two guide rails seven metres in height, up through a dark little nook to an exit on the roof.

But the psychoanalyst, perhaps with his father's help, has not left the elevator naked, a mere technological marvel. She has devoted some effort to beautifying its interior, as well as the shaft encasing it, so that both would blend naturally into the apartment. Two sides of the elevator car are panelled in dark oak, and lest a passenger forget his face en route, however briefly, a small mirror has been affixed to one side. But the third side has been left exposed to the piston attached to the shaft, which is essentially a natural extension of the wall of the room and has therefore been plastered and even decorated, with a picture of a dignified European gentleman.

"You brought your Freud in here too?" He can't help teasing the elderly psychologist.

"That is not Freud. Here I have hung Jung."

"Who's that?"

"If you sit down afterwards for a cup of tea, I'll tell you all about him."

Ya'ari glances genially at his interlocutor, then carefully closes the iron grille and presses the up button. First there is only a faint but protracted humming, indicating a problem with the flow of electricity, then suddenly the elevator shakes violently, lurches and screeches as if fighting off a hostile foreign invader, and finally, for no apparent reason, calms down and surrenders, and with a strange and heart-rending wail, begins to crawl slowly upwards, allowing Ya'ari to see that the entire open wall along the shaft is neatly plastered and hung with paintings, landscapes executed by an amateur.

The shaking and shuddering grow worse towards the end of the little trip, as if a powerful hidden hand is restraining the elevator from climbing beyond the roof. Finally it stops, but the wailing continues for several more seconds, ending at last on a sort of death rattle. To Ya'ari's ears these are not the howls of a cat on heat, as Dr. Bennett described them to his father, but the keening of a jackal, like the ones that prowled in the night when he was a boy.

The clean winter sunlight of Jerusalem dazzles him as he emerges onto the large flat roof, streaked with ancient tar. Paunchy old water tanks surround a shiny satellite dish, and the cables from the dish sprawl in every direction. In the eastern corner stands a white table, chairs chained to its legs so that a spirited wind will not send them flying.

His father claimed that the tenant was able to look out on the walls of the Old City during the years of Jerusalem divided, but now, in the unified-divided capital, the Ottoman era has disappeared behind forests of antennas and ranges of water tanks. Only the towers of the Augusta Victoria hospital and the Russian church can be seen, standing tall on the crest of the Mount of Olives. He turns to the west, towards Beit Frumin, former home of the Knesset, and looks fondly at the old three-storey building. A hidden elevator, he laughs to himself, that rises secretly to the opposite roof from the bedroom of a single woman, might have tempted someone to pick off a pesky political rival as he innocently arrived to attend the plenum.

The iron trapdoor over the ladder flies open and hits the roof with a loud clang. Armed in sunglasses and a straw hat, Mrs. Bennett, having climbed up by the ladder attached to the wall, rebukes the elevator engineer for not taking care to close the grille, so that she could summon the cab for herself.

"Oh. Sorry, but I thought you were afraid to ride in it."

"Why? What danger is there in a little shaking? Besides, your father also set me up an emergency switch that releases the hydraulic pressure and allows the elevator to go down by itself."

"I didn't notice it." He smiles sympathetically at the old girl who stands there all wrinkled and gaily speaks of "hydraulic pressure." "I see that my father really did think of everything here."

"Your father is a true friend, a friend for life. If he were a bit healthier, he would surely be here instead of you."

"No doubt."

"So what do you think of my elevator? Why is it in pain?"

Ya'ari shrugs, his gaze still fixed on the old Knesset.

"Tell me," he ignores her question, "were you already living here when the demonstrators threw rocks at the Knesset because of the reparation payments?"

"Certainly. I sometimes felt like throwing a rock at that Knesset, but not because of the reparations, which I got, too. For different reasons."

"Such as?"

"There was no shortage of reasons. But the sun out here is too strong for history. Let's go back down."

Despite the water tanks and the aggregation of antennas, it's pleasant on this Jerusalem roof. The Judean desert purifies and brightens the air.

"You go down in the elevator, and I'll use the ladder."

"Why? Let's ride down together. Your father set it up so the elevator could hold two people."

And really, why not try to squeeze into the tiny elevator with her, to check out what two passengers would feel like?

She gets in first and shrinks into a corner, and he enters next and presses against her with his back and leans over to push the down button. And again, from the depths, comes a faint buzzing, and the elevator shudders furiously, and with Mrs. Bennett pressed against him smelling pleasantly of soap, the yowling begins, and after a slow descent a mighty hand halts the car with a vengeance, as if to thwart a premeditated desire to break into the apartment downstairs.

He opens the metal grille and retreats into the corner so she can get out first.

"You heard that? So what do you say?"

Ya'ari shrugs and asks her in what year, exactly, his father installed the elevator.

"In fifty-four."

"And you're certain my father brought me along?"

"I remember you. A boy of seven."

"Eight . . ."

"Just a little tyke, sitting here in the corner watching his father with such admiration. Well, so how old are you now?"

"Not hard to figure out."

"Still a little boy."

"Careful, that's what my father calls you, a little girl . . ."

"Which is very gratifying and sweet. You can't imagine how nice it is of him to call me a girl."

"And my mother, you knew her?" he blurts out testily.

"Of course. A strong woman. Straightforward. She, too, would come to visit me sometimes with your father. Once we even took her in the elevator."

"Strange," he mutters with quiet indignation, "they never told me about you."

"Apparently I was some sort of secret of theirs," she says, and drops her wrinkled eyelid in a wink.

Ya'ari feels dizzy. He closes his eyes for a moment and tries to revisit his moonlight epiphany. As if she can sense his inner turmoil, Devorah Bennett asks again carefully, somewhat concerned: So what do you say? Can it be fixed?

And he recovers and delivers a quick diagnosis.

"The vibration seems to come from the piston that produces the oil pressure. It will have to be dismantled and checked. But how do you take apart a weird creature like this? Perhaps my father will have an idea. Though finding spare parts will be impossible. The only way is to have them custom-made, and that is definitely not simple."

"But possible."

"Maybe."

"And the yowling?"

"Maybe there's a little cat hiding in there after all?" Now he winks.

"No," she smiles kindly, "there is no cat and never was."

"So there's no choice: we'll have to bring in an expert with a sensitive ear to tell us the source of this weeping and wailing. Otherwise we'll have to start dismantling old parts of the electrical system, which will crumble in our hands and we'll never be able to put them back together."

"So we have a big production here," she sighs.

"So it would seem. Meanwhile, give me a tape measure, if you own such a thing."

6.

AND AFTERWARDS THE elephant stands up and goes on its way, but without the bandage on its eye. In appreciation of the animal that has suddenly enriched him, the owner spares it the onus of the bandage, rolls up the colourful cloth, and ties it to the pack already loaded onto the elephant's back. Then, without further delay, as if afraid that someone might want to share in his newfound wealth, he puts on dark glasses, takes the chain in his hands and pulls the elephant after him. The animal, too, is clearly happy to get moving and make tracks in the open plain, after being tied up for many days in a claustrophobic shed. Some local youths run after them, keeping up for a considerable distance before turning around and walking slowly back to the village.

The equatorial sun beats down on the hatless head of the Israeli; it's time to return to the farm. Witnessing the speedy departure of the animal owner, and his removal of the elephant's bandage, the Africans have apparently decided that this older woman—visiting for the third time, and this time alone—must possess power and influence, and they therefore accompany her on her way back.

Thus surrounded, the English teacher feels as if she were on a class trip—at the magnetic centre, on a brilliant morning, of a parade of youths and men and women too. For a moment she is frightened, but is careful not to speed up, lest this be interpreted as running away. She passes by the river, where some grey cows are drinking, and as she climbs the next hill, she notices the shady path that she missed, the same path she took with Yirmiyahu on that first day. The entourage is still at her heels when Yirmiyahu grabs her by the hand.

"You can't wander around here by yourself," he says angrily.

"Why?" she smiles with relief. "Don't tell me it's dangerous here."

"Not dangerous, and the people here aren't violent, but all the same, do not go out again by yourself."

"What's the matter?

"Nothing is the matter and nothing will be," he snaps, "even so you are not to go wandering around by yourself."

And the youths who escorted her, and have halted a few paces back, feel the anger of the tall, bald, peeled man, and their eyes glitter with inquisitive anxiety, waiting to see if the *muzungu* man will raise a hand against the benevolent *muzungu* woman. She suddenly feels humiliated, but maintains her composure.

"I'm not wandering around . . . I'm taking a walk."

"Then don't take a walk either."

"Why?"

"Why, why, why . . . because that's what I am asking of you and that's what I am saying." By now he is shouting with impatience. "You came without Amotz, and you won't go around anywhere alone. You know that Amotz would never allow you to wander around here by yourself . . ."

She continues to argue, though she doesn't know why.

"You are not Amotz, and you have no authority over me. And why are you so angry? Unlike Shuli, I really don't enjoy being alone. I always feel good in the company of people, and I thought you would be available most of the time, but this morning you disappeared."

"In general I don't have much work, but if sometimes I get busier, like last night, it only helps."

Helps you how? she would like to protest, flaunting her pain at the old, bald man whose white clothes dazzle her eyes in the sunlight. To erase Shuli and Eyali too? But she bites her tongue.

7.

AFTER JOTTING DOWN the tiny elevator's dimensions on a slip of paper, Ya'ari bids farewell to Devorah Bennett, without making any definite promises. The continuing absence of his wife increases his hunger for his children. It was only two days ago that Nofar lit Hanukkah candles with him, but the presence of the weird friend she brought precluded any chance—and perhaps by design—of a more personal conversation. Since I have already ended up on a Friday in Jerusalem, Ya'ari figures as he walks past the old Knesset building, why hurry back? So before he gets into the car he calls his daughter's cell phone, only to discover it's been disconnected. In other words, she's at the hospital. When she's on duty, she always turns the device off entirely, so as not to disturb the calibrations of any sensitive electronic apparatus. But instead of giving up and simply calling to leave a message with her landlord, he decides to write her a note this time; after all, this is a rare chance to have a peek at his daughter's rented room, which he hasn't seen since he helped her move to Jerusalem, when she made the final decision to defer her army duty by doing national service at the hospital.

He is gratified that the landlords, a married couple, both medical residents at the hospital where Nofar works, remember and recognize her father, whose appearance and body language remind them of her. They welcome him warmly, while wondering how he could have forgotten that on Friday mornings Nofar is always on duty and her phone is turned off. Ya'ari assures them that he knew all that, but since he happened to be in Jerusalem today he is taking the opportunity to have a look at the room his daughter has been living in for nearly a year, and perhaps to leave her a note. Might that be possible? From the time he helped her move, he hasn't had a chance to see how she has settled in.

As he enters his daughter's rented room, he has a few misgivings. He knows that Nofar will not be happy about this invasion, even if he only left a little note. She would not want him to see—though it is exactly what he expected to see—the chaos of clothes, bedding, books and papers, leftover food, and wilted flowers: an elemental disorder, created almost on principle, which for some reason does not at all trouble the young landlords, who stand now in the doorway singing their tenant's praises.

Surprised and touched, Ya'ari nods in agreement. Yes, he knows the merits of his daughter, who may resemble him externally but on the inside is very much like her mother. That is to say, she is a person whose boundaries are clear and firm, which is why she can live amid total disarray. The two get a good laugh from this charming explanation, which they can now use to justify the mess in their own quarters. And Ya'ari is grateful to the young couple who've taken his daughter under their wing, and interrogates them a bit about themselves, their schedules at the hospital, the nature of their specializations, and from there moves to medicine itself, what's new and what's passé, and since the conversation is free-flowing and frank, he permits himself a question he would like them to keep confidential. Doesn't Nofar seem to them anguished and lonely? Lonely, no, definitely not, the two declare as one, for in the evenings, when she is off duty, sometimes a friend will come, different ones, it's true, to take her to a film or a pub. But unhappy? That could be. It's as if—the landlady hesitates—as if, despite her youth, she has already lost something irreplaceable.

Ya'ari looks at the photo hanging over Nofar's bed, Eyal as a teenager—a picture he hadn't known existed—and mumbles something about the source of his family's melancholy. But there's no need for any explanation, because the landlords have already heard about the tragedy in detail. Nofar talks again and again about the *friendly fire*—those are the words she uses. Now, the couple inquire of the father, How is it that such a story is so deeply embedded in her? How old was she at the time, anyway? Because it seems to them that she gets a bit confused about dates.

Very young, says the father, eleven and a half, in the middle of sixth grade. The age difference between her and her cousin was substantial, almost thirteen years. Eyal studied medicine at university under army auspices, but afterwards did not serve at the hospital but instead insisted on combat duty. If he were still alive, he would now be a doctor like you. But the age difference, Ya'ari adds with a bitter smile, did not prevent Nofar from imagining that not only was she in love with her cousin, but also that he was in love with her. Maybe he sent off signals that we were unaware of, but which made a strong impression on her, and possibly because of this, she remains stalled.

From the landlords' expression the father senses he may have said too much. Because they love and respect their unhappy boarder, it's wrong for him to explain to them things that Nofar herself has not yet worked out. Now anxious to make a clean getaway, he checks his watch and looks for a piece of paper, but even such a minor thing as that is not easy to find in her room. He locates a prescription pad from the hospital, tears out a page and writes:

Nofar, my dear,

Grandpa made me come to Jerusalem to take care of an old elevator of some lover of his from long ago. So I thought if I was already here in your sad city, why not have coffee together? But I didn't remember that you're on duty this morning, so it turns out I've missed you once again. Moran is still stuck in

the army, and Imma is with Yirmi in Africa, till Sunday in
case you've forgotten. Tonight I'm lighting candles at Efrat's.
How about joining us? The kids will be happy. And Efrati, too,
of course. It'll be less sad that way. So as usual I'm on my cell,
waiting for a sign of life from you.

Kisses, Abba

He clears a space on the messy table and leaves the note in a
conspicuous place. Then he looks again at the picture of the
teenage boy and suddenly realizes that Nofar will not forgive
him for invading her deepest privacy. He quickly resolves to
erase his presence. He crumples the note and sticks it in his
pocket, then goes out to the landlords, seated now in the
kitchen with their baby, and when they invite him to join them,
Ya'ari abashedly asks that they pretend he was never there. I
know her well, he apologizes, she's sensitive about her
independence, and it would be hard for her to accept that
without warning I broke into her chaos. So please, don't tell her
I was here. Don't tell her anything. I didn't leave a note. I'll call
her later . . . that would be easier for her too. So thanks . . . and
apologies . . . I'm sorry . . . I apologize . . . And without giving
them a chance to regret his leaving, he departs.

Perhaps it is the easterly winds which arose overnight that
boost his speeding car on the highway from Jerusalem to the
coastal plain. To assuage his loneliness for his absent wife he will
have to settle for his father, whose admirable generosity of spirit
has piqued his curiosity. So Ya'ari gets down to business and
announces into the speaker-phone:

"That's it, Abba, I was over at your lady friend's house."

"So what's going on with her?"

"Your elevator is sweet, and so's the little girl . . ."

"Watch it, Amotz, don't be a wise guy."

8.

YIRMI RELAXES A bit, smiles and squeezes Daniela's shoulder, as if to heal the sting of his unexpected harangue and allay the anxiety of the old African who alerted him and now stands to one side, watching.

They return to the farm, and the old groundskeeper decides to defuse the family quarrel with a good meal. He fires the baking oven and kneads a big pita bread. Into a pot of boiling water he tosses roots and vegetable peelings, kernels of corn, and cubes of meat. Two other chefs rise from their cots in a nearby pantry and join in his labours. Meanwhile Yirmi, sitting opposite Daniela, is curious to know what drew his sister-in-law so strongly to the elephant that she went to see it a third time. But Daniela is not quite ready to lay bare her feelings to someone who has just scolded her in the presence of strangers, and instead of explaining what drove her to contemplate a spectacular genetic defect in search of primal human heartbreak, she needles her brother-in-law by telling him with childish pride about the hundred dollars she gave to the elephant's owner to remove the bandage.

"A hundred dollars? Are you out of your mind?"

It wasn't on purpose. Even though the money wasn't that much for her, she still has her limits. She'd been sure that all the bills she stuffed into her jacket pocket were small ones, because Amotz always held on to the big bills. It was only when she took out the money that she realized what it was, and by then it was too late; the man snatched it quickly and tucked it in his shorts and immediately complied with her request, and when the elephant crouched before her, its giant eye shed a tear, and then another.

"Tears? An elephant?"

That is what she saw with her own eyes. So how could she tell the owner, Wait, I made a mistake, ever since my sister's death I've been a little absent-minded, and by accident I gave you a hundred-dollar bill, but ten is enough for you, so give it back, please.

"He would also have been fine with one dollar."

"Who decides that one dollar is enough for him? You? On what basis?" she snaps at her brother-in-law. "Drop it, Yirmi, I actually like the idea that a hundred-dollar bill Amotz put in my purse should pass so naturally into the hands of this man, who might take better care of his elephant from now on."

"Which we will never know, but one thing is certain: you wrought a small revolution in the life of one African man, who will always remember you."

"It's nice to know that at least one man in Africa will think of me till the end of his life. One of these days you'll be somewhere else."

"How do you know? Anything's possible . . . I owe nothing to anyone, I'm free as a bird."

"In which case, both you and the elephant's owner will remember I was here."

"I will? Why is that? All right, Shuli's love for you was always unconditional, even if you were an annoying child and tagged along with her and went into her room without knocking. But me remember? I'm here to forget, not to remember."

"What are you talking about?" she asks with trepidation.

"You know very well. I'm here not only to build up my pension, but also to forget him and everyone who reminds me of him."

"Forget Eyali? How is that possible?"

"It's possible . . . why not? He is no longer anywhere, and I am still not a Sudanese who believes in winds and spirits."

"Why spirits? Is that the only way to talk about memory?"

"Memory is finished. I milked his death dry. You can't imagine how I investigated this death and everything I learned about it. But my responsibility is over. And if our Eyali—all of ours, yours too, why not? you also loved him very much—if this son happened to come back to life, believe me, I would say to him: My dear boy, bravo, you've managed to return to the world that had no pity for you, that took you by surprise and finished you off with two precise gunshots. But I ask you now, with all my love, please take pity on me and find yourself a different father."

"Are you sick?" she mutters. "A different father?"

"Why not? I'm over seventy now; I don't have many years left. I did my duty, I filled my quota of worry and suffering. At Eyali's bar mitzvah, after he finished reading the Haftorah, the rabbi told me to declare in a clear voice: 'Blessed is He who has released me from punishment for this one's sins,' and I repeated those repellent words against my will, as if the devil had made me do it. But now, after almost twenty years, I realize that bar-mitzvah devil wasn't altogether stupid. Now I bow my head and say simply, 'Blessed is he who released me.' If my son wants to be a 'wanted' man again and not the one who does the wanting—by all means, but he should be so kind as to find himself a different father."

"Yirmi," she says, tense and shaken, "what on earth are you talking about?"

"Do you want to poison the meal?"

"The truth liberates, it doesn't poison."

Yirmiyahu regards his sister-in-law with fondness. "If that's the case, if you also came here for the truth, then I'll give you a few new details about that 'friendly fire' that your Amotz saddled me with."

"Leave Amotz alone," she protests impatiently, "he was only trying to console you."

He puts a hand on her arm.

"I don't doubt it, and I have no complaints against him. Amotz is a practical man, after my own heart. But his 'friendly fire' made me crazy in the beginning, because it turned into a project. At any price, by any possible means, I wanted to know who this *friend* was who unleashed the fire, what his name was, what he looked like, where he came from, who his parents were, his teachers, everything."

"But why was that important to you? What did you want to do to him? What in the end could you do to him? Shuli never told me you were caught up in this."

"Because I never said a word to Shuli. She put an end to our sex life, and I put an end to total honesty."

"And Amotz knew about it?"

"Not Amotz or anyone else."

The black chef places before them two dishes of the meat and vegetable stew.

"This is breakfast, or lunch?"

"Both. After you've contributed a hundred dollars in honour of the tears of a wandering elephant, you deserve a full meal. And don't be put off by the distinctive taste of the meat; it was cooked on a hot fire. And let's not ruin the meal with talk that I know will only upset you."

"Keep talking, I hate eating in silence. I'm listening. I never thought that identifying the soldier who accidentally shot Eyali was of any concern to you. After all, they said he was not to blame."

"Of course he wasn't. The fault was entirely Eyal's. But still I wanted a connection with the one who killed him."

"What kind of connection?"

"A connection."

"And in the end you identified the young man?"

"No, in the end I gave up and stopped trying."

9.

WITH A TREMBLING hand the elderly Ya'ari tries to sketch for his son the inner structure of the hydraulic oil piston that raises and lowers the little elevator, and Hilario runs back and forth between rooms, fetching pages torn from his arithmetic notebook for further attempts. As the father recollects it, the two parts of the piston are screwed together internally, not joined by an exterior flange, whose bolts would rust over the years. That was how he guaranteed sturdiness and reliability for the long term, and ensured that the hydraulic oil would not leak out of unforeseen openings. But not even high-grade steel, the kind produced in Czechoslovakia before World War II, can resist forever the wear and tear of time. Therefore, it will be necessary to locate the joint, separate the two parts, remove the defective bearings and replace them with new ones.

"The sketch isn't worth the effort, Abba," says his son, "I'm sure the inside threads have melted together by now and we won't be able to take the thing apart. The only way is to take the whole mechanism out of the wall and try to install something else that'll work on the same principle."

"But there's no chance we can get ready-made parts that'll be right for my little elevator. We'll have to make a new piston from scratch just like the old one."

"Turning a new one is a different story. I have no idea who can do it, not to mention the cost."

"Why? I'll ask Gottlieb to make it in his factory. He owes me a lot, and he'll do it for me."

"Don't kid yourself that he'll work for you. And I'm not at all sure that he's capable of turning you a new piston. Everything in his factory is automatic and programmed, and the lathes work according to standard models. Gone are the days of workshops that do custom-made private elevators on the whim of single women."

"He'll make it for me," says the father, ignoring his son's cynical remark. "I know he can do it."

Hilario stands at the ready beside the wheelchair, poised to run into his room and tear out another page for the old man. Francisco sits nearby, listening intently. In the kitchen, amid the steamy aromas of lunch, Kinzie trills a song.

"And we haven't yet discussed the wailing electrical system," Ya'ari continues in a quarrelsome tone, "which is a separate story. I'll be damned if I can figure out where you hid it, Abba, and where it gets its current."

The old man smiles. Why be damned? Where it's hidden he doesn't remember, but because this is not spirit but matter, in the end it will be found. And the elevator gets its power directly from the electricity company.

"The electricity company?"

Of course. Devorah Bennett's apartment, like the other old apartments in the building, never had three-phase power, and his father was wary of overloading the system, so he found a way to circumvent the apartment's wiring and supply the elevator directly from the electricity company. Meaning that all these years the little girl has had a free ride, as if she were a long-standing member of the company's workers' committee.

"I see this woman aroused criminal urges in you," Ya'ari jokes. "But if that's the situation, you can forget about me. I'm not going near any wailing and shaking electrical system connected to some unidentified illegitimate source."

"Don't exaggerate . . . you told me that Gottlieb has some woman around his plant who's an expert on technical noises, so we'll take her to Jerusalem and together we'll locate the cat and silence it."

"What's this 'we'll take' and 'we'll locate'?"

"I'll go up to Jerusalem, too. Before I die I want to see the elevator that goes straight from her bedroom once more. Did you tell her I'm now in a wheelchair?"

"I gave her a hint."

"Why?"

"So she wouldn't bother you too much. But don't tell me this is a secret you're ashamed of."

"Not any more. But to tell you the truth, when I first got ill I was very embarrassed, and because of that I broke off contact. Because you should know that after Mother died, I tried to give myself more freedom, to bring more substance to what I already felt about her. Amotz, to tell you the truth, when I built her the elevator in her bedroom, I really fell in love with that woman. Not one phase but all three. I almost couldn't breathe when I was near her. Afterwards I tried to cool this love down. But when Mother died and I was alone, we had a lovely affair, not too intense, but appropriate for our age. And had it not been for all the psychiatric patients in and out of there all day, I would even have gone to live with her. But then the tremors got worse and also moved to my knees . . ."

Ya'ari face burns red as he hears his father's confession of love.

The Filipino woman comes out of the kitchen, small and flushed. A pixie in colourful silks, asking the boss in English if he's ready to eat.

"Maybe in a little while," he answers in his own creaky English.

"But the chicken schnitzel is right from the pan, just as you like it."

"Eat, Abba, I'm not running away, I'll sit with you."

"But it's unpleasant for you to watch them feeding me."

"Not so bad. It's fine. I'll even join you."

Francisco takes a large napkin and covers the father's chest. He brings a plate with schnitzel and sugar-snap peas, cuts the chicken into little pieces, places a fork into the father's trembling hand, and in his own hand holds another fork, with which he feeds the old man.

"You also want schnitzel like Abba?" the Filipino asks Amotz.

"Schnitzel I can get anywhere. I would rather try a dish that your wife makes for *you*."

The Filipino woman is pleased by the compliment, and in a yellow plastic bowl, the same bowl from which Amotz ate his porridge as a child, serves him hot soup, rich with seafood.

"You eat shellfish?" The father is surprised.

"What can you do? From childhood you taught me to eat everything that's put in front of me."

Francisco feeds the trembling old man, wiping his lips, now and then collecting from the napkin peas that fell from his mouth and returning them to their destination. Amotz does not shrink from the painful sight, but feels his heart go out to his father as he struggles to maintain his dignity. Therefore, when the old man begins to ask gingerly about the owner of the elevator, and wants a detailed description of the lady and her room, he suggests that his father invite the little girl for a visit, and promises that he himself will drive her down and back.

But the old man does not want Devorah Bennett to visit him at home and see him in his miserable wheelchair. Surely not before he has proven his ability to stand behind the lifetime guarantee that he gave her.

"Let's talk to Gottlieb," he urges his son.

"Gottlieb won't do any good here. Gottlieb has already lost his love for the profession and thinks only about money."

"Very good." The old man perks up. "If he thinks only about money, then threaten that you won't order the new Defence Ministry elevators from him. I'm sure he'll hurry to make you anything you ask."

"Threaten him?" Ya'ari is taken aback. "Go that far?"

"Yes, Amotz. If you promise a woman something for a lifetime, you have to keep the promise."

10.

"BELIEVE ME," YIRMIYAHU continues, "it wasn't easy to give up trying to identify the soldier who fired the fatal bullet. It was very important for me to meet him face to face. At first I tried to clarify it in a direct and open fashion, and found myself up against a stone wall among the members of the unit. Then I tried roundabout methods. But even though I was very clever, and went so far as to visit the site and calculate possible lines of fire, I was left without a positive identification."

"Why?"

"Why? Because they were all terrified and did everything in their power to prevent it. They were afraid I was planning some sort of reprimand, an accusation, or a lawsuit. Or even that I would go outside the law, stalk the killer in some sick way. That happens sometimes, and it might have happened with me too. There was no way I could persuade them that I was actually acting out of concern for the shooter, who, although it was indisputably Eyali's own fault, might carry around a psychic wound that would infect his entire life. I wanted to be capable of calming the boy, telling him, habibi, I am the father, and I confirm your innocence. You are exonerated not only by your commanding officers but also by the parents of the boy you accidentally killed. For your own good, we will keep in touch. If, in the course of your life, anxiety or guilt build up inside you over the friendly fire you aimed at a comrade who miscalculated the time of day, you can always come and visit me, and I will help you ease the guilt and lighten the anxiety."

"Strange . . ."

"It is strange, but it's also the truth. I became obsessed with wanting to hold the finger that squeezed the trigger, as if it were the last finger that touched Eyali's soul. Yes, Daniela, in those first months I thought in terms of spirit and soul, until I abandoned all that foolishness."

On her plate remain pieces of the meat, of which she is suspicious. One of the cooks hums a cheerful African song to himself, accentuating its tempo by drumming briskly on a pot, now and then stealing a glance at the two white people. Both of them are tired, she for no apparent reason, maybe because she's so far from her husband, but Yirmiyahu definitely deserves a rest—a few hours after their return from Dar es Salaam, something justified an urgent night-time ride out to the dig. But the rapt attention of his empathetic sister-in-law fuels his fevered confession.

"Theoretically, identifying the shooter should not have been difficult. Because this wasn't anonymous fire, coming from artillery or a helicopter, where all the sophisticated hardware can show for certain are the intended targets, not the actual hits. No, this is a simple story, almost a fable, of gunfire among friends, a small group of elite soldiers, eight all told, including the commander of the ambush. A likeable officer named Micha, who because of what happened became almost like a member of our family. He had also been to university, a law graduate, and he sent Eyal to the rooftop of a local family as a lookout, in case the 'wanted man' eluded the trap they had set for him. And it wasn't one ambush, but two, north and south, each fifty or sixty metres away from the building. So it was all clear and simple. Do you remember any of what was said at the time?"

"I think so."

"If so, you'll recall that I didn't give the family many details. Shuli cut herself off entirely from the story even at the early stages, and rightly so. Whereas I kept chasing after more, digging here and digging there, with a recklessness that maybe fits a certain type of male bereavement. For example, the desire I had, later on, to find out who was the 'wanted man' on that wretched night, what made him so great that they honoured him by bringing eight soldiers to Tulkarm at night."

"Why was that important to you?"

"That's exactly the question the officer from the General Security Service asked me. What's the point of telling you his name? Wanted men come and go, and the list goes on forever. Soon the whole Palestinian people will be wanted by us. 'Even so,' I insisted, 'wanted for what? Wanted why?' 'Wanted for the heavenly tribunal,' the officer joked, and didn't reveal a single detail. And rightly so. Because one detail leads to another, and such information has no practical significance if the death has already occurred. But I was still in shock and I felt compelled to exhume the entire reality of that night. I asked the TV news for the tape of their coverage of the military funeral. It was a very short report, not even a minute long, and at night, when Shuli was sleeping, I played it over and over on the VCR, not to watch our own suffering, including the drama of Nofar, who seemed about to throw herself in the grave after him, but to study carefully the faces of the guard of honour, who fired the three shots to which a soldier is entitled even if he caused his own death by mistake. Again and again I watched those soldiers, all of whose names and histories I knew, because I thought that maybe through facial expressions when they pulled the trigger I would discover the man behind the friendly fire."

"Absurd . . ."

"That's right, absurd. But that's how it was, then. What can I say? It's also normal and natural. The first months of mourning are a whirlwind of absurdity. On the outside you keep your cool, and inside you lurch from fantasy to madness, and until I came to a final, philosophical flash of recognition, at night on the rooftop of that house in Tulkarm, I was unable to get free of all that absurdity and begin the process of forgetting.

"For you have to understand. His friends didn't abandon us. We aren't the Americans or Japanese, who send telegrams of condolence to parents in distant cities and say, Bye-bye and we won't be seeing you. With us there are established customs of bereavement, rules by which you don't abandon the soldier's family but instead maintain a connection. An institutional connection and a personal one. The soldiers from his company come to visit now and then and become a bit like relatives, inviting you to their family functions, talking about themselves, sharing their experiences. At first they come as a whole group, awkward strapping boys who barely fit into the living room and keep an eye on one another lest a careless word slip out. But after they have studied the nature of the bereaved parents and confirmed that these remain civilized people and that death has not eradicated the essence of their humanity, they let themselves come for more intimate visits—in threes, in pairs, even alone, and in this way they pass your suspicions from one to the next, back and forth, like a tennis ball, and some of them are discharged and continue to visit you as civilians, and your presumptuous, pathetic, and pointless attempt to identify the shooter becomes harder and more complicated every day. The individual friendly fire is absorbed into the 'fire of our own forces,' a collective fire, and then slowly, slowly is transformed from army fire to civilian fire, and civilian fire to undefined fire, until the shooter himself is no longer sure whether one night he got up and shot his friend by mistake. And then I said to myself, if so, I need to shift direction, and instead of chasing after shadows to offer forgiveness to someone who doesn't need it or ask for it, let's demand that the army show me the place, let me go to the roof of this house in Tulkarm to understand what misled my son. But this is a story for another time. Now I want to sleep. What did you want to say?"

"Please, Yirmi, don't ever say that Nofar only looked as if she wanted to throw herself . . . because it was very real, Yirmi, believe me, the girl was in total despair at the funeral, and it still lingers."

"Forgive me, Daniela," he says, distressed, "I didn't mean... of course it was all real . . . Nofar is a wonderful girl . . . and her love for Eyal was wonderful too."

11.

IF INDEED HE intends to threaten Gottlieb, Amotz Ya'ari decides it should be done carefully and politely, and not in the presence of his father, who out of romantic enthusiasm might just yank the phone from his hand in the middle of the call and wreck the subtlety of the threat with the indignant impatience of an old man who knows his time is up. He clears the taste of the seafood from his mouth with a Filipino pastry, pats Hilario on the head, and drives to the office.

A drizzly Friday. Two in the afternoon. Throughout the neighbourhood offices are already closed, but in the big room at Ya'ari's firm, a man and a woman are engaged in spirited conversation in front of a computer. The two young engineers each took a healthy chunk of time off during the week for their children's Hanukkah diversions, and now, on a free day, have abandoned their spouses to make up for lost time. Ya'ari is proud of the sense of duty he has instilled in his workers, but does not join their discussion, lest they detain him with a question requiring a complicated answer. He smiles and waves, and without further ado sequesters himself in his office.

Although he did not expect a second call from his wife, whose actual self he will embrace in another seventy-five hours, he is slightly disappointed by the silence. He dials Gottlieb's cell phone.

It's urgent? It can't wait? grumbles the manufacturer. He's in a café, enjoying the company of fellow manufacturers, it's hard for him to talk and harder to hear. What is this? Because your wife isn't back yet from Africa, you have to bother me even on a Friday?

"Very impressive of you to remember her schedule," Ya'ari says. "I see that over the years you've become one of the family."

The maker of elevators lowers his defences and is prepared to listen to a short speech, provided it is spoken loud and clear. Ya'ari conveys the essence of his father's request: Gottlieb is to make new parts for a one-of-a-kind piston that grew old in a tiny ancient Jerusalem elevator. Why make them? Gottlieb wants to know. Why not replace the whole elevator, and at the same time widen it a little? It can't be widened, it's a narrow elevator belonging to an old lady; it goes from a bedroom closet straight up to the roof. It's impossible to make it wider or to replace it. That's the situation.

Gottlieb is in a hurry to rejoin his friends, whose gales of laughter are interfering with the phone conversation, and so he promises that on Sunday he'll check out the capabilities of his old metal lathe, which for quite some years has been out of commission. You should know, he scolds Ya'ari, this is not for you, because you are a difficult person, but only because your old man is asking. What can I do, sighs the manufacturer. I have been attached to him for fifty years.

Ya'ari now also requests the services of the woman technician who specializes in noises, to locate the source of the humming in the electrical system of this same elevator.

"If you want to hire the musical ear of my expert," Gottlieb informs him with satisfaction, "you'll have to pay her separately. Not on my tab. She can take a formal day off, and you can play with her all you like."

"But wait a minute, we also need her for the wind problem in the tower, and that's not on my account."

"The wind complaint? Why does that keep coming back? We took that one off the docket. We agreed that we have no responsibility for anything that wails due to the failures of the construction company."

"No, Gottlieb, listen, it's not that simple. I visited the tower this morning, and the wailing and roaring are really insufferable. And I also ran into that head of the committee, the bereaved tenant . . ."

"What made you go there?" Gottlieb interrupts him angrily,

"after I warned you not to go near the tower or that guy, who automatically makes you feel guilty over everything. They want us to incur major expenses, without our being at fault over anything. If they want to open up the elevators and examine the shaft, by all means—but on condition that they pay for every minute of the technicians' time. Listen, Ya'ari, I'm warning you, if you're looking for trouble, go and get mixed up in this by yourself. These winds do not interest me in any shape or form. I'm out of the whole deal."

"You're not out of anything," Ya'ari answers evenly, "you have no choice. I promised this tenant, head of the committee, that the two of us, together with the architect and the construction company, will find the source of the problem. You can't let yourself off and just disappear. Because if you damage my credibility, in the future I'll cut you out of things that matter to you."

"Like what, for example?"

"For example, the new elevators for the Defence Ministry. Believe me, Gottlieb, if we order them from the Chinese, we'll save the state money."

Now silence looms on the other side. Ya'ari hears the breathing of the maker of elevators, who feels a sharp wound to his wallet.

"Now you're threatening me?"

"If you like, call it a threat."

"You know I can threaten you too."

"Obviously, everyone in this country has someone he can threaten. Nobody has immunity."

"You included."

"Of course."

"And this is how you threaten a man that you said was a member of your family a few minutes ago?"

"It's because you're a member of the family," laughs Ya'ari.

"Watch out, I'll complain about you to your father."

"You watch out, he's the one who gave me the idea of threatening you."

"So the two of you decided to ruin my weekend."

"Nothing will get ruined, Gottlieb, my friend. For the time being we're talking not about money, just time. What do those winds wandering in the tower want from us, after all? That we track them down with patience and concentration. To provide them with an honourable exit."

12.

OUTSIDE A HARD rain falls, a rapid downpour that began without warning, but the farm's great kitchen has been heated by cooking, dishes destined for the hungry band of scientists who will arrive tomorrow from the dig and stay for the weekend. Yirmiyahu's hand props up his head as if it might otherwise snap off from exhaustion and roll down the table between the greasy plates. His night-time ride to the excavations—its goal is still unclear to Daniela—was particularly fatiguing; Sijjin Kuang's friends, the stars and the moon, were hidden by heavy clouds, and she had to navigate by the trees and winds, which deceived her time after time. Now he can't keep his eyes open, and so he lumbers upstairs to his temporary room, while his sister-in-law stays at the big dining table and watches the chefs at work, smiling distractedly. The Africans are drawn to the mature white woman, and are delighted to ask her to sample one newly cooked dish after another, until she, too, decides to go up to her room. The rain has ended as abruptly as it began, and a sparkling sun comes out to savour the world, but after her brother-in-law's scolding she dares not leave the compound by herself, even for a brief stroll.

She wonders if her visit has gone on too long. Today there was a flight from Morogoro to Nairobi, and from there she could have reached Tel Aviv by dawn tomorrow, with one stopover in Amman. But yet another connection, and in Amman of all places, had frightened Amotz, and she herself had thought it not quite right to make a sympathy visit all the way from Asia to Africa for just three nights. If only she had a Friday newspaper, she could even enjoy the time off from her husband and home, but there's not a shred of newsprint to be found in any language, and she can only hope that by the time she returns on Monday Amotz will not have thrown away everything worth reading.

She asks the cooks if there might be a little transistor radio in the kitchen to link her to the wider world, and although they understand her request, they have no such device, but they promise her that the scientists arriving from the excavation site will be able to furnish her with up-to-date news. Out there in the canyon stands a big dish that collects stories of everything interesting and important in the world. However, in the meantime, she will have to do without connection to the world.

But what she cannot ignore is a worsening headache. Is it just an ordinary headache, or a symptom of the high blood pressure that she first developed after her sister's death. The family doctor was not overly impressed and saw it mainly as an emotional reaction, so rather than prescribe a daily medicine he recommended a daily walk and weight loss and instructed Amotz to monitor his wife's blood pressure now and then.

A daily walk and losing weight do not much appeal to a woman disinclined to accept physical limitations on her free will. It's easier to roll up a sleeve and extend a bare arm to her husband, so he can strap the cuff around it and assure her that her sensations are imaginary. But here on a remote farm in Africa, she must rely only on herself, and since two blood pressure pills are appended to her passport, there's no reason not to swallow one of them and take the other back to Israel. She heads to her room, to her passport.

But before taking the pill, she decides to have a few words with the Sudanese nurse. Surely Sijjin Kuang must have an instrument like her husband's. She returns to the kitchen, where the cooks direct her to the camp clinic, a small shack at the back of the main building that in colonial days had been a stable for horses. There she finds the Sudanese asleep on the mat-covered floor, wrapped in a black robe, her long body folded like a giant bird's. Without waking her, Daniela glances around the modest infirmary, which reminds her of the one at the school where she teaches. A glass-fronted cupboard holds rows of jars and bandages and adhesives, syringes and bottles of disinfectant. On a small table lie a stethoscope and a number of gleaming instruments for probing the orifices of the human head, and there in the corner hangs the blood-pressure machine.

The sleeping nurse-driver is clearly recovering from her navigational adventures of the night before. Daniela quietly retreats to wait on a bench outside. Her headache has not lessened, the little pill her husband gave her is tucked in her hand, and she wonders if she should just swallow it and do without the check-up. But she has the feeling that the touch of Sijjin Kuang's velvety desert fingers might do her even more good than the strong hand of her husband.

She closes her eyes, allowing the peaceful hum of nature to ease her pain a bit. Aromas from the kitchen flow to her through the pure, clear air. Her distaste for kitchen work always rouses her dormant female guilt, so she changes position, lying down on the hard bench and folding her hands beneath her head as a pillow. It can't be that Shuli hid things from her. After the tragedy she would call her sister two or three times a day to give emotional support and have long heart-to-heart talks. Had Shuli known, found out even indirectly, that Yirmi had spent a night on the roof of a Palestinian house in Tulkarm, she would have told her immediately. But Shuli hadn't known. When the couple's sex life came to an end, so did the complete openness with each other.

Relaxation saturates her body, even on the hard bench. She grows drowsy, lulled by the rustle of native grasses. She believes she hears the faint sounds of a flute. Or maybe there is a radio here after all. A soft hand touches her. The Sudanese nurse, tall and serious, has placed a comforting hand on Daniela's shoulder and a finger to her own lips, warning her to keep silent. Don't budge, no sudden moves.

About twenty metres away stands an unfamiliar black animal, like a giant cat, its thick bristly tail erect, raising two front paws with very long curly claws. Its sharp narrow mouth, like a small reptile's, is thrust towards a gold-coloured snake, which rises from the grass with a quivering tongue and audibly exhales, as if into a silent flute.

The two creatures are equally hypnotized, each wary of drawing nearer to the other. The black animal seems capable of subduing the snake with its jaws and claws, and might indeed be designed by nature to do so, yet it hesitates—perhaps it prefers to confront prey less audacious and dangerous. But how to back away from the snake without losing face? How to break off contact without damaging the dignity of its purpose? It therefore growls more loudly and bares its jaws, so that the snake will stop cocking its flashy head and coiling its body with that whispering hiss. But the snake, too, has its pride, and though it cannot swallow or digest such a big black cat, it would at least like to shut it up.

Sijjin Kuang silently leads Daniela into the clinic. It could take a while for those animals to find the courage to disengage, she tells her, keeping her voice down. Did you want me for something? And though Daniela's headache has gone, she asks her anyway to check her blood pressure, and tell her if she should take the pill she has in her hand. The Sudanese nurse willingly complies. Unlike Amotz, she doesn't check her while seated, but has her lie down and asks her not merely to roll up her sleeve but also to remove her blouse.

This is very pleasant for Daniela, and as she hoped and expected, the coal-black skin of the young woman's hands has a rich velvety touch. Sijjin Kuang also takes more care than her husband to strap the cuff properly around her upper arm. Does my white peeled flesh bother this sad young woman? Daniela asks herself. She is upset that Sijjin Kuang, now focused on the movement of the needle in the gauge, has seen only her ageing belly and sagging arms, and not her breasts that have kept their youthful shape.

"Your blood pressure is normal," Sijjin Kuang says in her good English, and helps Daniela get up and put her shirt back on. Beyond the open door it is quiet. During the examination the two animals outside must have mustered the courage to part, or else, who knows, maybe the black catlike animal is now dragging the golden snake, mangled, back to its lair.

"I hear that you had a hard night," Daniela says sympathetically to the nurse as she puts away the instrument. "Yirmiyahu said you got lost a few times," she adds.

Sijjin Kuang smiles, exposing perfect white teeth.

"Your brother-in-law is a spoiled person," she says, astonishing Daniela with a remark that ignores her sympathy, and instead casts an unexpected light on the man she has known since her childhood.

13.

FROM WITHIN THE elevator descending to the depths of the old Knesset he wakes to the ring of his irate daughter-in-law reprimanding him: "What's wrong with you, Grandpa? The kids are waiting for you to light candles."

Agitated, he shakes off a deep, boundless sleep. Here's the rub. When a man like him races between an old prune of eighty and an elderly father spoon-fed in a wheelchair, his sixty-one years seem light as air. But when he's alone in bed, in a dark room, he feels their full weight. Is it merely cumulative fatigue, or has the lack of the wife lying beside him greatly weakened his inherent readiness for the world?

Guilt feelings about the two grandchildren waiting for him by the menorah spur him to action, and with amazing speed he throws on his clothes and, not pausing to wash his face, jumps into his car and races towards his son's house in the twilight of a slow drizzly Friday. As he sits at the Halacha junction in north Tel Aviv, facing a red light that takes forever to change, one scene from his dream returns, half-remembered. It was in the old Knesset. He had come dressed in a technician's uniform, tool box in hand, and a doorman in a visored cap and blue flannel suit let him through the inner door and ushered him into an old elevator, broad and well appointed, the kind he always liked. But instead of taking him up to the third floor, so he could look out at the roof of the apartment of his father's old lover, the doorman pushed the basement button and told him, be prepared for an endless descent, in Turkish times this was a deep cistern.

He phones Efrat to find out whether to buy cake on the way, or ice cream, or something else to please her and the children. No, too late, his daughter-in-law scolds him, this time it's enough just to bring yourself, but hurry, the children are losing patience and will light the candles by themselves. What happened to you? You're usually so punctual.

By now his blood is boiling. As it happens, Efrati, he mutters ironically, I actually work for a living. And he wants to persist and remind this indolent beauty of his sixty-one years, but he remembers his wife's warning to respect her pride, so he hastily hangs up, before a curse can slip from his lips. Yet to preserve his status in the eyes of his grandchildren he can't let himself show up empty-handed, so he stops in front of a brightly lit convenience store.

There, amid a throng of teenagers, the sweet-toothed spirit of his wife descends upon him, and he extravagantly scoops up sweets. Especially inviting are two ornate tubes shaped like canes and stuffed with colourful toffees, and two figurines, a boy and a girl, fashioned of dark chocolate.

Neta and Nadi cling to him with love. The absence of a father automatically raises the grandfather's stock. He hugs and kisses them, then lightly hugs Efrat and brushes her cheek. He first felt free to give her a kiss only after Moran announced their engagement, and over the years, even after the two children, he has never dared show greater affection.

"The sweets only after dinner," he declares didactically, but too late. The detached head of the chocolate boy is already in Nadi's mouth. "You little cannibal," he says, planting a kiss on the toddler, but forbids him to continue eating the body of the headless boy.

The menorah is ready, crowned by the shammash. Ya'ari turns over the box of candles in order to recite properly the blessings printed on the back. It would be poor form to garble the text in front of the children. But suddenly Neta insists that Grandpa say the blessings with a kippah on his head, just like her kindergarten teacher's husband.

Efrat shuffles around in a shabby bathrobe, looking tired and wilted, her pretty face pale and her hair unkempt. Moran phoned in the morning and asked her and the kids to come and visit tomorrow, she tells him as she searches for a kippah. Not easy to find one in this house, not even the paper kind they hand out at funerals. But clever Neta resourcefully cuts a skullcap of sorts from a sheet of red construction paper, fastening it into shape with staples. Ya'ari puts it on with a clownish smile and is about to light the candles when Nadi observes that he is a boy and not a girl and thus requires a kippah, too, so they wait for Neta to produce another cap, which almost covers her little brother's eyes.

Now all is ready, and the excited children demand that the light be turned out so that the candles will "banish the darkness," as the popular song goes. Efrat looks sad, sitting on the sofa in the dark, lost in thought. Is she pregnant again? Ya'ari wonders, excited, as he removes the shammash from its place and lights it, trying to read the first blessing by its glow and then the second. Mechanically, he starts singing "Maoz Tsur," as he hands the candle to Neta, who lights the first candle and the second, then hesitantly hands the shammash over to Nadi, who is already standing on a little chair, poised to light the third and fourth. And when only the fifth is left, Ya'ari takes the shammash and turns to Efrat, Come, Efrati, you light a candle, too. She looks at him distantly and doesn't budge from her seat. I've already lit enough candles on this holiday, give it to Neta, and he gives the shammash to Neta, who lights the fifth candle, and suddenly her brother goes berserk, first trying to knock over the burning menorah, and when his Grandpa stops him, he gets down on his knees like a Muslim at prayer and bangs his head against the floor, wailing furiously—why did his sister light the fifth candle and not he? And there is no way to quell his jealousy other than to extinguish the fifth candle and hand him the shammash. And he's still not satisfied: Why wasn't he the first to light the fifth candle?

Over dinner Ya'ari tells his daughter-in-law and grandchildren about the little elevator that his father built for a Mrs. Bennett in Jerusalem, describing how it rose from the closet in the bedroom directly to the roof, and which part of the Old City you could still see from there. Afterwards he talks about the woman herself, and jokes about the ancient love that was awakened between the builder and his client. His daughter-in-law is interested in the story. The possibility that Moran's grandfather had an adventure in Jerusalem in the 1950s tickles her imagination. She goes back and calculates the dates and years—when the elevator was built, when old Ya'ari's wife died, when the Parkinson's set in. With methodical nosiness she wants to reconstruct the whole picture, to ascertain how long during the life of Moran's grandmother, whom she'd known only in her last two years, did Moran's grandfather keep a secret lover in Jerusalem.

Ya'ari attempts to protect his parents, with little success. Efrat cross-checks the dates and proves to him that his father is no saint. Why should he be a saint? asks Ya'ari. Because you and Daniela want to give the impression that you always do the right thing, that you're perfect people. Ya'ari chuckles. What do you mean, perfect? We have our faults. Of course, his daughter-in-law giggles too and her reddening face reassumes its wonderful sheen. But somehow, she insists, you manage to persuade all of us that your faults are actually virtues. Amotz laughs heartily and keeps his cool. Maybe Daniela, but not me. And he looks approvingly at the blush that has returned to his daughter-in-law's face.

Nadi eats the limbs and body of the chocolate boy and wants to eat Neta's chocolate girl too. But she succeeds in moving it to higher ground, safe from his jaws.

On television, standing beside a fighter jet, the Minister of Defence lights the Hanukkah candles and sings, in a pleasant voice, "He Who performed miracles for our forefathers." Nofar calls and chats affectionately with her sister-in-law and also asks her niece and nephew to kiss her over the phone. Ya'ari hesitantly takes the receiver, wondering with mild trepidation whether the landlords have revealed his impulsive visit to her room. It turns out they kept their promise, but Ya'ari's father did tell his granddaughter about her father's visit to an old client in Jerusalem, and she's disappointed that he didn't think to come and visit her at the hospital. She would have taken him to the trauma unit, where she is now working at her own request, so he could start believing in the resurrection of the dead.

Nadi has ended up on the sofa, asleep. Ya'ari helps his granddaughter put on her pyjamas, covers her with a blanket and reads her a story about a family that doesn't care that a mouse is roaming freely in their house. The dishes are piled in the sink, the tablecloth is stained, the Hanukkah candles dwindle. His restless daughter-in-law paces from room to room, making call after call to find a babysitter, but it turns out that on a Friday night at the height of the holiday no young girl is willing to pass up her friends' party. Listen, Efrati, he says kindly to the desperate woman, I'll stay here this evening with the kids. You also deserve a little joy in your life. She looks up with amazement, not knowing if he's being ironic or serious. But it could be till late, she warns her father-in-law. Whatever you want, he answers graciously. I caught up on my sleep this afternoon; staying up won't be a problem.

Why stay up? his daughter-in-law says. She'll spread a sheet and blanket on the sofa and give him one of Moran's clean T-shirts and a pair of tracksuit bottoms, and he can sleep peacefully here till morning. Now he is taken aback. I don't understand—you're only planning to come home in the morning? No way to know, she says with a mysterious smile. It depends how things go at the party. What things is she talking about? Ya'ari wonders to himself. Maybe he ought to set a curfew for the mother of his grandchildren and get her back here by midnight. But it's too late for that. Efrat has come alive: in an instant the depressed and worn-out housewife has been transformed into a happy young woman, a radiant beauty, her heels clicking proudly about the apartment. She puts on a dress that fashionably exposes all that may and must be exposed of a woman, excepting her nipples, which still belong to her husband, and on her unblemished skin she strews some sort of sparkling stardust, meant to ease the entry of a lovely woman into tonight's banquet of the gods.

From the look she casts his way it's clear she is waiting for a rave review for her performance, but Ya'ari prefers to keep quiet. Daniela has already warned him against giving his daughter-in-law the sort of compliments that a man gives a woman. You do not look at your daughter-in-law through the eyes of a man. Even what was permitted to her father is forbidden to you. Indeed she was right. For as she bends over her sleeping son, lying beside him on the sofa, to determine whether she ought to move him to his bed, the perfumed breasts that nearly brush his face, and in particular the tiny tattoo engraved above one of them, ignite a strange desire that for a brief moment takes his breath away.

"Don't move him. Let him stay here with me. Even if he wakes up, I'll manage with him."

"The main thing," she says, astonishing him, "is not to show signs of fear or weakness, because then he gets crazier."

"Gets crazier? You're not exaggerating?"

To be on the safe side, in case of emergency, she puts *Baby Mozart* into the VCR. From Neta's infancy Ya'ari remembers fondly the little railway cars carrying adorable animals, and the dancing of these animals, and the car that vanishes and then reappears and reconnects and disappears again, and the sea lions sliding and climbing and sliding and climbing, all of this to the masterful music of Mozart, which according to researchers calms the souls of toddlers and at the same time sharpens and broadens their minds. If such a video had been available in my day, Ya'ari likes to complain, I wouldn't only be an engineer today, but rather a major scientist.

Overriding his objections, the gorgeous mother insists on tiptoeing in her high heels into the children's bedroom to say good-bye to her drowsy girl, and to allay any potential separation anxiety by telling her that her grandpa, strong and alert, will protect her from evil spirits or bad dreams. Half-asleep, the girl mews a little protest. For the life of me, Ya'ari protests, I don't see the point of all this frankness. But Efrat's beauty apparently obliges her to report her every movement, so that her husband's imagination will not torment him. Now she wraps herself in a thin blue shawl that matches the colour of her eyes.

"You won't be cold?"

"It's fine, I'll be driven door to door."

And before leaving, glowing with happiness and gratitude, she wants to kiss and hug tightly the available old babysitter, but he pulls away, lightly touching her hair, so that her flesh will not get too close to his.

"Go . . . go . . . you're wasting time."

The moment the door closes a heartrending cry bursts from the bedroom: *Imma, Imma'leh, where are you?* And when he hurries in and turns on the light, he finds his granddaughter, a darling duplicate of the vanished mother, standing in her bed and stubbornly wailing a lament: *Imma, Imma, Imma'leh, where are you? Why did you go?*

Neta is considered a well-behaved and rational child, and compared with her wild brother is sometimes defined as an angel come down from heaven. Ya'ari is therefore certain he will easily be able to calm the crying that has left her anguished and shaking. But when he tries to take her in his arms, she only increases her shrieking, propping her head with her little hand as if it were about to fall off.

He shuts the door to the children's room, so that her cries will not wake her brother, but it's too late. The toddler is pounding on the closed door now with his little fist, and when he enters—barefoot, agitated, red-eyed—he climbs at once onto his bed and sits in a weird cross-legged position, coolly studying his blubbering sister, waving his little foot like a pendulum.

"But I'm here, I'm with you, I'm taking care of you," Ya'ari tries to convince his granddaughter that she has not been abandoned, but her weeping has its own momentum now and nothing will stop it. She is still holding her head in her hand, as if she felt a stroke coming on, and out of that vertigo of lamentation, throttled now and then by deep internal sobbing, throbs the relentless dirge: *Imma, Imma, Imma'leh, where are you? Where did you go?*

Ya'ari is desperate. He anticipated a battle with Nadi, but not with Neta, who is always willing to cooperate. And so, after unsuccessfully trying to calm her with promises, he decides on a new tactic.

"But how can this be, Neta, my darling, a big girl like you, look how your little brother is sitting quietly."

He instantly regrets his words, as a squawk of deep humiliation cuts into the weeping.

So they sit, the three of them, trapped in a loop of lamentation and monotonous wailing whose immediate cause is by now forgotten, as if performing a ritual of ancient, prehistoric loss. And her brother sits on his bed, still waving his foot. He is only two years and a few months old, but his broad, strong face testifies that he is bound to grow into an aggressive man, if not a violent one. He reminds me of somebody. But who? It is a question Ya'ari has asked himself countless times. He smiles softly at his grandson and asks for advice: So what now, Nadi, how do we calm your sister down?

"Nana wants her *Imma*," the toddler sums up the situation for his grandpa.

14.

"I WANTED THE feel of that roof at night, but the military would only approve a visit in the daytime. Finally we compromised on late afternoon, which extended a bit into darkness. The company commander was friendly and tried very hard to satisfy my curiosity and to help me understand. And because he was an experienced and serious officer, who knew the local residents well and wasn't afraid of his shadow, he gave himself the authority to deviate slightly from the instructions of his superiors, and allowed me to remain standing on the roof, on the spot where Eyali stood, until after sundown, when lights began to go on in the houses."

At the African farm, evening is also not far off. Yirmi sits with his back to the open window, facing his bed, where his sister-in-law now lies, with the novel she read slowly through the afternoon spread open at her side.

Yirmi has obviously slept soundly, without interruption. His eyes are wide open, his face is free of anger, and he exudes a pleasant, freshly washed smell. He has exchanged the sweaty clothes of his night-time trip for clean and ironed ones; he knocked delicately on the door to his room and only after verifying that Daniela was not asleep and was quite willing for him to enter did he do so, and turned his desk chair towards the bed and sat down with the luminous African plain stretching behind him.

"And of course it never occurred to Shuli that you were going there."

"Of course not. You think I would scare her, let her worry that she might lose me too in the same place? Even after I went there I told her nothing, because I knew she would be sure, and rightly so, that I would want to go back."

"And you did want to go back . . ."

"I didn't only want to, I did. But alone, without any Israeli beside me."

"And you didn't tell Amotz either."

"That's right. Because I knew that there were no secrets between you two, and the minute you knew—you, who can't keep a shred of a secret—it would get to your sister at the speed of sound."

Daniela tries to object, but she knows he is right: it is hard for her to keep a secret from her loved ones. She pulls at the blanket to cover her bare feet and suddenly longs for her mother, who died two years after Nofar was born.

"But how could you get permission to go onto that roof?" she asks testily.

"It wasn't hard at all, amazingly enough. In the bereavement department of the Defence Ministry there's this little office set up specially to deal with odd requests from parents, or children, or siblings who have lost a loved one. A middle-aged official sits there, himself a father bereaved long ago. He works as a volunteer beside a woman officer who is very skilled and efficient. She makes the connections with army powers that be. A visit by parents to the place where their child fell is not unusual, provided that the area is no longer a war zone, such as Sinai or the Golan Heights or even the Lebanese border. But in the occupied territories it's a complicated affair, because there's no battlefield and yet the whole thing is a battlefield. But they still have enough flexibility to accommodate a parent, or even a brother or sister, who wants to experience the feel of the place where their loved one was killed, and perhaps also to understand why, for what. You get what I'm saying?"

"Every word."

"And my request received special attention. Because we're talking here about intimate gunfire, where even after the official investigation is over there's always some hidden aftergrowth. So one could say that not only did the office move quickly to assist me, they were expecting me."

"What did you want to know?"

"I wanted to check."

"To check what?"

"Why, for the soldiers lying in ambush, he turned from a hunter into the hunted."

"But they explained it to you. He got the time wrong and came down from the roof too early."

"He did not get the time wrong, Daniela. I've already warned you more than once to drop that idea. Eyali was not a man who got the time wrong. The watch they returned to us, which was on his wrist when he was killed, showed the correct time."

"Maybe he got excited, maybe he was scared."

"No, he was not scared. Your Moran was a cowardly child, but not Eyali. Enough of your maybes and don't try to teach me what I know better than you do. Just listen."

She reddens. But she can feel his inner torment, and without saying a word she nods her full attention.

"I had never been to Tulkarm, even though the town is half an hour's drive from Netanya. We once dared go to Hebron, and we visited the Church of the Nativity in Bethlehem. We went to eat at a restaurant in Ramallah, we drove through Jericho, and many years ago we might have also visited Nablus and Jenin. But not Tulkarm. What is there to do in a small border town? Just a town, not terribly neglected, rather clean, with wide streets, avenues, and groves and orchards here and there. And houses of all shapes and sizes. Private homes of one storey, or two or even three. Also houses higher than that. And of course a little refugee camp on the side. But not so bad. It's liveable. There are surely worse places in the land of Israel.

"And sometimes soldiers are assigned to the rooftops. As a lookout, for an ambush. For one night only, or a few nights. And there are some prominent rooftops, strategic ones, where a whole platoon sits for a month. And under those rooftops live people. Families with children, with loves and hates. Not so bad. The world does not collapse. The main thing is to live.

"Remember that our story took place before the second intifada, when the whole thing was a mess, when chaos reigned on both sides. And this officer—he was a successful lawyer who had returned to the army in search of adventure—Eyali's company commander, was on the other side of town altogether that same night, also staking out that notable wanted man, who came to what end I still have no idea. Maybe he's hanging out with the heavenly tribunal, which is what that clown from the security services said, or maybe they gave up looking for him. And this officer, he knows everything, and runs me around Tulkarm as if he were in Ramat-Gan, in a fancy jeep, heavy and armoured, with a silent soldier sitting in it with a machine gun. And he shows me the place where Eyali was shot, near a pile of building materials, standing by a water tap, and he points out to me the doorway of the building he rushed out of and explains where the ambush was, and with his two hands he demonstrates the angle from which the bullets were fired, one and then another. I've still got my agenda of identifying the shooter, so I ask him, By the way, if that's where the shots came from, who was the soldier that fired them? And the officer, an intelligent man, winks at me and says, Why do you care? After all, you've got to know them all, they're all good guys. Why should we incriminate one of them?

"All right, I say to him, then at least let's go up on the roof. It was five o'clock in the afternoon, and I, Daniela, remember every detail. I climb the stairs, and some of the flights have no banister, and here and there the wall isn't plastered either, and I pass open doorways and nod shalom to entire families, children and adults, old men and women, cooking, sewing, doing homework—whole lives in this building, three actual floors, though not completely finished, but with this wide roof in place at the top, full of laundry hanging out to dry, colourful sheets flapping in the wind. And the tenants did not seem surprised that once again the Jews wanted to see the world from the Palestinian rooftop, and if they are bringing along an elderly civilian, it must mean something important."

"When was this exactly?"

"In the autumn. Three months after he was killed. The weather was getting cooler. That mute soldier, with the machine gun, was a Druze, and they picked him in particular so he could translate into Arabic who I was and what I wanted. But there was no need for an interpreter, because among the locals there is always someone who knows Hebrew. For example, a pregnant woman, a lovely young lady studying history at Ruppin College, near Netanya. The soldier who was killed, no, she doesn't remember him, but her father will be home soon from the orchard, and he perhaps knows more about the 'work accident.'"

"Work accident?"

"That's the expression we use when they get killed by their own mistakes—for instance, while preparing a bomb—so they pay us back with the same language; why not? Okay, we're now on the roof, and the Druze soldier leans his machine gun on the railing, and the officer describes the sector for me, and I'm walking around from one side to the other: maybe I'll find some clue, some sign of whatever caused Eyal to come down from the roof in a suspicious manner. And evening starts falling with sort of a blue mist, and the pregnant student, who came up after us, asks if she should take down any laundry, and the officer says there's no need, and he points out to the west, where Israeli lights are going on in the coastal plain, so close, close enough to touch."

"You could see the sea from there?"

"Apparently at one time you could, but today, the new tall buildings block the view. That's what the officer told me. And in his opinion, it's a good thing."

"Why good?"

"So they wouldn't desire the sea as well."

"That's what he said? Disgraceful . . ."

"Maybe it was because his patience was running out. The father, who was supposed to arrive any minute from the orchard, never showed up. Someone apparently told him that Jews were waiting for him on the roof of his house, so he preferred to visit some sick uncle and not undergo another interrogation, where he'd have to repeat everything he had already told the army, that is, nothing of importance. Does this old story interest you at all?"

"Every word."

He gets up and takes a long look out of the window. Then he paces the room for a moment, picks up her novel, has a look inside, and replaces it face down, the way it was.

"What's it about?"

"Not now. If you want, I'll try to finish it before I go home and I'll leave it for you."

"God forbid . . . you insist on not understanding. Don't you dare leave behind one letter of Hebrew."

She gives him a piercing look.

"So the father didn't come. And this pregnant student, who spoke Hebrew quite elegantly and gently, saw that we were getting impatient, so she called in her mother, a woman in traditional Arab dress, chubby, knowing not a word of Hebrew, but with a mischievous spirit. The mother did remember the soldier. She didn't see him, but she had heard something from her husband. In the middle of the night, on his own initiative, he brought Eyali some strong coffee, and also a pail, which the soldier had asked him for."

"On his own he brought him coffee?"

"So he would stay awake. That's the way the daughter explained it. And when I asked her, what did your father care if he was asleep, he wasn't protecting you, but the other way around, the mother looked at me with her warm eyes, and even though she knew I was the father of the soldier who was killed, she said to me unabashedly that her husband was afraid that if the Israeli soldier fell asleep, he would have the urge to kill him. But a soldier who was awake would be able to defend himself. So he brought him strong coffee. And the pregnant student translated all this in her delicate accent, while exchanging mischievous smiles with her mother."

"A complicated Arab. Bringing coffee so he won't have the urge to kill?"

"That's how she translated it. Maybe in Arabic it wasn't exactly an urge but a slightly different word. But so you don't misunderstand, this whole conversation on the roof was in a friendly spirit, everyone smiling. The officer was smiling too; only the Druze with the machine gun stayed serious."

"And then?"

"And then we really did have to get out of there, because by that time we had completely broken the rules, but I knew that this roof would continue to preoccupy me, that I would need to better understand the coffee, the bucket. Maybe that pregnant student, with her sweet lovely Hebrew, was also a factor—I mean, not she herself, but her pregnancy, or more precisely, the idea that the baby she would give birth to would also be crawling around on this rooftop. By the way, did you know that Efrat . . ." He hesitates.

"Efrat what?"

15.

GRADUALLY, NETA'S LAMENT over her treacherous mother subsides. The choked-up cries are quieter, the duration between them grows longer, and the intensity of the anger and anxiety they express diminishes, though as if to preserve their honour they do not cease at once but instead die down slowly. Neta no longer has the strength to stand and hold her head theatrically, and she slowly slides down to sit on her bed, and then, finally, her reedy body folds up into the foetal position. The grandfather does not intervene in this process, but sits patiently, not moving, not uttering a word. From time to time he closes his eyes to lend encouragement to the girl's drowsiness. Nadi watches sternly, then suddenly gets off his bed and leaves the room, and Ya'ari motions with a finger for him to be quiet, so as not to interfere with his sister's collapse into slumber. He waits a while, until sleep has overtaken her entirely, then turns out the light and covers her with a blanket.

In the living room the candles have long since gone out. The only light comes from the kitchen. He looks for the boy, but cannot find him. The exterior door is locked, and so is the door to the terrace. He looks in the bathroom, but the child isn't there. He calls, Nadi, Nadi, but there is no reply. For a moment he is seized with panic, but since his son's apartment is not large, he quickly checks the clothes closets and behind the washing machine, until he remembers the child's favourite hiding place, under his parents' bed. And there indeed lies the boy, like a grey sack. The grandfather turns on the light, but the child screams, Turn it off, turn it off, Nadi isn't here. So then Ya'ari tries to play a game in the dark and pretends to be someone who can't find his grandchild, but this time, safe under his parents' bed, the boy refuses to cooperate with the familiar game and starts screaming. Ya'ari attempts to crawl under and get to him, but the child pushes him away, scratches his hand, crawls out the other side, stamps over to the locked door and begins to kick it with his bare foot.

He doesn't want his mother or his father. His anger goes back to the fifth candle that his sister lit before him. Ya'ari therefore tries to undo the insult by cleaning the remnants of wax from the menorah and replacing all five candles. At first Nadi can hardly believe that his grandfather would go to such lengths to compensate him, but when he sees Grandpa turning on the lights, putting the kippah back on, reciting the blessings again, and placing the burning shammash in his little hand so he can light all five candles, his wrath is soothed and a little smile quivers on his tormented face.

But the smile turns out to be transitory. The spirited toddler, complicated and uncompromising, suddenly decides that a second lighting of candles on the same evening is not the real thing, that it is a ruse on his grandfather's part to pacify his jealousy of his elder sister's birthright. For a minute or two he studies with hostility the five colourful candles and the shammash burning quietly in the menorah, then suddenly blows them out like candles on a birthday cake, knocks the smoking menorah over and shoves it to the ground, then bursts into a scream and runs to the front door and kicks it hard and calls his father's name.

Now he understands that Efrat's warning was not an exaggeration. Moran, apparently out of embarrassment, generally reports to his parents only his little boy's health problems. Ya'ari grabs the child forcefully, rips him away from the door, lifts him up and holds him tight in his arms. Nadi thrashes wildly, trying to get free, menacing his grandfather's hand with his teeth, trying to bite it. But Ya'ari, though surprised by the child's strength, won't loosen his grip.

The toddler's resistance grows weaker, but when Ya'ari lays him down on the sofa and turns off the light, the boy springs up and runs to kick at the front door again, and the blow to his bare foot inspires more desperate howling. Once again Ya'ari is forced to grasp him in his arms. And to distract him, he puts on the *Baby Mozart* tape that Nadi has grown up with, which still works its magic.

And while he clasps the child in his arms in the dark, trains and ladders begin moving on the screen, and fountains and seesaws, cloth dolls of friendly animals, and the marvellously simple music of a composer who died in the prime of life reconcile a grandfather and his grandson.

The child's attention is focused on the sights and sounds so familiar to him, but it's hard to tell whether he's still trying to break free of his grandfather or clinging to him tightly. Ya'ari remains on his feet because when he tries to sit down on the sofa, the child bursts into a shriek of protest. And so they stand there, while delightful images flicker past them, conceived by well-meaning educators in tranquil California, and after the last note is played, and the screen goes dark, the child mumbles feebly, Again, Grandpa...

And Ya'ari has no choice but to rewind the tape.

Now, with his grandson's head on his shoulder, Ya'ari has a moment to study closely the contours of his face; he finally identifies the memory that eluded him, understanding why it escaped him before. Many years ago he also stood in the dark clutching a toddler in his arms, one who resembled this grandson. But that had been in silence, without musical accompaniment. It was on a visit to Jerusalem, before Moran was born, when he and Daniela had offered to babysit little Eyali so that Shuli and Yirmi could go out and enjoy themselves—and so he and Daniela would have a quiet hideaway for lengthy lovemaking.

The infant image of the nephew who was killed by friendly fire, flung out of the distant past and caught again in his arms, suffuses Ya'ari with a pain diluted by sweet nostalgia for his own youth. To the music of Mozart he hugs his little grandson tight, as if to inoculate him with the strong confidence he has acquired during his own life.

When the Mozart tape completes its second screening, and Nadi mumbles, half-asleep, More, Grandpa, he decides not to replay the pleasant tunes a third time, but to try a fresh approach with a different video. And from the stack of tapes he grabs one from an unmarked box.

As soon as it starts to run he realizes that he has made a mistake, yet he does not stop it. This is not a tape for children, this is not even a tape for grown-ups, this is a tape that he would never have suspected his son and daughter-in-law of taking an interest in.

Although in recent years sex scenes even in mainstream films have become more brazenly explicit, they are brief—it always seems to Ya'ari that the actors are afraid they won't be up to the task when called upon to feign passion that is not their own. But this video has no story or plot, no hidden relationships among its characters: their sole purpose is to have sex, natural, open sex without impersonation or shame, accompanied by the thumping of an unseen drum.

His sleep-heavy grandson is straining his arms, and he extends a finger to stop the cassette, but the expression on the face of a young cropped-haired woman as an older man undresses her arrests him. Something in her embarrassed smile and her instinctive attempt to hide her breasts and shield her nakedness indicates that this pretty young woman is not accustomed to making love in front of the camera. It might well be the debut of a hard-up American student looking to finance her education.

The young woman closes her eyes, throws back her head and opens her mouth wide, but her body keeps wrestling with the man who will soon demand everything from her, and this panic mixed with pleasure fascinates the viewer in the dark. Distant memories of his young wife in the days following their wedding stir his desire.

And then he hurries to turn off the cassette, he snatches it from the tape player and returns it to its box, then sticks it into the middle of the stack of tapes. He carries the sleeping toddler to his bed, changes his nappy for the night, and covers him with a blanket.

16.

"WHAT DOES EFRAT have to do with this?" Again she demands an answer.

Beyond the open window, on the horizon, the moon has shed the diaphanous haze and gleams sharp and bright.

"Efrat herself obviously has nothing to do with this," Yirmiyahu says finally. "By the way, when exactly was Nadi born? Do you know you almost didn't tell us about him?"

"Nadi was born after I was here with Amotz, and at that point I didn't think Shuli was much interested in relatives."

Yirmi falls silent. He gets up from the chair and again walks around the room. Once more he distractedly picks up the novel, reads a few sentences, then puts it down. Daniela says nothing, waits.

"Yet still, her pregnancy turned out to be relevant. Because not long after your visit here, we got a letter from her, telling us that she was expecting."

"A letter from Efrat? Why did she write to you? What did she want from you?"

"She asked our permission to call the boy she was expecting Eyal."

"Really?" Daniela is astounded. "I had no idea . . . she didn't say a thing. She wrote in her own name, or Moran's too?"

"Only her own. She wrote that Moran didn't know of her wish. What surprised us was that at the end of the fourth or fifth month she was already talking so confidently about her son and planning his name."

"Yirmi, nowadays, not like in our time, the scanning they do of the embryo is so comprehensive and precise, that you can know not only its sex but also the condition of every organ in its body. You can even predict if the developing child will be nice or not."

"And if he won't be nice, what then?"

"That depends on the parents." Her eyes smile, but a bit sadly, and her heart suddenly goes out to her daughter-in-law.

"So how was the birth?"

"Difficult. They had to get him out by Caesarian, he got into trouble and turned the wrong way round. But how did you respond to her? I hope you didn't hurt her."

"I don't know exactly what went through Shuli's mind when we got the letter, because I didn't even give her a chance to think it over. That very minute I wrote to Efrat my absolute refusal. I thanked her warmly for her touching intentions, yes, definitely touching, but unthinkable. You think about it, too, Daniela: Why put the burden of the dead on a child not yet born? And if I was already starting to detach, the last thing I needed was to entangle my mind with a new human being. By the way, what kind of child did he turn into? Nice or not?"

Sixth Candle

1.

WHEN SHE GETS home she is careful not to turn on any lights, so as not to call attention to the lateness of the hour, but when she sees her babysitter lying curled on the sofa in his clothes and shoes, she nudges him gently. For a moment Ya'ari imagines that his wife has returned from Africa, and the thought of the end of the journey showers joy on his sleeping soul. But the voice of his daughter-in-law, imploring him to take off his shoes and put on Moran's T-shirt and tracksuit bottoms, dissolves his dream in a flash. The Hanukkah party has redoubled Efrat's radiance; luckily, her flimsy shawl is still draped around her shoulders, so he won't have to deal again in the dark with the perfumed cleavage of the young woman who is leaning over him at 2:15 in the morning and wondering why he didn't get himself better organized for bed.

"Your children wore me out so much, that even your hard sofa managed to put me to sleep."

Efrat is surprised that a technical expert like him didn't realize that this sofa can be opened out. She left him a sheet and blanket, after all, plus clean tracksuit bottoms, so why didn't he make up a bed and go to sleep? Get up, get up, I'll teach you how the sofa opens . . . it's really simple.

"No, forget it, Efrati, I'm going home."

But pangs of conscience over the delightful party that ran so late harden her in her refusal to accept the night-time departure of the grandfather who executed his duty so faithfully. No, she will not let him drive on a holiday weekend night, when the drunks have begun to take to the road. Moran would not forgive her if something should happen to him. And she tugs his arm and stands him on his feet, and with uncharacteristic speed opens the sofa, to prove to him that comfortable sleep is also possible at her house. She fits the sheet and spreads the blanket, and hands him the folded T-shirt and tracksuit bottoms. No, says her stern gaze, you are not as young and strong as you think. Lie down, and I'll close the blinds so the sun won't wake you. And in the morning I'll make sure the kids don't bother you.

"Please, Amotz," she says, "do it for me, wait till it gets light."

He cannot remember this beauty ever pleading, to him or to others. Maybe, through him, she is trying to expiate some guilt that's weighing on her.

"The sun is unimportant," he mumbles as he sees her flipping the switch and lowering all the blinds. "In any case I get up before it does."

And though it seems so easy and natural to go home, he surrenders to his daughter-in-law, who apparently turns into an efficient homemaker only at the dead of night. She drops the shawl from her shoulders and brings him another pillow, then bare-armed she slaps it again and again, as if it were the source of sin in her home, and gives him a clean towel and quickly departs, to enable him to change from his wrinkled clothes into his son's nightwear.

Although the tracksuit bottoms belong to the fruit of his own loins, he is reluctant to slip into them, not least for fear they'll be tight on him. He puts on only the T-shirt, and lifts the blinds a bit so the sun will not forget him. Then he lies down on his back on the wide sofa bed and covers himself with the blanket.

In fact, he has never before spent a whole night at his son's home. In the early days after Nadi's Caesarian birth, when Daniela stayed to help Moran out, sometimes remaining all night, he would always go home to sleep. And now, for no reason, even though his own bed is only a few kilometres from here, he has agreed to stay with his grandchildren, lying close to where his daughter-in-law readies herself for sleep. She takes an endless shower, and even after the slit of light under her closed door has gone out, music is still playing in her room, soft and annoying.

If he were to leave now, she couldn't stop him. But his fear that she will sleep through the morning while the children wander around the house neglected gets him to his feet only to knock on her door and whisper irritably: Efrati, if you want me to stay here, at least turn down that weird music.

2.

THAT SAME ANTICIPATED sun will rise too late to wake his wife in East Africa. Well before dawn, she is roused by the engine noise of the two pickup trucks delivering the scientific team to the base camp for their weekend break. From her high window, under a sky still swirling with stars, she can make out the silhouettes of a few of them as they alight from the vehicles, dragging knapsacks and duffel bags.

Tonight, the head of the team, the Tanzanian Seloha Abu, and the Ugandan archaeologist, Dr. Kukiriza, are tired, silent, and lost in thought, like soldiers returning from a difficult mission or arduous training. They even had a casualty: the Tunisian woman, Zohara al-Ukbi, ill with malaria. They carefully lower her onto a stretcher. The circle of respect and concern that forms around her is soon joined by the white administrator and the Sudanese nurse, who lean in the dim light towards her suffering face, wish her well, and obtain her permission to house her in the infirmary.

One after another the scientists disappear through the main doorway en route to their rooms on the first and second floors, leaving behind them cardboard boxes filled with fossils and fragments of rock. And the elderly groundskeeper, as their loyal friend and devoted chaperon, takes all of these into the kitchen.

Perhaps because of the old elevator shaft that never housed an elevator, echoes of the scientists' voices filter into her room, and the sound of a lively flow in the water pipes testifies that it's not sleep the exhausted diggers want most, but a quick return to a civilized condition.

Though it is not yet four A.M., and she is entitled to go back to bed, Daniela realizes that the presence of the team will make it impossible for her to recover her interrupted sleep. And so when the first rays of light begin to pierce the big kitchen windows, the Israeli guest appears, washed and smiling and properly made up, and is greeted convivially by the two South African geologists, who have decided on a big breakfast before they shower or sleep. Because they still appreciatively remember the tourist's rapt attention to the comments of their colleague Kukiriza, and have not forgotten their own silence on that occasion, they invite the white woman to join in their meal, so they can expand her understanding of the scientific purpose of the dig, this time from a geological standpoint.

"We wanted to tell you," says one of them, "that Jeremy surprised us when he brought you along three days ago, and the interest you showed in the work of the team made us very happy. It is clear to us, of course, that this interest is only out of politeness, yet the way in which you asked and listened left a good taste with all of us, and when we heard you were still here, and we would meet you again, we had another reason to be glad about our weekend. Am I exaggerating?" He suddenly turns with concern to his friend, who has been nodding in spirited agreement while scrambling egg after egg and mixing in chopped vegetables and bits of sausage.

"You see," the first geologist continues, "we work in total isolation. Our excavation site does not appear on any tourist route, and so visitors do not happen by, not even black people, so that we may explain to them what we aim to achieve. The only two whites we've seen came to us one year ago, and they were representatives of UNESCO in Paris, financial people who were not here to take an interest and to learn, but only to make sure that we were not needlessly wasting money. Our connection with universities and research institutes is only by correspondence, and before we get an answer so much time passes, that we almost forget what the question was. Therefore, we greatly appreciate all interest, even what comes by chance. Your brother-in-law is an honest and efficient man, but he finds it hard to understand our intentions. The more we try to explain to him what we are looking for, the more he gets confused about periods, not by thousands of years but by millions. But of course dating is the heart of the matter, the main struggle we face. This is what gives importance to the stones that capture or encase the fossils; here is manifested the contribution of the geologist, without which no evolutionary conclusion may be drawn to explain who survived and why they survived, who became extinct and why, and what price was paid by the survivor, and who benefited from the extinction."

Daniela flashes a pleasant smile at the exuberant young man, whose English is almost a mother tongue. And before the huge omelette bubbling in the skillet finishes capturing and encasing the vegetables and meat, he hastens to set on the table, as an appetizer, a fragment of rock to illustrate his lecture.

Now, in the brightening light of day, she learns that the two young men are M.A. candidates from the University of Durban, Absalom Vilkazi and Sifu Sumana, and Daniela listens to their explanations appreciatively and patiently, with the mature serenity of a woman who will be sixty in three years but is unconcerned by her advancing age, trusting in the faithfulness of her husband.

3.

EVEN ON THIS grey, wintry Saturday morning, the children get up early. He senses the feathery footsteps of his granddaughter, who approaches the sofa to check whether Grandpa has been replaced in the middle of the night by a subcontractor; and she doesn't settle for the familiar head resting on the pillow, but pulls down the blanket a little to confirm that the body is his as well. She does this cautiously and with restraint, despite the laughter which seems about to erupt from inside her, and Ya'ari clamps his eyelids tight and keeps his face towards the wall, curious to see how his granddaughter will handle his slumber. First she tries to tug lightly at his hair, and when there is no response, she tickles the back of his neck; she seems caught between a desire to wake him and reluctance to make outright contact with an old man's strange body. Ya'ari remains frozen, still and unmoving. I know, Grandpa, that you're not asleep, a sweet whisper wafts by his ear, but he, face to the wall, stubbornly refuses to respond. She hesitates, then climbs onto the sofa, hops over his body in her bare feet, and installs herself between him and the wall. With a small but determined hand she now tries to pry open his eyes. I know you're not asleep, she says with self-justification.

Ya'ari pops open his eyes. See, she declares victoriously, I knew you weren't asleep. And then, without a word, he sweeps up the blanket and pulls it over his five-year-old granddaughter, the carbon copy of her mother. He speaks straight into the blue eyes that dance with laughter, demanding an explanation:

"Why did you cry last night, after Imma left? You know that I know how to take care of you just like Grandma Daniela. So tell me, why did you keep crying like that? Just to make me crazy?"

The girl listens attentively, but seems disinclined to answer. The laughter in her eyes subsides a bit, and still clutched in his embrace, she tries to evade the gaze that seeks to probe her hidden thoughts. Since she is his first grandchild, she has always received the royal treatment. From her earliest years she got used to climbing into their bed at their house, lying between him and Daniela and chatting about life. But now, instead of a forgiving and indulgent grandma, on her other side there is only a bare silent wall, and she seems to start feeling mildly anxious next to the grandfather who insists on an explanation for the crying marathon.

"Do you remember how you held your head, as if it were going to fall off?"

Her pupils contract with the effort of recollection, and she gives a little nod of confirmation.

"And do you remember," Ya'ari persists, "how you wailed away for half the night, *Imma, where are you? Why did you go? You remember?*"

The child nods slowly, shocked or scared by the grandpa who imitates her voice and her plaintive words.

"Why couldn't you calm down? What was upsetting you? Why wasn't I enough for you? Explain it to me, darling Neta, you know how much I love you."

She listens to him intensely, then sits upright, and with the quickness of a small animal throws off the blanket and jumps off the sofa bed.

But he seizes her little arm.

"If you love your mother so much, why are you waking me up this morning and not her?"

Her eyes open wide with astonished humiliation, and Ya'ari senses that his facetious rebuke went too far and the girl might begin a new round of weeping, and so, before she can bolt for her parents' closed bedroom door, he smiles at her forgivingly, and points at her little brother, just darting in from the children's room, his big head of hair dishevelled and his eyes red, squinting balefully at the light as he climbs automatically into his high chair, which stands next to the dining table.

"And here's your lovely little brother," he adds, trying to

dampen her resentment, "who right after you stopped crying and went to sleep, began to cry and go wild. You remember, Nadi, how you went wild last night?"

The child nods.

"You remember how you kicked the door?"

The toddler glances at the door.

"What did the door do to you, that you kicked it like that?"

Nadi tries to think what the door did to him, but his sister spares him the trouble of answering.

"He always kicks the door after Imma leaves."

Ya'ari is relieved.

"Doesn't your foot hurt when you kick the door?"

Nadi soberly examines his bare foot.

"Yes," he whispers.

"So is kicking a good idea?"

The child has no answer, but the similarity to that other, faraway child still flickers in his face.

"So tell me now, kids," says Ya'ari, trying to get to the root of the mystery, "am I right that you cried and acted wild because you miss your Abba who has gone to the army?"

His suggestion seems reasonable enough to Neta, who despite everything wants to please her grandfather, but Nadi furrows his brow as if wondering whether this is the right answer, or if a deeper one lies behind it.

"So today, if you'll be good children, we'll take you to see your Abba in the army, and now let's eat some cornflakes."

And he pours the golden cereal into two colourful plastic bowls, adding milk according to each child's specific instructions.

4.

DANIELA TAKES A knife and fork and begins to eat the omelette, which is rosy with meat and vegetables, while studying the black concave basalt stone that sits between her plate and coffee cup. This is a meaningful stone, laden with history, placed there to serve as a useful accessory in clarifying for the courteous listener not only how one can tell when *Australopithecus boisei*, that "eating machine," branched off the path clearly leading from chimpanzees to *Homo sapiens*, but also whether the conventional assessment, which holds that this ape ran into an evolutionary dead end, is in fact correct.

Because when we discover fossils from animals or creatures of a humanoid nature—a wisdom tooth, a wrist bone, a solitary finger—embedded in ancient rock, the excavators must be religiously careful also to preserve the evidence of their surroundings. Especially the encasing rock, because that's where invaluable information is hidden that only a geologist can decipher, not merely regarding the date, which is determined by radioactive analysis, but also the question of whether this rock is a medium that just happened to capture a fragment of the prehistoric creature, or whether it might also be a tool dropped from its hand. For if the ancient being knew how to use this stone to crack open his nuts, he should be upgraded a rung on the human ladder. Here is where the paleoanthropologists are dependent upon the professional eye of the geologist, and two heads are better than one. Only geologists are trained to determine whether a simple stone, like this one on the table, which is about one million six hundred thousand years old, is carrying a foetus inside.

"A foetus?" Daniela is so shocked she drops her fork.

"A metaphorical foetus," explains the second geologist, Sifu Sumana, who till now has been quietly focused on eating the last of the giant omelette straight from the pan.

"In other words," elaborates Absalom Vilkazi, "a stone that has swallowed up another, more ancient, stone, whose erosion in a particular spot indicates that it was not just any stone, but rather served as an implement, a tool in the hands of an *Australopithecus boisei,* and even if he himself was removed from the chain of evolution en route to the great destination of the creation of man, his spirit has nonetheless not disappeared; it continues to exist."

"His spirit?" she whispers.

"Perhaps you have forgotten, dear lady," the South African geologist says in a triumphant tone, "that two and a half million years ago our Africa was naturally joined to Asia and Europe. No sea or ocean separated them. And our *Australopithecus boisei,* whose traces we are seeking—this great African ape who despaired of his future on this continent—travelled from Africa to Europe and contributed the genes of the bulimic 'eating machine' to the civilization that developed there."

She looks closely into his eyes to see if there is a spark of humour.

"Now you are joking."

"Why?" the South African says innocently, even as mischievous laughter dances in his eyes.

His youth, flowering in the morning light, appeals to her. His English sounds natural and fluent, even though with his parents he would probably speak Zulu or Sesotho. Without a doubt, Daniela thinks, the elimination of apartheid has made this black man stand taller, and now, as he is confident in his identity, he is trying to challenge smug and prosperous Europe, as an equal. And suddenly her heart aches for Moran, confined by the army, who doesn't understand that the conflict that poisons his homeland also diminishes his stature and undermines his identity, and in her train of thought Nofar and Efrat and Neta and Nadav are linked with Moran, and with beloved former students, and with the youngsters she'll return to after the Hanukkah vacation. Here they are in her mind's eye, sitting in the classroom decorated with posters and newspaper clippings, and among them she can make out the heartbreaking shadow of her nephew, who has descended from Jerusalem to the coast and joined her class to claim his place in the tears now clouding her gaze.

Absalom Vilkazi senses the unhappiness that suddenly silences the white lady, older than his own mother, and he is worried that she interprets the absurd migration of the prehistoric ape to Europe as an insult to her intelligence. And he therefore takes the liberty of gently laying a pacifying hand on her shoulder, as he does with his mother, and says, I was only joking, I apologize.

5.

"You're at our house?" Moran is surprised when his father picks up the phone. "Did something happen?"

With businesslike conciseness Ya'ari informs him of his spontaneous volunteering for the post of babysitter, and very considerately spares him the tale of his children's night-time rampage.

"But which party did she go to?"

"I didn't ask and she didn't say. I only made sure she had her cell phone with her, because it always makes me nervous when she goes around without it."

"So why did you stay till the morning? You fell asleep and didn't realize she had come home, or she's still not back?"

"No, no, what's the matter with you? What a thought! She's here, but asleep. She got back after midnight and begged me not to drive home at night, then was so quick to open up the sofa that I gave in."

"You're also impressed by her aggressive pleading?"

"Why aggressive?"

"Not important."

"Why not important?"

"Forget it, Abba . . . it's not important . . . keep talking."

Ya'ari senses his son's deep disappointment in himself, in his wife, maybe even in his father.

"What's going on, son?" he says softly.

He's sick of it. This inane punishment in the name of solidarity is getting on his nerves. Yes, at first he was a little glad of the enforced detachment from the world, from Efrat, the kids, the office, and, sure, a demanding father too. It was nice to be able to nap mid-morning, or before dinner, without accounting to anyone. But over the past two days his tranquillity has evaporated. Last night he kept tossing on his smelly army mattress, his mind full of nonsense, such as how to save his white queen from the black knights of that hare-brained adjutant.

"Ah," says Ya'ari, laughing, "the redhead has already drafted you to play chess with him?"

"After I started beating him at backgammon."

"Wait a second, Moran, you want to say something to the children? They're here with me in the kitchen, eating cornflakes. Looking at me."

"No, Abba, not now, there's no time, I'll see them soon anyhow. Just do me a favour, go into Efrat's room and get her out of bed. Because if she doesn't start getting organized to leave, she won't make it here to see me. We're attached to a base of recruits, and visiting hours are strict. Only till early afternoon. Tell her to hurry. The drive won't be so simple; it's been raining cats and dogs for the last few hours."

"In Tel Aviv it's actually like spring, clear blue skies. This country isn't as tiny as people think. So listen, I have an idea, I'll bring everyone to you in my car . . . it'll be safer that way."

"But will you have patience for all of us after not sleeping all night on the sofa?"

"It wasn't so bad—it even turned into a bed at three in the morning."

Despite the authorization that he received from his son, Ya'ari does not even consider entering Efrat's bedroom, but instead knocks hard on the door. When he is persuaded that she has regained consciousness, he conveys her husband's instructions in a stern no-nonsense tone.

"Oh, Amotz, it would be wonderful if you would drive us."

"And even more wonderful if you would finally get up on your feet."

The two grandchildren are glad that it won't be their mother driving them to their father, but Grandpa, in the big car, and so without argument they don the clothes chosen by their mother, and like two little bear cubs, clumsily bundled in warm coats, they agree happily to help Ya'ari move the child seats from car to car and show him how to strap them into place. Meanwhile Efrat proves that when she wants to, she can be quick and efficient even in the morning, and she prepares sandwiches and peels vegetables, spreads hummus inside pitas, adds oranges and little bottles of chocolate milk. And when she comes down to the car with the big cooler, pale and without makeup, wearing clunky sneakers, threadbare jeans and an old oversize army jacket that seems intended to obscure her figure—it occurs to Ya'ari that she means to punish herself and join in her husband's confinement.

Even on this wintry Sabbath morning the coastal road is packed. There's no knowing whether it is the children dragging their parents into the nervous traffic, or the guilt-ridden parents dragging their children to amusements and shopping on the day of rest. But the northerly rains reported by Moran are now compounded by a stiff wind from the east, which buffets the car with such force that Ya'ari has to hold the wheel with both hands. Since there are no tapes of simple Israeli songs likely to distract the children in his car, Efrat attempts to entertain them with a game of "Opposites," and Ya'ari gathers that opposition is well entrenched in his daughter-in-law. Quickly and effortlessly she comes up with nouns and adjectives, confident that each word has an antonym her children will know.

And so the highway slips northwards between day and night, hot and cold, dry and wet, summer and winter, clever and stupid, tall and short, ceiling and floor, happy and sad, clean and dirty, straight and crooked, husband and wife, sun and moon, door and wall, dead and alive. And since Neta already knows the answers, she fires them off before her little brother can even come close, and though his mother and grandfather try to make her give the toddler a chance, his sister is incapable of curbing her enthusiasm for opposites, and Efrat apparently doesn't want to deprive her of the pleasure.

In the rearview mirror Ya'ari notices his grandson's mounting fury. If he were able to free himself of the straps that bind him, he'd climb out of the chair and start kicking the car door hard.

"Enough is enough with these opposites," Ya'ari orders Efrat and Neta, "the boy's about to explode."

After the Caesarea exit the traffic gets heavier. It's the first parents' day for the new recruits, and entire families are hurrying to the camp to supplement their food and other needs. The rain has stopped, but the area in front of the base is full of puddles, among which barbecues have been set up and picnic tables unfolded and chairs positioned, and here and there shelters against the rain. And between the charcoal barbecues and the coolers that spot the scene with orange, green, and blue, are Israelis of every sort, veteran and rooted, immigrants recent and otherwise, Russians and Ethiopians; and the recruits in their new uniforms, sitting opposite their adoring parents, diligently downing the meats and the salads, the home-cooked chicken schnitzels, as if over the past month a great famine had afflicted the military camps.

But where is Moran?

Efrat waits in the car with Neta, and Ya'ari goes off with Nadi in his arms towards the front gate, walks by the checkpost, surveys the tall guard, stares into the camp, but among the recruits going in and out there is no sign of the confined soldier who protects his white queen from the black knights. Until finally someone grabs him from behind, pulls the boy from his arms and lifts him high in the air.

Moran is unshaven, red-eyed. In an old work uniform.

"Abba," says Nadi, fluttering in the air, overjoyed, "you are alive?"

6.

YIRMIYAHU STUDIES DANIELA with wonder as she sits in a puddle of light opposite the dirty breakfast dishes and listens with infinite patience to the geologist, who has broken a rock just for her and out of its fragments is trying to furnish her with a short history of time.

"Very good," he praises his sister-in-law. "I see that the young ones are also making good use of your patience. It's okay if you don't understand the explanations; the main thing is the listening. Just wait, soon the others will come down and arrange a symposium for you. In the meantime, Sijjin Kuang will take the malaria patient to a clinic not far away, and be back this afternoon."

"There's another clinic in the area?"

"Not exactly a clinic, more like a sanatorium."

"A real sanatorium?"

"Actual but not real," he says jokingly. "Sort of a health retreat, a rehabilitation or recuperation facility for those who want to get away from the world into the bosom of nature in Africa, at low cost and without the annoyances of modern civilization. Not a sanatorium like the Swiss Alps, but operating on the same principle."

"Is there room for me?"

"Where?"

"With you in the car."

"Why not? But as always, you'll have to sit in the back, and this time you'll need to take up less room, because the patient will be beside you. Nothing to be afraid of, malaria is not a contagious disease. The cause is not a virus or bacteria, but rather a parasite, carried by mosquitoes. And the mosquito that bit Zohara al-Ukbi—it's always female, never a male mosquito—is already gone from this world."

"If you're sure you're not endangering me, then why don't I come along, really? I'm leaving here in two days, so I should finally have some idea of the area where you've decided to hide yourself."

She apologizes to the young men for leaving, and secretly hopes that maybe on the way to the sanatorium she'll have a chance to see another breathtaking genetic mutation. As she leaves the kitchen, Sijjin Kuang is already revving the car engine, and before Daniela takes her regular seat in the back, she greets the Sudanese driver, and seeing her sad expression she wells with deep affection for the gentle animist, bends over, and lightly touches her lips to the ebony cheek. And the nurse, surprised by this unanticipated gesture, lays a hand as delicate as a bird's wing on the youthful hair of the older woman and says, it's good that you are coming with us.

The young North African woman, by turns hot and shivering from the parasite in her blood, is also happy to see the passenger wedged alongside her, and from under the blanket that swaddles her she extends a friendly, fevered hand. *Ahalan wa-sahalan, Madame,* she whispers to the Israeli, it is good that you, too, are with me.

The Land Rover turns south, where the dirt road is so smooth that the murmur of the tyres envelops Daniela in drowsiness despite the early morning hour. Since this isn't the right moment to be interviewing the malarial paleontologist about her profession and role in the research programme and expecting answers a layman might understand, the healthy passenger prefers to join the sick one in closing her eyes and basking in the pleasant warmth of the sun that keeps them company.

The ride is short, less than an hour, and when the car arrives none too soon at its destination, Daniela has the feeling that although the guilty mosquito is no longer alive, the parasite of indolence has nonetheless sneaked into her blood and jumbled her senses. When her brother-in-law opens the rear door, lifts the young Arab woman in his arms, lays her carefully on a stretcher and covers her, and he and an orderly carry her into the building—the Israeli is overtaken by a strange desire that the same be done with her, and since there is no one around who can guess what she wants, she stays frozen in place and waits for the helping hand of the driver.

The sanatorium, too, was once a colonial farm, and on the outside its main building is the base camp's twin, but the interior is very different. Here they are not greeted by a huge kitchen with sinks and stoves but rather by a small lobby, with a reception desk of black wood that looks as if it once served as the cocktail bar. Black leather armchairs sit in a semicircle with their backs to the counter, facing a large window with a view to a horizon so distant that even in the strong noon sunlight it takes on a grey penumbra.

The elevator that never found a home at the headquarters

of the scientific team works nicely here, with an ancient and agreeable rumble. When its grille opens, an affable-looking Indian doctor steps out to welcome the malaria patient, who has not come here to die, heaven forbid, but only to get stronger. While the doctor introduces himself to Zohara, Yirmiyahu brings to his sister-in-law's attention the fact that the senior personnel here are not Africans, but Indians who have crossed the ocean. Europeans, especially elderly middle-class Englishmen, have great faith in the ability of Indians to provide superior care, physical and spiritual, to those who wish to be braced and pampered as they prepare for death.

Through the big window a small swimming pool may be seen, and several wild animals stroll about, kept on the premises so that their beauty and serenity will offer comfort to the patients' souls as their bodies slowly expire. And while a room is made ready for the malaria patient, she is fed clear chicken broth, routinely kept on a burner that sits among the bottles of whisky and gin.

The Sudanese speaks quietly in Arabic with the sick woman, whose chills have been eased by the hot soup. And Yirmiyahu, settled deeply into a leather armchair, continues to lecture his sister-in-law about the uniqueness of this institution even as she imagines some sleep-inducing parasite wide awake in her own blood.

Though the building appears modest and does not have a great many rooms, it can't be called a clinic, or a small hotel either. It is a sanatorium, a treatment home, giving medical care to both body and mind. And just as the reputations of convalescent facilities in the rest of the world are measured by the beauty of their settings—snowy mountaintops, hidden lakes—here, too, nature is extraordinary, both for its primal quality and for the wild creatures who move through it without fear of human beings.

But the real test of such institutions is the nature and level of the services they offer to the patients who come and remain of their own free will. Make no mistake: this place, despite its modesty and isolation, acquits itself most honourably when it comes to efficiency and the range of services it offers; it also stands out for its low cost. For who comes here? In general, lonely old people, who are not affluent and who can no longer rely on the forebearance of their relatives and friends. Widowers and widows whose children have grown distant, or elderly couples who never had children at all, or had them and lost them in tragic circumstances. People who are drawn to this place are most often those who spent their lives serving others. Here, at a reasonable price, they can get reciprocal service to their heart's content: a young man or woman who will sit at their bedside all night long and hold their hand to ward off nightmares; not just someone to tidy up their room but also someone to sing and dance for them on request, or even an old grandmother who will sit in a corner and knit them a scarf, with a black baby crawling at her feet.

At first glance the place will seem quiet to her, Yirmi continues, or even a bit desolate, yet this, too, is one of its virtues. All in all, this is a cloistered place. But half a kilometre away is a small village full of men and women, teenagers and children, who may be brought in for any task, so that a guest who is able and ready to submit his body and maybe his soul to the ministrations of others may enjoy services that in the past were enjoyed only by noblemen and princes. And precisely because these are servants who for the most part do not understand the guest's language, there is a limit to the intimacy. Yes, for a very modest fee, acceptable in the region, there are people here willing to provide service that would make the care Amotz's father receives from his Filipinos look meagre and boring; the villagers are most eager to cater to the whims of the whites, even to be summoned in the middle of the night. It is almost, if you will, a reversion to slavery, but out of free choice.

"And this is acceptable to you?"

"What's wrong with it, if it satisfies both sides?"

She regards the big man in the faded leather chair with hostility.

"And it satisfies you too?"

"It's a possibility. After the excavation team completes its project, maybe it'll be worth my while to come here for treatment . . . but only on condition that they upgrade my painkillers."

An Indian chambermaid comes to take the patient up to her room, but the latter is reluctant to go and asks that Sijjin Kuang accompany her. The two Israelis stand up, and the administrator promises Zohara that in ten days they will come back to get her.

"And you, Madame?" The Arab woman turns to the Israeli visitor, "You will still be here when I get well?"

"No," says Daniela, "by then I won't be in Africa; my school holidays end in two days. And perhaps my students don't miss me so much, but I hope that my husband and children and grandchildren want me back."

"Then come again to Africa, Madame," whispers the young woman.

7.

EVEN FROM A distance Neta can see Nadi's triumphant expression as he sails over people's heads, and she cries out, "Abba, Abba, I'm here, too," and gets out of the car, and weaves her way, lithe and nimble, among the barbecues and coolers. Moran hugs and kisses her lovingly, and since she also claims a place on her father's shoulders, and her brother is unwilling to cede his perch, the confined soldier piles her on too and walks to the car, his father following. Watch it, you'll put your back out, warns Ya'ari.

Efrat sits in the car talking on her cell phone, not budging even when Moran sets the children down and opens the door. Who are you talking to now? My sister, she answers impatiently, without looking at him. It has to be now? he fumes. Yes, now. You haven't talked to her enough? He's livid. But she doesn't respond and turns her back on him. And then he grabs the phone from her hand and says, enough, don't go too far.

To distract the children from their parents the grandpa steers them to the boot to help him take the sandwiches and vegetables and oranges out of the cooler, and to arrange them all nicely on an old oilcloth. It is Daniela who generally tries to decipher her son's marital frictions, but she's far away in Africa, and he has to manoeuvre alone through this outbreak of hostilities.

One evening, in the empty office, in a rare moment of soul-baring, Moran confessed that his wife's good looks were not only a source of pride for him, but also a heavy burden. Her beauty makes her more vulnerable to men. She easily arouses the wild fantasies of random passersby. He doesn't always watch her every move, but it sometimes seems to him that her glamour distances them from their closest friends.

Now she sits fuming in the car, swathed in the cumbersome old windbreaker that obscures her body completely. On her sour face, devoid of makeup, are a few unsightly blemishes, as if she has deliberately made herself ugly for her husband, to stave off any suspicion or complaint.

"No, Amotz, I'm not hungry," she says, pushing away the sandwich, "you eat."

"I'm not hungry either," Moran says, rejecting the same sandwich, "you eat it, Abba."

Moran's work uniform smells of gun oil—a fundamental Israeli aroma, an ever-present whiff of dread, the smell of one's first contact with the army, of basic training, which forty years cannot erase from one's consciousness. What's this? Ya'ari extends a hand to feel the dense black stubble covering his son's face. That redhead doesn't make you shave before he sits down to play backgammon with you? Moran pulls away from his touch. What about you, he goads his father, you didn't shave this morning either. What, Imma isn't here so you're trying out a sexier style?

"Sexy?" Ya'ari is insulted.

"Sexy like Arafat," Efrat says maliciously, looking at her husband.

The little ones have not had their fill of their father, and they cling to him and climb on him. But Moran is distracted, graceless. His mind is fixed on his wife, but they are both silent now, and the poisonous silence is affecting the children, who provoke each other, wanting attention.

Nadi is drawn to the smell of meat roasting on a nearby barbecue, and Ya'ari has to stop him. The Israeli din gains volume. Bluish smoke pollutes the winter air. Recruits, stuffed full with meat and sweets, improvise a mini-soccer match at the edge of the visiting area, or walk arm-in-arm with their girlfriends within the perimeter set by their commanding officers. Fathers laugh heartily, sharing memories of their own army days, and mothers exchange phone numbers, so that together they will be able to keep track of special events during the months of training.

Yes, reflects Ya'ari, there's anger and bitterness between these two, but also attraction, and in this teeming parking lot they won't be able to defuse their spite and make up before parting. He cannot presume to fathom the workings of his son's marital relationship, nor does he intend to try without Daniela. But even Daniela, who does venture into mind-reading, can be mistaken. Could she imagine, for example, that tucked between Baby Mozart and Baby Bach is a cassette of hard-core sex, which these young people watch to get turned on, not relying on their own desire? But he won't tell Daniela about the cassette, so as not to upset her.

He offers the car keys to his son and says, listen, there're so many people here, and you might want some quiet time together, so take yourselves to some nice café in the area, and I'll look after the little ones. When I visited you at the base that night, I thought I saw an old tank the children might enjoy. Is there really an old tank here, or did I just imagine it?

"I haven't run into any old tanks, but I haven't done much exploring around the camp. If you say you saw an old tank, it must be there. You, Abba, are not capable of hallucinations."

And he takes the keys from his father. Efrat hesitates, but Moran insists, yes, we deserve a little privacy.

Nadi is thrilled by the chance to climb on a real tank, but Neta is sorry to be separated from her father. We'll be right back, Moran promises, and we'll bring you something better than the cucumbers and carrots that Imma peeled. And he puts the food back into the cooler.

Ya'ari holds his grandchildren's hands tight, and they cross the road with great caution. The children urgently need the toilet, he says grimly to the soldier guarding the gate, and leads them on with determination. Parents' visiting day loosens the disciplinary leash, and many recruits walk around without their berets or weapons; some have even traded in their army boots for civilian shoes. A few assertive mothers have succeeded in penetrating the base to inspect their children's living conditions. Is there an old tank monument here? Ya'ari asks everyone he runs into, but he gets no clear answer. Still he persists. They reach the far edge of the base. Beyond the eucalyptus trees lie the houses of the neighbouring town. A raindrop lands on his head, and he looks up at the sky. The clouds are crammed together, yet patches of blue show through here and there. All at once heavy drops begin to fall, and he hurries with the children into a nearby tent.

The tent is filled with meticulously made beds, which are guarded by an Ethiopian soldier sprawled on one of them. He wears a light battle vest, and the rifle between his legs rocks to the beat of unfamiliar music.

Ya'ari requests cover until the rain lets up. And Nadi draws close to the guard and fearlessly, yet with deep reverence, strokes the bolt of the rifle.

"You didn't go out to visit your family?"

No, says this lone recruit, he has no family in Israel. His father died right after they arrived in the country, and his mother, who was supposed to follow them here, remarried and stayed in Addis Ababa.

Ya'ari is curious to know whether he misses Africa.

Mother and Africa, explains the soldier, have become one for him, and he is unable to separate them.

8.

SIJJIN KUANG IS slow to return to the sanatorium lobby. The powerful midday sunshine that pours through the window nearly lulls the two relatives to sleep as they sink deeper into the worn leather armchairs, which resemble a pair of hippopotamuses. Behind the reception desk sits an African man, typing into an elderly computer. What amazes Daniela is that for a long time now not a single patient or employee has entered the lobby. Only the tapping of the keys chips away at the great silence. Yirmiyahu closes his eyes and drifts off, and Daniela can now study his face from close up and see what has changed in this man she has known for so many years. Is this the first time you've been here? she asks him when his red eyes open for a moment, and he tells her no, he has been here a number of times, bringing diggers who had been felled by malaria. And they got well here? No way of knowing; we lost contact with them. Their tribesmen were in a hurry to get them out of here, and replace them with others. UNESCO doesn't insure the health of diggers.

He yawns and stretches, places his hand on his forehead and

says, I think I also have a bit of fever. She puts one hand against his forehead and the other to her own and says, I think I'm the one with fever, not you. But tell me why is there no one here, no patients or workers? Yirmiyahu shrugs. Maybe they're eating now, maybe sleeping. Do you suppose, she asks further, that there's a cafeteria here where I can find something sweet?

An ironic smile lights the man's eyes.

"No, Daniela," he yawns, "I don't believe there's a kiosk here for you."

"You're sure, or you only believe so?"

"I am sure that I don't believe."

The elevator whirrs and starts to rise, and when it comes back down it brings with it the aristocratic Sudanese driver, who asks the white man to come up and help her calm down Zohara al-Ukbi, who is refusing to stay here. On the way to her room they had passed the rooms of terminal patients, and the young Arab woman had a panic attack and demanded to be returned to the farm.

Yirmiyahu sighs, rises from his chair and follows the nurse. Daniela, who guesses that reassuring Zohara will take some time, approaches the desk clerk to ask if he has anything sweet, she feels a bitter taste in her mouth. The African apologizes that he has nothing to offer the white woman, but when he finishes on the computer he will try to find something. She looks at the documents he is inputting, and asks if he has any reading material, perhaps a brochure, maybe something with pictures? No, this institution has no need for public relations, and the paperwork piled up here consists of medical reports about illnesses and treatments, now being recorded on the hard drive for future generations. Then he remembers that one of the patients who died here left behind a book in English that might possibly interest the visitor; he will go upstairs for it at once, but it might only be a prayer book.

A prayer book is not exactly what his bored guest is yearning for—but if it is in English, she will give it a chance.

Meanwhile she tries to make herself more comfortable. She turns around the hippo relinquished by Yirmiyahu and joins it to her own, takes off her shoes and socks, and sinks her bare feet in the rough cracked hide of the other herbivorous creature. She closes her eyes and allows the noonday sun to caress her through the unshaded window. The tapping on the keyboard stops, and she hears the rustle of papers and the glide of a closing drawer and the moving of a chair. Now that she is all alone, a sweet drowsiness overtakes her, as in the car at night beside her husband, when he accelerates on the highway. And when the rumble of the elevator intrudes into her twilight consciousness, she is disappointed that her brother-in-law has already returned to rouse her from her well-arranged cocoon and tell her they are heading back. But the gravelly voice speaking to her now in fluent well-enunciated English belongs neither to Yirmiyahu nor the desk clerk. As in a dream, she sees an old man approach her, clad only in a white bathrobe, and extend a cordial hand. To her astonishment she recognizes the elderly Englishman who sat beside her on the flight from Nairobi to Morogoro. He had boasted to her that he was the owner of a small estate, and here he is, but one of its residents. He has just learned that a white lady had arrived from the base camp of the excavations for the prehistoric ape, and immediately guessing who it must be, has hurried down to tell her, with unabashed candour, that their brief encounter on the plane has been very much on his mind.

9.

"But Grandpa, it's not raining anymore," Neta says, pulling at Ya'ari's fingers while he is deep in discussion with the lone soldier about the scenery in Ethiopia. The soldier talks with joy of the landscapes of his childhood, and it is so pleasant to chat with this older man that he is willing to open the rifle bolt for his enthralled grandson and explain to him, using a live round, how the pin hits the primer to ignite the gunpowder in the cartridge, which propels the lead bullet to its target. Boom-boom they kill and then give a kiss, Nadi summarizes the shooting process with great satisfaction. And after fondling the rifle bullet with his little hands, turning it over and over, he spirits it slyly into the pocket of his coat, but Ya'ari quickly snatches it from the "little killer." Yes, we must hurry, it's getting late, and again he grabs his grandchildren's hands, but before they leave he remembers to ask the lone recruit whether in fact there is an old tank on the base.

And indeed, Moran was right. Ya'ari is not inclined to hallucination, neither by day nor by night. Behind the sheds of the base command stands a Syrian tank from the Yom Kippur War, set up as a memorial to past heroism. The Ethiopian goes outside and explains how to get there, and then, on a sudden whim, he leans over and kisses the children. Nadi hangs onto him with affection, but Neta is alarmed. Come, children, let's see this tank, says Ya'ari to the dismay of his granddaughter, who has had more than enough of this military tour and wants very much to return to her parents, having sensed the tension between them. But Nadi's manly spirit pleases Ya'ari, and he wants to satisfy the boy's military curiosity, and so, as they stand before the tank, an obsolete Soviet model whose camouflage paint was designed for the basalt terrain of the Golan Heights, he complies with his grandson's request to lift him on top of the turret.

"Just for a minute, Neta darling, we're only going to peek and see what's inside this tank, and then we'll go back to Imma and Abba right away. You don't want to see what's inside?"

But Neta, standing tiny and tense next to the corroded caterpillar tracks, wants no contact at all with the tank, which even after rusting in place for more than thirty years is terrifying. The darkening sky compounds her distress. But Ya'ari will not give in and lifts her little brother onto the hull, then goes up to join him, and from there, carefully and with considerable effort, climbs with the child onto the bulky turret. The hatch, he is pleased to discover, can be opened.

It is dark inside, and Ya'ari, who served in the infantry, is no expert on the innards of tanks. A cursory look tells him that the Soviet army had not been greatly concerned about the comfort of the individual soldier, only about the thickness of the steel protecting him. He can make out the olive-drab colour of the steering bar, two large copper artillery shell casings, and what looks like the disintegrating vest of a tank soldier—dead these thirty years, no doubt—is lying in a corner. Nadi very much wants to crawl in and touch the steering bar, but Ya'ari is afraid he'll have trouble getting him out. As a compromise, he holds him upside down, and in a reverse childbirth motion lowers his big head into the dark hole. Lower, Grandpa, the child pleads, while his head seems to float in the darkness, I see a dead man. That's it, no more, Ya'ari says, frightened by his grandson's wild imagination. You've seen enough. Now let's get out of here fast, before an officer comes and yells at us. No, Nadi says, stiffening his body. There's no officer, you're silly.

Ya'ari has noticed that Nadi sometimes speaks disrespectfully to his father and mother, but till now has watched his tongue with his grandfather. He pulls the child up sharply, and clambers down with him. Nadi, that's it. You've seen enough. And on top of that, you can say "silly" to your friends in nursery school, but not to your grandpa who loves you so much. The child falls silent, lowers his gaze, then purses his lips and looks venomously into his grandfather's face. Neta, too, is on the verge of tears, tugging impatiently at his hand, and drops begin to fall from the sky. If she starts whimpering now, her brother will immediately join in, and it will not be to his credit to return two bawling children to their parents.

He puts the teddybear hoods over their heads, and covers his own, to his grandchildren's delight, with a sheet of graph paper he finds in his pocket.

When they reach the front gate Ya'ari is amazed to discover that the chaotic civilian world has been utterly erased, as if by magic, from the consciousness of the army recruits. The picnic ground is deserted; all the cars have vanished, with no trace of paper napkins or empty mineral water bottles. Also absent is the car he lent his son, and now he remembers that he left his cell phone in it, plugged into the speaker-phone socket.

Greenish lightning slashes the sky, followed by shattering thunder. The terrified children cling to his body, the soaking graph paper dribbles on his head. Without thinking twice about hurting his back he lifts both his grandchildren in his arms and dashes to the guardhouse. A tall soldier in full battle garb looks at them severely. The amiable Ethiopian has been replaced by a

Russian recruit who scowls at the three civilians who have sought refuge with him. Is he too a lone soldier, whose mother has remained in Russia? Ya'ari does not ask; nor does he need to. There is a woven basket in the corner, filled with food.

"Imma, Imma'leh, where are you; Abba, Abba'leh, where are you?" Neta's lament is not a hostile, confrontational complaint but rather a thin, heartrending wail of justified anxiety. Ya'ari sweeps up his granddaughter, her wispy body feeling immeasurably lighter than that of her little brother, and holds her close to his chest. Now the keening pierces him to the marrow—Imma, Imma'leh, where are you; Abba, Abba'leh, where are you, and the more he tries to soothe her, the more he can feel the panic flowing from her into him. There really is no reason to suspect engine trouble in his new car, so the only remaining possibility is an accident.

In the rain-soaked guardpost, beside the tall Russian who keeps angrily brushing away the little hand reaching for his submachine gun, his practical engineer's mind churns through the outcomes of all possible situations, from a simple flat tyre to a car-mangling wreck. Dammit, he berates himself, dammit, you're standing here with two little children who are counting on you, and you have no right to show any sign of desperation. And even if Daniela is not at your side when you hear the terrible news, you will not run away to Africa or any other continent, but by your very sanity, your practicality and sense of responsibility you will vanquish the chaos that swells all around you.

In his imagination scenes of horrible catastrophe mingle cruelly with practical considerations. How he will have to ask Daniela to give up teaching to devote herself to the grandchildren; how Moran's apartment will have to be rented out, and for how much; how his firm's lawyer will examine the life-insurance policy; and who will argue in court over the extent of the damages. He makes a mental note of which architect could best add a wing to their house for the children, and considers how he might persuade Nofar to become their legal guardian after he and Daniela have passed away.

A cold wind blows through his wet hair. His knees are shaking. Fear torments him, and the precise solutions he elaborates in his mind offer no comfort. The eyes of the Russian soldier are fastened on the pudgy little hand that keeps pretending to stroke, with consummate delicacy, the submachine gun propped on a stand. And the soft moaning drones on.

"Imma, Imma'leh, where are you; Abba, Abba'leh, where are you."

"They'll be right back, Neta, you'll see, I promise. They haven't forgotten us."

And, in fact, a few minutes later, there is a flash of light and a honking sound, and Moran, who has found his family's hideout, quickly crosses the road, enters the guardhouse and sweeps up his children and hurries all three into the warm bosom of the car.

"I'm sorry, Abba, I'm sorry. We lost track of time."

Moran and Efrat's heads are both wet, and his daughter-in-law's big jacket is spotted with mud and bits of leaves. Ya'ari fixes his eyes on the young woman sitting in the front seat next to her husband and avoiding his gaze, even refraining from touching her two children squeezed beside him in the back, as though her turbulent soul is not yet ready for them.

"Grandpa put me in a tank," the boy announces proudly.

"Well done, Nadi," gushes his father, "see what a great grandpa I gave birth to?"

The two children laugh.

"Not true, you didn't give birth to Grandpa, he wasn't in your tummy," declares Neta.

"Grandma Daniela gave birth to Grandpa," chortles Nadi.

Moran hugs them and kisses their heads. And Efrat's eyes, their sandy blue colour deepened by the rain clouds above, melt for her children, and she extends a caressing hand.

They've made up, Ya'ari concludes in a flash, judging by the confined soldier's effusiveness. And really, why sit in some unfamiliar café and waste the limited time together with gripes and recriminations, when you can go out into nature, and in the cold and rain of winter salve your wounded relationship with a quick coupling. There will come a time when this Hanukkah holiday is remembered well, the car's owner smiles inside, as he warms himself in the back, cramped between the children's safety seats—maybe a third grandchild will be born of it. Yes, a bright bloom is returning to Efrat's face, and her calm look, lingering on her husband, is not merely free of disdain but even appreciative of a man who knows how to make the most of a short interlude, and how to recognize, under his wife's rain-drenched army jacket, the yearning of her flesh.

And really, why not? Disaster, as we have seen, sometimes lies in wait only a footstep away, so why bicker with your beloved, when you could take pleasure in him. In two days Daniela will return from Africa, and he knows she will want, as always, on her first night home, to know what happened to her husband day by day and hour by hour while she was away. And though she does not like him to speculate about their children's sex lives, this time he will insist on telling her how he stood with the grandchildren at the gate of the camp, exposed to thunder and lightning, while her son and daughter-in-law were out making love in the fields. Yes, he will withhold nothing from her. And therefore, on second thoughts, he will not spare her the blue video hidden between Baby Mozart and Baby Bach, lest she stumble upon it as he did. But really, why shouldn't she know? In three years she will be sixty, and is mature enough to understand that there is wilder libido in the world than she has previously imagined. After all, she herself, before disappearing through the departure gate at the airport, was the one who spoke the words "real desire."

10.

DIDN'T FORGET HER? Daniela laughs, astonished, and removes her feet from the opposite armchair, a movement that tilts her backwards a bit. But how come? We exchanged at most a few words at the end of the flight.

"True," says the elderly Englishman as he elegantly gathers the skirt of his white bathrobe and sits down carefully in the vacant chair. They exchanged only a few words, but he remembers every one of them and regrets that he had not begun to converse with her at the start of the flight, to hear more about the late sister and the soldier killed by his comrades' friendly fire, and especially about her, who she is and what she was smiling about the whole time with such tranquillity. But since during most of the flight she preferred to look out of the window, as if deliberately avoiding him, it would not have been polite to interrupt her. Was the view really so fascinating, or did she think him not sober enough for conversation?

"Both."

But does the lady really believe that such an inveterate drinker as he could become intoxicated during a flight of less than one hour? How many drinks did the stewardess bring him? Two? Three?

"At least five," she says, and smiles at the purplish, white-haired Englishman, who sits before her naked beneath his bathrobe, gazing at her with admiration.

Five? Really? She counted them? Nevertheless, he did not depart the aircraft drunk.

"There was no way of knowing, since two stewards came quickly and took you away in a wheelchair. Now I gather they were from this farm of yours. But what matters is that today you are completely sober, and you can apologize to me . . ."

To apologize to a pretty woman is a singular pleasure . . . but, all the same, for what?

"For giving me a business card from this farm and telling me it was yours, even though you are just a patient here."

Correct, says the Englishman, laughing heartily, he is just a patient, but a senior patient, a perennial patient, who returns here every year of his own free will for treatment, and he may thus be considered a bit of a shareholder too. But if she demands an apology, he will readily supply one. Yes, he is sorry that he misled her. He is sorry. There is nothing easier for an Englishman than to utter those words. From the moment he saw her maintain her dignified composure when she was detained at the departure gate, he found her attractive, and even more so during their short conversation at the end of the flight.

And so, although he knew that the chances they would meet again were exceedingly slim, as she had told him that her visit to her brother-in-law would be brief, he had the notion of planting a little lure, like a hunter seeking to trap a rare animal. And in the end it succeeded, for here she is.

Daniela blushes, but smiles forgivingly.

"You are mistaken. I did not know that you were here. I did not notice that this place is the farm on the business card you gave me. I simply came along with my brother-in-law who was bringing a malaria patient, a young woman from the excavation team. But it is true that I did not forget you. I have been a teacher for many years, and I have trained myself to remember my students, and therefore people I meet by chance I remember as well. And when my husband isn't with me and does not demand all my attention, an exceptional person like you may be engraved in my memory."

To be engraved in the memory of such a lady is a great honour.

"If you want you may call it an honour . . ." Daniela tries to dampen the slightly sweaty excitement of the bathrobed Englishman, who is beginning to resemble a dirty old man. "But anyway, what are you doing here? You don't seem particularly ill."

That is correct, he is not actually ill yet, but he will be one day, and he plans to end his life with dignity. As a bachelor without children, living on a modest government pension, in England he has no chance of receiving dignified care. In state-run old people's homes, old Englishwomen pester elderly bachelors like him.

"What kind of work did you do?"

In more recent years he worked for British Rail, but his true career was with His Majesty's armed forces. He was too young for the second world war, but when he joined up just afterwards he asked to be sent to places where there was some hope of active duty, to colonies in Asia and Africa. But after India and Palestine were lost, the other colonies began to demand independence, and by the time he reached the rank of major, not a colony remained where the British Empire might rule honourably and justly, without encountering much terrorism. Thus at the age of fifty, if she can imagine it, he became an engineer with British Rail, and fifteen years ago, when he retired, he decided to return to East Africa not as a colonialist but as a patient.

"And you chose Africa over all the other places you served?"

Yes, of all the peoples of the former Empire he prefers Africans as carers. They are more genuine and honest than the Pakistanis or Burmese, and when they care for one's body, they do not try, as do the Indians, to steal your soul. They are modest and not suspicious, like the Arabs, or afraid that perhaps they will be afflicted by European diseases. They are introverted people, and they care for you without too much talking, like vets caring for pets. It is true that the scenery here is less impressive than elsewhere on the continent, but he feels that a monotonous semi-arid expanse enables one to depart from life with less anguish and more hope.

"Hope for what?"

Hope that one is not really losing anything by dying. This hope enables one to be indifferent to death, like an animal.

He speaks intimately, but with fluency, as if acting on stage. She finds it odd to be speaking so openly to a stranger, a man old enough to be her father, who is nevertheless sitting in front of her wearing only a bathrobe.

"This is your standard of comparison? Animals?"

"Don't underestimate them."

"Of course not. Three years ago, when my sister was still alive, and my brother-in-law was an official chargé d'affaires, we came, my husband and I, for a few days' visit, and the four of us went out to a nature reserve, and it was fascinating to see how they conduct themselves."

Those reserves are filled with tourists, and the animals there have begun to adapt their behaviour for our gaze. But here it's a different story. Here they're in the heart of authentic nature, a place where once there was a great salt lake, and if you were to stay overnight, you would see an extraordinary spectacle. Around midnight, animals of all kinds gather here, dozens of animals large and small, who come from the far reaches of the wild to lick the salt from the dried-up lake bed. And they do so in silence and solidarity, neither bothering nor intimidating one another, each one licking its required dose of salt and going on its way. For this reason alone, it is worth staying here.

She shrugs. Here in Africa she is at her brother-in-law's disposal, and he determines her daily schedule. But if sugar were embedded in the basin of this lake, she too would go down for a taste; and she wouldn't wait till nightfall, but do it now, in the middle of the yellow afternoon.

"Would you?" The old Englishman is astounded by such a passion for sweets in a woman who seems so level-headed. Alas, he has no sweets to offer her. It is forbidden for the patients to keep food in their rooms. But perhaps the bottle of local liqueur stashed in his room might be considered a sweet.

Daniela is ready and eager to taste this liqueur, and at the same time to have a peek at his room, since the small lobby, where she has been sitting for more than an hour, has told her nothing about what the rest of this place is like and what exactly goes on here.

But to her great surprise, the man recoils from the idea of letting her go up to his room. No, his room is no sight for a stranger's eyes, and it is also strictly forbidden to invite to one's room guests who are not mentally prepared for the visit. If she would kindly wait, he will bring the liqueur to her.

Once again she is alone. In another forty-eight hours she will be in the air, and Africa will fade into memory. In Israel it is Shabbat, and if Moran is still confined, she hopes that Amotz is making things easier for Efrat by taking Neta and Nadi to the playground. Her mind springs into action and the feel of the worn-out black leather chair suddenly repels her. She puts on her shoes and goes to look out of the window. She can indeed make out a gleaming white area that might be the lake bed. Obviously it would be an incredible spectacle, seeing the animals gathered by moonlight to lick the salt they need to stay alive. But for her the spectacle is over. She'll never come back to Africa, not even if Amotz wants them to. There are other places in the world. And if Yirmiyahu insists on ending his days here, he can arrange the shipment of the urn containing his ashes to Israel himself. That is, if he even wants to be buried beside her sister.

The elevator begins to move. It halts, then moves again— whether up or down is not clear. Finally it arrives, bearing the desk clerk, who has not found her anything sweet, doubtless because he didn't try, but has brought her, as she asked, a book in English: *The Holy Bible,* the Old and New Testaments in one volume.

So many years have passed since she last opened a Bible. At school ceremonies selected passages from the Prophets are invariably read aloud with great feeling, mainly by girls for some reason, but she can't even remember on which shelf her Bible rests at home. Now here in this desolate plain in Tanzania, of all places, she takes the book she has known since childhood, in this edition joined altogether naturally to the Gospels and Epistles, which she has never read.

Before the desk clerk sits down to resume his archival assignment, she asks him what is taking her brother-in-law and the nurse so long. The rebellious malaria patient is still doggedly refusing to remain, he says. Maybe I should go up to convince her, Daniela suggests helpfully and turns towards the elevator. But the desk clerk springs up in a panic and blocks her path. Visitors who are not prepared may not go upstairs.

If so, perhaps there really is something here that they are afraid to expose, she thinks. She drags a chair over to the window. She has never before read the Bible in a foreign language. No translator or date are listed in the book, but from the lofty English phrases she gathers that this old-fashioned translation is the King James Version. As she starts turning its pages she immediately comes up against words like "aloes" and "myrrh," of whose Hebrew meanings she has not a clue.

She randomly opens to 2 Samuel and reads about Amnon the malingerer, who invited Tamar to his chamber so that she might prepare two *ugot*—"a couple of cakes," by this translation—and she finds the prose clear and engaging. The English metre of Jeremiah's poetry seems to her stately and beautiful, and she is very pleased by the little English vocabulary test she gives herself. Now she'll try her skill with the speeches made by the friends of Job, the man who cursed the day he was born, and see if they explain the failings of the world better in English than in the difficult Hebrew she recalls from her youth.

The patient lightly taps her on the shoulder. Now dressed in a shirt and suit, he flashes her a subversive wink and triumphantly waves a bottle containing a golden liquid. What have you found here? he asks his new friend, and she shows him the book and asks boldly which he likes better—the Old Testament or the New. He is taken aback. In two months he will be eighty, and no one has ever asked him to prefer one text over the other. Not even his priest. Christianity has taught us that the Bible is an organic whole, whose elements complement each other and flow from one to another—as in Shakespeare's plays, where King Lear fleshes out and amplifies the madness of Hamlet, and the great love of Juliet for Romeo is transmuted into the devotion of Lady Macbeth to her murderer husband.

His answer surprises her, like an extraordinary answer from a mediocre student of whom she expected little. And the colonial officer, pleased by the effect of his words, hands her a glass and carefully doles out a few experimental drops, and as these are drops, she can only lick them, and their taste is strange and definitely unfamiliar to her, but clearly sweet. She hands him back the glass and says, Let us drink, sir, I am ready.

And very slowly she drains two glasses, and after hesitating requests a third, but the Englishman, who was not prepared for such enthusiasm, which might well empty his bottle, suggests deferring the third glass; the lethal influence of the local alcohol becomes apparent only gradually, he warns her, and it's best to take a break. Meanwhile he gently takes the book from her, as if to renew his old acquaintance with it.

At this moment, Yirmiyahu appears, without Sijjin Kuang, and he is amazed to see that even in such a remote and isolated place his sister-in-law has succeeded in landing an elderly English admirer, who now introduces himself and offers a friendly drink.

But Yirmiyahu, who looks worried, declines the drink. They must take to the road. Sijjin Kuang will stay the night to help the sick woman adjust to the place, and he will now be driving. Though the distance is not great, he had best remain sharp.

"I don't understand," Daniela confronts her brother-in-law in English. "What has one to get used to here? Are there painful sights that require mental preparation? Is it because of the carers, or the patients? They even prevented me, a mature woman, from going upstairs, as if I were a schoolgirl."

The Englishman smiles and places a friendly hand on her shoulder. Calm down, Daniela, my dear, he says, with the familiarity of a close friend. There are too many young people here, boys and girls, and it would be imprudent and unfair to expose them.

Yirmiyahu says nothing, and when he sees that his sister-in-law, still waiting for a clear answer, remains seated in her chair, he grabs her hand, just as if she were her sister, and pulls her to her feet. But Daniela hangs back. She takes the Bible from the Englishman and presses it to her chest.

"What book is this?"

"I asked the desk clerk for something to read, and he found me, you'll never guess, a Bible, in English, with the New Testament too."

"So what? You can leave it on the table."

"No, I want to read a bit of it before I leave. You see things in the English that you can't in Hebrew. In the meantime nobody here will miss it, and you can return it when you come to pick up your patient. On condition that you don't burn it."

Yirmi's eyes sparkle.

"Why not burn it? Why should the source of all troubles be more immune than the newspapers? This book is where all the confusion and curses begin. This especially must be destroyed."

Daniela regards him quizzically, but still warmly.

"Here it's in English, not Hebrew."

Yirmiyahu looks affectionately at his sister-in-law.

"If it's in English, we'll give it a pardon."

11 .

"THIS IS ISRAEL," declares Moran, handing his father the keys. "Thunder and lightning and commotion, then out jumps the sun to calm everyone down. Too bad that nature isn't more cruel in this country, to force the people to fight against it instead of each other. This is winter?" He continues to embellish his observation, perhaps in order to distract them all from the fact that he arrived late and exposed his father and children to the raging thunderstorm. "In global terms, this is just a pleasant autumn."

He and Efrat are standing beside the car, and as Moran leans into the back to buckle his children into their car seats, the redheaded adjutant pops out of nowhere looking for his confined soldier, and is surprised by the beauty of his wife. That's it, I have to confiscate your husband, says the adjutant to the woman studying him with mild contempt. Believe me, I could have sent him to the West Bank, to stand at roadblocks and chase wanted men, but I felt sorry for him and preferred to adjust his attitude here. What can I do, I'm a man who doesn't give up even on lost causes. And he suggests that Ya'ari change his route and take the trans-Israel highway back to Tel Aviv. You won't be sorry; you can now get onto it near here, and even though it's a longer way around, and he had also objected to its construction because of the damage to the landscape, it really is quick and not crowded, and it's silly to keep boycotting it.

Ya'ari is pleased with the idea. It's been a while since he took the highway, and the new section is unfamiliar to him. But Moran is finding it hard to part from his wife and children, and at the last moment he remembers to talk about the office. Go, and bravely defend your white queen, his father interrupts him, waving at the barracks. The elevators won't run away.

At the Ihron interchange they merge smoothly into the highway. A beep signals that the cameras have identified the car's owner as a registered toll-payer, and Ya'ari picks up speed on the well-designed road that traverses the heart of Israel. Efrat has hidden away in the boot her wet army jacket, muddied by the lovemaking, and sits now at her father-in-law's side in a lightweight turquoise sweater that exquisitely matches her eyes. Diligently, she leafs through the road atlas she found in the glove compartment—not out of a deep interest in the geography of her homeland, but evidently to escape the curious glances of the driver, ostensibly a family member but essentially a stranger.

Deep sleep has spirited the children away. The tour of the army camp, and especially the frightening wait for their parents, have dissipated in the warmth of the car, and the humming of its tyres on the road. The girl's head is the first to droop, and her hand reaches forward in a gesture of saintly supplication. For a while longer, Nadi seems to wrestle with the shadow of the dead Syrian soldier he saw in the old tank, and then sleep tips his head backwards too.

Ya'ari smiles into the rearview mirror at his sleeping grandchildren. You know, he says to his daughter-in-law, yesterday, when I spent time with the children, I thought I saw a new resemblance between Nadi and Daniela.

"Daniela?" Efrat turns around and peers at her son for a moment.

"Maybe not Daniela herself," he backtracks a bit, "but via Daniela to Shuli and to Eyal when he was little. You, of course, can't see that similarity, but I knew Eyal when he was Nadi's age. And last night—it was amazing—when you went to the party, and Nadi cried and carried on, suddenly this new resemblance surfaced."

Efrat again turns her head towards the backseat. The possible resemblance to Moran's cousin excites her but is also confusing. She hesitates a moment before reacting, but finally has the courage to tell her father-in-law something that even her husband does not know. In her fifth month, when it was already known that the unborn child was a boy and not another girl, without consulting Moran she wrote to Yirmi and Shuli and asked for permission to name the baby after their son. But they refused. Politely, sympathetically, but firmly. She thought she was making a gesture of consolation, then realized she was only adding to their pain.

Her pale face grows very red from the thrill of telling the

father something she concealed from his son. As a gesture of support Ya'ari removes a hand from the wheel and rests it on the young woman's shoulder, not far from the little hidden tattoo. It was good that you made the gesture, and good that you understood why it was refused. Although, in their place… He does not continue, and even resists thinking what he had intended to say.

Traffic on the highway is light, and though it moves at high speed, calm nerves and good manners prevail. On the east and west sides of the multi-lane highway two identical petrol stations come into view, flanked by shops and cafés. He glances at Efrat, to see if she wants to buy something for the children, who have had nothing to eat or drink since breakfast, but now her head has flopped backwards just like her son's, and her eyes are closed, as if her brief confession exhausted her. Is she really sleeping, or has she closed her eyes to break off contact? A short while ago, in the bosom of nature, did she take the liberty of shouting her joy out loud, or sigh discreetly, murmuring her pleasure? He says not a word more, but turns down the heater and picks up speed.

His daughter-in-law, like his wife, surrenders trustingly to his driving and sinks deeper into sleep. This gives him an opportunity to examine from close up just what her beauty is made of. But when her radiant eyes are closed and her dimple disappears, the Madonna-like face seems a bit gaunt, her cheekbones sharp and oversized. Only her unblemished, swanlike neck, adorned by a delicate gold chain, remains alluring. Is all that beauty actually something precarious and fragile, hanging by the thread of her forceful personality?

As they head south, the skies grow bluer and clearer. Ya'ari pays attention to the road signs, especially those pointing east of the highway. Only when one gets to the heart of the country does one see how sturdy and deeply rooted are the Arab communities, small villages that have turned into crowded towns, the minarets of their new mosques jutting upwards. And as a security barrier, not very high, suddenly begins to wind beside the road to the east, he slowly pries the road atlas from the fingers of the sleeping beauty and turns the pages to see if he is right. Yes, this is Tulkarm, the old and stubborn enemy, but pastoral too.

The weight of passengers' sleep can make a driver drowsy, particularly a driver who did not spend the night in his own bed. So he gingerly turns on the radio, looking for some soft music. Efrat opens her eyes for a moment and closes them again. If grinding rock doesn't keep her awake at night, why should mellower music during the day?

The scenery along the trans-Israel highway is monotonous. Herds of bulldozers have sliced through hills, obliterated farmland, uprooted humble groves, and made the crooked straight so that the drive will be smooth, without significant rises or dips or unexpected curves. But the sun, already heading west, compensates for the bland practicality of the road. Golden winter light inflames the fringes of the clouds.

In spite of the music, Ya'ari does not feel sufficiently alert to be driving at the high speed limit, and so, though the Kesem exit towards Tel Aviv is not far off, he plucks his cell phone from its cradle and calls Nofar. To his surprise, she answers, and her voice sounds soft and friendly.

"Is Imma already home?"

"No, don't you remember she's due back on Monday?"

"I don't get why she needs to be in Africa for such a long time."

"What are you talking about, Nofar, it hasn't even been five days."

"Five days? Is that all? So why are you talking in such a pathetic tone of voice?"

"Because I'm calling you from a car that seems more like a dormitory. Efrat and the kids have crashed out all around me. It was family day at the army base where your brother is confined, so we saw him there, and now we're going home via the trans-Israel."

"So I have an idea. If you're already on the fast road, why don't you keep on going to Jerusalem and hop over to see me? I'm on duty now, and I also deserve a little family day."

"To Jerusalem? Right now?"

"I mean, they told me that yesterday you looked for me in my room, so today you can find me at the hospital. Come on, Abba, don't be lazy, the road will lead you to me all by itself. Less than forty minutes and you're at Sha'arei Tzedek hospital. I miss the kids. Give me Efrati, I'll talk her into it."

"I told you, she's asleep."

"So let her sleep, and when she wakes up and asks where you took her, tell her Nofar also exists. Don't tell me you're afraid of her the way you are of Imma."

"Enough, Nofar, enough of this nonsense."

But Nofar is right. Since Efrat is still atoning for her sins in dreamy slumber, there is no need to ask her consent for the detour. Jerusalem is not far away, and though the winter day is short, there'll still be time to get back to Tel Aviv.

And so, at his daughter's command, he kidnaps his

daughter-in-law and grandchildren and takes them, unconscious captives, to Jerusalem. The excitements and conflicts and loves and fears of the past twenty-four hours have so exhausted all of them that they do not sense the change in the sound of the car when it leaves the plain and begins climbing into the hills. But when they stop at the first traffic light, the boy's eyes open first, then the girl's, and finally Efrat's. You slept like the dead, he says, but does not reveal where he has taken them, leaving it to his daughter-in-law to regain her bearings. Oddly, she doesn't immediately recognize the city; only as they turn towards Mount Herzl does she look at him with amazement, as if she were still fluttering in the remnant of a dream. Before she can ask, he says yes, Jerusalem. Nofar begged to see the children, but you were asleep and I couldn't ask your approval.

Her eyes gleam with ironic amusement.

"Jerusalem? Why not."

At the entrance to Sha'arei Tzedek, Nofar is waiting, dressed in a white uniform, her dark hair pulled back in an old-fashioned coil. She is elated by the sight of her niece and nephew and hugs and kisses them, and as usual picks up Nadi in her arms as if he were a baby. They head for the large cafeteria, and find it locked up tight. Nofar says, how could I forget that they close it on Shabbat? So Ya'ari hurries to the car and returns wobbling under the weight of the loaded cooler. Digging into it, they discover that in the morning Efrat indeed filled it with many goodies. They set up their picnic near a big window. The children chomp intently on the hummus-filled pitas, and Efrat warms her hands with a mug of coffee poured from a large thermos. Nofar is content with a peeled cucumber, and Ya'ari tucks heartily into the very sandwich that at noon had been shamed in the round of no, you eat it, and tries, without much success, to get his grandchildren to talk about their military outing. To most of his leading questions he is forced to supply his own answers, getting only vague nods when he asks, at the end, right? Then Nofar asks permission from her sister-in-law to show her father *something* in her new department.

En route to the trauma unit Nofar equips him with a green-coloured gown and helps him put it on, and leads her father into an isolated dark room, very warm, with only one bed, where lies a young half-naked man, connected by a thicket of tubes to hanging bags and machines. His head is swathed completely in white, his two eyes blazing in the centre. Nofar draws close and speaks his name loudly, and the young man slowly turns his head. Here, Nofar says gaily, meet my father. He wants to be amazed by your resurrection.

With a welter of medical detail, she spins her father the tale of this young construction worker who fell from scaffolding and was brought in actually dead, and yet has been restored to life. Right? She says in a challenging tone to her immobile patient. You wanted to fly away from the world, didn't you, but we didn't let you, right? We caught you in mid-flight. And the young man, his admiring eyes fixed on the girl who teases him with great fondness, nods his bandaged head, but Nofar is not content with his confirmation. Her eyes fill with deep emotion, and she persists with the little scolding. Tell me, is it nice to run away without asking permission? In the white skull glint sunken, suffering eyes, and a broken voice emits the faint keening of a small animal. But Nofar doesn't let up, and as if the man lying here were not suspended between heaven and earth, she keeps talking to him in the tone of an experienced teacher: You have to live! You were not born so you could escape from us in the middle of life.

And she straightens the sheet covering the young man, plants a kiss on his eyelids, adjusts his urine tubes, and gestures to the visitor that they should leave the room.

In the entry hall Nadi and Neta are gleefully pushing a worn-out wheelchair and drinking chocolate milk from plastic bottles. Efrat, who has already poured herself a second cup of coffee, is methodically applying makeup to her face, mirrored in a greying window with a view of Jerusalem.

"Listen, Amotz," she says firmly to Ya'ari, as he removes the green gown and returns it to Nofar, "since you've already tricked me into coming to Jerusalem, then at least, while we're here, why don't we meet your father's Jerusalem lover."

"The lover?" Ya'ari is stunned. "Why would you want to do that?"

"Why not?" Efrat answers coolly. "I want to see what makes your family cheat."

12.

YIRMIYAHU STARTS THE ignition and the carburettor floods immediately. They wait a few minutes, and he tries again. Sijjin Kuang is always so eager to take the wheel and gallop through the wide open spaces, he says apologetically to his sister-in-law seated at his side, that I've lost my feel for this engine. Anyway, she has good intuitions, but believe me, she also makes mistakes.

"You know the way back from here?" asks Daniela, rather anxiously.

"In theory it's not complicated."

"And not in theory?"

"Don't worry. How far did we drive from the farm to here? Thirty or forty kilometres, on an easy road. And since you're armed with the Old Testament and even the New, you have nothing to worry about."

Again the engine balks, but Yirmiyahu persists, and after some wheezing and throat-clearing the car regains its equilibrium and moves out onto the dirt road. Yirmiyahu leans forward, the better to navigate precisely, and asks his sister-in-law not to distract him with talk till they get to the first crucial intersection. Daniela shrugs, slightly insulted, and begins leafing through the Bible, and a few minutes later an unanticipated fork appears in the road. Yirmiyahu turns to his sister-in-law and points left, asking for confirmation: You remember? This is the right way, yes? Daniela is flustered. You're asking me? I get lost in Tel Aviv, you want me to take responsibility in Africa? Please, you decide.

So he does and picks the left fork and soon recognizes bits

of landscape from the morning. Relieved, he starts humming a tune and picks up speed. Then he glances at the woman whose short stay in Africa has added colour to her face.

"During your career did you ever teach the Bible?"

Yes, years ago she substituted for a Bible teacher who was ill, and for a week read the story of Joseph and his brothers with her class. It was easy enough.

"Joseph and his brothers? A charming tale of a whole family that settled in Africa following one brother, the administrator. The texts in Genesis are miniature stories that can be interpreted any which way. They tell of a family that is not yet a people, and in this family, the great obsession of the patriarchs is to produce as many descendants as possible, so there'll be someone to graze the sheep, but again and again they discover to their dismay that they have married women who have a serious problem getting pregnant. Once Shuli and I went to a memorial service for the father of friends of ours, and instead of talking about the father who had died they brought some sort of lecturer, an author or poet, who rebound the binding of Isaac, and then I saw how it's possible to find new ore in texts that have been mined over and over again. This lecturer tried to describe what the whole story of the captive son and the big knife looked like from down below, from the point of view of the two youths who were guarding Abraham's donkey at the foot of the mountain."

It's already three o'clock, and a wind starts up across the plain, and makes the air hazy. Sunlight strikes the windscreen, revealing spatters of dead bugs.

"You have to clean this windscreen once in a while," comments Daniela.

"I also noticed," says her brother-in-law, ignoring her, "that all those public lectures about the Bible are generally about nice, clear-cut subjects. Jacob and Esau, the Song of Songs, Jephthah's daughter, Samuel and Saul, David and Absalom, Jacob's love for Rachel, Cain and Abel, Samson and Delilah. They all take the easy road, avoiding the really hard stuff, the violent texts where the prophets rant and rave."

"The prophets? I don't think I ever looked at them after my matriculation exams."

"Me neither, until Eyal was killed. And then I reread them, prophet after prophet, and suddenly one day I saw the profound curse that has penetrated the genes of this people."

"After Eyal was killed you studied the prophets?"

"Only for a little while, but intensively. It all started with the Foreign Ministry's assistant director-general, a religious and cultured man, who delicately proposed organizing a minyan in our home during the seven-day *shivah* mourning. And because he was my superior, and I knew I'd need him if I wanted another foreign assignment, I couldn't say no. And I didn't really mind, because Shabbat fell in the middle of the *shivah*, which left only four mornings for prayer. And since he also agreed not to ask me to strap on phylacteries, I said, Why not? You two were staying in a hotel in Jerusalem, and Amotz also became a little friendly with this man when he came for the prayers."

"His name wasn't by any chance Michaeli, or Rafaeli?"

"Rafaeli, that's right. Amazing how you remember unimportant names."

"It comes from teaching. From faculty meetings where they would seal the fate of students I had never even seen. Amotz rather liked him."

"Yes, he is a fine fellow. Even after the shivah ended he kept on going with the religious instruction. Very tactfully, without pressure, and most important, without the usual sentimental schmaltz. Only now are you setting forth on the journey of grief, he said to me, so allow me to suggest a few texts you aren't familiar with, perhaps you may find some insight in them.

"I mainly got from him various reprints and photocopies of articles from Modern Orthodox journals, and I would even discuss these with him, but soon enough I realized that this was not for me. The bridge between the nonbeliever and the make-believe believer is sticky and rickety. So I said to him, Listen, my friend, maybe for starters I'll just read a little Bible, and we'll take it from there.

"So that's how I started reading the Bible, from the beginning. The Book of Genesis is very nice. Forefathers, mothers, sons and their brides, brothers and sisters, rivalries and jealousies. Except it didn't seem to me that the fathers took much interest in their sons, except for Jacob and your Joseph; if they're not going to slaughter them, they banish them from their homes, or just stop caring.

"Afterwards I read a little more of the Torah, the five books of Moses—how the struggles and conflicts begin between Moses and the mob that came out of Egypt with him and now long for the meat with garlic and onions, instead of which they get a severe religion. These poor souls seem to sense what will soon befall them, and begin to rebel against this cosmic faith, this authoritarian and demanding creed, which got pinned on this one little people. Interesting that this Rafaeli, for all his religiosity, told me that there's an audacious theory that claims that Moses didn't die a natural death but that the Israelites murdered him. I wanted to tell him, If that's so, it's too bad they didn't kill him thirty or forty years sooner, but I didn't say a word. One good thing you can say about these stories in the Torah is that their prose is clear, not overwritten or rambling. There's no deceptive double-talk as with the prophets. The Torah does have rebukes and curses, but they're concentrated in one place, and the hopes and consolations in another place. There's order in the world.

"And then I read a little of Joshua and mainly Judges. Those little wars are quite amusing, breaking out all the time in all sorts of places in the land of Israel, just like today; and accordingly in some remote town there pops up a homegrown judge—Ehud, Gideon, Deborah, Jephthah, Samson—to do battle for a while and then disappear. True democratic rotation."

The car arrives at a new fork and stops. What's this? The driver interrupts the stream of his lecture. Where did this come from? And he shields his eyes with his hand and peers towards the horizon.

"You can't see a thing through this filthy windscreen," says Daniela, and asks the driver for some water and a cloth. He removes a dirty rag from under his seat and hands her an army canteen, and she pours water on the windscreen and starts scraping off the dead bugs. Yirmiyahu gets out and starts to walk down the road to the left, looking for tracks from the Land Rover from the morning, then does the same for the right fork.

"If we go the wrong way, remember this is where it started," he warns Daniela as he turns the car to the left, out of mere faith that this is the right direction. Sijjin Kuang was so involved in struggling to convince her Arab patient to stay at the sanatorium that she forgot to provide the Jews with detailed directions home.

"Nevertheless," Daniela says, smiling ironically, "it makes me happy to hear that you still think of yourself as a Jew."

"But I am peeling it off. Soon enough I will be a Muzungu to the Jews."

She gives him one of her radiant looks, guaranteed to inspire trust. Over many years she has trained herself to listen calmly to the idiosyncratic opinions, some of them childish, of this man. But the ideas he has formulated in recent times have gone over the limit. Daniela is certain that if he were to find, even at his age, a new partner, her sister, too, would have been pleased.

"Yirmi, look closely, you sure you're on the right road?"

"Not certain, but I believe so. Despite those two huge trees tangled up in each other, which I don't remember from the morning."

"I actually think I do remember them."

"If so, little sister," he says, tapping on the wheel with self-satisfaction, "we're on the right track, and for the duration you have no choice but to listen to a synopsis of what I think of the prophets, and you'll see why supposedly awesome poetic passages just make my blood boil. Because people like us, lazy secular people, who wave the flag of the ethical teachings of the prophets, don't actually read them. They remember one lovely verse, some lines that have been set to music, swords beaten into ploughshares. They attack the Orthodox in the name of prophetic morality, they speak about universal justice, about courage and nonconformity—without examining too closely what this courage was for and where the nonconformity leads.

Because if you look at them, you find that all of these teachings keep hammering the same nail. Who owns the justice? By what authority is it maintained? Is it universal justice, or only the justice of the God of Israel, in a package deal of loyalty? Yes, it turns out that this justice is tied to loyalty to God, and the rage is not about the welfare of widows and orphans but about unfaithfulness to God, who is basically a kind of crazed husband, jealous of his one and only wife whom he latched onto in the desert and has tormented ever since with his commandments. The great social drama is simple jealousy. And because the language is so majestic, and the rhetoric so hypnotic, we don't pay attention to what's said between the lines."

"And what is said between the lines?" Daniela takes off her shoes, pushes back the seat, and puts up her bare feet, which reach almost to the windscreen.

"Between the lines and in the lines. Death, destruction, exile, punishment, more punishment, devastation, plague, and famine. Starving people eating their babies. It's true that sometimes, amidst those horrible passages of rebuke phrased in such flowery language, an implausible snatch of consolation will creep in, something utopian and grandiose. Conditional consolation, annoying consolation, because it all comes down to the fire normally aimed at the people of Israel being redirected towards other nations. As if there can never be in this world a minute of genuine peace, and the axe always falls on someone.

"And this we have drunk in with our mother's milk, we've been fed it like baby food. So it's no wonder that we're all set for the next destruction that will come, yes, speedily in our own time, maybe even yearning for it, look, it's already right here, we've been hearing about it, we've read it word for word in wonderful language."

The dirt road is well packed. The Land Rover's tyres ride as smoothly as if it were asphalt. The haze blurs the sunlight. The visitor takes off her sunglasses and studies the large man who so enjoys having an attentive audience for his fervid obsessions.

"You would also lecture my poor sister about all these theories?"

"Not much, because I didn't want to burden her with more gloom and doom. And soon enough reading the Bible began to nauseate me. But before I finally abandoned the book to gather dust on the shelf, I shared my thoughts with Rafaeli, the deputy director-general, and to his credit I must say he listened with great patience, like a therapist with his client, and didn't try to argue with me, but merely recommended that I drop the prophets and move on to Ecclesiastes and Proverbs, and I said to myself, Fine, let's give the Bible one more chance. So I went to the Scrolls, and it was actually in the Song of Songs that Eyal's death suddenly overwhelmed me and I read this poetry drowning in tears."

"Death in the Song of Songs?" gasps his sister-in-law.

"Because the beauty overwhelmed me. The love . . . the wondrous eroticism, the descriptions of nature. And then it hit me hard what Eyal would never be able to enjoy."

"And you never returned to the Bible?"

"Never touched it again. I cut myself off from it together with all the other useless texts."

Instinctively she presses the book to her chest and looks up at a vulture perched on a treetop, spreading its broad wings.

"Did you also read Jeremiah?"

"Of course. After all, I am his namesake, tied to him from birth. And I quickly caught on that he was the sickest and most dangerous of all the prophets. An unstable man. Exasperating. Jumping from topic to topic. A professional grouch. A low-rent strategist. Don't be misled by the beautiful language, the pretty words, the metaphors and similes, the rhythm of the sentences. All these only interfere with hearing what actually lies behind them. Now, with the English translation in your hand, you can uncover all the violence and despair. And indeed if you translate it back into Hebrew, into real everyday language, the hatred and extremism will appear from behind the feathers of the peacock's tail. Try it... why not? Here's an exercise for a teacher of English. You wanted to test your vocabulary? By all means, give yourself an exam."

How strange and special, thinks Daniela. Two grown people dealing with the Bible in the middle of the African plain. I came all the way from Israel to Tanzania to translate the Bible back into Hebrew.

She opens the book, finds Jeremiah, and says, maybe I'll read it first in English. No, he says, the English will also get fancy and lure you with linguistic decorations. Translate it spontaneously, a page at random, but into simple Hebrew, please, Hebrew that your children can understand.

She translates slowly, pressing her finger to the page, attempting to make herself heard over the wind that has started to howl.

"Therefore said God, the Lord of the regiments? Lord of Hosts . . . God of Armies. Because you say this word, then see,

I'm going to turn my words in your mouth into fire, and this people into wood, and it will gobble them up. You'll see, I'll bring a nation against you from far away, O House of Israel, says God, and it's a strong nation, an ancient nation, a nation whose language you do not know, and you won't understand what they say. Their quiver of arrows is like an open grave, they are all violent men. And they will eat up your harvest and your bread, and eat your sons and daughters, and eat your sheep and cattle, and eat up your grapes and fig trees, and with their sword they will ruin your fortified cities, which you depend on for safety. And yet, at this time, God says, I will not put an end to you. And if they ask, why does our God do all these things to us? Then you tell them, just as you left me and served strange gods in your own land, so you will also serve foreigners in a land that is not yours."

"Oof, enough." She closes the book and puts it in the glove compartment. But Yirmiyahu is delighted by her translation.

"You see? Just a random passage, and the violence is immediately revealed. A prophecy of destruction, with relish. Disaster and death and cannibalism, and suddenly, this is typical, he panics at his own prophecy, and says, Wait, for all that, it won't be the end. But why shouldn't it be? If their sins are so great, why not finish them off once and for all? Very simple, because then there won't be anyone to prophesy to; he'll have no one to torture with his curses. He will be unemployed. And why is the foreign nation entitled to such a great victory? The simple answer: Jealousy and control. Not justice, only betrayal. You worshipped other gods—so you deserve that your sons and your daughters will be eaten."

Daniela feels drained. The journey is not over, and Yirmi's driving has become slow and distracted. The haze in the air is turning into a yellow fog. The ancient prophet is wearing her out with his hatreds, and the philosophizing driver with his complaints.

"But there is one marvellous passage there," Yirmi goes on, riding the crest of his speech, "in chapter forty-something there's a section in the prophecies of Jeremiah that the editor needed a lot of courage to include. The exiles in Egypt rise in protest against the prophet, who has also ended up there, and they dare to tell him to his face: 'Enough, we've heard everything you said, and we have no intention of obeying you. It's good and pleasant for us to burn incense to the goddess— who is called by a unique name, the Queen of Heaven.' The men and husbands suddenly come to the defence of their wives who burn the incense, and say to the infuriating prophet plain and simple, 'Enough, that's it, we will keep doing the pagan ritual, because when we and our wives served this Queen in Jerusalem, we were happy, we had plenty of food.' The main thing—and this is the line I find so touching—they say to Jeremiah, listen to this: 'In Jerusalem, without all your admonitions, we were *good*, we felt we were *good*, but as soon as we started listening to you and stopped burning incense for the Queen of Heaven, we lost everything, and then came the sword and the famine.' Do you hear me? You hear?"

"Of course I do, you're yelling."

"I came upon that passage simply by chance—two or three months after we buried Eyal—and I was so moved I wanted to hug those exiles in Egypt from a distance of twenty-five hundred years. People who stood up bravely against the cursing cry-baby, the professional killjoy, who also inflicted his name on me."

The road has become bumpy, and is suddenly blocked. The driver goes out to inspect the wheels and finds them tangled in some thick vegetation with small purple flowers. Well, he says to his sister-in-law, with all this talk about the Queen of Heaven I neglected the earth, and didn't notice that we should have arrived at the farm a while ago. But not to worry. Don't panic. We'll find the right road, we're not far away. There's a walkie-talkie in the car, and also an old pistol.

13.

NOFAR NOW HEARS about the old girl for the first time, and listens with great interest to her sister-in-law's description. Ya'ari is astounded how from a few random details that he dropped last night at dinner Efrat has been able to concoct a whole story of long-standing infidelity. Wonderful, says Nofar to her father. How encouraging to know that we have such a romantic and sophisticated grandfather, and really, why not go and have a peek at her? Given her age, tomorrow may be too late, and we'll all be sorry for missing a good story.

"Even if we're dying to peek at her," Ya'ari says, surrendering to his daughter and daughter-in-law, "that still doesn't mean she can or wants to peek at us at this very moment."

"If she really loved Grandpa," Efrat declares confidently, "she'll also be interested in meeting his granddaughter and great-grandchildren and their mother. Tell her this is only a short visit. No more than fifteen minutes. Just to see Yoel's unique elevator. And she shouldn't put herself out."

Devorah Bennett is surprised to hear Ya'ari's voice on the phone, after all they had scheduled their meeting for tomorrow.

Then it is Ya'ari's turn to be surprised; secretly, without saying a word to him, his father promised to come to her in person, to feel the vibrations of the elevator with his very own body, and to listen to the cat.

"You didn't know about your father's visit tomorrow?" The old woman is astonished.

"Not even a hint."

"Because your father is probably afraid you won't let him make the trip. So listen to me, young man, and permit me to call you a young man even if you are a grandfather, I insist that you come along so he won't roll down my stairs."

"Don't worry, I won't leave him, not even for a minute."

And of course, it would give Devorah Bennett great pleasure to show them his father's elevator, and get a glimpse of his family.

Nofar runs to her department head for permission to be released a teeny bit early from her shift. When she returns without her nurse's gown she looks thin and pale, but squeezes with youthful joy between the car seats of her niece and nephew. It's nearly four o'clock, and wintry Jerusalem, soon to be deprived of its Sabbath, seems to be blending religiosity and secularism into one grey experience. Ya'ari parks the car right in front of the Old Knesset, drawing on his own faith that an Orthodox mayor will not countenance violating the Sabbath by the writing of a parking ticket. Nofar and Efrat unfasten the drowsy children from their seats and zip up their coats. And Nofar, who is especially attached to her little nephew, smothers him with hugs and kisses before picking him up and carrying him across King George Street.

"Why are you carrying him?" Ya'ari scolds his daughter. "He's very heavy."

"To me he's cute and light, and he enjoys being in my arms. Right, Nadi?"

The child says nothing, but hugs his young aunt tightly.

With considerable clamour Ya'ari leads his family up the stairs of the old Jerusalem building. Nadi insists on being carried up the stairs as well. You're spoiling him, grumbles Efrat. No problem, mutters Nofar, staggering under the weight of her favourite boy.

Devorah Bennett is pleased to have a gang of young people visiting her apartment at this grey Jerusalem hour. How did you arrange to get yourself such sweet grandchildren? she teases Ya'ari, as if sweetness has never been the strong suit in his family. The children are drawn to the sprightly old lady, who gives them squares of chocolate and leads them with the rest of the group to her bedroom, to show all of them the tiny elevator that their great-grandfather invented. In the corridor between the living room and bedroom they pass the consultation room; its open door reveals a dignified, heavy-set woman sitting inside, smoking a cigarette in a long holder. The hostess introduces her to the guests: This is Mrs. Karidi, an old patient who has become a friend, and now instead of my taking care of her, she takes care of me. The lady exhales a big smoke ring and with the throaty laugh of a chronic smoker waves it away.

In the bedroom the doors of the closet are also open, and a small grille is pulled back, and there is the tiny home elevator, now containing a small armchair. Come, children, let's go up to the roof, the grandfather says brightly to his grandchildren, and along the way maybe you'll hear the wailing of a starving cat.

Neta is afraid to go in without her mother, but Nadi has faith in his grandpa and enters the elevator with him. Ya'ari closes the grille and presses the right button. And again it starts with a loud knock, and the vibration is accompanied by the hidden wailing, the whole slow way to the roof.

The frightened grandson scratches his grandfather's hand, and Ya'ari draws closer to the toddler, and the child hugs his leg. Then, still clinging to each other, they go out onto the roof to see the darkening city. A cold wind blows between the old water tanks, and Ya'ari lifts the child, so he won't trip over the black cables of the satellite dishes. There's the Old Knesset, he explains, pointing at the dark building. From down in the apartment they call out to Grandpa to shut the grille, so they can bring down the elevator. Then the whole group quickly gathers on the roof, led by the old girl, wrapped in a colourful blanket. Nofar and Efrat are thrilled, as if they were standing on the roof of the world, and Nofar is sorry because new construction has blocked the view of the Old City walls, where at night they light huge Hanukkah candles on David's Citadel. How many candles tonight? asks Efrat. Tonight, Neta reminds her, we light the sixth candle. So let's light them at home, says her mother. We need to be getting back.

Night falls rapidly. The first scattered stars appear through shreds of clouds, and lights go on in the streets. The Jerusalem air is chilly, but dry, and a light wind is blowing, but everyone except Nofar is dressed appropriately. Again she sweeps her nephew into her loving grip and waves him in the air, not far from the railing. Enough, really, scowls her father, this child is heavy, you'll end up putting your back out.

And suddenly the former patient, Mrs. Karidi, also appears

on the roof with a fresh cigarette burning in her holder. Like a round boat with a lone headlight shining on its prow, she glides her full bulk between the water tanks and satellite dishes, making for the edge of the roof to get a fine view of the world. Indeed, soon her smoker's raspy voice is heard, and a hand waves from afar. Children, she calls, come and see the fire. And in fact the dignified lady has discovered a breach in the curtain of new construction that hides the Old City walls, that gives them a glimpse of six splendid torches that celebrate the holiday of Hanukkah.

14.

DANIELA GETS OUT to guide her brother-in-law as he turns the car around. We'll backtrack a bit, he says, and if we can't find the fork where we went astray, we'll wait till they get in touch with us from the farm and guide us home. Don't worry, this has also happened when Sijjin Kuang was driving, and they always found us. Anyway, I'm sure I recognize that hill across from us, I can see it from my bed. You should recognize it, too, since you've been sleeping there for four nights.

The car retraces its path, but after two kilometres or so they reach an indistinct four-way intersection where they have never been before, and Yirmi brakes, turns off the engine, and says, that's it. We'll wait here, so we don't pile one mistake on another.

And from the tool chest he takes out a rag and unwraps a large pistol, saying, I always forget how to undo the safety catch, so I don't use this very often, but if an impressive enough animal comes near us, we'll try to scare him off. He then takes out a two-way field radio and turns on its red flare. Like the gun, it is a souvenir of British times, or maybe even German, but miraculously enough, it still works.

Suddenly the radio emits a screech of chatter, and Yirmiyahu flips a switch and identifies himself with a few words of English. It's too early for them to get worried about us, he explains to his sister-in-law, but soon, when it gets dark and they see we haven't returned, somebody will be sure to make contact. Don't worry, we're really not far, and there's no danger.

"I'm not worried," his sister-in-law answers calmly, "I'm convinced that Shuli, like me, chose a reliable husband."

They sit silently in the car, as the sky grows purple. Daniela senses that her brother-in-law is in a good mood, perhaps because of the rage he vented at the prophet who gave him his name. And so she dares to turn to him softly and ask, Tell me, but only if it's not hard for you, do you know now what happened there that night with Eyali?

"Yes, I understand the whole thing," he answers simply. "That Palestinian, who gave Eyali coffee to keep him awake, knew exactly why Eyal came down from the roof, but he didn't tell anyone, mainly because it didn't occur to anyone to ask him. I knew that Eyal was always precise about time, and the watch they returned to us had also stopped at about the right time, so I was forced to sidestep the army to find out why the soldiers mistook him for their wanted man. I approached a Christian pharmacist, an Arab named Emile from East Jerusalem, an intelligent man who managed to reclaim his father's pharmacy in the western part of the city. I was one of his customers, and we became friendly, and he knew that Eyali had been killed, and I also told him about the friendly fire. So I went to him, and asked if he could help put me in touch with the Palestinian from Tulkarm, who had dodged the meeting with me and the officer.

"And about two weeks later, in exchange for a considerable sum—not for the pharmacist, who acted purely out of goodwill, but for the Palestinian, a man of about sixty, cold and suspicious, who was wary of revealing his name—we met in a greenhouse at Moshav Nitzanei Oz, where he worked as a day labourer, so he could explain to me what he saw on the roof from his vantage down below. And what happened was so simple in its stupidity, so human but also so embarrassing, that I took pity on Shuli and told her nothing. As for me, I could have banged my head against the wall from despair."

Daniela stares at him.

"My precious innocent son, dumb, civilized, the soldier who commandeers the roof of a conquered family and fills the residents with dread—is ashamed to leave behind the bucket they gave him, filled with what it was filled with, because he was afraid . . ."

"Afraid?"

"Afraid for his good name, his dignity in the eyes of the Palestinian family, and so he doesn't leave the bucket on the roof, and doesn't pour it away from the roof, but a few minutes ahead of time he goes down with it, and not to get rid of it in some corner, but to rinse it thoroughly, to rinse it, do you hear? So he can return it to the family as clean as he got it. Innocence? Consideration? Respect? Mainly stupidity. Abysmal lack of understanding about what to take risks for and what not. And so, a minute before the shooting, the Arab hears the water in the courtyard. And the soldiers lying in ambush saw not their friend *coming down* from the roof, but rather a figure slipping *into* the building—why wouldn't they think this was the wanted man they've been waiting for all night?"

"And the Arab saw all this with his own eyes?"

"He didn't see a thing. He was inside the house. But the turning on of the tap and the sound of rinsing woke him—he was sleeping lightly that night in any case—and right after that, he heard the shots, and in the morning, when the soldiers had already taken Eyali and got out of there, he found his bucket in the doorway, rinsed and clean. Here was a soldier who was ready to disobey explicit instructions so he could say, 'I too am a human being, and I am giving you back a clean bucket. I may have conquered you, but I did not contaminate you.'"

"And the Arab—was he at least touched by what Eyali did?"

"I asked myself exactly that, not at that moment, but later, when I had digested the story. Because the man told it all with a blank expression, without feeling, just the facts, and took the money and hurried back to Tulkarm, as it would soon be curfew."

"But why didn't you tell Shuli?"

"Don't you know your sister? She would have immediately blamed herself, because of the way she had brought him up, all that insane order and cleanliness of hers."

Daniela falls silent. She knows exactly where his words are heading.

The hill that serves as their reference point gradually loses its outline and turns into a murky silhouette. A large flock of birds flaps through the soft air. Yirmiyahu takes the stretcher from the vehicle, places it on the ground and lies down. Daniela looks at the big bald man, whose eyes are closed. She wants to say something to him, but decides against it. She gets out of the car and walks a short distance away, finds a spot concealed by taller grass, takes down her pants, crouches and relieves herself slowly. And as the last drops fall she raises her eyes to the heavens and discovers the first cluster of stars shining overhead.

A sharp chirping pierces the African emptiness and quickly fades into a sob. And then a crackling, metallic voice speaking excellent English calls out, Jeremy, Jeremy, where are you? Yirmi leaps up from the stretcher to seize the connection.

"Come, Daniela," he calls to his sister-in-law as he starts the engine, "get in and see the surprise that's waiting for you."

And as they slowly make their way along the dirt road towards the murky hill, a flare shoots into the sky and spreads a canopy of yellow light. Slowly, slowly sinks the flame, and the trail of light dies down, and then another candle shoots through the darkness, and following that, a third.

Seventh Candle

1.

JUST LAST NIGHT, his elderly father said to him: I want you to know that I definitely do *not* need you tomorrow. Francisco and I have organized a whole crew to take care of the little Jerusalem elevator. You can relax and tend to business at the office and get the house ready for Daniela. But if you insist on coming along, then early in the morning, please. Before noon my shaking is not as bad.

"But morning, Abba, not dawn."

"We'll compromise on in between. The difference isn't that much."

When Ya'ari arrives at his father's home at half past seven he finds him trembling in his wheelchair, ready to go. Washing must have been accomplished at first light, and breakfast too, and on the table, cleared of crumbs, the Filipino baby is avidly sucking her toe, surrounded by five plastic containers filled with sandwiches, biscuits, and peeled vegetables.

"You don't trust your woman in Jerusalem to feed us?"

"Food there will surely be, but I know this lady very well. Given her regal manners my staff may be too intimidated to go to her table. We're taking care of them, so they won't be dependent on her refreshments."

"The staff, the staff," scoffs Ya'ari, "what staff?"

It turns out that a real delegation has been assembled, six escorts for one old man, not counting Ya'ari himself: a private ambulance driver; two Filipino friends recruited by Francisco; Hilario, in the role of interpreter; and one little surprise . . .

"What surprise?"

"A surprise," smiles his father, "when you see her, you'll understand right away that this is a surprise."

"But what sort of surprise?"

"A little patience, please. Have I ever disappointed you?"

Ya'ari looks fondly at his father, who is dressed festively for the occasion in a white shirt and black jacket; a red tie lies folded in his lap. His shaking does not seem any better this morning.

"And your medicines?"

"I took a little more than the usual dose. And I have another dose in my pocket, in case the old girl tries to exceed the bounds of propriety."

"How many years since you've seen her?"

"Not since the beginning of the millennium. When my illness got worse, I understood that it would not be dignified for us elderly people to peddle illusions to ourselves."

"Illusions about what?"

The father removes his glasses and brings his wristwatch close to his eyes to verify that the second hand is moving. Then he looks up at his son and grumbles, "Illusions . . . illusions . . . you know exactly what I mean, so don't pretend this morning to be somebody you're not."

"Meaning what?"

"Meaning a conventional, naïve, limited, engineer."

The elder Ya'ari, who had no formal education, still sometimes teases his son about his degree in engineering. But the son doesn't drop the subject.

"Illusions that love can be a consolation for death?"

The father waves his hands irritably.

"If that explanation makes you feel better, then we'll agree on it. But do me a favour and save the philosophy for later, and instead tell me, should I put on the red tie, or is it too much?"

"If you don't also plan to put on makeup for the visit, then a red tie will brighten your pale face."

"But a festive tie may give the wrong impression, that I'm coming as something more than a technician fulfilling a guarantee."

Ya'ari takes hold of his father's quivering hand.

"Lover-technician, nothing is more attractive than that."

There's a quiet knock at the door. Hilario, who is sitting by the table making sure that the baby won't spread her arms and legs and fly to the floor, runs to answer it. Two Filipino youths with sad adult faces enter awkwardly and are drawn immediately to their infant compatriot, who greets them with a friendly smile. Kinzie hurries in from the kitchen to introduce the newcomers, Marco and Pedro, good friends and fellow carers who got the morning off from their employers to help a friend carry his boss up four flights of stairs to his lover in Jerusalem.

2.

EVEN AFTER FIVE nights here she still wakes up in pitch
darkness. This time she's roused by a sudden anxiety about
Nofar, whose devotion to her service in the hospital could get
her unwittingly infected by some rare disease. The day after
tomorrow, immediately on returning to Israel, she will demand
that Nofar spell out for her which inoculations are given to
assistant nurses and explain the procedures for handling people
afflicted with dubious illnesses. It has been several years since
she and Amotz have grown wary of intervening in Nofar's
private affairs, but illness is not a private affair.

She considers whether to turn on a light in the room or to
try and cling to the tail end of the sleep that is slipping away
from her. After fifteen minutes of lying still with her eyes closed
she concedes that this night's slumber has abandoned her for
good, and she turns on the light, intending to replace her own
worries with the material and moral losses of the heroine of the
novel. But after two pages the arbitrariness of the plot again
stops her short. Fictional troubles can't trump real concerns,
and given no choice she lays aside the novel and picks up the
King James Bible. At first she returns to the Book of Jeremiah,
to assess calmly the validity of the heated protest against the
prophet by the man bearing his name. And indeed, the level of
aggression directed by the biblical Jeremy against his
countrymen, coupled with such ornate linguistic virtuosity,
confirms her brother-in-law's accusation: that these furious
prophecies were delivered with pleasure and satisfaction, rather
than sorrow or pain.

She looks for the Book of Job. There, at least, she can find human suffering with a personal, not a national, dimension. She hopes, too, to find in it rare words to challenge her English.

In this version, for some reason the Book of Job is in a different place, hidden in a spot that considerably precedes Jeremiah. Once she locates it, though, she has no trouble at all collecting words indecipherable to her, such as:

froward
collops
assuaged
reins
gin
cockle
neesing

It is wondrous and pleasing to encounter in the Bible vocabulary she fails utterly to understand in a language that she loves and teaches, and she writes the words down on the last page of the novel. Perhaps she can use them to test the regional supervisor of English Studies back home, an ironic bachelor from South Africa who likes her and cultivates her company. But would it be nice to embarrass a friend with a test he might well not pass?

Then she lets go of Job, which does seem to her a more estimable text, but stuffed with tedious repetitions. And in general—a lazy drowsiness flutters her eyes—one could compress the Bible a bit without losing anything significant. With the book in her hand she gets up to close the blinds against the imminent sunrise, but before laying it down and turning off the light, she decides to have a look at the Song of Songs.

Right from the sensual start—*Let him kiss me with the kisses of his mouth*—the English flows melodically. Here there's not one cryptic word; each one seems right and trustworthy, with the spirit of the original Hebrew hovering over the lines. The old-fashioned English resonates with grace and grandeur, even a hint of humour. Here is love, open and generous, sometimes pleading for its life, sometimes daring and expansive, bronzed by the noon sun, or burning at night. Yes, now she understands why it was here that the bereaved father began to sob.

I am black, but comely,
O ye daughters of Jerusalem,
As the tents of Kedar,
As the curtains of Solomon.
Look not upon me because I am black—
Because the sun hath looked upon me.

In the imagination of the white woman, on her bed at night in the Dark Continent, the Sudanese Sijjin Kuang arises now from the desert, black and comely, her stature like a palm tree, and goes about the city at night, sick with love, wandering through streets and markets, searching for the one that her soul has loved, and she cannot find him, and the watchmen on the walls find her and beat and wound her, and tear away her scarf, and she is as a rose among the thorns . . .

And the Israeli visitor is drawn to her and runs after her, skimming through the eight chapters not in tears, but with a pounding heart.

O that thou wert as my brother,
That sucked the breasts of my mother,
When I should find thee without,
I would kiss thee;
Yes, I should not be despised.

She closes the book and sets it aside. Turns off the light, curls up, and plummets into merciful sleep. And not one hour passes but three, as the violent morning light tries in vain to peek between the slats. At last a knock at the door wakes her; surely it is her brother-in-law calling her to breakfast, or else Sijjin Kuang who has returned, and without a second's thought she invites whoever is at the unlocked door to enter, but the door does not open, because out by the stairway stands the Ugandan archaeologist Dr. Robert Kukiriza, who very politely asks permission to enter for a private conversation.

And because she is flattered by the fact that the star intellectual of the team has seen fit to come alone to her room, she asks him to wait a moment, and she takes off her nightie and runs barefoot to wash her face, puts on the African dress, quickly makes the bed, after closing the Israeli novel lying there face down and standing it on the shelf beside the Bible. Just before going to the door, she opens the shutters wide to let in some pure fresh air, and then, still barefoot, she turns the handle.

3.

Now FRANCISCO ENTERS with Maurice, the owner of today's private ambulance, who years ago used to transport the lady of the house to clinics and hospitals for her tests and treatments. He is an Egyptian Jew, and brought with him to Israel the easygoing, patient temperament of the denizens of the land of the Nile. Sometimes, with just a few words, he instils hope in his round-trip clients. In her final years, Ya'ari's mother became quite attached to him, and preferred his ambulance to a taxi even for shopping or visits to friends.

"And here's our Maurice," says Ya'ari's father, spreading his arms with affection to greet the short, solidly built man. "When we see you, we remember the one who loved you so."

Maurice leans over the wheelchair and clasps the old man to his breast carefully, as if he were made of glass, then warmly shakes young Ya'ari's hand. How happy he is to be summoned again into service by the Ya'ari family, especially not for a trip to a hospital but to an old loved one.

The old man turns crimson and wags his finger back and forth at Francisco, who talked too much. But Ya'ari laughs, here's proof for you that the heart just gets younger every day.

It's raw and drizzly in Tel Aviv, and Jerusalem will presumably be worse. Ya'ari insists that Francisco wrap his father in a big coat and, over that, the black plastic poncho, with its hood like the ones on his grandchildren's jackets. And after Marco and Pedro load a tool box, prepared ahead of time, into the ambulance, and the cooler with the plastic containers of food, they take the suitor down in the elevator and wheel him, too, into the familiar blue vehicle that has grown a bit old, like its owner. For a moment Ya'ari deliberates whether to join his father in the ambulance or preserve his freedom and drive his own car. In the end he decides to supervise his father from close by, though he will need to crouch and squeeze in among the silent Filipinos.

"And what about the surprise?"

"The surprise is waiting at 9 Rabin Square, next to the Book Worm."

And the driver is advised accordingly.

Beside the bookstore, still closed at this hour, cloaked by a veil of fine rain, waits a figure of indeterminate age and gender. Even as it nimbly hops into the ambulance and removes its hat to shake the rain from it, uncovering cropped hair and a slightly wrinkled face, it is still hard to tell whether this person is male or female, young or old.

But the old man solves the riddle. Say hello to Gottlieb's expert, who today will help us interpret the shakes and howls in Jerusalem. Rochele? Roleleh? Is that the name? May I introduce my son and heir, Amotz.

"I already met the heir of the heir," the small woman says, smiling as she removes her wet jacket to reveal a blue jumpsuit, "and I hoped he'd be here, too."

"He is confined by the army for shirking his reserve duty."

"That doesn't seem to fit him."

"There are facts that don't fit reality," sighs Ya'ari.

Marco and Pedro gaze appreciatively at the tiny expert. With her subtle mix of boyish body and mature face, despite her blonde hair and blue eyes she could be taken for Filipino.

"Moran told me that you listened together to the winds in

Pinsker, and that you think the problem is not with our elevators, but entirely with flaws in the shaft."

"I don't think," the expert explains patiently, "I'm certain. You have to put the building contractor on the roof of an elevator, give him a powerful torch, and take him straight up to his blunder, so he can see it and take responsibility."

"That's exactly what I suggested to Gottlieb," Ya'ari agrees, impressed by the woman's professional confidence. "I said we should light up the shaft. But our firm has no authority to touch the elevators, which are guaranteed by *your* company, and unfortunately your Gottlieb is stubbornly refusing to take any action, even to prove the responsibility lies elsewhere."

"But of course," interrupts the expert vigorously. "What does he care? He's stingy over every turn of a screw that doesn't bring him any income. I've known him since childhood; he's sort of my stepfather."

"Gottlieb is your stepfather?" The elder Ya'ari trembles with astonishment and futilely attempts to edge his wheelchair closer to her. The rain clatters on the roof of the ambulance; the small windows are steamed up.

"You didn't know? He never gave a hint?"

"Nothing."

"It's just like him to conceal our family relationship. My father worked for him in the factory, and after he died, Gottlieb advised my mother to send me off to a kibbutz, to save money and also so he could get close to her. Whenever I came back on holiday, he would go into a sulk and disappear from the house, to avoid any responsibilities. I was always abnormal in his opinion, for one thing because I remained short and skinny. At first he totally disapproved of my working in the regional auto repair shop. This didn't fit his view of women. He thought it was more appropriate for me to work in the kitchen, or the kibbutz laundry. But when it turned out I had this talent for hearing technical flaws, and I proved it with elevators he was making, he got all excited and invited me to work for him. And yet to this day it's hard for him to admit openly that I'm also a member of the family. I think I frighten him a little."

"Why?" inquires Ya'ari.

"What do I know? I think he's a little scared of things that seem irrational to him, mystical stuff. To him it's as if I heard voices, and people like him are afraid that even if they can make good use of it, one day it'll come back to haunt them and they'll lose all their money."

Old Ya'ari bursts out laughing and squeezes her hand with affection.

"But really, how did you get to be such an expert? Moran was also impressed by you."

"It may surprise you, but my hearing was discovered by way of music."

"What kind of music, my dear?" asks the old man, apparently enchanted by this childlike woman.

"Maybe you've heard of the musical celebrations at Kfar Blum, the chamber music festival that Israel Radio puts on every year at the kibbutz? Civilized people come there from all over the country to hear performances of classical music, hoping it will turn them into classy people. The kibbutz is responsible for all the administration, operations, and housing, and it's a good business. And there're a lot of jobs, too. Stewards, ushers, staff to organize the rehearsal rooms, set up chairs and music stands, move pianos, see to the lighting. At the festival the public is invited to attend rehearsals, and those who know best say that this is the peak experience. There are even connoisseurs who don't go to any concerts at all, only to the rehearsals. After the army I began to work in the support staff, and I ended up at a lot of those rehearsals, where I would hear comments about tempo and tone colour, the subtleties of vibrato and half-muted crescendi, and mischievous glissandi, and also how not to screech or play out of tune. And really, since Bach fugues and Mozart sonatas have been played for a few hundred years, can anything new be added to them in the social hall of Kfar Blum, except maybe some tiny nuance of interpretation? So I would sit there, fascinated, my ears wide open, and when they showed me how music is written, I discovered that I had not only good hearing, but perfect pitch, meaning that I can not only hear the intervals between notes but also identify every note by name, and even sing music from the page in the right register."

"Perfect pitch without ever studying music?"

"Yes, apparently I was born with it. And when I learned that I had hearing like this, I started to listen to sounds at the garage too, to put my sensitive ears to use finding the connection between grating noises and other weird sounds in trucks and tractors and malfunctions in their engines, and it turned out I could hear tiny noises, and if you took care of them in time, you could avoid a whole lot of trouble later. I mean, in this country, until something actually breaks down or falls apart, nobody pays attention or takes preventive measures. Even right now I can hear the automatic transmission in this ambulance scraping when it changes gears, and our driver ought to check the oil in the gearbox, when we get to Jerusalem, so we don't get stuck in the rain on the way back."

4.

DANIELA CANNOT REMEMBER the ages of the rock fragments that were laid out beside her dinner plate four days ago, on that unforgettable evening at the dig, but she did grasp the archaeologist's explanation of evolutionary "transmission" and believes that when the time comes she will be able to summarize it for Amotz. Her Ugandan visitor is the only member of the research team who holds a Ph.D., and from the archaeology department of the University of London, no less, and this strengthens his self-confidence and his independence, as he boldly invites himself into the chamber of a foreign lady to make a highly unusual request.

"I am sorry for the disturbance and invasion of your privacy," apologizes the slender black man, as he seats himself on the stool at the foot of the bed, "but since we know that you are returning to your country tomorrow, and we are returning to our excavations this evening, we have decided to speak with you in private even before getting Jeremy's approval. It is very important to us that you will hear our request first, so you may consider it on your own, before consulting with your brother-in-law. You see that I am not speaking only for myself, but for my friends, who are happy for your short visit and your very generous interest. But first of all I wish to ask you, is there any chance that you will return to Tanzania or to Africa within the next year?"

"Return to Africa in the next year?" She smiles. "I don't think so. More likely I will never come back. This is a private visit, sort of a visit of consolation for me and my brother-in-law, and it has fulfilled its purpose. I also don't think my husband will agree to another separation from me. We visited Tanzania together three years ago, when my sister was still alive, and together with her and her husband we went to the nature reserves. If Jeremy decides to stay with you, he will have to come to see us."

Despite the archaeologist's appreciation of her presence now, Daniela senses that he is pleased that she has no intention of making another trip, as if his request were dependent upon her leaving here forever.

"By the way, Jeremy also will not be able to stay with us a long time."

"Why?" she inquires, a bit concerned.

"Because the research team has a budget for only one more year, and after that we will return to our respective countries. But I believe Jeremy is already looking for another position."

"Where?" she scowls. "He'd be better off coming back to Israel."

"But he doesn't think your country has a chance."

"Nonsense . . . don't listen to what he says."

Dr. Kukiriza is surprised by the sudden storminess of the Israeli woman, which is followed by a long silence. Only slowly does he overcome his hesitancy, and in a gentle voice begins in a roundabout fashion to explain his request. He starts with the plight of the African scientist, who for all his personal boldness and independence is still officially dependent upon the evaluations of the white researcher who controls the official archival record and the state-of-the-art laboratories. There are members of the team who correspond by e-mail with scholars in America and Europe who study the great apes of Africa, and who report to their colleagues what we have discovered here and hope to find in the future, but even if these whites encourage Africans, they cannot confer final scientific verification on their work until they see and feel the actual evidence, and this verification is essential not only for our confidence and feelings of self-worth, but also to increase our funding.

"So why don't you send them what you found, it's so simple."

"It could be simple," says the Ugandan, "but it is not. Because there is a strict ban on removing what we find from the country without the permission of the government."

"Why?"

"Because these fossils are considered a national treasure."

"Monkey bones?"

"Of course, madam." His face darkens and his voice becomes tense. Even the bones of apes millions of years old are a national treasure of the first order, and when a great anthropological museum is built in Tanzania or a neighbouring African country, it will include a place of honour for the findings of this research team. In Africa they do not have artistic masterpieces, nor historical memories of ancient battles and wars that changed the face of the earth, nor writers and thinkers whose works have become classics, and yet humanity originated in Africa, so why should they not take pride in what they have given to the world? If humanity still matters.

Now she feels embarrassed by what she said in haste and nods her head with enthusiasm.

And he continues to explain that when findings are sent outside Africa, there is a need not only for special permission but also for insurance and guarantees that everything will be returned intact, and thus the cost of such a shipment is beyond their ability to pay, not to mention having to navigate the long and complex bureaucratic procedures. There is a concern that if bones like these begin to travel the world, scientists will not come to Africa from far and wide to inspect them closely. In Ethiopia recently, the signature of the president himself was required to ship the jawbone of a chimpanzee for examination in France.

"To that extent?"

"To that extent." He rises from the stool and begins to pace about the room, lost in thought, as the moment arrives to unveil his question.

"Are you perhaps familiar with an institute in Israel called Abu Kabir?"

"Abu Kabir?" She is surprised to hear the well-known name on the lips of the black man. "Of course . . . it's our main pathology institute."

"An Arab institute?"

"Why, no," she corrects him, "this is an Israeli institute where all are equal, Jews and Arabs, and the Arab name is left over from some village that was maybe there once and destroyed in a war. But it's in Tel Aviv."

The Ugandan closes his eyes for a moment.

"Abu Kabir, meaning Father of the Great One, a beautiful, strong name for an institute of pathology."

"A beautiful name?" She is taken aback. "For us it's a name that arouses great fear. This is where they identify the bodies of victims of terrorist attacks."

"So it is also explained on the institute's website. But apparently because of the many victims you have, Abu Kabir has developed into a very advanced and sophisticated institute, which supports scientific research involving identification from the past as well."

"That could be," Daniela says, crossing her arms and hugging her shoulders, "but I wouldn't dare go near there, not even to their website."

"And we asked ourselves," says Dr. Kukiriza, ignoring her response, "if we might take advantage of your return tomorrow to send a few findings to Abu Kabir for analysis."

"What findings?"

"Bones. Three little bones that weigh next to nothing, no more than twelve centimetres in length."

"And you want me to take these to Abu Kabir to pose them a riddle: Who is the deceased?"

"In our opinion, these are bones of our prehistoric ape, *Australopithecus afarensis*. You have already had the chance to feel them. They are clean and odourless. Dry bones, but not fragile ones, which will not take up much room in your suitcase. We have already been in e-mail contact with a researcher at Abu Kabir, Professor Perlman, and she has agreed to accept them for testing."

And now that his wish has finally been expressed, he peers with fiery eyes and heightened expectation at Daniela, who remains uncomprehending.

"But if, as you say, bones like these are national property, don't I need official approval to take them with me?"

"Yes," admits the archaeologist candidly, "approval is necessary." But as he has just explained, the process is long and convoluted, and so they were hoping, he and his friends, to circumvent it by her good grace. For who will suspect a middle-aged lady, an ordinary tourist, of smuggling important bones? And who is looking for bones anyway, at the airport? And even if they are discovered, who can tell that they are millions of years old? And who will care? These are animal bones, not human. And even if we assume that someone, in Africa or Israel, insists on a clear answer as to why she has these dry bones, she can say that she innocently picked them up in the wild as a souvenir of Africa, and thought of using them as a paperweight on her desk.

A smile lights up the woman's face. She already knows her answer, but deliberately withholds it.

"We, of course, will ask for your brother-in-law's permission, but first we wanted to know if such a mission was possible from your standpoint."

"Possible," she answers faintly, "if it is really important to you."

"It is very important to us."

"If so," and her voice grows stronger, "don't involve my brother-in-law. Why make him anxious?"

5.

THE STORM, WIND and rain, preceded them on their mutual journey from the coast to the capital, and made worse the boisterous traffic of downtown Jerusalem. But an ambulance, even a private blue one, is entitled to use the fast lane reserved for buses and to park anywhere it pleases, including on the pavement across from the Old Knesset building. The old man quickly plucks the hat from his head and removes the plastic poncho, and in his wrinkled black suit, enhanced by the red tie, he wheels himself straight to the stairs, and there surprises his escorts by asking to be allowed to get out of his chair and climb to the top floor with the help of his cane alone.

This is not the first time that Ya'ari's father has rejected his wheelchair. Daniela regularly encourages him to do it, even though this unsettles Ya'ari, since it's harder to steer a trembling old man supported only by a cane. This time the old man's decision is firm. He will not appear before his friend as an invalid. The shakes of the illness will in any case be mixed up with the tremors of his excitement, but the wheelchair shames his manhood. Even a mere technician would not dream of showing up in a wheelchair. It is precisely for this purpose that he has asked Francisco to bring along his two short and powerful friends, who now support him by his armpits and from the rear, so that he seems to be floating up the stairs, floor by floor, to the door he knows so well, which still displays the old plaque: Dr. Devorah Bennett—Psychoanalyst.

Here, the father surprises his staff again, by insisting that they go back down to the next landing and wait invisibly in the stairwell, for he wants to make his entrance as a man leaning only on his cane. Amotz and Gottlieb's expert join the four Filipinos, and they all crowd into the landing half a storey below, positioning themselves where the psychoanalyst will not notice them. And the old man himself, bent over, leaning on his cane, slightly loosens his tie and rings the doorbell three times—their signal, arranged in years past, that he is not a patient. And the door is opened by the lady of the house, who in his honour has put on a woollen dress and let down her hair, and though she looks shrunken and wrinkled in the morning light, her step is light and her voice lively.

"Here's the boy," she exclaims, "but where's the wheelchair that came between us? Are you still ashamed of it?"

The old man is shocked into silence.

"What's the matter, my dear," she says, squeezing his shoulder. "I'm the same young woman you left years ago. No need to be alarmed. And you have such a nice cane."

The old man succumbs to his twofold trembling and the cane slips from his hand. So as not to collapse on the doorstep, he pitches himself forwards and clings for dear life to the fragile old woman, who struggles to keep her balance under the unexpected load, and begins weeping on her shoulder.

From the staircase Ya'ari hears his father sobbing, perhaps for the first time in his life. Little Hilario looks up at him with perplexed concern, as if curious to know why he doesn't run over to help. But Ya'ari freezes. He sees his father's weeping as a great volcanic blast of liberation. I will do him wrong, he says to himself, if I go up now and embarrass him. He looks at the Filipinos sitting quietly on the stairs, half-listening, perhaps pining for their homeland. Only in the big bright eyes of the expert flickers a little smile, as if in the cries and whimpers she can make out hidden melodies.

Summoning all her strength, Devorah Bennett pulls the old man into the apartment and leaves the door open, which is a sign for Ya'ari and crew to enter cautiously. His father has already been taken into her treatment room, and is apparently propped in her chair, since she is saying very loudly, as if his hearing were also impaired: See, now you're the therapist and I'm your patient.

Ya'ari seats the Filipinos around the dining table, which is elegantly arrayed with expensive refreshments. As one already familiar with the apartment, he directs the expert towards the bedroom. In the hallway he puts a hushing finger to his lips as they tiptoe past the treatment room, but his father is on the alert and notices them. For the moment I'm only letting her hear the noises; I'm not dismantling anything, Ya'ari tells him, as he leads the small woman to the miracle of the tiny elevator.

"So," he says, looking into her wide blue eyes, "I bet you've never seen a contraption like this."

She smiles with amusement. This is something impressive. He pulls open the grille and escorts her into the tiny cage, which seems made to order for a nymph like her, with her cropped hair and nearly flat chest and aroma of freshly mown grass. Show me your stuff, he challenges her, pressing the up button, and the elevator begins to groan and shake and wrestle with itself, but before the expert can voice an opinion he puts a finger to her lips, Wait, he says, there's another surprise for you. And then, during the slow ascent, the wailing of the cat on heat begins to waft into the tiny space. The expert's mouth is agape with laughter. She looks around to find the electrical connections, but the walls are blank. She then reaches over and removes the picture of Jung, revealing a primitive electrical box, and as she does so the hungry yowling grows louder. The expert has already produced a small voltage tester from her jumpsuit pocket, but Ya'ari stops her. No, he will not let her near the wiring until they disconnect the current that comes from the electricity company.

"Where else would it come from?"

"You don't understand. It circumvents the regular connection to the apartment."

"Why?"

"Because the building doesn't have three-phase current, meaning that the electricity company would have had to be called in to switch the hookup, and they would have started drilling problematic holes all over the walls. Back when the elevator was built, the wait for such an operation could take two years, not to mention the cost that the lady was not equipped to undertake, even though my father offered to pay for it. So he tapped straight into the electricity pole."

"By what authority?"

"His own. This was a generation that didn't always distinguish between private and public property."

"Yes," smiles the former kibbutznik, "I know a few of those old socialists myself."

They go out onto the roof, and the winds try to shove them off. Ya'ari steps back. In stormy weather like this they'll never find the rogue cable, and there's obviously no chance of taking his father up here in the hope he'll remember where it is. But neither cold nor wind can intimidate the expert, and like a small gazelle she skips among the pot-bellied water tanks, hops around satellite dishes, puts her ear against old fraying clothes lines that haven't been used for decades.

A rare creature, thinks Ya'ari as he follows her movements, wondering what Daniela would make of her. Not only is her age elusive, but her sex seems to change from hour to hour. No wonder Gottlieb is scared of her. And now, despite the deluge from above, she succeeds in finding the cable.

"Don't touch a thing," shouts Ya'ari, but his voice is muffled by the roaring winds.

She points to an insulated wire that runs innocently among the clothes lines and surreptitiously comes to rest on to the roof railing, from there heading somewhere unspecific to steal electricity.

She rests her belly against the railing and leans way down to trace the route of the wire, her legs in the air. Ya'ari races over in a panic and pulls her back, and she lands like a feather on the roof and rolls over.

"I'm warning you," he says, extending his hand to hers, "don't touch anything here."

"But if we don't disconnect the electricity, how can we fix the connector box?"

"Let it keep yowling at her forever," he retorts, "she's not worth getting electrocuted for."

"If that's what you want," she says, her eyes wide with disappointment. "But you're giving me a day's pay for nothing."

"And if it's for nothing, what do you care?" he says, leading her by the arm back towards the elevator. "But don't worry," he adds, a new idea dawning, "your workday isn't over. When we get back to Tel Aviv we'll go and listen to the shaft in the Pinsker Tower. Strong winds like these shouldn't go to waste."

6.

AFTER THE ARCHAEOLOGIST has left her room, Daniela reconsiders. Maybe it's not right to conceal from Yirmi the little mission she has just undertaken. She puts on shoes and makeup, and goes down to the kitchen.

In the kitchen the cooks are preparing the last meal for the research team. New provisions are also arriving, but Yirmiyahu is not at the table by the entrance to list them and pay the suppliers.

"Where's Jeremy?" she inquires of her friend the elderly groundskeeper. He tells her that her brother-in-law was there a few moments ago, but a bad headache drove him to the infirmary.

"It really is high time he tended to himself," she says offhandedly to the African, who marvels at the white visitor's morning appetite as she asks for a bite of the lamb chops emerging from the oven. But the cooks are quite pleased by her hunger and hurry to offer her also a taste of an unidentified dish already prepared for the farewell dinner. Here, madam, they say, now that you are getting used to the smell and taste of Africa, you are leaving? When will you come back to us?

She could gratify them by holding out some hope, but instead she gives a straight answer: I won't be back, and she spoons undissolved sugar from her cup to sweeten her mouth, then exits into the burning sunshine, heading for the infirmary. Recalling the vicious stand-off between cat and snake that she witnessed in the grass nearby two days ago, she makes sure to walk on open ground.

On a dirt mound near the infirmary sit several young African women, two of them pregnant, apparently waiting. The door is wide open. Inside the infirmary are two rooms. In the well-lit front room stands the cot where her blood pressure was found to be normal. In the darkened back room she can make out the bald head of her brother-in-law, who lies with his face to the wall.

She taps on the open door, and he turns and faces her, but doesn't get up. For the first time since she arrived six days ago she catches a flash of hostility in his eyes.

"Sijjin Kuang hasn't come back yet?"

"No."

"Can it be that Zohara won't let her leave?"

"Anything is possible."

"But what's so scary over there?"

"Why scary?"

His curt answers seem intended to put her off, so she sits on the adjacent bed, as if to announce, I'm not budging from here.

"In the kitchen they told me you had a terrible headache. Did you find anything here to make it better?"

"No."

"Why not?"

"Sijjin Kuang locks up the medicine cabinet. Because sometimes women from the area sneak in and take medicines they don't need."

"And you have no key?"

"Why should I? Sijjin Kuang is always nearby."

"So what will you do now?"

"I'll wait for the pain to pass. And if you don't mind, close the door, the light makes it worse."

He shields his eyes with his hand.

A quiver of pity runs through her. "If you've decided to lie down, why not in your bed?"

"For one thing it's not my bed, and here in the infirmary I'm safe from the commotion of the researchers. Tonight they'll go back to the dig, and tomorrow, after you leave, I'll go back to my place."

She gets up and closes the door, but he doesn't remove his hand from his eyes, as if to say that even behind a closed door he is not open to conversation.

"Maybe drink something?"

He doesn't answer.

"I suggested you should drink."

"Later."

"Should I bring you something?"

"Later."

But she goes out into the front room anyway. The African women have left the dirt mound and are now at the doorstep, perhaps hoping that the white woman can also dispense medicine, murmuring at her as she fetches Yirmi a glass of water. When she offers it to him he doesn't drink, but asks her to set it on the floor, but she insists, drink, so you won't get dehydrated. He continues to refuse, and she keeps insisting, and finally he yields, lifts himself up and drinks from the glass and mutters, you always managed to get your way in the family. Everyone always went to the restaurant you wanted, drove the route you wanted. Maybe, Daniela smiles, it's because you knew deep down that what I want is good for others. And she takes the empty glass and asks, more water? But he does not reply, and this time, she gives in.

Silence. Outside, despite the heat, the wind is whistling. In the inner room the blinds are closed, but points of light glow white in the cracks. The murmur of the African women grows louder. Maybe they have entered the infirmary now and are longingly examining the lock on the medicine cabinet. For a moment she considers whether to tell him now about the mission she has accepted, but figures that in his current state of mind he is likely to object, and she has a strong desire to keep her promise. She has a strange belief that these dry bones, from an ape that gave rise to all humankind, are meaningful for Israelis as well.

"Were you thinking of showing me something else on my last day here? Doing something?" she asks her brother-in-law cautiously.

He props himself up, shoves the pillow behind his back, and looks hard at her.

"You would surely like to see another unusual animal, like the elephant with the cyclops eye."

"Definitely . . . happily."

"But what can I do, Daniela, I don't have another animal like that."

"If you don't, then you don't."

Beyond the door the African women babble on, like a crystal brook.

And suddenly, almost without thinking, she says, "Listen, last night I read the Song of Songs."

"In English?"

"Yes. And it's no less beautiful and moving than the original, which kept echoing for me in the translation."

He is silent, his glance wandering.

"And when I read all eight chapters I understood what you felt. A poem like this pours salt on the wounds."

Yirmiyahu gets up and begins pacing around the small room, as if trying to chase her away. And suddenly he explodes, "What's going on here? You came to Africa because of Shuli, but in the end you're forcing me to talk about Eyal."

"Forcing you?" She is shocked. "And it's not connected?"

"Everything is connected and also not connected," he says irritably, "but I should never have told you about Eyal's last night."

"What's happening to you?"

"That story makes him ridiculous."

"That's totally absurd." She objects with all her might. "His innocence was noble; he is not ridiculous."

But he persists. There is a deep substratum to this episode, which goes beyond personal psychology. There is no doubt that if an Israeli soldier takes over a strange house, and intimidates its residents, in essence he only continues to dishonour them by suddenly risking his life to hand over a clean bucket.

"I can't begin to understand what you're getting at."

"Obviously you don't understand, and apparently you never will." He speaks in a low voice, yet his words resonate with inner turmoil. "For all of their brainpower, the Jews are incapable of grasping how others see them. I'm talking about real others, those who are not us and never will be us. Because only this way is it possible to begin to understand, for example, why that Palestinian, who got a considerable sum from me just to tell me what happened with that friendly fire, did not seem at all impressed by what Eyal did. He just took the money and went off without a word of thanks, or a word of condolence, or any praise at all for the consideration and good manners that were supposedly displayed. And I, with idiotic obsessiveness, could not reconcile myself to such indifference. So again I turned to my Jerusalem pharmacist, and pestered him to arrange an additional meeting with this man. At night, in the heat of the intifada, with a twofold mortal threat, from our forces and the opposing ones. And this was a first glimpse into the abyss we are toppling into, or, more accurately, that you are."

Here is the genetic defect, it strikes Daniela, as she sees his red eyes flaring at her in the dark room. There is no need to go out into nature to find it.

7.

WHEN THE TINY elevator lands with a thud, shake, and groan and the narrow grille is opened, the two passengers find its inventor waiting in an armchair beside the big bed, a glass of tea in his hand, an electric heater glowing red by his feet, and his cane on his lap. Well, little lady, he addresses the expert, did you hear the yowling of a cat, or do you think our hostess is hallucinating?

"No hallucination and no cat, grandpa," she answers emphatically. "There are all kinds of sounds in your adorable elevator, but only because of loose electrical contacts, and because of phenomena that are common in an old system like this, where the commutator collects dirt and even tiny particles of metal that flake off the piston. I've already found the connector box you hid behind the picture of Carl Gustav Jung, and on the roof I located the power cable you camouflaged among the clothes lines. But your son is terrified of electrocution. With the turn of one screw I could have disconnected the system, but he prevented me, by force. What's going on? Did you cause him some electrical trauma in his childhood that makes him such a coward?"

The old man laughs, then chides her.

"First of all, speak with respect about my son, because he's a grandfather too. He got through his childhood in my house without any traumas, but when he was a student at the Technion he was mainly taught how to predict disasters. In this case, however, I agree with him. I would also prefer that you not touch live electrical connections, because I didn't take out insurance on you."

"Nonsense. You weren't worried about electrocution when you connected the elevator straight to the electricity pole in the street."

"First of all, it wasn't me, but a bitter old pensioner from the electricity company, who wore special insulated gloves and some sort of sleeves that enabled him to work with live wires and set up free electrical power for his friends. Only after he was caught in the act did they start to take care at the electricity company that their retirees shouldn't be in any way embittered."

"Yes, then, too, there were robberies and indecent acts," remarks the lady of the house, "but the newspapers only had six pages and no space to cover them all. Come, my engineers, and have some tea."

"Maybe we should first check the vibrations in the piston," says Ya'ari, leaning towards his father's feet to warm his hands above the heater's white-hot coils. But the hostess insists they take a break, and leads the old man into the living room. The four Filipinos sit stock-still around the refreshment table, as the old man knew they would, waiting for a clear signal allowing them to take a biscuit or little sandwich.

The signal is given. The hostess passes around a big plate, and Francisco and Hilario and Pedro and Marco do not refuse a single round, until the plate is empty.

"All right," says the old man, "now let's go and have a look at the piston. So it can tell us what's bothering it."

And this time he invites the Filipinos to come with him into the lady's bedroom, and all at once the intimate chamber is filled with the strong presence of members of a different race, who are naturally keen to inspect a little elevator tailored to their own small proportions. Amotz heads over to check how to detach the oil piston from the wall, but his father tugs him by the jacket and says, This time, let me lead.

Ya'ari smiles and watches his father brace himself against the squat sturdy shoulders of Marco and Pedro and make his way into the elevator he had devised, where he presses against the wall to keep his balance and tells the Filipinos to let him stand alone. With a trembling hand he closes the grille. Behind the faded gold-coloured lattice, with his bald head, gaunt face, and drooping shoulders, he resembles an old monkey in a cage. He pushes the up button, but his shaky finger lacks the strength to start the elevator, so he moves back slightly and presses the button again with the tip of his cane. The elevator shakes, moans, bumps from side to side, and begins to rise, and only when he is completely out of sight does the yowling in the shaft die down.

Francisco, Marco, and Pedro grin as if they'd seen a circus stunt, but little Hilario is worried. He approaches cautiously to peek inside the open closet and see where the elevator has disappeared to. Ya'ari does not hide his pleasure at his father's accomplishment, and smiles broadly at the hostess, who has sunk helplessly into her armchair.

"*Insane*," she declares, coming to regret the forfeit of her peace and quiet for this tumult.

"Naughty boy," the expert agrees.

For a moment Ya'ari worries that his father will go out on the roof and be blown away by the wind. But after two minutes the wailing is heard again, and the elevator lands in all its musical richness.

Ya'ari hurries to extract his father, and since the old woman does not relinquish her chair, he seats him on her bed, props him all around with silk cushions, and waits for precise technical instructions on how to begin dismantling the piston without electrocuting himself.

8.

YIRMIYAHU GOES INTO the well-lit room to refill his water glass. The African women, sitting now by the entrance, crowd at once into the clinic to demand the unlocking of the medicine cabinet. Slowly and with difficulty he utters a few words of refusal in their language, and they laugh and protest, till he loses patience and shouts at them angrily, and they scatter back outside. One of the young ones crumples to the floor and bursts into tears, and her friends lift her tenderly and lead her back to the dirt mound to await the return of the nurse.

Yirmiyahu leans over the sink and wets his face, then fills the glass and gulps the water, fills it again, and goes back into the inner room. He seems surprised somehow to see his sister-in-law still sitting there, poised on the second bed. For a moment he considers leaving the door open, then closes it.

A long silence.

"Don't tell me," she says suddenly, "that the malaria parasite can in fact pass from person to person, because if so, I'm next in line."

He glances at her.

"You're not in any line. This happens to me sometimes. My temperature goes up if I'm exhausted."

"Maybe it's a good defence against the prophets of Israel: you get sick before they can punish you. But you better watch out for them."

A sad smile lightens his face. "What can they do to me that they haven't done already?"

"Don't be so sure," she ventures. "I guarantee you that disasters await us that haven't yet been announced, not even in the English translation."

"Aha, I see you're beginning to get the principle. Prophecies of destruction, delivered with pleasure and lust."

"But in fact you prophesy the same way."

"I? Why me? I'm not a player or a partner. I freed myself of the leash of the forefathers. I look on from afar, indifferent and liberated, safe and sound in a place where there is not and never has been a shred of prophecy, or of fury, or of consolation. And here, even if they dig up the entire ground, they won't find a trace of a dry Jewish bone."

In two months he will be seventy, she thinks, but that doesn't stop him from reliving the rebellion of a high school student. Still, in the few hours remaining, he needs to be listened to. Because for all his bragging about detachment, it's not the arrogance of an ancient prophet that burns in his marrow, but the friendly fire. So she diverts the conversation back to its beginning. She is curious to know more about the Jerusalem pharmacist, who at the height of the intifada managed to smuggle him safely back and forth at night.

Emile is a Christian Arab from East Jerusalem, about fifty years old, who through patient and industrious litigation won back the pharmacy that had belonged to his parents before the founding of the state. He is a flexible man, who speaks Hebrew well, and his pharmacy, in the German Colony, is clean and well-organized and sometimes open at night. Medicines that are sold elsewhere only by prescription he sells on the basis of trust alone. He is a knowledgeable pharmacist, dispensing good advice about insomnia, weight loss, nausea, and heartburn. And when word spread in the neighbourhood that Eyali fell not from enemy fire, he came to pay a condolence call at the home of Yirmi and Shuli, his old customers, and on his own initiative brought tranquillizers that he himself had concocted. From then on, every time they entered his shop, singly or together, he would attend to them promptly, with concern and devotion, inquiring about their physical condition and emotional state, serving them with compassion.

After the first, hurried visit to Tulkarm, when the Palestinian paterfamilias had evaded his meeting with Yirmi, Emile had keenly felt the frustration that had now been added to the agony, and with the help of relatives and friends managed to find the owner of the roof and persuade him to talk to Yirmi in exchange for a fee.

The story the Palestinian told did not anger Yirmi at first. Nor was he bothered by the absurdity of the incident. On the contrary, he found his son's gesture noble. But he was surprised by the utter lack of sympathy on the part of the Palestinian. Out of either anger or hatred, he never looked Yirmi straight in the eye, and without adding a word took the money and disappeared among the hothouse flowers.

And then Yirmi said to himself, This man is a day labourer, struggling to live under occupation; what can I expect of him, anyway? But the middleman, the educated Christian pharmacist, by all appearances a moderate fellow, with an Israeli identity card, had also shown no sympathy; had no kindly word for the innocence of the soldier.

And as he drove back to Jerusalem that day, a desire took root in him, actually not a desire but a necessity, a compulsion, to redeem Eyal's honour, to endorse an action that appeared stupid but also embodied the gallant spirit of a young man who surely knew he was risking his life in order to return a bucket rinsed clean to suicide bombers.

"Suicide bombers?" Daniela is astonished.

"Of course," says Yirmi. "If not today, then tomorrow. And at that moment I resolved to go back to Tulkarm and again go up on that roof, to prove to the Palestinian that we had not only given our son an absurdly good heart and manners, but courage too. So after a few days I went to Emile and told him that all his medicines would not help me calm down until I could go back to that roof to rescue my son's honour, and that such indifference over his simple human gesture was unacceptable to me. And if I had to bribe middlemen to sneak me in there, my wallet was open, on condition that the middlemen wanted my money and not my blood. I told Shuli that I was being sent for one day to our embassy in Cyprus. On that night, she was actually staying with you in Tel Aviv, and I'm sure that she didn't suspect a thing. And though Tulkarm sits right on the border, getting there was not easy, believe me. On the way in, they didn't do much checking at the roadblocks, and because I rode in with some labourers and dressed accordingly, they couldn't tell me from the others. But on the return trip, they had to smuggle me into my own country on roundabout back roads, to protect me from enemy fire and friendly fire too."

"And all that was worth it?"

"Very much so. Because on the roof I received, in addition to a cup of strong coffee, a little lesson in Judaism."

"From whom?" she says, laughing. "From the Palestinian or the pharmacist?"

A tap is heard on the door of the back room. Sijjin Kuang has returned.

9.

ONCE MORE THE father tells his son: "Don't butt in. This time I'm in charge. It wasn't you who put this elevator together, and you won't take it apart."

"But on condition you stay on the bed," the son answers. "You decided against the wheelchair, and I'm in no mood to see you fall down."

"Don't worry," says his father, "I'll give instructions by remote control. But you sit on the side and don't get involved. This elevator is guaranteed by me personally, not by the firm. Right, Mrs. Bennett?"

"A personal lifetime guarantee."

For some reason she still hasn't offered him the comfortable armchair she has claimed for herself—as if she likes seeing him propped up among the cushions on her big bed. She pulls the electric heater close, spreads a blanket on her lap, lights a cigarette, and seems ready for a long encampment. Suddenly a barrage of hail rattles the windows, and a few white icy pebbles fly in through the shaft and roll on the floor, and darkness descends on Jerusalem.

Without explicit orders, the expert goes to the elevator and turns on the light. Then she takes the two reading lamps from either side of the bed, plugs them both into an extension cord, and directs their light towards the bottom of the elevator. New shadows begin to move on the walls. The old man beckons to Hilario, takes his hand and strokes his hair, and whispers at length in his ear what he should tell the Filipinos who are waiting for their orders. The lengthy Hebrew instructions are drastically condensed by the interpreter, and it now becomes clear that it was not merely so he could be spirited up the stairs that the old man mobilized Francisco's friends, but also so they could hoist the little elevator by hand, making possible the detachment of the piston from the lift mechanism.

Now the expert wedges her childlike, sexually ambiguous body between the side of the elevator and the wall of the shaft where the piston is attached. Drawing on her experience in the regional auto shop of Upper Galilee, she locates the oil cap and unscrews it with a monkey wrench produced from her jumpsuit pocket. A trickle of viscous white liquid begins to flow out, instead of the completely blackened oil one would expect after so many years.

"What's that?" asks Amotz.

His father shrugs. He cannot identify the nature of this fluid, either. He found the pump in his native Czechoslovakia, in a warehouse of used elevator parts, and since he bought it for next to nothing, he didn't bother to examine its innards.

The white stuff continues to trickle. Even the expert, who now and then smells and tastes it, can't come to a conclusion regarding its nature or provenance. But she is collecting it, in a small jar brought beforehand from the kitchen, so perhaps they'll be able to identify it later on.

The lady of the house also wants to taste the liquid. She gives Hilario a small spoon, he brings her a sample, and she sticks the tip of her tongue into it. It could be machine oil, or maybe sesame, or truffle, or eucalyptus, or coconut, or kerosene or petrol. Not bad, she says. Careful, my dear, jokes the old man, the guarantee I gave you does not include indigestion from elevator gravy. And they laugh, he on the bed, shaking on the silk cushions, and she in the armchair, the two of them relaxed and intrigued by the drama in this miniature theatre, as Hilario explains to Marco and Pedro that they should prop the elevator a bit higher on their shoulders so Francisco can detach the forklift from the bottom of the car and pull free the entire original and delicate unit.

"And the electric current?" Ya'ari suddenly wells with anger at his father. "Before Francisco starts to turn a single screw we have to be sure he won't get electrocuted."

But the anger is unnecessary now. There is no current in any screw. The expert has already disconnected the power in secret and without permission, and is unharmed and happy.

Why does he have to worry so much over something that's not his responsibility? Why try to take control of an historic relic he is neither supposed nor obliged to know a thing about? If he joined the team in order to look after his father, he can see with his own eyes how good it is for the old man to lie on the big bed, in a warm and familiar room, beside a beloved friend, in the intimacy of a dark winter morning. And if so, why should a busy man like him, a bothersome worrier, not take advantage of this fortuitous moment of grace on the Hanukkah holiday and sit serenely in a corner? And if Daniela in Africa is bonding with her past but free of the present, he himself now has the chance to take time out from both. No secretary, draughtsman, or engineer is ringing his cell phone for advice; in other words, the world is carrying on fine, even without him.

A smile of contentment lights up Ya'ari's face. Good, from this moment on I am but a silent onlooker. He brings a wicker chair from the kitchen, stands it beside the big bed, sits down and crosses his legs and closes his eyes.

Francisco once told him and Daniela that the territory of the Philippines encompasses seven thousand islands, only about five hundred of them inhabited. In fact he and Kinzie come from two islands that are hundreds of kilometres apart. Thanks to the wide variety of dialects spoken across the whole archipelago, what unites their islands as a nation is the English language.

That lingua franca is proving effective in the bedroom of the psychoanalyst as well. Hilario, the clever first-grader, passes along in English the technical instructions he gets in Hebrew from the great-grandfather and explains to Marco and Pedro how to raise the lightweight elevator.

Though the car is rather easily lifted upon the short men's shoulders, Francisco prefers not to rely solely on his two comrades, and adds the support of a stepladder and a small bureau before crawling underneath to disconnect the lift arm.

The Filipinos speak softly among themselves, and old Ya'ari adopts their polite, respectful tone as he tells Francisco, via Hilario's translation, the correct procedure for undoing the screws. He must work slowly, with caution. The screws are rusted, and one must oil them and wait for them to yield gracefully, to exit undamaged from the place they have grown used to for so many years.

The Filipinos seem to enjoy the unusual task they have happened into. Instead of washing and feeding paralyzed old men, or taking walks with grouchy old ladies, they are dismantling a unique invention and carrying an elderly elevator on their shoulders. The hostess sighs with relief, relaxes, and falls asleep in her chair. Ya'ari's eyelids also droop, and his vision grows blurry. He listens to the quiet voices, rests his hand on the bed and imagines his father lying upon it years ago, among the cushions. He recollects the pleasured panic of the young woman in the cassette tucked between Baby Mozart and Baby Bach in Moran's apartment.

Should he tell Daniela, or spare her the distress?

He opens his eyes and realizes he must have dozed off for a few minutes, for the elevator has vanished behind the doors of the clothes closet, and on the floor by the bed rests an ancient creature, with one forked leg like the devil Ashmedai, a greenish cylindrical piston like a the long tail of a lizard, and a control mechanism that resembles the head of a small cat, sprouting severed nerve-endings in a rainbow of colours.

The lady of the house is still deep in dreamland, and his father, looking with affectionate pride upon the original machinery that stayed intact for so many years, smiles at Ya'ari and says to him, See what happens in old age? At the height of emotion you run out of stamina and fall asleep, and wake up when it's over and feel guilt and regret. And he directs Francisco, who has been washing his hands in the bathroom, to help his colleagues take the dismantled apparatus down to the ambulance that waits on the street with Maurice, and to bring up the wheelchair.

"My dear," he says, waking his lady friend, "we took apart the machinery for you. There will be no more humming and wailing. But whether it will also be possible to resurrect the elevator, so you can go strolling on the roof—this depends now not only on me, but also on an old friend, who is in love only with money."

The psychoanalyst opens her eyes and smiles a knowing smile. "And I thought you would stay for lunch."

"Lunch?" says old Ya'ari with surprise. "Why? So you can tie a bib on me and feed me with a spoon? When love crosses into degradation, I retreat."

10.

THE PATIENCE OF the African women has paid off. Sijjin Kuang opens the medicine cabinet and distributes pills, and also gives two aspirins to the white man. "Please, give me some, too," says Daniela.

"I'm going to bed after a sleepless night," announces Sijjin Kuang, "and you should also," she adds firmly, standing tall over the Israeli visitor. "Early tomorrow morning I will take you to Morogoro. The plane is small and you must get there early, so they don't give your seat away."

"That can happen here?" The visitor is alarmed.

"Yes, here too," says her brother-in-law.

"And you won't come with me to the airport?" She turns to her brother-in-law in Hebrew.

"What do you need me for? You've already heard more than I wanted to tell you, and even more than I thought I knew. So much that you won't remember what to tell Amotz."

"You're so sure I tell him everything?"

"Has anything changed?"

She studies him sourly and does not answer. Yirmiyahu turns to Sijjin Kuang and surprisingly, in his limited English, summarizes the last few sentences spoken in Hebrew. The Sudanese woman regards the two of them with puzzlement, and before locking the medicine cabinet asks if anything else is needed of her. A sleeping pill, requests Daniela, you've got me worried about getting up early and I'm afraid I won't be able to fall asleep. But sleeping pills are not popular among Africans and are not to be found in the medicine cabinet. Like a magician the Sudanese produces another white aspirin between her long black fingers and gives it to the woman who is fearful for her sleep.

"Maybe you should really go now and get some rest instead of hanging around here," says Yirmi to his sister-in-law, in the patronizing tone of an older brother. "On Sunday nights, before returning to the dig, the team has a custom of holding a fancy dinner in 'high table' style and they'll surely insist that you be there."

"High table." She laughs. "What is this? Oxford? Cambridge?"

"If they feel like honouring themselves in such a fashion, what's wrong with that? So go on, take a nap, so later you won't yawn in their faces."

Again she senses his clear desire to keep his distance from her, maybe because he feels he has already got carried away and doesn't want to be dragged any farther. But she says to herself that if she gives up and doesn't hear the end of the story, she'll be guilty of disloyalty to her sister, who was kept in the dark about her husband's desperate adventure. So she takes off her shoes and plants herself on the bed and directs a penetrating gaze at her brother-in-law, who stands at the threshold of the inner room, half in the light and half in darkness: Yirmi, what do you mean, a lesson in Judaism?

. "In Jews."

"And who, may I ask, was the teacher—the Palestinian landlord, or your pharmacist?"

Remaining in the doorway, he studies her.

"Neither one. The pharmacist was afraid to come to the meeting that he himself had arranged. Someone warned him at the last minute that despite his blue Israeli ID card, he might be prevented from getting back into Jerusalem from the West Bank, if he were caught. His absence worried me at first and even frightened me, because I had put my security in his hands. Although he was a Christian and not a Muslim, he was held in respect as a medical man. But I realized he would not be coming only when I was already sitting on the rooftop waiting for him, and by then there was no retreat. It was a winter night, very cold but dry, and this time there was no laundry flapping on the clothes line, just a few old armchairs, and the middleman, an Israeli Arab with two wives, one in Israel and the other in the territories, sat me down and said, Coffee will arrive right away, sir, and in the meantime enjoy the air, which is cleaner here than where you live, and disappeared. I sat and listened to the sounds of the city, which were different from the sounds of an Israeli city, and I tried to absorb what Eyali heard in his last hours. I sat alone and waited, and no one came up, and then I knew that if they were to kill me now, or kidnap me, I absolutely deserved it, because I was tempting fate and provoking a humiliated enemy."

"At least you were aware of this."

"Apparently I was slightly infected by their suicidal impulses."

"And how did it end?"

He has finally understood that his sister-in-law, like a hunting dog, will not let go of him, and he brings a chair from the other room and places it beside her bed.

"All right. So when the landlord saw that the pharmacist wasn't coming, he didn't know what to do with me and sent me his daughter—the young and pregnant one I met when I came with the army officer."

"The student of history with the mellifluous Hebrew."

"You don't forget a single word."

"A single word of *yours*. So don't worry about Amotz, he'll hear it all from me."

Her brother-in-law falls silent, as if upset that his words will not remain between the two of them in Africa but will be reported in Israel. But he recovers quickly, and continues.

"So this young woman, the student, arrives on the roof, followed by her mother, fat and jolly as ever, presumably there to protect her. The student is now huge, almost ready to give birth, but her face is fresh from all the rest she gets under curfew and closure, glowing with imminent motherhood, and her black hair spread on her shoulders. And the mother brings coffee on a tray."

"So they won't be tempted to kill you if you fall asleep," she jokes.

"They could slaughter an unarmed old man like me even if I were awake; even a woman could do it. No, they brought me the sweet coffee so I could sit and explain with a clear head what I really wanted from them. Why I kept coming back there. And when I saw that pregnant student—whose studies at Ruppin college had been interrupted by the intifada and would not likely be resumed, and whose husband, so I gathered from her, had run off to one of the Gulf states to look for work and would not return soon—who knows, maybe he was the wanted man they were staking out—when I saw her coming to sit down quietly beside me, I had this revelation, that it was in fact *she* who had drawn me to risk my life and return here. Yes, it was her sympathy I was looking for. I wanted to hear from a well-educated young woman, in her gentle Hebrew, that even if, like the others, she saw us as enemies, she was still capable of sympathy for a naïve and stupid soldier, who risked his life so as not to leave filth for *his* enemies."

"She knew what had happened?"

"Of course."

"And you got the sympathy you wanted from her?"

"No. On the contrary. It was the student who was the toughest of them all. She began with a rebuke based on the history she had learned at college. Why is it you Jews can penetrate all sorts of foreign places and settle into other people's souls? Why is it so easy for you to wander from place to place without forming bonds of friendship with any other people, even if you live among them for a thousand years? Because you have a special god who is yours alone, and even when you don't believe in him, you are certain that because of him you have the right to be everywhere. In that case, who will love you? Who will want you? How will you survive?"

"This is all familiar stuff."

"Yes, but there on the roof in Tulkarm, through the bottomless bitterness of this pregnant young woman, it took on a new hue. Maybe because she was soon to give birth, maybe because her husband wouldn't be there at the delivery, maybe because of her studies that had been cut short, she felt she had nothing to lose with me, that I was laid bare before her, a stubborn old Jew. What are you doing here again, she asked, what can a man be looking for at night among his enemies? Why are you bothering and frightening my father? What do you want from me? That I'll offer you compassion for your soldier? Why should I feel sorry for a soldier who invades a space that does not belong to him and doesn't care about us, who we are and what we are? Who takes over a family's roof in order to kill one of us, and thinks that if he does us a favour and leaves us a clean bucket, washing away the evidence of his fear, we'll forgive him for the insult and humiliation? But how can we forgive? Can we be bought with a clean bucket?"

"That's how she explained it to you? As an added insult? That's crazy."

"No, Daniela, don't make life easy for yourself. She's not crazy. She's strange, but not crazy. Idiosyncratic, but not crazy. She spoke with clarity and logic. We are sick and tired of you, she said. You took land, you took water, and you control our every move, so at least give us a chance to join you. Otherwise we'll all commit suicide together. But you, for all your ability to bore your way into other people, you are closed up within yourselves, not blending in or letting others blend with you. So what's left for us? Only to hate you and pray for the moment that you will move away from here, because this will never be a homeland for you if you don't know how to blend into everything that's in it. So go on, she says, pick up your walking stick again and get out of here. Even the baby in my belly is waiting for it."

"What was her name?"

"She wouldn't tell me."

"You quote her as if she actually persuaded you."

"She didn't persuade me, but she impressed me. With her female confidence. And the pregnancy saddened me greatly. Because if Eyali were alive, I could have a daughter-in-law like that, who would give birth to a child who speaks sweet Hebrew."

"Again with the sweet lovely Hebrew? In what way sweet?"

"When Arabs speak proper Hebrew, without mistakes, even more flowery than normal, there's often a sweetness to it. The accent becomes softer, and because they are self-conscious about pronouncing *p,* afraid it'll come out as *b,* they stress it more, with a sort of anxious musicality. The verb in their sentences comes at the beginning, and the shift in word order creates a dramatic difference. And there's also a singsong phrasing that turns a statement into a question, so that instead of saying, It hurts me, she'll say, And how can I not be hurt? And instead of saying, I hate you, she says, How can people not hate you? Something like that."

"And this is sweetness?"

"To me it is."

11.

AT MIDDAY, IN an ambulance descending from the mountains to the coastal plain, sits the elevator apparatus in its entirety, one of a kind, in the back with the four Filipinos, who keep their distance from it. Old Ya'ari is there, too, sitting in the wheelchair, feeling satisfied that the dismantling was achieved without mishap, thinking over the next step: how to convince Gottlieb to make a new piston that will fit the fork lift.

He is still ashamed of his tearful outburst on his friend's doorstep, but he is also grateful to her for wisely recasting his weakness as a strength. In any event, it was good that he resisted her offer of lunch. Who knows, he might have cried again over the cake.

Ya'ari and the expert are crowded in the front with Maurice, listening to the ambulance driver reminisce about his last trips with Ya'ari's mother. When I see your father alive and kicking in his wheelchair, I miss her. She was a real lady, and when she died she was your age, Amotz, but she had no complaints or bitterness.

Ya'ari confirms that diagnosis and distils the purpose of life into one short sentence: Do everything possible to leave this world without complaints or bitterness. But his own final test has not yet arrived, and for now he has nothing to do but wonder why it's already afternoon and no one has called from his office asking a question, requesting advice, or reporting a complaint—as if his business can actually go on without him. Maybe there's another children's play on today? he wonders and phones his secretary, who assures him that all his employees have come in, despite it being the tail end of the holiday, and are working diligently, and that no problem has arisen among them requiring the boss's wisdom and experience. However, there is a stranger who has been sitting in his office for several hours and insists on waiting for him.

"A stranger?" Ya'ari is baffled. "In my office?"

Yes, the tenant from the Pinsker Tower, who showed up with legal papers and is determined to serve them on Ya'ari by hand, personally.

"But why did you let him into my office? Why can't he wait outside?"

"Amotz," protests the secretary, "he's a bereaved father, his son was killed a few months ago, he told me the whole story. It's very crowded in the office with all the computers and drawing boards, and outside the weather is bad, rainy and very windy. But don't worry, he's sitting in a corner and not touching anything."

The elder Ya'ari decides to pass up on Kinzie's lunch and take the machinery straight to Gottlieb's elevator factory. He'll eat lunch with the workers, which will remind him of the good old days. But his son is fed up with the whole private elevator festival and announces: You wanted to take charge of the process? Then please, finish it yourself. Let's see if you can draw a rational line from the psychoanalyst to the manufacturer. He says good-bye to his father in front of his childhood home, gets in his car, leaving old Ya'ari and the rest of the contingent to proceed alone to the factory nestled amid orchards in the Sharon region, after warning Francisco and Hilario, "It's up to you two to make sure nothing happens to him."

Through the open door of his office Ya'ari can see Mr. Kidron sitting stiffly in a heavy winter coat, a knitted ski cap on his knee, his eyes fixed on the swaying branches of the tree outside the window. He has not touched the tea and biscuits the secretary brought him. Ya'ari, with an effort, dismisses his foul humour and enters the room cheerfully. The man stands up but does not greet the chief executive, merely hands him the legal complaint. Ya'ari takes it from him, reads it quickly, and asks with a faint smile: "So I'm the only defendant here?"

"Even if there are other defendants, they don't diminish your guilt," says the tenants' leader coldly. "All of you are one corrupt gang, who don't care about the damage you leave behind. You have a tree that makes a pleasant noise outside a closed window, but with us, when we get home and get near the elevator, we don't hear the wind but howls of pain, and there's no reason we should pay with a never-ending nightmare for your sloppy calculations."

"Believe me, Mr. Kidron, our calculations are accurate. There are cracks in the shaft."

"So open up the elevators and prove to the construction company that they are to blame."

"Only the manufacturer is authorized to open the elevators. I am only the designer."

"That's what I said, you're a corrupt bunch who shift the blame from one to the other, so we can't catch you. But the tenants are sick of it, the blame is now on you, Mr. Ya'ari, and if you want to be free of it, take it to court."

Ya'ari studies him. A man with innocent blue eyes, not tall, but slender under the wet coat. His hiking shoes are covered in mud. Before his son was killed he was surely a pleasant and friendly man.

"As you wish, I'll go to court. But do tell me, anyway, why is the lawsuit directed only at me?"

"Because you're an approachable person. Even your secretary is nice."

Ya'ari looks over at the tree fighting the wind and places a gentle hand on the bereaved tenant's shoulder.

"Yes, I am an approachable person. It's a failing of mine, but maybe also a virtue. This is an ideal day to locate the defect that is tormenting you, so why wait for the court to acquit me while in the meantime you'll be supporting a hungry lawyer—let's go and take advantage of the storm tonight and check the shaft once and for all. Tomorrow my wife is returning from Africa, and she won't let me leave her in the middle of her first night back. That leaves us only tonight, and because we'll have to shut down all the elevators, the best time is the small hours, say between two and three in the morning, in the hope that all the tenants will be in their apartments. Because we don't have porters to carry late-night partygoers up the stairs to the umpteenth floor."

Kidron brightens. "Okay," he says, "I'll put up notices in the building and warn the residents not to get home late tonight. How long will it take?"

"You will be surprised to learn that despite my age this is the first time I have gone hunting for winds at night. Like surgery or war, you know when you start, but not when you'll finish."

The head of the tenants' committee takes it upon himself to summon a representative of the construction company to be present as well.

"Talk tough to him, the way you do to me," Ya'ari advises. "Threaten him." And he eases the man out of the door.

And now, of course, just as he is about to hurry to Gottlieb's factory to make good on his promise to Kidron, his employees come to him with questions and try to show him plans and diagrams. By the time he manages to get free of these responsibilities and arrives at the elevator factory, it is dusk. And to his surprise, the blue ambulance is still there.

"Not only did I feed your father lunch with a spoon myself, and wipe away the crumbs," Gottlieb informs him, "we're also cutting him a new piston. Learn from this, young man, the power of old friendship. And it's best that a man have only one such dear friend, because two would break him."

"True." Ya'ari laughs. "But what about the dear son of the dear friend?"

And he tells him about his promise to hold a Night of the Winds. A skilled technician is needed, someone who can remove the roof of the elevator, then reassemble it.

"In the middle of the night? You know what that'll cost me?"

"It won't break you. Because we already paid that relative of yours in advance."

Gottlieb shoots Ya'ari an icy look.

In the past few years, Ya'ari has paid few visits to this factory. These days orders are placed online, and besides, the younger engineers in his firm are not enthusiastic about Gottlieb's elevators and fight for more up-to-date models that operate without machine rooms. Now he is amazed by how the factory has expanded. Big impressive cutting machines slice sheets of steel with high precision. Drill punches produce control panels. Remote-control robots assemble electric motors. The high-ceilinged halls are clean and orderly, if a bit dim, and skilled workers circulate among the machines, seeming slightly tense at the approach of the factory owner.

Gottlieb, far from letting himself be cowed by the Chinese elevators that Ya'ari's engineers have been recommending to the construction companies, has opened new markets for himself, and now exports elevators to Turkey and Greece. He even gets orders from England. From the corner of his eye Ya'ari sees a new design wing, filled with engineers, technicians, and draughtsmen, hired to compete with his own. And yet deep inside the thriving factory there is a small hall where an ancient metal lathe hums merrily, and here Ya'ari finds his father in his wheelchair, fascinated by the work and vibrating to its rhythms. In the corner sit Francisco and Hilario, silent and exhausted.

"Abba," he leans over and hugs his father, "are you convinced the lathe won't work if you don't stare at it?"

"That's what I tell him, too," says Gottlieb, "but your father apparently enjoys the chirping noises. His Filipinos are too quiet for him. Come, Amotz, let's take your father to our candle-lighting. You're about to see a Hanukkah menorah no less unusual than the elevator he built in Jerusalem."

The old man does not answer, merely looks with puzzlement at his friend and his son. Ya'ari wheels his father's chair after Gottlieb as the manufacturer leads the way to the cafeteria, where workers on the shift are assembling for the lighting of the candles. In the centre of the hall stands a menorah fit for the factory, composed of nine tiny models of elevators, with a small bulb installed in each.

At the entrance is a basket of kippahs, and on the tables are arrayed trays of small but still warm jam doughnuts. The workers put on the skullcaps and crowd together silently. They know this menorah well and are no longer impressed. How many candles today? Gottlieb asks an Orthodox worker who stands ready to chant the blessings. Seven, says the man, and waits for a signal from the boss.

Gottlieb goes to a panel of numbered buttons and presses the red emergency switch, which lights up the shammash, a replica of the latest elevator produced at the factory—and the worker bursts into sacred melody, his Sephardic voice sweet and clear. As the blessings end, Gottlieb presses the seventh-floor button, and slowly, one at a time, seven more miniature elevators light up.

"Well, what do you say?" He turns proudly to the father and son. "A miracle like this would have astonished even the Maccabees."

Ya'ari chuckles and thinks good-naturedly, It's all right, there's this side to Gottlieb, too. But tomorrow night we'll finally light real candles with Daniela.

12.

AFTER THE ISRAELI visitor's headache has been dissolved by a long, deep sleep, she showers and returns refreshed to the ground floor, where she finds the tables rearranged for the farewell dinner. The big table has been moved to the edge of the hall and placed upon a small wooden stage, then covered with an embroidered map of Africa. The remaining tables are positioned in three rows, as in a theatre, with benches on one side only, so that diners will face the stage. In the open space outside the building the scientists are loading the pickup trucks with food coolers and duffel bags and new digging tools, and Daniela can also see a group of Africans in colourful clothes decorated with ribbons; some of them are leaning on long sharpened sticks. Yirmiyahu arrives from the infirmary, moving slowly, and on his way to take a shower and change his clothes he cautions his sister-in-law not to make light of the ceremonial dinner: For some reason they attach greater importance to you than you deserve.

"You know it's impossible to make me more important than I am," she teases him, "and what about you? How's your headache?"

He regards her soberly. Patience, he says. Tomorrow, when

you're gone, the pain will pass. And without waiting for a reply or a protest he touches her shoulder in a gentle gesture of reconciliation, then hurries to his room.

Out of nowhere appears the wrinkled old groundskeeper, adorned with a sash, waving a huge branch. Grandly he leads the Africans inside and instructs them to take seats at the three rows of tables. Who are these people? Daniela asks Sijjin Kuang, who with stately authority is assisting the old man in seating each guest in his proper place.

On Sunday nights, she tells the visitor, before departing for the new week of excavation, the members of the research team invite the tribal chiefs and heads of local clans to join in the farewell dinner, so they will feel they have a stake in the scientific work.

Sijjin Kuang seats the Israeli woman in the first row of tables, leaving empty places to her right and left for Yirmiyahu and herself. The cooks, in white toques, place ceramic pots on the tables and distribute pitchers of a yellowish drink. Yirmiyahu enters, his bald pate shiny and his clothing fresh, and sits down beside her and says, Europe becomes important to them even as they sense its growing alienation.

The old black man waves the branch and the assembled rise to their feet. The scientists enter in a row, clad in black university gowns with sashes attached in the colours of their native countries' flags. Minus the North African paleontologist, the marchers are nine in number, led by the Tanzanian Seloha Abu, who assigns each member his place at the high table. And since the guests are very hungry and the food is piping hot, speeches are postponed till the meal's end and the eating begins, to be accompanied, in keeping with the British tradition that Dr. Kukiriza has brought with him from London, by small talk alone.

"Tell me," Daniela says suddenly to her brother-in-law in Hebrew, "you're sure you won't come back to Israel slightly delirious from all this?"

He puts down his fork.

"And who told you I'm coming back? You've been here for six days, and you still insist on not understanding where I stand. Nothing will draw me back to a country that has turned into a recycling plant."

"That's a novel definition."

"Here there are no ancient graves and no floor tiles from a destroyed synagogue; no museum with a fragment of a burnt Torah; no testimonies about pogroms and the Holocaust. There's no exile here, no Diaspora. There was no Golden Age here, no community that contributed to global culture. They don't fuss about assimilation or extinction, self-hatred or pride, uniqueness or chosenness; no old grandmas pop up suddenly aware of their identity. There's no orthodoxy here or secularism or self-indulgent religiosity, and most of all no nostalgia for anything at all. There's no struggle between tradition and revolution. No rebellion against the forefathers and no new interpretations. No one feels compelled to decide if he is a Jew or an Israeli or maybe a Canaanite, or if the state is more democratic or more Jewish, if there's hope for it or if it's done for. The people around me are free and clear of that whole exhausting and confusing tangle. But life goes on. I am seventy years old, Daniela, and I am permitted to let go."

And he takes up the fork and plunges it into the meat.

Daniela wants to strike back indignantly, but stops herself.

The flow of his words suggests that even if he has never performed this monologue for others, he has doubtless muttered it to himself many times.

The old African sets fire to the big branch and waves it, and the Tanzanian team leader rises to deliver the traditional address. Yirmiyahu whispers to his sister-in-law that although the man speaks in the local vernacular, all the members know this speech and can understand the meaning of every sentence. He is speaking on a favourite topic, man's dominance over fire and his ability to understand it, and even Yirmiyahu is able to comprehend part of the speech and to fill in the rest:

Fire is conceived of as a living thing. It moves about incessantly, changes its shape and colour, eats, makes noises, provides heat. Man can create it or extinguish it, can blow on it to revive it or blow on it to put it out. Fire is the only thing in the world that man can kill and then bring back to life. Most of what man creates or produces depends on fire, and most destruction and ruin are connected with fire. Fire is a friend that brings life, that cleanses and purifies, and it is also a terrifying foe. Perhaps in the knowledge of fire is a key to the knowledge of death.

Of all creatures in the world, only man is conscious of the phenomenon of death. It is strange, since all animals see death all around them, and some cause it every day. Nevertheless, recognition of death is unique to humans, and is expressed, for example, in the custom of burial, which first appeared about 100,000 years ago.

The consciousness of humans differs from that of the animals in two main ways, knowing fire and knowing death. There is a connection between these two types of knowledge, one gives rise to the other. Fire made man into the being who controls the world, but also into the miserable human who knows that his death is inevitable.

The old African waves the burning branch during the entire speech.

Eighth Candle

1.

HE WAS CONVINCED he would wake up on his own, but a dream that refused to end kept him sleeping. Fortunately, he had arranged a wake-up phone call. While hunting for a warm long-sleeved T-shirt he thinks how happy Moran would be to chase after wind in the middle of the night, but for a grandfather hounded all day by a great-grandfather, a night-time adventure like this is a bit much. And yet, having recognized his obligation in broad daylight, he will not shirk it at night. If his own father gives a lifetime guarantee for a homemade elevator and honourably stands by it, even as he trembles in a wheelchair, should he, this man's son, evade responsibility for defects appearing in an apartment tower during its first year? True, a sharp lawyer could juggle these windy complaints, tossing them from one party to the next till the complainant's spirit broke, but here we have a bereaved father, and there is strong fellow feeling between him and a bereaved uncle, so the uncle is taking the trouble on a stormy night to instil team spirit in all those responsible to determine who among them is the guilty party.

Tel Aviv calls itself the City that Never Rests. The epithet is more than just words, Ya'ari decides as he finds himself in a swirl of lights and traffic in the small hours of a winter's morning. Even in his youth he was never much of a night owl, and in recent years he has tried to convince Daniela to go to bed earlier. Tomorrow night, he knows, they won't hurry to get to bed. Neither will be able to fall asleep. There will be too much to tell and too much to hear. But he will not hint, even lightheartedly, at that "real desire" she promised at the airport. He knows he must prepare himself to be patient. For though she has been the traveller and he the abandoned one, she will still be angry about the separation, and anger, as it always does, will sabotage desire.

The rain has stopped, but on the street puddles glimmer in the headlights. Again he drives around the former Kings of Israel Square, now renamed after Rabin, to find waiting beside the dark window of the Book Worm the same vaguely defined individual, who has added to her attire of the previous morning only a red scarf, wrapped about her neck.

"Well," he teases her affectionately. "Now you can't complain that we overpaid you. Tonight we will all need your expertise. Let's just hope the wind will be sufficiently strong; it seems to be displaying symptoms of fatigue."

"Don't worry, Ya'ari." The expert smiles at him with her big bright eyes. "Even a weak wind will do. When it's trapped in a shaft, I can easily make it talk."

"Talk," he repeats, intrigued. Then he asks if tonight she might disclose her age.

"No," she hastens to respond, "not yet."

Once again, he and his car are swallowed up by the underground parking beneath the tower, but this time it's hard to find a spot. Can it be that even as the winds have grown worse all the vacant apartments have found tenants? As he cruises the two floors of the garage the gloomy voice of the tenants' spokesman blares from his car phone: Take my parking spot, Mr. Ya'ari. I left it free for you.

On the elevator landing of the lower floor the groans can be heard at full volume, and the expert's childlike face radiates satisfaction. They go up to the lobby level, where the night watchman directs them to Mr. Kidron's flat on the twenty-fourth floor. Signs lettered with an ink marker and bordered with thick black lines are posted on the walls of the lobby and the doors of the elevators. At first glance they resemble formal death notices, but a second look reveals they are merely warnings: Between two and four A.M. all the elevators will be shut down to enable the search for the winds.

The door marked KIDRON FAMILY is wide open, and all the lights are on inside. On the dining table, late-night snacks are laid out next to pots of black coffee. Gottlieb, who arrived earlier with a technician, is half-sprawled on a sofa, eating energetically while inquiring about the family connections of the lady of the house, a chubby, nervous woman clad in black and adorned with an engraved gold necklace. Her husband, too, is formally attired, in a dark suit and tie, as if dressed for battle with the representatives of the construction company, who are running late.

"Representatives?" Ya'ari says with surprise. "In the middle of the night they're sending us more than one person?"

Yes, both an engineer and a lawyer are on their way. These days no self-respecting company would come to such an investigation without a lawyer, and since the country is flooded with them the price for nocturnal consultations has dropped precipitously.

Ya'ari introduces himself to Gottlieb's technician, a powerfully built man of about fifty, who sits communing with himself in a corner by the balcony, tool box at his feet, coffee mug gripped tightly in both hands.

"Rafi." The man whispers his name with a downcast gaze.

No family warmth is evident between Gottlieb and the expert. The little woman avoids her stepfather, puts a biscuit on a plate and sits down near the technician. Tomorrow morning, Gottlieb informs Ya'ari, the work I am doing for your father will be done. But he will still need the mercy of heaven for his piston to function again in Jerusalem.

"Even if it doesn't work," Ya'ari responds coolly, "it's not the end of the world. Believe me, my father's tyranny has worn me out."

"Your father's tyranny? You're complaining? Hey, it's the same tyranny that woke me up tonight for this bit of theatre."

"It's not worth your getting up in the middle of the night to clear yourself of blame and responsibility?"

"Not if I'm bringing two technicians getting paid at the night-time rate."

"We're taking care of your young lady."

But the young lady, her star-bright eyes attentive to the discussion, says, leave him alone, Gottlieb, I don't need any payment. I'm happy enough just to listen for them, the father and son.

"Sure," Gottlieb waves her off sourly, "I know you both think I'm a miser, but you forget how much disability insurance I have to pay so we're covered if there's an accident. In my factory there are machines that can cut a man in half in two seconds, and then what? Who's going to pay for sewing him together? Me from my own pocket?"

"Gottlieb, my friend, there are no machines here."

"Yes, well, we're about to survey a dark shaft thirty storeys high."

Ya'ari wearies of the pettiness and wants to break off the conversation, so while his host phones the tardy representatives of the construction company, he asks the wife's permission to go through their apartment to see if any draughts can be felt through its walls. Follow me, says the nervous woman, and leads him first into the couple's bedroom, the scrupulous neatness of which betrays that they have not been to bed that night. A small terrace off the room faces the southeast part of the city, and Ya'ari invites himself out for a look and again stands above the urban vista he surveyed six days before from the tiny balcony of the tower's machine room. On that long-ago morning the sky was overcast; now sharp points of light sparkle in the night. Amid the city centre skyscrapers, the looming colossi of the Azrieli project, and the proud tower at the Diamond Exchange, multicoloured advertisements and the latest headlines alternate on huge digital screens: cropped-haired, leggy women touting dishwashers and clothes dryers segueing into reports of the Iranian nuclear threat.

Plump, quiet Mrs. Kidron stands by his side, fondling her gold necklace and lifting her eyes towards a passenger plane that lowers its landing gear as it glides downwards over the city. Ya'ari looks at his watch. Sixteen more hours until Daniela's arrival, provided that no wild beast has eaten her passport and ticket, and no arbitrary official has decided to alter the flight schedule.

"Your son . . . the soldier," he mumbles, almost casually, his eyes still fixed on the plane, "did he get to know this new apartment?"

"No. He was killed two months before we moved here. We wanted to cancel the purchase, but it was too late."

"Why cancel it? Doesn't it make it a little easier, moving to a new place?"

"So we hoped, but in the autumn these winds started up, and they only made us more depressed."

"Depressed because of the winds? But it's purely a technical problem."

She regards him with a fearful expression.

"Is that what you believe?"

"I don't believe it, I'm certain of it."

Another passenger plane, a jumbo jet, zooms in from over the sea and prepares for landing. Ya'ari asks his hostess if he may have a look at the other rooms. She leads him through a small book-lined den into a children's room filled with toys, similar to the room Daniela set up at their house for the grandchildren. Ya'ari listens carefully. Yes, the groaning wind is only in the shaft and stairwell. The apartment itself is quiet. He feels a sudden need to see a photograph of her son, and he lightly touches the lady's hand and asks for one. But the mother refuses his request. All photos of their son are hidden deep in a closet, because the parents resolved to keep him with them not through photographs but through memory and, above all, imagination. Both of us, says the mother, agreed not to get stuck on an image fixed in time. We try to go back and connect through activity, take him to places he never saw and imagine how he would behave there. We want to keep him in perpetual motion, allow him to grow and even grow old, so he will not be forever frozen in pictures from childhood or the last photos from his military service.

Ya'ari's heart skips a beat, and he nods his head silently. Then he asks to be directed to the lavatory. He is quick to lock the door, and when it turns out that the switch is outside he does without light. He pulls down his trousers and sits in darkness, tense, angry, perhaps in pain, lost in thought.

The wall behind him appears to be an exterior wall, and despite the late hour he can hear water flowing as well as the wailing wind. He feels a gathering sense of anxiety over Daniela's arrival. He is worried about malfunctions and delays on flights from Africa. But he still trusts the practical wisdom of his brother-in-law, who will know how to get his wife back to her homeland.

New voices are heard in the apartment, young and laughing. The representatives of the construction company have arrived to grapple with their guilt.

2.

IN THE END they forgot to give me their bones, Daniela realizes, with disappointment, when she sees from her window that the two pickup trucks are ready to take to the road. But I won't run to remind them. Apparently it's not that important to them, or they don't trust me, or maybe this is another third-world shortcoming, an inability to follow through. Yet not only was I not afraid to take the package with me, I was delighted to help them.

This is her last night in Africa, and perhaps her final farewell to her brother-in-law. There will be no one to bring his ashes in an urn to be buried in Israel. Has she fulfilled the goal of her visit: to reconnect, with her brother-in-law's help, with old memories that in years to come will nourish the love her sister deserves? All in all, Yirmi avoided discussing his wife, preferring to toss twigs of wrath onto the pyre of friendly fire, which he will never allow to die down. And still he complains about the prophets' lust for anger. Even if he truly took pity on Shuli, hiding from her what he dared to reveal to her sister, it's impossible that Shuli was not burned by the fierce flame he stoked inside him against a world that she still loved in spite of the death of her son.

The Israeli visitor, who generally excels at sound sleep, worries that she is in for a wearying bout of sleeplessness, which will burn itself out only as morning approaches, spoiling her good-byes as she takes leave of the place and its people. She could probably put herself to sleep with the unfinished pages of the novel, hoping that its artificiality will help her eyes to spin the first threads of sleep. However, she is determined to stick to her decision to save it for the two-hour stopover between her flights, and is already planning to tuck the book into the outside pocket of her suitcase on wheels, for easy access in the cafeteria in Nairobi.

Yirmi quickly disappeared after the festive meal, and is clearly avoiding her. He is swept up in his idea of disengagement and is probably afraid that before leaving she will make him swear, on his love for her sister, to keep in touch with the family. Maybe he also understands that she will exploit the moment of parting to speak up and rebut his arguments. Until now she has just listened to him, and with leading questions urged him on, and has been careful not to express any disrespect, lest he fall silent. As a high school teacher she has had to learn how to listen to the immature blather of teenagers. Which may be why she is so impatient with the adolescent rebellions of the elderly.

Actually, not only should she demolish his arguments, she should also be angry over his disappearance. Because Shuli would have been disappointed had she known about her indifferent dismissal by someone who was always beloved by the family, who was thought of as a man to be relied on, and who is now losing himself in a godforsaken place and disconnecting from everything that was important and dear to her sister. But Daniela's anger is surprisingly deflected, blown sideways, and lands squarely on her husband, the weight of whose absence is especially heavy tonight. Though tomorrow evening he will again be at her side, she feels that if he had been wiser in his love, he would not have let her make this visit on her own. He was under an obligation, even if against her wishes, to drop everything and join her, to help her fight the despair of ideas that give hope only to a pregnant suicide bomber.

Perhaps Amotz could have dealt with Yirmiyahu. Not for himself, but for Shuli, and also for Elinor and her husband Yoav, so that they might return to Israel after their studies. Only Amotz, with his straightforward intelligence, could have wrested a commitment from Yirmiyahu to keep in touch with the family, at least till his black mood died down.

But Amotz, she thinks to herself with mild disdain, is obviously taking advantage of her absence to go to bed even earlier. She can see him in her mind's eye in his red flannel pyjamas, climbing into their big bed at this very hour, surrounded by the photos of the children and grandchildren on the walls as he gathers the financial pages of the newspapers from the floor and gets under the big quilt, without feeling that he ought not to be in Tel Aviv but here, on a remote African farm, awake and ready to do battle with a man bent on destruction.

True, nihilism can be a mask for terrible personal trauma. But she knows that self-hatred cannot lead to rehabilitation. Yet she herself is helpless in confronting Yirmi and refuting him with serious arguments. She is a teacher of English: she deals with the meaning of words, with grammar, and sometimes with the analysis of characters in short stories and plays. But Amotz's head is filled with facts and figures, and he can remember the number of dead and wounded on both sides, not only in Israel's wars, but also in the wars of other, far-away nations. When he reads at all, he reads biographies and nonfiction, which is why he can come up with examples from times and places she didn't know existed, why he is able to compare Israelis with other peoples and distinguish real blame from imaginary blame. He should have been here by her side to rein in his brother-in-law, not merely for the sake of truth, but also so there would be hope for their children and his, so that Elinor and Yoav could come back to Israel, with or without their doctorates, and produce at least one grandchild to restore meaning to his life and wipe away the strange sweetness he found in the Hebrew of a young Palestinian woman filled with hatred and scorn.

In this fierce need for her husband, mixed with resentment, she fails to notice a gentle knocking on her door, until the door moves slightly and is cautiously opened. Through it, to her delight, walks in Dr. Roberto Kukiriza, with the bones of the prehistoric ape, the one who did not manage to fit into the evolutionary chain.

She blushes and says to him, "I thought you had given up on me, or that you had forgotten your bones."

"We have not given up on you," he answers in a friendly tone, "and how could we forget our discoveries? But a few colleagues were worried that we might be involving you unfairly in a strange and uncomfortable mission. The fact that you concealed it from Jeremy also caused us some concern."

"No problem there," she promises quickly. "I am willing to tell him."

"Very good. This will pacify the doubters. For we wish to be sure that Jeremy is also at peace with what we are imposing upon you. Over at Abu Kabir they are already waiting for you."

She extends her hand eagerly, and he takes from his pocket a small cloth bag, opens it, and shows her three bones, each different from the others in size and colour and shape, and suggests that she pack them in her suitcase.

"Certainly."

But he is still reluctant to hand them over, and inspects the suitcase lying open on the table to find the right spot.

"Perhaps we should put them in an unlikely place," he suggests. "Perhaps in your toiletry bag. An obvious female zone they will not search."

"That's a good idea," she says, and pulls the bag from his hand.

3.

AND SO IT has come to pass, muses Ya'ari with pride, all because of my quiet authority. Between two and three in the morning the team of six "wind people" have assembled in the brightly-lit

411

lobby of the tower, and beside them, beaming, stands a seventh, Mr. Kidron, chief of the apartment owners' association, holding two emergency torches powered by large batteries and silently giving thanks to the winds for not betraying him by dying at the moment of truth. The heavyset night watchman has been dispatched to the gate of the garage to ensure that no resident will show up at the last minute and get trapped between floors.

The four elevators have been stopped on different floors and must be brought together and then shut down individually. Only then will it be possible to ride on the roof of one of them, travelling slowly the full height of the shaft, casting a light on its walls. Though he carries both a master key and a triangle key in his pocket, Ya'ari prefers not to use them in the presence of the manufacturer, to avoid giving the impression that maintenance is his domain. The technician brought by Gottlieb summons each elevator in turn, shuts down the group control, and then detaches, with the triangle key, the electrical connection between the shaft door and the door of the car, and in the end all four elevators stand before them open-mouthed, awaiting their inspection of the winds.

The cell phone of the tenants' leader rings. The guard wants to know what to do about a man and a woman who have arrived at the garage with five heavy suitcases. They landed at the airport just an hour ago and knew nothing about any inoperative elevators. What floor do they live on? asks Ya'ari, and when he hears it is merely the eighth, he sternly rules that they should leave their bags in the lobby till morning and go up on foot. But no, the woman is pregnant, and so Ya'ari decides to go and fetch them himself in the big central elevator, and orders the technician to get one of the side elevators ready to move.

"Right or left?"

Ya'ari and Gottlieb look at the expert, who turns her face upwards, listening attentively.

"Left," she declares. "The defects are on the left side."

This time Ya'ari takes out his keys, despite the presence of the manufacturer, and reactivates the big elevator and goes down to collect the couple who have returned to their native land. And indeed he finds a pregnant woman and heavy luggage. So, he teases them, you came back to the suffering homeland? But he has only half hit the mark. The couple live and work in America and have even become citizens, but they want their child to be born in Israel, in the apartment they bought as a holiday home, so they can get help in the first few months from the parents on both sides. Practical Zionism, chuckles Ya'ari, and helps them slide the heavy bags out of the elevator.

When he gets back to the lobby he sees that the preliminary work on the left-hand elevator is proceeding apace. Gottlieb is a professional par excellence and knows every bolt of the elevators Ya'ari designed for him. He stands next to a dexterous and disciplined technician and tells him what to unscrew in a shiny, apparently seamless elevator, and the car swiftly bares its hidden electromechanical apparatus before the astonished eyes of the construction company representatives.

The technician enters the elevator and lowers it a bit without closing the door of the car, and a few seconds later the group sees him riding on its roof. He operates it using the three-button service controls—two pressed for each direction, up or down. And now, with the elevator suspended between the lobby and the car park, even the lawyer can get a sense of the dark shaft rising upwards, divided by the three sets of iron bars that stabilize the movement of the elevators and the counterweights along the guide rails.

The roof of the car that has been opened up is small, unlike the roof of the big central elevator, and Ya'ari deliberates whether to send only the technician and the expert for an introductory tour of the exposed shaft, or to join them. He finally decides to go along. He takes the two emergency torches from Mr. Kidron and says, okay, I'm going to cast a light on the ill winds. He hands one to the expert, who is already in position, keeps the other for himself, and says to the technician, Let's go, habibi, we're taking off.

The elevator floats upwards. The technician carefully controls the service buttons, so that the car's movement is slow, almost imperceptible. The listener from Kfar Blum is sure that the winds are breaking in at the fourteenth floor, but Ya'ari insists on checking every floor thoroughly. Strong beams from the two torches scour the walls of the shaft, revealed in their nakedness as pocked and wrinkled. Here and there sprigs of iron wire sprout from the concrete—once even an old scrap of newspaper. Now and then it looks like a human face or animal form is drawn on the wall, and sometimes a sentence carved in an unknown language. This is no simple job, says Ya'ari to the technician, who looks tensely up into the dark expanse of the shaft as though fearful of colliding with an unexpected object. Floor by floor they glide past iron elevator doors numbered in sloppy and varied handwriting. By the beams of light they scan the walls meticulously and Ya'ari never asks the technician to halt the gradual climb. But when they reach the thirteenth floor, Rachel says: This is it, Nimer, stop here.

And indeed, as soon as the elevator falls silent there is no doubt that here is the entry point of the menacing, aggressively groaning wind, as the tiny woman, her torch beam licking the wall methodically, points out to Ya'ari something in the shaft resembling open lips or perhaps nostrils, the consequence of faulty casting, or even malice. Like the pipes of a giant church organ, these nostrils produce a surprising variety of resonant—or dissonant—sounds.

"This is the spot you were thinking of?" Ya'ari asks the expert, who is standing up now, smiling sadly.

"This is the place. When I came a few days ago to listen to the winds with your Moran, I thought the problem was at the fourteenth floor, so I was only slightly off."

"Believe me," Ya'ari says, patting her fondly, "God makes bigger mistakes. If your Gottlieb and I were to spend a whole night riding up and down the shaft, we would never come upon this pipe organ. So let's bring the engineer up here and even his lawyer, so they'll see where the wailing comes from and then go back down with the blame and responsibility, and let the rest of us sleep at night."

He instructs the technician to take the elevator back to the lobby. And when he gets down from its roof he first of all praises the manufacturer, who has been dozing in the cozy armchair next to the night watchman's table. "A good thing you didn't leave your perfect pitch in Upper Galilee, otherwise you and I would be travelling up and down in that shaft forever." And to the engineer he says, "Why waste words, you won't believe it till you see for yourself. So come on, don't be scared, take a torch and sit on the roof of the elevator. The young lady will bring you safe and sound straight to the failures of your construction company."

The engineer hesitates for a moment, then takes the torch from Ya'ari and climbs onto the elevator, and is lifted off into the dark shaft with the little woman and the technician, beaming light in hand.

Ya'ari sits down in the watchman's chair and interrogates Gottlieb about the technician he brought along with him. Who is he really? Rafi? Nimer? A Jew? An Arab? A hybrid, a mixture, mumbles Gottlieb, half asleep. In what sense? Ya'ari asks. A mixture of all the good things still left in this country, mutters Gottlieb, and closes his eyes.

The lawyer paces restlessly. From time to time he goes to the elevator shaft and peers upwards as if wondering whether his engineer has been swallowed by the void.

"Careful," says Ya'ari. "Even falling only two floors down to the garage is a bad idea. But if you'd like us to take you up to the defect as well, so you can see why you'll be totally unable to defend it—no problem."

The lawyer is lost in thought. The head of the residents' association stands to the side, pleased at getting the inspection he had hoped for, but wary of its results. He would have preferred the discovery of a technical flaw in the elevators. A flaw in construction will require repairs that will interfere with normal life in the tower.

"Maybe you, too, would like to go up and see how the winds make their music?"

"No," Kidron says nervously. "It's enough to hear it, I don't need to see it."

The elevator returns to the lobby. The expression on the engineer's face as he gets down from its roof is that of a man who has seen an apparition. He whispers with the lawyer, who gathers that he can't justify his fee if he doesn't see the defect with his own eyes. It might be possible to cleverly shift the damages to the insurance company. The hybrid technician sits sombrely on the roof, bent over the control box, but the expert's big eyes shine as she invites Ya'ari to rejoin her and take another ride up to see the wondrous natural organ.

Why not. And this time he won't stop at the thirteenth floor but will soar all the way to the thirtieth. Maybe there he will discover new acoustics.

"You come, too, and see the organ," Ya'ari prods the lawyer. "I'll take you there myself."

And the lawyer, a handsome young man, accepts Ya'ari's challenge and prepares to climb up as the latter tells the technician to make way. I also know how to press three buttons, he jokes, and very carefully he heads on high with the lawyer and the expert.

First he ascends to the top of the shaft, the thirtieth floor, to hear from there the full lung power of the abyss. Far below them they can still see the glowing white light of the lobby. Then he cautiously takes them down to the thirteenth floor, and the expert casts her beam on the lips, or nostrils, of the pipe organ—the handiwork of Romanian labourers, or Thai, or local Arabs, and perhaps intended to lend a spice of life to the innards of the building. But the anxiety of the lawyer, who has never before ridden bareback on the roof of an elevator through a dark shaft, has apparently compromised his powers of understanding. Where? Where? he keeps asking insistently. I don't see a thing. Faced with such lawyerly obtuseness, the expert, still flashing the beam of light, stretches her body out to the side of the shaft, to point with her hand at the strange flaws

417

bathed in water stains or mould—and the end of the red scarf wound about her neck catches in the iron track of the counterweight, she stumbles, and the torch falls from her hand, plunging like a meteor into the pit below, as she grabs the iron bars that separate the elevators, letting out a yelp of pain that staggers Ya'ari.

4.

A FEW MINUTES after the departure of the handsome archaeologist, the visitor hears the engine of the vehicle that waited for him and hurries to her window, just in time to see how the beams of its headlights, piercing the fine rain, stripe the dirt road like a golden whip.

The bones sit among her toiletries, wrapped in their cloth bag, and for a moment she considers wrapping them in something else to insulate them from the odours of makeup and perfume, but decides not to. If everything that has clung to these bones deep in the ground for millions of years hasn't impaired their identity, they won't be compromised by the scent of her toiletries.

In spite of her promise to inform her brother-in-law about her little mission, she would be in no hurry to see him, if she didn't also feel compelled to tell him a few pointed things that might get lost in the swirl of her departure in the morning. She puts on her gym shoes and—though the night is warm—her sister's old windbreaker, and goes down to his temporary quarters, shown to her three days ago by the groundskeeper. But the door that opens at her touch reveals an empty room and bare bed. Disappointed, she continues on to the dining room.

The high table is still on its lofty perch by the west window, and to her amazement it is still covered with the remains of the festive dinner, as are the other tables, and the sinks are filled with unwashed pots and pans. Yet despite the disorder and grime, she feels at home in this place and is not afraid to be alone in the cluttered darkness. And because she thinks Yirmiyahu will pass by en route to his room, she finds a seat by one of the tables and waits for him.

The silence is absolute. She thinks about the prehistoric bones that have settled in with her makeup, and again feels bad about her loyal housekeeper, who will not be getting the lipstick she requested. Should she add pain to disappointment and tell her why and where this special and expensive lipstick was thrown away?

She brushes the crumbs off a section of the table and lays her head down and closes her eyes. She'll wait for him a little longer, but if he takes his headache as licence to closet himself in the infirmary—perhaps with the added confidence that she wouldn't dare go there in the dark—she'll have to give up tonight and postpone her planned speech till the hour of parting.

As she rests her head on the big table, eyes closed, sleep flutters over her like a little bird, and for a few minutes she drifts off. And when she lifts her head heavily and opens her eyes in the dark, for a moment she doesn't know where she is, and in the faint light of the windowpane she sees the silhouette of a little elephant, its trunk lifted silently skywards and its wondrous floating eye—an independent creature, flickering in all its blueness.

But the mirage quickly fades and again becomes the

silhouette of the high table, the blackened skeleton of the giant branch that burned during the festive speech, left leaning there, and the glowing embers in the belly of the stove, whose door was left ajar.

Now, at last, her whole being is broken open by the pain of longing that she came to find in Africa; the loss of her sister finally batters her, here in the big kitchen, with a force she has never yet experienced. She gets up and lightly kicks shut the door of the stove to hide the dying fire, and lets her tears find release in a long, lingering sob that convulses her entire body.

Yes, perhaps her excessive devotion to her two grandchildren in the past year was also intended to muffle that longing, which is why she had to come to Africa alone to join in her brother-in-law's grief. But Yirmi, shackled by his attempt to find meaning in the fire that killed his son, instead launched friendly fire at his wife and her family. Oh, Amotz, maybe your intentions were good, but you could not imagine the falsehood bound up in the phrase you blurted out when you brought the terrible news.

Tonight, following the monologue about separation and disengagement that Yirmiyahu subjected her to, it's natural and understandable that he would try to avoid her. He knows her well, and knows she can respond harshly and judgmentally even when she seems to be a cheerful and receptive listener. Therefore tomorrow morning he will be quick to send her on her way. You have to rush, he'll say, overnight the rain mucked up the dirt roads; Sijjin Kuang is a stickler for timetables and hates to be late.

But she is reluctant to leave the protected space of the main building and head in total darkness for the infirmary. She vividly remembers the afternoon when the snake sprang from the grass near the infirmary and recoiled in fear before the jaws of the catlike beast.

Where, now, is the wizened African who assisted her in the mornings? She would follow him, eyes closed, through the wet grass while raindrops tapped her shoulders. But after he extinguished the burning branch and set it by the high table, he disappeared. Does he live at the farm, or does he come here from a hut in a neighbouring village? She forgot to ask these things about him, just as for six days she never asked the way to Sijjin Kuang's room, another person she would follow anywhere with complete confidence. But though it's not yet midnight, she won't sully her reputation on the eve of her departure by knocking on unfamiliar doors.

A simple torch might have increased her self-assurance. Even a big candle would be fine. She remembers where matches are kept in the kitchen. Had not Yirmi destroyed her Hanukkah candles on the first night, she might have been able to combine the little candles into a sturdy source of fire and light whose flame would banish her fears. She opens the door and looks out at the dark universe. Out of the clouds emerges a sliver of moon, a Muslim crescent, that may illuminate the path somewhat. She zips up her sister's old windbreaker, covers her head with its furry hood, and without letting herself think twice walks out of the farmhouse to the path she knows, then begins to run, as if dodging the warm raindrops, in the belief that her quick movements will confuse any animal even if she steps on it by mistake.

If her grandchildren were to see her running like this in the middle of the night in Africa, they would surely laugh, but their laughter would not last long, because the distance to the infirmary is short. The front door is closed but unlocked, and silently she enters the treatment room, which is dimly lit by a table lamp. Beside the stethoscope someone has left a tourist brochure of Tanzania. On the cover is a photograph of the Ngorongoro nature reserve, a huge, deep crater with walls the height of a two-hundred storey tower. The wildlife trapped in it, unable to climb out, have retained their prehistoric uniqueness. When she and Amotz visited three years ago, Yirmi and Shuli took them there, and the two couples went down to the bottom of the crater for a long tour. She hesitates for a moment, then turns off the lamp, and in the deepened darkness she goes to the door of the inner room, taps on it softly, her heart pounding, then opens it without waiting for an answer. And Yirmiyahu, waking with a start while she is still in the doorway, says, Have you lost your mind?

But it isn't madness that has brought her here, but rather a jolt of pity for the young soldier, who asks her to free him from the fierce grip of his father and let him rest. And so she enters the inner room and sits down not on the empty bed opposite, but right beside the man she has known since she was young, who flinches now as if in self-defence.

"What's going on?"

"I can't fall asleep, and I'm worried I won't be ready in the morning when Sijjin Kuang comes to take me to the flight."

"Why worry? If you don't wake up on your own, she'll come and get you up."

"Why her? Won't you be up early?"

"I'll be up. And if not, she'll wake me too."

"Be that as it may, perhaps it would make more sense for

422

me to sleep here at the infirmary. It will make me feel calmer, more secure, and this way she can wake both of us. No, don't be alarmed. You remember how when my parents were away at night I would sometimes climb in bed with Shuli? She was always happy to have me."

"Not always." He grins. "You once showed up in the middle of the night when I was also in the bed, and we had to chase you away."

"But now, with Shuli gone, there's no need to get rid of me."

And she cannot believe that she has said such a thing, just like that, so naturally. It seems to her that even in the dark she can see his astonishment. Perhaps to protect himself from her he grabs his trousers from the chair, takes out matches and a crushed packet of cigarettes, lights one, and the room fills with its strange smell.

"You started smoking again?"

"No. But sometimes at night it's good to see a little glowing ember between my eyes."

"Then give me one too."

"Better you should smoke your own. This is a very strong plain African cigarette, that has some sort of wild grass in it together with the tobacco."

"Just what I need right now."

She pulls the pack from his fingers and lights herself a cigarette, takes a deep draw of the odd-smelling smoke, and tells Yirmi about the promise she made to get his consent to the transport of the bones already hidden among her cosmetics, adding that even if he objects, she is determined to take them with her. She feels the need to repay these scientists for their friendliness.

"Why would I object?" he says, surprised.

"Because they suggested this was illegal."

"So what if it's illegal?" he says, a note of hostility creeping into his voice. "If they catch you, they'll immediately forgive you, as always."

"What do you mean, as always?"

"Because you're an expert at saving yourself from pain and from blame, and you also chose, as you yourself admitted, a man willing to shield you from the world."

These hard words, delivered in an accusatory tone, add venom to the smoke seeping into her. She throws the cigarette to the floor and grinds it out with her shoe and stares at the family member she has known since childhood. Yirmi remains indifferent and self-absorbed as he pulls the wool blanket over his bare legs and takes another pleasurable drag at his cigarette.

Tears of hurt well in her eyes.

How can she be accused of protecting herself from pain if she came all the way to Africa to see him? And if he feels that she also knows how to enjoy the visit, there's no contradiction in that. She is a curious woman, always fascinated by people. But her true purpose was to be with him, to listen with patience and sympathy to his every word. And even when he aroused her anger and resistance, because of his blindness in the past and stubbornness in the present, never for a moment did she forget his misery.

His bent head moves slightly.

"Anger?" he mutters, but still does not look at her directly.

That's right, anger and defiance, she reiterates, her voice choking, rising to a kind of wail. Instead of hiding his wretched obsession with that roof from her sister, and instead of humiliating himself, and indirectly her too, in a fruitless attempt to win sympathy from a suicidal pregnant young woman just to give meaning to the friendly fire, which was no more than a random stupid absurdity, he should have reconciled himself to that absence of meaning, and his obligation should have been something else entirely.

"Something else?" His face is twisted with mockery.

Yes. Because even if Shuli suppressed her womanliness after the death of her son, his duty was to fight for it, and not to use her withdrawal as an excuse to wipe away his whole biography and identity and the world he grew up in, and the history that has been and the history that will be. His duty was to fight for Shuli, for her sexuality and her desire. To console her instead of helping her extinguish herself. So she could live and not die.

Yirmi looks up in horror at the tearful, wailing woman who continues to pour out accusations as if her mind had lost control of her lips. He surely never anticipated that his tolerant and attentive guest would rise up at the moment of departure and suggest that he was to blame for her sister's death.

Now she is trembling and sobbing with fright over her brazen onslaught. He stands up, puts out the stub of his cigarette and crumbles it between his fingers, wary of getting nearer to her.

"Come on," he says heavily, "it's late, and you're tired. I'll take you back."

But Daniela refuses to budge. On the contrary, she defiantly takes off the windbreaker and also her shoes. Because just as the Palestinian roof had a magnetic effect on him, so, too, has this infirmary on her: a strange place, but not dangerous. For all his own suicidal illusions he had to know that a Palestinian woman who had brought him something to drink would let no harm come to him. Hospitality remains holier than revenge. And she trusts his hospitality and knows he will not touch her even if under cover of darkness she continues to remove before him all her clothes, as she is now doing, item by item, until she is lying in his bed naked, covered with a blanket. Because this is how she wants to mourn the lost womanhood of her sister.

He recoils, agitated. For the first time since her arrival she thinks his self-control is about to give way. But she still trusts him even as he comes near her in the darkness and suddenly resembles a great terrifying ape, even when he lifts up the blanket and looks at her nakedness, the sheer nakedness of a weeping older woman and is perhaps reminded of what he abandoned and of his guilt about her sister. And then he closes his eyes, and as if bowing in obeisance, he flutters his lips on her bare breasts, then groans and bites her shoulder, and quickly, gently covers her up again. A moment later, he leaves the room.

5.

YA'ARI IMMEDIATELY REMOVES his hands from the controls, to prevent any accidental shifting of the elevator. Don't move, he calls to the trapped expert, we'll get you out of there. And you be careful too, he yells angrily at the young lawyer, who looks on in horror at the little woman whose leg is caught somewhere between the counterweight and the separation bars, and don't you move either or touch anything.

Gottlieb apparently saw the torch tumble down the shaft, because as Ya'ari fumbles for his cell phone, the manufacturer's voice cries out from the depths, What is it, Ya'ari? Did the lawyer fall? But Ya'ari, who has found his phone, does not shout back so as not to frighten the residents. With quivering fingers he dials Gottlieb's number and informs him that his stepdaughter is trapped in the shaft. And since he does not know her exact location, he orders that no elevator be moved and says to call the fire department. Not the fire department, Gottlieb objects immediately, they'll wake up the whole street with their sirens and cause mayhem in the building, for no reason. No, habibi, we're going to rescue the little one ourselves. My Nimer and I, and even you, have enough skill and experience to know what we can handle and what we can't. Forty years ago I myself stumbled into a shaft like this, and you can see with your own eyes that I got out safely. And so Gottlieb wants him now to be practical and logical as always, and determine his precise location so the technician won't have to climb any more stairs than necessary.

Ya'ari trains his light between the separation bars, at the counterweight pinning the leg, and sees the outline of the body and the red woollen scarf. The quiet sobbing of the woman mingled with the lamentation of the wind rattles him. What do you feel, Rachel? Tell me. He tries to get her to answer, but she only keeps murmuring, Abba'leh, Abba'leh.

Finally the outer door on the thirteenth floor is opened, and Nimer, who arrived by the stairs, out of breath, decides to get the lawyer out of there first. With a monkeylike agility that belies his age, he lowers himself over the elevator track, orders the lawyer to grab hold of his hand, and with one strong pull drags him up the side of the shaft and hauls him onto the floor of the building. Gottlieb told me to get you out too, he says to Ya'ari. No, says Ya'ari adamantly, I'm not moving from here until we rescue her. I'm part of this.

427

Gottlieb, meanwhile, has reactivated the big central elevator and loaded into it the technician's tool box, and is now sailing upwards on its roof like the helmsman of a great ship, coming to a halt near the twelfth floor at a spot allowing access to the trapped woman.

Only now, in the reassuring presence of her stepfather and employer, does she end her cries of pain to respond to his questions.

"What happened, Rolaleh?" he says, attempting a joke, "you decided to take a night-time stroll on the walls of the shaft?"

"I fell, Gottlieb, and my leg got caught."

"This is what happens, Rachel, when you take the Ya'ari family's winds too seriously."

"My leg hurts, really badly."

"We'll free it up right away and get you out of here; just don't move."

"I'm afraid my leg is gone."

"Gone where, by itself?" he continues in the same jocular tone. "It's not going anywhere without you. And you can rest easy, because I took out not one but two insurance policies on you, and any minute Nimer will get into the big elevator to take off a side panel and free up your foot. Don't worry, you'll still be able to dance on it at the wedding."

"Whose wedding, Gottlieb, what are you talking about?"

"Yours, of course."

"There won't be any wedding."

"Yes, there will, and even I'll dance."

"So you are suddenly a dancer?"

"Only at your wedding."

In the meantime Nimer has walked down two flights of

stairs, opened the door of the car and slid into the big elevator with Gottlieb waiting on the roof. Acting on instructions shouted by his employer he swiftly opens up the side to get to the trapped expert. From above, lit by the beam of Ya'ari's torch, the technician emerging from the elevator looks like a prehistoric man at the entrance to his cave, as he signals to Ya'ari to inch his elevator up a bit to free the counterweight, then pulls in the delicate creature still wrapped in her red wool scarf. And the manufacturer brings the elevator down safely.

In the lobby, anxious and agitated, wait not only the engineer of the construction company and the lawyer and the head of the residents' committee and the night watchman, but also a few curious tenants, who woke from the noise and came to witness the excitement. The expert, her foot bleeding, is laid down on a blanket provided by the guard. Ya'ari has meanwhile come down in the left-hand elevator and returned it to automatic control, and within minutes three of the four elevators are again functioning, and the groaning of the winds returns in full force.

Since Gottlieb has no faith in the efficiency of public rescue services, he declines to call an ambulance, and carries the childlike figure of the wounded woman in his arms to his big car, to drive her to a nearby hospital.

"Just don't tell me I'm to blame for her fall," says the lawyer defensively to Ya'ari.

"You're not to blame for her fall," Ya'ari answers with disdain, "but you are to blame for not believing what was shown to you."

"So what happens now?" Kidron asks Ya'ari, his face pale.

"What happens is what I told you. The design and

429

manufacture are in order but the construction company is at fault, so now you can finally leave me alone."

6.

A FEW SECONDS after being snatched from her sleep Daniela realizes that she is hearing the actual voices of two Africans, a boy and a woman, who have entered the adjoining room. She is wearing her brassiere and blouse; she remembers putting them on again moments after her brother-in-law fled the room in panic. Only the windbreaker still lies on the floor, and she shakes it out and wraps it around her before cautiously opening the door between the two rooms. An African boy is lying on the treatment table, and an older woman stands by his side, apparently his mother.

She smiles her silent thanks at the pair for waking her up. Now she can slip back into her room, so that Sijjin Kuang can wake her there.

But when she leaves the infirmary into bright morning light and steps onto the wet glistening grass, she sees from a distance the stately figure of the Sudanese, who is coming to rouse her after not finding her in her room.

"They are waiting for you there," Daniela says, red-faced, to the nurse, who is too discreet to interrogate her as to how and why she spent the night at the infirmary, and simply reminds her that they are short of time.

With a pang of conscience she enters the kitchen. Morning activity is at full tilt, and all signs of the festive meal have been removed. Yirmi is sitting in his shabby khaki suit at one of the small tables, bargaining in sign language with a tall Masai warrior in a red robe who has brought him a sheep and a lamb. He waves warmly at his sister-in-law. You have to hurry, Daniela, he calls to her, last night's rain damaged the dirt road.

She quickly climbs the stairs to the room she left the night before, and viewing the disorderly sheets she gets the feeling that some stranger was in the room and even in her bed, but she has no time now for fantasies and delusions. She must depart properly from a room that was after all quite adequate, return it in good order to its regular occupant. After washing her face and closing her suitcase, she folds the bedding, taking care to do so meticulously. Then she scrubs the sink and toilet, so as not to leave any unpleasantness behind. For a moment she considers getting someone to carry her bag down, but knows she is capable of wheeling it down the stairs herself.

You are late. Yirmi rushes her as though she were a schoolgirl. In his look, in the tone of his voice, there are no signs that he is troubled or bears her any grudge. Instead, there's a new friendliness, mixed with compassion for the visitor who is returning to a dangerous place. She is surprised to discover that the hurried pace he firmly imposes on her leaves her no time to eat breakfast calmly in her usual spot nor even to say a proper good-bye to the old African groundskeeper. Yirmiyahu has prepared for her trip—just as on the night she arrived—a bag of sandwiches and a thermos of coffee. This is for you, he says, handing them over with a smile, just don't be late, and don't get lost on the way back. I promised Amotz I'd get you home on time. And he carries her small suitcase to the Land Rover.

Sijjin Kuang is already seated at the wheel, and in the seat beside her is the African boy from the infirmary, who needs the space for his bandaged leg. Yirmi sets the suitcase in the backseat and gestures for her to sit where she has been accustomed. For a moment she feels insulted by the speed at which she is being dispatched and by the backseat allotted to her.

But all of a sudden her brother-in-law hugs her tight. All things considered, thank you for the visit. You didn't only torment me, you also made me happy. And if I at least convinced you that you two don't have to worry about me, then your visit accomplished something positive.

"Not to worry?" she whispers with disappointment.

"No," he says firmly, "worry about each other in Israel, which is a natural place for perpetual worry. And if you are nonetheless seized by worry for me, too, then send Amotz over; for him, I won't have to prepare any speeches, because you'll have told him everything. Only he should come without newspapers or candles, and we'll tour the area."

And he strokes her head gently and helps her get into the vehicle.

In a quick clean break the Sudanese driver exits the farm, and since the African boy has taken from Daniela the seat to which her age entitles her, she finds herself yet again the companion of boxes. But her frustration over the backseat is not just technical. The Israeli visitor had planned to talk to Sijjin Kuang on their last ride together, to discuss the future of the Israeli administrator, whom three days ago she had called, in a blunt and startling fashion, spoiled.

But how to talk from the backseat amid deafening engine noise? In the end, she must sit and watch the back of an African boy who has an infection spreading under his bandages. With any luck, a clinic will be found that can save his leg.

The road winds about the forest that the two women drove through on the first night. Then the trees looked dark and bristly, but by day, washed by the rain, they are endearingly green and peaceful, and she is gripped with sadness over her silent ride and missed opportunity. She reaches for the driver's thin shoulder, leaning forward: please, may we stop here for a minute?

Sijjin Kuang agrees reluctantly and stops near a barren patch in the forest and turns off the engine, so that Daniela can get out and stretch after her unsettled night. The boy is also pleased, and he hops on his good leg between the trees and cuts himself a branch with a knife. Only Sijjin Kuang stays by the car. She lifts the bonnet and checks the oil, then adds a little water to the radiator. Suddenly Daniela is flooded with admiration for the serious young black woman, and she returns to the car and says straight out, Sijjin Kuang, I had a dream about you.

The Sudanese nurse looks frightened. Perhaps, according to her faith, a white person's dream about a black person has some evil power? But Daniela is quick to calm her. It was a good dream. I saw you with us in Jerusalem, seeking love and finding it.

Sijjin Kuang is shocked. She shuts the bonnet of the car with a loud clang and wipes her hands with a towel, and with a wise, ironic smile she asks the dreaming woman, "You are sending me all the way to Jerusalem to find love?"

"If it is love," Daniela answers softly, "then why not?"

"And Jeremy, your brother-in-law—have you convinced him to return to Jerusalem?"

"I don't know. What do you think?"

"That it is good for him to stay here."

433

The African boy hops back to the car with the big branch in his hand. But Sijjin Kuang doesn't let him bring it into the car, and reluctantly he throws it away.

7.

SINCE THE TECHNICIAN was so skilful in the rescue operation, Ya'ari stays with him until he finishes re-attaching the open side of the big elevator. But putting things together is harder than taking things apart, and Gottlieb's absence slows the process down. Ya'ari himself is not familiar with the fine details of the elevator that his firm designed and cannot offer advice. The night watchman is not much of a conversationalist. So little remains for Ya'ari to do but doze in Gottlieb's armchair near the watchman's table, exuding silent solidarity with the middle-aged technician.

The first rays of dawn, which illuminate the oversize glass doors of the tower's lobby, also open the eyes of Ya'ari, who sees the technician replacing the last of the tools in his box and locking it. The elevator designer rises heavily from his chair to return the car to group control, but the worker has beaten him to it. And the elevator lifts off at once to the early-rising tenant on the thirtieth floor. Come, Rafi, says Ya'ari with affection, I'll take you home. No need, says the man. I'll wait for the first bus. But Ya'ari insists and drives him along the coastal road to a neighbourhood in the south of the city, a place where people get up early, not far from Abu Kabir. The technician, silent all the way there, invites Ya'ari in a gesture of gratitude to come up to his apartment for a morning cup of coffee, and Ya'ari, who can't decide whether to go home to make up for lost sleep or go on to the office, accepts, in part to examine the worker's apartment and decide whether there was anything to that word *hybrid,* or if it was said only in jest.

The clean two-room flat is furnished in good taste. In the front room are shelves with books, mainly in Russian. There is nothing Middle Eastern about the upholstery of the sofa or the art reproductions hanging on the wall. But the coffee prepared by the host is clearly Arab in aroma and taste. A young pregnant woman, who has woken up in the other room and now brings soft ring-shaped rolls to go with the coffee made by her mate, contributes no further clue.

Ya'ari questions the man about Gottlieb's qualities as an employer, and to his surprise finds that the technician appreciates him. Admittedly the wages he pays are mediocre compared to salaries paid by others, but because he is always present on the factory floor and circulates among the workers, he adds drama and tension to the work, and so the time passes more quickly.

"So what is your name, really," Ya'ari wants to know before leaving, "Nimer or Rafi?"

The technician grins. "That depends on who is asking."

"When I asked you, you said Rafi, so what does that say about me?"

"True," the man admits, "I said Rafi, but now that we've worked together all night, Nimer is okay too."

His cell phone rings: the voice of Moran, who was released half an hour ago and is on his way back to Tel Aviv. His first question, is his mother back yet? Not until the evening, his father answers matter-of-factly, but after you change clothes and kiss your wife and children, please go to the office and take the reins. I'm going home to sleep, and you've done enough loafing. And he summarizes for his son the events of the Night of the Winds.

When he gets to his home in the suburbs, his eyes barely open enough to see the tree in the front garden, the cell phone rings again, this time Francisco, reporting that his father is running a temperature.

"How high?"

"Thirty-eight point five."

"Maybe take it again?"

"I already took it twice, it was exactly the same."

"Okay, I'm on my way."

"Should I telephone Doctor Zaslanski?"

"Have pity on him and wait a little while. The poor man is eighty years old, so let him sleep."

According to Ya'ari's instructions, any rise in his father's temperature up to thirty-eight degrees Celsius the Filipinos are to attend to themselves; if it's more than that, they should call in Ya'ari and the old man's personal physician, his childhood friend Doctor Zaslanski.

Ya'ari washes his hands and looks longingly at the bed he abandoned in the middle of the night. He feels a truly strong desire to curl up in the white down quilt.

But the doctor has warned him that Parkinson's disease can get worse during a high temperature, and the last thing Ya'ari wants today is illness complicated by rekindled love. So without shaving or changing his work clothes, he drives to his father's house to check the boundary between the physical and the mental.

The old man's eyes glisten. The temperature imparts an

attractive ruddiness to his cheeks. He sits up in bed, propped by pillows, and asks right away about the winds in the tower. Ya'ari tells him about the organ holes left in the shaft by chance or on purpose.

"This is how it ends," says old Ya'ari with resignation. "When you treat foreign construction workers poorly, they leave a little souvenir in the building before going back to their country, and now try hunting them down in Romania or China."

"Why are you so sure it was done deliberately? Maybe it's just by accident?"

"Accident?" the old man sneers dismissively, "*accident* is always the easy way out for someone too lazy to think."

The son is too exhausted to argue with the father. Doctor Zaslanski will not arrive for another hour, and since Hilario is already awake, Ya'ari asks Kinzie to change the sheets and make him a fresh bed in his old childhood room. A little nap of an hour wouldn't hurt. The Filipinos are happy to carry out this request. You are very tired, Mister Amotz, they chide him. Instead of your wife's trip giving you some rest, it has tired you out. What time does she land?

"Five in the afternoon."

"You want a clean pyjama of your father?"

"No."

His childhood bed gives off a sweet smell, perhaps from something Southeast Asian. The room is familiar and foreign all at once. Still standing is the bookcase they bought him when he entered high school, and his old chair is still in place by the desk. But there's a mishmash of other furnishings, from other rooms, such as the night table that stood next to his mother's bed, and a wicker basket from the bathroom, and there are also various accessories from the Philippines—colourful posters and lamps, and a real or fake telephone in the shape of a dragon. Ya'ari takes off his clothes and gets into bed in his boxer shorts and long-sleeved T-shirt, and hopes for a sound and soothing sleep that will render him fit for the reunion with his wife.

He drops off at once, and his sleep is heavy, though at times real voices drift through. He hears the reassuring bass voice of Doctor Zaslanski, familiar from his childhood, explaining what to give the old man for his fever, adding, Don't worry, let Amotz sleep, don't wake him. And Ya'ari clings to his blanket and silently thanks his childhood doctor, and sinks deeper into the marvellous slumber.

And he dreams. Workers carry a mass of metal and drop it with a clang on the floor and speak Romanian or Chinese. And here he is again in the shaft of the winds, but this time the shaft does not extend up high but lies flat like a tunnel, and the elevators are like cars in a coal mine, and he can walk beside them as they move. But instead of coal they transport tenants dressed in black, wearing glittering gold chains around their necks. And Ya'ari escorts them, torch in hand. He walks between the fencing and the tracks and suddenly feels an urgent need to urinate. But where? Cars filled with tenants pass by incessantly, emanating from a source of light and riding into the darkness, and because the cars have no roofs, and the tenants are all looking in his direction, he has a hard time finding a hidden corner. On the side of the shaft he notices a tangled spider's web, and he edges towards it and decides to wash it away with the powerful stream from his bursting bladder.

He wakes up in time and rushes to the toilet. Through the living room window he sees a different light. It's afternoon. At the end of the corridor, near the entrance to the apartment, sits Gottlieb's piston.

"What is this?" he demands. "They delivered my father's piston here?"

"Yes, two workers brought it around mid-day, because Gottlieb says there's no room for it at the factory."

"Bastard," Ya'ari grumbles, "suddenly he has no room for the piston. Why didn't you wake me? I would have made them take it back."

"It would not have helped," Francisco answers evenly, "because your father agreed. The piston made him so happy."

Ya'ari sighs and leans against the wall, drained.

"How is he?"

"He is getting better. His temperature is going down."

Ya'ari looks at his watch. Unbelievable, three-thirty in the afternoon.

"How could you let me sleep like that?" he scolds Francisco.

"Your father wouldn't let us wake you." Francisco smiles, showing all his white teeth. "But only till four," he said, "so you don't miss your wife."

8.

THIS TIME, THE small plane lands far from the terminal in Nairobi, and a dilapidated bus is brought over to fetch the passengers. Daniela, who hoped for a direct transfer to the next flight, is forced to go through passport control and customs once more. How long will you stay here? asks a policeman, who is also the customs officer. I'm not staying here, she answers with a sad smile. I am just passing through, I will stay for only two hours. Nevertheless they open her suitcase and search it, and even remove the contents of her toiletry bag, but the dry bones do not arouse any interest.

And again she goes through the metal detectors, and wheels her suitcase behind her till she locates the same teeming cafeteria where she can wait for the flight home. The stopover is not six hours but this time she is not the same confident woman, carving out a territory for herself. She doesn't dare pull over two extra chairs, to put her feet up on one and her bag and suitcase on the other. She makes do with an empty seat in the heart of the hubbub, crowded among other people's tables, and when she tells the waiter with a faint smile, Just coffee, she bows her head.

Fear and anxiety in anticipation of returning to Israel. Merely imagining the possibility that Amotz will discover what happened fill her with horror. That strange look of Yirmiyahu's when she left him—what did it mean? Anger? Hope? Shock? He did not say a word about what had happened that night, perhaps because he felt sorry for her. And though ordinarily she hates the idea of anyone feeling sorry for her, now it is what she wants. Leaving aside the bite on the shoulder, the mere fact that her breasts were touched by his lips means that she gave him, out of pity, a deed of ownership. Now she is in his hands, whether he returns to Israel or not. And maybe precisely because of his sense of honour, and his deep ties to her and Amotz, he will refrain from coming back. Who knows, the strange thought occurs to her, maybe *this* was her hidden agenda: to prevent him from coming back, so he could not poison her family, her children and grandchildren, with his friendly fire.

The waiter sets down her cup of coffee and requests immediate payment, as he is about to conclude his shift. She pays and tips him well, but is unable to lift the cup to her lips, as if it contained bitter medicine. Crowded and cramped between Africans and Europeans, she suddenly hears some Hebrew. She doesn't lift her head. In this grimy cafeteria she wants total anonymity. God willing, time will numb her shame.

The digital display now shows a delay of half an hour in the takeoff for Tel Aviv, which pleases her. Two young Hasidic men dressed in black—obviously local emissaries of Chabad who have managed to get into the terminal—circulate among the tables scrutinizing the clientele, seeking Jewish passengers. They take a good look at her too, and she quickly averts her eyes. To avoid giving them any pretext for approaching her, she pulls out the novel she bought for the trip and opens it without enthusiasm at the final chapter.

She counts the remaining pages. Only twenty-five. Then she skims through them to check the amount of dialogue and the length of the paragraphs. Finally she starts to read, first returning to the last two pages of the previous chapter to reconstruct the context. There is a new tension in the voice of the author, who writes in the first person and identifies completely with the heroine. But it's still hard to decipher the nature of this tension. In any event, the irony and cynicism are muted, and gone are the tiresome descriptions of the landscape, which in previous chapters seemed to have been written more out of literary duty than to serve a narrative or psychological purpose. Apparently something grave is about to happen. Perhaps the author is planning the heroine's suicide. And in fact, why not? A vacuous and clueless young woman might just try to kill herself. Some sort of pain is suddenly apparent between the lines, particularly in places where the text seems most minimalist and unclear. The pages go quickly, and then, for no reason, slow down. For a moment she flips back to the beginning of the book, recalling that there was some hint there that might explain what would happen in the final pages. She feels that the young and pretentious author is gearing up for an absurd twist that readers of her own age and spiritual temperament will happily accept, but not a serious reader like Daniela, who is already rebelling against it. Nevertheless she takes a sip of the cold coffee, and as if hypnotized continues to turn the pages. She is helpless, caught in the novel's spidery web until she reads the last lines, which are blurred by a flood of tears she did not at all expect.

She closes the book and slides it into the outer pocket of her suitcase. After all the effort and the emotion she feels hungry. The length of the flight's delay holds steady on the digital display. The cafeteria becomes even more crowded, and there is no hope that the waiter rushing between tables will notice her now that she has paid him. She remembers that the refreshments kiosk is not far away, but has no desire for sweets.

On the contrary, they'll just make her feel sick. She remembers the sandwiches prepared by her brother-in-law, who forced her out of concerns real or imagined to miss breakfast. She returned the thermos to Sijjin Kuang but packed the food in her suitcase, and she now takes out a meat sandwich and bites into it, glancing around her.

One of the young yeshiva students has sat down at a nearby table, laid out a cloth napkin, and placed upon it a bottle of mineral water, and now he too takes a bite of a homemade sandwich. He notices her picnic and smiles, as if they have a shared family secret that will soon permit him to approach her. He chews with great deliberation. If he were aware of the animal provenance of the flesh she is consuming, he might not spring from his seat towards her beckoning finger.

The young man is not Israeli but American, and his halting Hebrew is heavily accented. She speaks to him firmly, in the tone that an impatient teacher takes with a student of whom she expects little.

"Do you by chance have a Bible with you?"

"Bible with you?" he is shocked. "What do you mean?"

"What do you mean, what do I mean?" she laughs. "If you have a Bible in your bag, I'd like to look up something quickly and then give it right back to you."

"A whole Bible?"

"Yes, but in Hebrew."

"The whole Bible I don't have. But maybe you want to see Psalms? I have Psalms."

"Not *Tehillim*," she says, imitating his pronunciation. "A complete Bible."

"What exactly are you looking for?"

"It doesn't matter. Do you have one or not?"

"I don't have a complete Bible," he admits in defeat.

"If you don't, well, it's no tragedy."

"But I can give you a prayer book, which has many chapters from the Bible in it."

"No prayer book or chapters," she answers impatiently, because she realizes that she will not easily get rid of the young man whose thin, soulful face is adorned with the first signs of blond beard, and who intends ardently to pursue the religious obligation he has happened to incur in an airport on an African afternoon.

"Okay," he says, after a moment's thought. "Wait for me a minute and I'll find you a complete Bible. There's time before the flight to Tel Aviv."

He quickly disappears into the big crowd, perhaps to seek the help of his friend, and about ten minutes later returns and presents her with a big new Bible, apparently purchased just for her—a dual-language Bible, Hebrew and English.

The English version is not the King James, but the Hebrew is the same ancient Hebrew she has been looking for. She remembered it as Jeremiah chapter 42, but she finds what she wanted in chapter 44. And she reads it silently, with great excitement, as the American yeshiva boy, his face translucent with piety, stands beside her, fascinated and nervous.

Therefore thus saith the Lord of Hosts, the God of Israel: Behold, I will set My face against you for evil, even to cut off all of Judah. And I will take the remnant of Judah, that have turned their faces to go into the land of Egypt to sojourn there, and they shall all be consumed, in the land of Egypt shall they fall. They shall fall by the sword, and shall be consumed by famine, they shall die, from the smallest even unto the greatest, by the sword and by famine, and they shall be an execration, and a desolation, and a curse, and a mockery. For I will punish them that dwell in the land of Egypt, as I have punished Jerusalem: by the sword, by famine, and by pestilence. And of the remnant of Judah that have come into the land of Egypt to sojourn there, none shall escape or remain to return to the land of Judah, to which they have a desire to return, and dwell there. For none shall return, except a few survivors.

Then all the men who knew that their wives made offerings unto other gods, and all the women who were present, a great assembly, and all the people who dwelt in the land of Egypt, in Pathros, answered Jeremiah, saying: As for the word that thou hast spoken unto us in the name of the Lord, we will not listen to thee. But we will certainly perform every word that is gone forth out of our mouth, to make offerings unto the Queen of Heaven, and to pour out drink-offerings unto her, as we have done, we and our fathers, our kings and our officials, in the cities of Judah, and in the streets of Jerusalem. For then had we plenty of bread, and were well, and suffered no misfortune. But ever since we stopped making offerings unto the Queen of Heaven and pouring out drink-offerings unto her, we have lacked all things, and have been consumed by the sword and by famine.

9.

Amotz already sees his wife from afar, but Daniela can't yet spot him among the crush of welcomers. Out of habit, she heads towards the right-hand exit at that slow, even pace he likes, pulling her little wheeled suitcase behind her. He backs away and circumnavigates the crowd, and for some reason there is a new heaviness in his step. So rare is it for her to be the one away and he the one left behind, that he has an urge to delay their reunion, perhaps so she'll sense that he's not always on call when she wants him.

Surprisingly, she, too, does not stop to wait for him, but keeps walking, apparently absent-mindedly, and when he intercepts her from behind, as Moran did to him at the army base, his experienced hands, gripping her hips, can sense the sadness and exhaustion of both her body and her mind. And so, as he brings her head close to him, his lips brush not her mouth but her forehead, just the way she kissed him at the moment of parting, seven days ago.

"Done?" he half asks, half declares.

"Done," she confirms, and her eyes, which gleam at the sight of him, are already surprised. "What's this? In my honour you didn't shave today?"

"Not in your honour, I just didn't have time. At night we dealt with the winds in the tower, and in the morning Francisco needed me because my father ran a high temperature, and while waiting for Doctor Zaslanski I fell asleep in Hilario's room, and then I had to rush to the airport."

"And you didn't shower?"

"I can't shower there, with all of Abba's stuff in the bath."

"You can only sleep there."

"Sleep and dream."

"And what about your father?"

"His temperature went down."

"And you didn't go to the office today?"

"They let Moran out of his confinement this morning, and I sent him to the office to replace me."

"So, in short," she says, gently touching his stubble, "you had a wild time."

"If that's what you call a wild time."

"You know, in work clothes and unshaven you actually look young and cute."

"So I'll stay like this."

"And the winds?"

"Just as I thought, the fault is in the shaft. There were lips and holes in the wall, left there by accident or maybe on purpose, that have the effect of a church organ."

"A church?" she says, laughing, "so what will the tenants do? Cross themselves and pray?"

"The construction company should pray for mercy from the insurance company. Gottlieb and I are off the hook. But wait a second, Daniela, we have to call Moran and tell him you landed. This time, maybe because he was sitting in the army camp with nothing to do, he worried about you even more than I did."

"More than you?" she says, slightly stung.

"After hearing your voice and Yirmi's from Dar es Salaam, I calmed down completely."

"And did you miss me?"

"I didn't have time to miss you." He smiles, knowing this

hurts her, attempting to prick this thin crust of estrangement that he did not anticipate. He unlocks the car with the remote control, and instead of putting the suitcase in the boot, he seats it like a passenger in the back.

"As it happens I did have time to miss you," she says seriously as she buckles her seat belt, "and also to be angry."

"Angry? About what?"

"That you didn't come with me."

He is surprised and not surprised.

"And I thought that's what you really wanted. Quiet time for yourself. To revive childhood memories, undisturbed by someone who doesn't belong."

"After thirty-seven years of marriage," she bursts out, "it's high time you understood that my sister is not only mine but yours, and Yirmi, who is stuck out there, is your affair too. You should have insisted, not let me go alone."

"But how?" he says dumbfounded, "it was you . . . you . . ."

"You . . . you . . ." she mimics him, "yes, but I'm also allowed to be wrong sometimes, and you could have understood and prevented the mistake."

He grins at this. "How could I understand that you were mistaken, if for thirty-seven years you've made sure to convince me that you always know what's right and what's not when it comes to the family?"

She falls silent, only looking at him with a pained expression.

"But what happened there? Why was it a mistake to go there alone?"

"Later."

"At least give me a hint."

"Soon. First you. Tell me about the children, and what happened with Moran and the army."

"He ignored his reserve duty again, but this time they caught him. It was the adjutant of the battalion, an old friend of his from officers' training, who made sure he was confined, and they're going to put him on trial for his previous absences. In the end they'll probably strip him of his rank. That's it, Daniela, no more officers in the family."

"And this is a tragedy in your opinion?"

"Not a tragedy, just a small painful disgrace."

"Not in my opinion. I don't need any more military glory. You should know that Yirmi out there is not just grieving for Shuli, and she wasn't the one we talked about most of the time. He's bogged down in pain and rage over the Eyal story, with ramifications and private investigations we didn't know anything about. The 'friendly fire' you planted in his brain won't let him go."

"I planted in his brain? Me? What is this, you came home ready for combat? Excuse me, I didn't plant any fire, nor could I. He planted it himself. I just tried to soften 'shot by his own forces' with something that's maybe also slightly ironic . . ."

"Okay, don't get upset, maybe I was wrong."

"Your mistakes are coming at me so fast, I'm not used to it. What's going on?"

"Enough, let it go, I didn't mean to cast blame, just to express regret that you didn't come with me and help me deal with a difficult and miserable man. But not now. I'll try to explain later. Meanwhile, say a word about the grandchildren."

"Sweet."

"And Nofar?"

"Friendly for a change."

"You kept in touch?"

"Kept in touch?" he says, taking offence. "I personally took care of every family member. First Efrati, I made it possible for her to go to a party on Friday, and all night I babysat the kids who screamed and cried. And on Saturday I drove her and the children to Moran's base, and wandered around in the pouring rain with the kids to give her and Moran—I will elaborate later on—quality time. As for Nofar, I was with her in Jerusalem not once but twice. And on top of all this I had my father, who after you left turned into a lion in love and lassoed me into taking care of a private elevator belonging to an old flame of his, an amazing old lady in Jerusalem. You should have seen the way my father schlepped me back and forth. I was not just a devoted father and grandfather to them all, but a good son too."

"So you really did have a wild time," she says with a smile.

"Too wild. Life overwhelmed me from every direction. But what's going on there, in Africa? When does Yirmi intend to come back?"

"He's not coming back. He doesn't even think about returning. Africa, he says, enables him to disengage from everything."

"What's that mean, *disengage,* and what's everything?" Ya'ari says dismissively. "Is there such a thing as *everything?* And even if there were, how is it possible to disengage from it? Forget it, Daniela, I know Yirmi no less well than you do. He has no choice, he'll come back in the end."

10.

WHY DOES SHE suddenly find the glaring urban milieu that surrounds her so oppressive? The elephantine towers scattered about the Tel Aviv megalopolis, the giant advertisements morphing one into the next, the aggressive drivers to the right and left, entering and exiting the highways? Even the luxurious front seat in the big car flusters her, as if she still yearned for the backseat of a sputtering Land Rover driven by a sad woman from Sudan.

Her husband talks and she listens, but her attention wavers. Because he is used to her fascination with little details, he tries to convey moods and tones of voice, and weather and colours and smells, happy to recount his activities to her to prove his effectiveness and skill. So he loads his wife with every minutia, not even sparing her his discovery of an erotic cassette between Baby Mozart and Baby Bach.

"So what did you do with it?"

"I put it back where it was. What am I going to do with a tape like that?"

"Nonetheless, you watched it."

"Only the beginning."

"And what was there in the beginning?"

"What else? Some young woman, a little scared."

"So you really did lead a wild life when I wasn't here," she says, sticking to her theme.

"And what about you?" he asks in jest. "A wild death?"

"I fought against death," she says, seriously.

"What do you mean by that?"

"First finish your story."

"I've already covered the main points. But first let's get organized."

Their house is dark and cold, and she asks him to turn on the heating. Exhausted and sad, she doesn't linger in the kitchen with him but goes straight up to the bedroom, takes off her shoes, and plops down fully dressed on the unmade double bed that her husband abandoned in the middle of the night. The blanket brushes the floor, and his pyjamas are in a heap near the pillow. But instead of feeling at home in the most familiar place in the world, she is unsettled by the many possessions around her. After her spartan lodgings in Africa, her bedroom seems stuffed with extraneous objects. Unnecessary closets and shelves, baskets filled with empty perfume bottles and dried-out compacts. Even the family photos on the walls—she and her husband, children and grandchildren, and the last picture of her nephew—seem excessive in number.

Amotz carries up the suitcase and sets it in a corner, sits down by her feet, and strokes and massages them.

Her eyes close.

"You're not hungry?"

"No. Is the water hot yet?"

"Almost. I turned on the electric boiler, in case the solar heater isn't enough."

"You wash, too, please."

"Why?" he says disingenuously, "you told me that like this, dirty and in work clothes, I'm younger and cuter."

"Young and cute, but wash anyway."

He leans over her and kisses her face and neck, stepping up the tempo of his caresses. She is soft, passive, but when he reaches to unbutton her blouse, hoping to bury his face between her breasts, she grabs the masculine hand and stops it short.

"And what happened to that real desire?"

"It exists, it'll come."

"Why not now? What's wrong with now?"

"Now I'm not all here yet. Wait for me."

Disappointed, he continues to kiss her face, her neck, his stubble scratching the bare smoothness of her skin. She closes her eyes in pain and pushes him away.

"Either shave now, or forget the kisses till tomorrow."

"Just for kisses it's not worth shaving," he says sullenly, gets up and paces the room restlessly.

"Tell me—what's this excavation team about? What are they digging for?"

She tells him about the team and its scientists, about the evening visit to the dig, about the eating machine that didn't fit into the evolutionary process, and also about Dr. Roberto Kukiriza, who asked her to smuggle prehistoric bones for inspection at Abu Kabir.

"In violation of the law?"

"What could happen?"

"Where are they?"

"In my toiletry bag. But there's nothing to see. Just three dry bones of an extremely early monkey."

But he insists, and quickly finds the bag in her suitcase, extracts the three bones, feels and smells them, holds them close to his eyes.

"That's all?"

"That's all."

"And if they had caught you and arrested you? Prisons in primitive dictatorships are worse than cemeteries."

"You would have found yourself a new wife, a better one," she says, smiling, aching with remorse.

"Is there such a person?"

"Of course. There's always someone better."

He now notices the dual-language Bible in her open suitcase.

"What's this? You took a Bible with you on the trip?"

She tells him about the American yeshiva boy, and why she asked for a Hebrew Bible at the airport. He listens with amazement.

"The Book of Jeremiah? I don't understand. What does Yirmi want with that? Is he for him or against him?"

"Against him, totally against him."

"That is to say, against himself a little too."

She wants to drop the subject. The water is hot, she says, go and take a shower downstairs and I'll wash here. But dim the lights a bit.

And only when she hears the water flowing on the first floor does she enter her shower to check the bite on her shoulder. The teeth marks have already grown indistinct, and all that remains is a reddish crescent, explainable in any number of ways. Nevertheless, she does not want her husband, who knows every inch of her body, to examine it. And she soaps herself for a long time, till her flesh grows red.

She puts on a nightie and gets into bed. Picks up a copy of *Ha'aretz* and recalls the burning of the newspapers and lets the paper drop.

Her husband ascends to the bedroom, wearing not pyjamas but running shorts. His face is still unshaven.

When she wakes up at midnight, she does not find her husband beside her in bed. She goes down to the living room and sees him sitting in total darkness watching a film on television.

"What, you're not sleeping?"

"No, I slept all day, and now I'm awake as the devil."

He is a devil, she thinks, and in the darkness the shining screen lends his face a mysterious aura. The devil can still discover, she thinks with dismay and goes to the dining table, where the Hanukkah menorah sits alone, bereft of candles. "What's this? The holiday is over?"

"Not over," he says, "tonight is the last candle. But you fell asleep so quickly."

"So how many candles do we light?"

"Eight. Eight."

"Let's light them, then. I didn't light a single one in Africa."

"In the end he really did burn all the candles you brought?"

"Not in the end, at the beginning." And she takes the box and wonders, "why are there so many candles left? Didn't you light any at home? After all, you like playing with fire."

"I lit them here only once—the third candle, with Nofar. The rest burned in other homes. At my father's, and with Efrati and the kids, and in the army dining hall when I visited Moran, and even at Gottlieb's factory. I didn't need to come home and light them by myself."

"So come now." She brightens suddenly. "It's not too late." And she sticks eight candles of various colours into the menorah, adding a red shammash.

"You do it," he says, not budging from his chair. "Because you didn't light a single candle, I'm letting you light all eight."

"All right, but turn down the TV, we can't say the blessing like this."

"You also want us to do the blessings?"

"Why not? As always."

"Then you do them. We live in feminist times, you're not exempt. There are women rabbis out there who go around in prayer shawls and phylacteries."

"But where are the blessings?"

"They're printed on the box."

"So convenient."

He lowers the sound on the television, but leaves the picture on. She lights the shammash with a match, shares its flame with all the other candles, and reads the blessings by their light. Come, she orders him, now we'll sing. He rises reluctantly from the armchair. But please, he insists, just not "Maoz Tsur." It's a song Nofar also hates.

"What is there to hate in a song like that?" she protests. "You sound like Yirmi."

"Like Yirmi or not like Yirmi, I don't like that song."

"But it won't do you any harm to sing it together with me, a duet."

Haifa, 2004–7

456